DATE			

✓

Footsteps in the Rain

Footsteps in the Rain

SARA HYLTON

ST. MARTIN'S PRESS NEW YORK

Library of Congress Cataloging-in-Publication Data

Hylton, Sara.
    Footsteps in the rain / Sara Hylton.
        p.   cm.
    ISBN 0-312-19413-7
    I. Title
    PR6058.Y63F6   1998
    823'.914—dc21   98-33706
                                                                CIP

First published in Great Britain by Judy Piatkus (Publishers) Ltd

First U.S. Edition: November 1998

10 9 8 7 6 5 4 3 2 1

Oh, must I always, always hear
Your footsteps going away,
Along a city's narrow street
That edged a rainy day?

A silence would be lonelier,
But not so hard to bear,
As steps that walk across my heart
And don't go anywhere!

Anon.

Prologue

I remember that it was raining when I left Belthorn ten years ago, cold icy rain falling from a leaden sky, swept by the wind to lie in great puddles across the cobbled station square. It was as though I had never been away, because today the rain is coming down as miserably as it had then.

On that day it had failed to quench my high spirits or dampen the enthusiasm with which I viewed my future life. Today the dreams and aspirations of that young girl have passed into limbo, and I am left with the feeling that a lifetime has been lived in those few years.

Nothing seemed to have changed around that almost deserted square. Two people were boarding a tramcar that waited at the terminus and I was glad to see that there were two taxi-cabs standing at the rank below the station steps. Into the gloom of the winter afternoon I hurried down the steps to the taxi rank. The driver's eyes lit up when I gave him instructions to my grandparents' house – several miles outside the town – and I sank miserably into the back seat.

The driver was disposed to chat.

'Do ye know Belthorn miss, or are ye just visitin'?'

'I used to live here when I was a girl, but it's ten years since I left,' I answered.

'Ay well nothin' much changes i' Belthorn. There's a new office block goin' up i' Water Street and the parish church is bein' looked after. Course nothin' could be done durin' the war, we're only just getting round to things.'

Passing the parish church I could see the scaffolding around the imposing square tower.

'It's very quiet,' I couldn't help remarking, and with a grin he said, 'It's 'alf-day closin' miss.'

I had forgotten. On half-day closing, after one o'clock the town was dead. The outskirts told a different story, however. Here smoking mill chimneys loomed upwards against the threatening sky and vast mills stood ugly and stark, illuminating the dusk with row upon row of lighted windows.

'You'll know some o' them mills, won't ye miss? Most o' the mill owners live outside the town, one or two of 'em in Grafton where you're 'eadin' for.'

'I wouldn't know which is which.'

'Well, we've just passed Bentham's but they've left the area. Sir Alec's gone to live in Scarborough and they're saying the mill's goin' into a combine. The war's been over some time. The orders are fallin' off. Things aren't so rosy. Your folks i' cotton, miss?'

'My grandfather and uncles.'

'Which mills were they then?'

'Dexter's.'

His voice was impressed. 'Dexter's is it. They have three or four of 'em. So you're a Dexter miss?'

'I was before I married.'

'Sorry love, I'm bein' nosy. But I likes to chat. Your 'usband not with you then?'

'No.'

I didn't want to tell this stranger that my husband of three months was dead and buried in some grave I had never seen, and where nobody would visit, somewhere in the high reaches of the Khyber Pass. My laughing, charming, young husband who had loved me rapturously throughout a few heady months of imperial pageantry in a distant exotic land.

'Ah well,' he was saying. 'No doubt he'll be joinin' ye. Are ye stayin' long i' these parts?'

'I'm not sure. My plans are uncertain.'

'I know the Dexter's house, miss. It's one o' the nicest i' Grafton. A far cry from the cottages by the factories, but then ye can't really blame 'em for wantin' to get away fro' the noise and the mill chimneys can ye? Is yer 'usband i' cotton too?'

'No.'

2

The terseness of my reply silenced him for a while. I was not going to tell this stranger that my young husband had been an officer in the Indian Army and that cotton had never figured in his life.

We were driving through the outskirts of Belthorn along narrow streets edged with small, gardenless, terraced houses, where women gossiped at their front doors and children played in the gutter. It was a scene that had impressed me as a child. I had passed along here on my way home from school. It had filled me with curiosity, but I had always been glad to leave the poverty behind and see the hills and green trees again, the long gardens where mill managers lived and, beyond, the mansions where the mill owners lived.

I stared through the taxi window at the grey misery of the day and the flickering lamplight illuminating wet pavements and dusty windows. I was glad of the darkness as I felt the scalding tears rolling unchecked down my cheeks, I could taste the salt in them, and in my heart I could feel the searing pain of loss and tormenting fear.

Heaven knows I had not wanted to come back, and yet it was something that seemed inevitable, when the future lay ahead like an uncertain dream and only the past was real, when the future was a shadow and only the past had substance.

What was ten years in the life of a community, and yet the ten years since I last drove along this road had changed me utterly, so how could I be sure that there would not be deeper and wider changes in all that I was going back to?

How had it been in those years that made up my childhood, those years that saw me waiting impatiently for the day when I would leave this place behind me and hopefully never return?

Book One

Chapter One

My Dexter grandparents had three sons, but only the elder, William, and the younger, Edwin, went into cotton. Their middle son, my father – Harry, was a major in the Twenty-ninth Lancer Regiment in the Indian Army.

My father never wanted to make cotton his career: since he always maintained that it was an unpredictable industry where the very nations that the confident cotton mills were helping to train would one day beat us at our own game. My grandfather pooh-poohed the idea: it would never happen. Lancashire was cotton, and anything that came out of the Far East in the distant future could only be a shoddy and poor imitation of the real thing.

Undeterred, my father refused to be put off his chosen career and my grandparents were not too insistent. To have a son with a good commission in a prestigious regiment was not to be disparaged. Among their friends and neighbours all the sons went into cotton. They were the young masters, little emperors to the millfolk and pillars of local society.

Grandfather and my two uncles were Freemasons and members of gentlemen's clubs, both political and social, and the people they mixed with were like-minded. The girls they met were sisters of the men they had grown up with, monied mill owners, and because Dexter's was supreme among those mills they had their pick of the girls. Money married money and it was expedient to love where money was.

There was no shortage of well-heeled young women only too anxious to marry a serving army officer with expectations and a lucrative background, so it came as a considerable shock to my grandparents when my father elected to marry my mother: the daughter of his regiment's padre. Of course churchmen of whatever denomination were eminently respectable, but my grandparents would have preferred her father to have been the brigadier.

I was eight years old when my parents brought me to England and England was in mourning for the death of King Edward. I remember none of it, But I learned later that my father rode his charger behind the royal coffin as a representative of his regiment.

After the funeral we travelled north to stay with my grandparents. Memories of India were fleeting: shuttered rooms and wicker furniture, sunshine and cool green lawns, parades of men and horses at sundown and elephants gorgeously attired. Memories of my tutor who came to the bungalow every day, a sombre softly spoken Englishwoman, faded quickly.

It seems now that all my early memories were of Fairlawn, my grandparents' large stone house at the end of a winding road that climbed a hill, and looking out on the crags and fells surrounding it. None of the windows of that house overlooked the distant mill chimneys which covered the surrounding towns and villages with a permanent umbrella of smoke, and it was here, on Darnley Hill, that the mill owners and their families lived with their large houses, well-kept gardens and stables for their horses.

When my father's leave was over, my parents returned to India without me. I stayed on with my grandparents so that I could receive an education. It was a whole new world.

I remember sitting on the window seat in the large room that had been my father and his brothers' nursery staring across the misted moors, and although a fire burned in the grate and a servant constantly came in to add coal to it, it was always cold, as if the mist crept in through cracks around the windowpanes. Even when sunlight brightened the corners of the room, it never quite expelled the chill.

There was a large white rocking-horse across one corner and shelves filled with books of all descriptions – nursery rhymes, fairy stories, encyclopedias. There was a globe on a wooden stand, and a large table surrounded by chairs in the centre.

8

Sunday had a firmly established ritual: uncles and aunts with their families came for lunch and stayed for afternoon tea, and it was then my cousins came up to the nursery and I was made to realise that I was the newcomer in the family and was given instructions accordingly.

The rocking-horse belonged to my cousin Ralph and his sister Sophie did not like me poking among her books even when I later learned they were not her exclusive property. Ralph and Sophie were the children of Uncle William and Aunt Myrtle.

My other cousins were Charlotte and Caroline, Uncle Edwin and Aunt Edith's children. Only Caroline appealed to me, probably because she was the youngest of my cousins, and, since the others were largely disposed to ignore me, Sunday was a day I did not look forward to.

Over lunch Grandfather and the two uncles talked business: hiring and firing of employees, short-time and overtime, and how the state of world affairs was likely to affect the cotton industry.

My grandmother and the aunts talked about very little until the coffee stage when they retired to the drawing room. Then they talked about their clothes, the shops in the town, where they expected to spend their holidays and the education of their children. They discussed at length forthcoming functions, eventually we were banished to the nursery, so that they could no doubt discuss any scandal they felt they should know about, and we shouldn't.

Grandfather's temper was dictated by the affluence of the mills. If he came home smiling and genial I quickly learned that things were going well; if he came home red-faced and hectoring there were problems. As I grew older I got the measure of my cousins and, because I was the one living with my grandparents, gained firsthand knowledge which they only acquired later.

With the children of other mill owners I went to a private school at the bottom of the hill until I was eight, and then joined my older cousins at Wentworth, an expensive private school in the town. It was a school for girls, and my cousin Ralph was now enrolled at the large grammar school for boys in Manchester, so the only time I saw him was on Sunday.

9

Travelling to and from school in Grandfather's chauffeur-driven limousine introduced me to the layout of the district. The mansions on the hill where the mill owners lived, the big, slightly less pretentious houses lower down, where the professional men and mangers lived and then the narrow streets inhabited by the mill workers.

It was these streets that intrigued me most because they were filled with activity and noise. Children played in the alleyways or hung round the public houses and corner shops, shawl-clad women clattered along in their clogs, their baskets over their arms, and always the pall of smoke descending from the tall mill chimneys, covering with grime the lace-curtained cottage windows.

People were smiling, even though we were at war. War meant full order books: cotton was needed for the armed forces, and if there was death and misery in Flanders life had to go on: one thing cancelled out another. People too had a philosophical approach: survival on the field of battle and in war-torn England were one and the same.

Shortages of food in the shops hardly seemed to effect us. Grandfather would arrive home with a brace of pheasants or some other delicacy and there were always new-laid eggs and bacon for breakfast. Grandmother and her women friends were organising charitable events to raise money for the men at the front and she lost no time in enlisting servants and family to sew and knit for the Red Cross.

Our horses were taken by the army, much to Grandfather's annoyance, and only Caroline and myself kept our ponies.

My mother remained in India, although my father was serving with his regiment in France and I was instructed to say special prayers for his safety in church on Sunday.

I shall never forget the first morning I was taken into the mill. Ralph, as the young master, led the way importantly, up the steep stone steps, down which the wind bore dismally, and then we were in a large room that echoed with the deafening sound of machinery. Beside the great looms women and girls stood in the aisles watching the movement of shuttles; I paused in amazement as they spoke and laughed with each other when I was so certain they couldn't hear a word.

I was told by the foreman that they learned to lip-read: they

10

didn't need to hear, and as we were ushered along the aisle some of the women smiled; others stared at us in surly disdain.

Many of the young girls sweeping the aisles looked very little older than myself and when one girl dropped her broom in front of us the foreman spoke to her harshly and the tears came readily to her eyes. I felt so sorry for her. I pulled a paper bag filled with sweets out of my pocket and handed it to her.

Caroline pulled me away saying, 'Don't be silly Amanda. She's only a workgirl, we don't have to talk to them.'

That was the moment that my views of Cousin Caroline changed. I had thought of her as my one true friend; now I saw she was as fallible as anyone else.

It was Saturday and when the whistle sang out promptly at one o'clock they made a rush to take off their aprons and head for the room where they had hung their outdoor clothing, then laughing and chattering they jostled for the staircase; from high above we heard their footsteps clattering down the steps.

It had been a grim morning, but there was no hint of depression on their faces as they left for their weekend.

'I don't want to come here again,' Caroline said feelingly. 'I hate the noise and it smells horrible. I'm glad I shall never be expected to work here.'

Although I shared her feelings I sensed a strange, earthy excitement about the place, and as I watched them hurrying away, I could not help noticing their vitality. Their clogs made a strange throbbing rhythm on the cobblestones – and over it all came their laughter. Not even war had the power to quench it, and as their shawl-clad figures disappeared into the distance I felt that something irretrievably joyous had gone from my day.

The steep stone steps leading down on to the loading bay demanded all my attention but as I reached the bottom I was aware of Ralph standing alone, staring dismally after the others, and when I caught up with him I sensed that something had upset him. I smiled, and taking hold of my hand he asked, 'Well, what did you think about the mill?'

'I'm not sure. I didn't like the noise. Will you work here

when you leave school?'

'So my father and my grandfather say.'

'Don't you want to?'

'No. I shall hate it.'

'Then why do you have to?'

'Because I'm the only Dexter of my generation.'

'What about Sophie and the others?'

'They'll get married and they won't be Dexters then.'

I pondered for a moment. 'What do you want to do then?'

'I want to go to university or join the army.'

'But won't the war be over long before then?'

'Of course not. Next birthday I'll be sixteen. Boys are joining the army at seventeen and I've been in the officers' training corps at school. It's all going to be wasted if all I do when I leave school is come here.'

'I wish my father worked here at the mills, instead of being shot at somewhere in France.'

'Surely not. I've seen the way some of the women who work here look at my father and Uncle Edwin. Their men are in the forces, while they're here doing nothing for the war.'

'But they are. Grandma says they're as much involved in the war as if they were at the front.'

'Oh she says that because she feels she has to. It's nonsense of course.'

We walked in silence to where the others waited for us outside the factory, near the quite ostentatious office block. Grandfather frowned at Ralph's sulky face, and his father looked at him sharply too before they got into their respective cars and drove away. I sat in the rear seat with Grandfather and we drove in silence.

I did not like Saturdays. During the week there was school and the friends I had there, but Saturday was a lonely day. Grandma usually had some committee meeting for some charity or other, and there was always something needing her attention at St Mary's church. Grandfather went to one of his clubs to play snooker or bridge in the winter and in the summer to some sporting activity so that I was left to amuse myself.

Invariably I spent it in the nursery, sitting at the large table with my paintbox, drawing and painting things I could see in the room, or the view from the window. It was early spring and the room was cold in spite of the sparse fire that burned in the grate. My fingers were so cold they could barely feel the paintbrush and I constantly had to blow on them to warm them up.

When Bridie came in to stoke up the fire she exclaimed angrily, 'Faith and it's as cold as charity in here. You're goin' to catch your death sittin' there and besides it's dark in here, ye can hardly see what you're doin'.'

Although I agreed with her I kept silent, and after she had added small pieces of coal to the fire she said, 'I'll bring you up some soup Miss Amanda, or I'll ask Cook for a better idea.'

After she had gone I went over to the fire and crouched in front of it, feeling the warmth slowly penetrate through my fingers and along my chilled limbs. In a few minutes Bridie was back saying, 'You're to come with me Miss Amanda. There's a roaring fire in the kitchen and hot scones straight from the oven. You can bring your paintbox if you like.'

She waited while I collected my belongings then I followed her downstairs and through the door at the back of the hall to the kitchens beyond.

It was the first time I had been into the kitchen but my eyes lit up at its cheerfulness. The warmth from the fire could be felt across the room and Cook sat at the kitchen table with an array of scones hot from the oven in front of her.

Until that moment I had only seen her in church on Sunday, a darkly clad figure with a black felt hat pulled firmly down over her eyes and wearing a dark fur tippet round her neck. Now she sat resplendent in a white starched apron with a white cap over her grey hair, her rosy face smiling a welcome, and Bridie ushered me forward towards a seat at the table.

Cook said sternly. 'You're to come in 'ere when it's cold, that big room upstairs needs a lot of 'eatin' and besides it's lonely for a young lass to be up there without company. Don't your cousins ever think to invite you to their homes on a Saturday?'

'I really don't mind Mrs Eltham. My cousin Caroline goes out with Aunt Edith on Saturday afternoon. I think they go to the shops and to take tea with friends.'

With a somewhat grim smile she said, 'No doubt they'll be up at the Marston house. It's where your aunt spends most of her time these days.'

When I didn't speak she said, 'Get the lass some hot soup, Bridie, and we'll taste a few o' these scones. The mistress said she wouldn't be 'ome until later and it's a lot better than sittin' up there on yer own isn't it, love?'

That was the first of many such afternoons I spent in the kitchen and I learned more about my family from Cook than I ever did living with them. She had a caustic tongue and was self-opinionated. She had the utmost respect for my grandmother, was proud to serve the family but had long since ceased to view them through rose-tinted spectacles.

It was not what she said to me that enlightened me, but rather what she said to herself and to Bridie having assured herself that I was unlikely ever to repeat what I heard in the kitchen.

Indeed I was so grateful to be welcome there that never in a thousand years would I have disclosed to anybody that in Cook's eyes the family was less than perfect.

She remembered my father as a handsome, charming young man who had had the good sense to cut loose, but whether he'd been wise in joining the army and going off to India was another matter. She asked questions about my mother, saying she had only met her on two occasions but she had seemed a very nice young lady and my father was obviously very attracted to her.

She was rather more forthcoming about my aunts. Aunt Myrtle was the only daughter of Sir Joshua Fielding, and the Fieldings owned three mills in the next town. Both families had been highly delighted at the marriage since Myrtle was well blessed with worldly goods but little beauty. Aunt Myrtle was tall and stately with fine dark eyes and a haughty manner. As the one daughter-in-law clever enough to produce a son her stature within the family was sacrosanct.

Cook had rather more to say about Aunt Edith. Of course it was all said to Bridie and anybody else who cared to listen and she talked to them as if I weren't there. Aunt Edith had come from rather less exalted stock. Her father was a grocer with two shops in the town, and sat as a Liberal on the town council. Aunt Edith was the one with airs and graces and considerable ambitions that both her daughters marry well, particularly Caroline who was pretty and more malleable than her older sister. Hence, Cook muttered darkly, her absorption with Sir John Marston and his family, ever-mindful of their one son Phillip.

Those afternoons I spent in Cook's kitchen made me see my cousins as the servants saw them. I could now view with amusement Grandfather's ill-humour and self-opinionated notion that outside the world of cotton everything else was unimportant. Over the years Grandma had learned to close her eyes and her ears to his blustering arguments with his sons and their children. Aunt Myrtle largely ignored him. She had heard it all before from her own father, but Aunt Edith talked the way he talked and tried desperately to ingratiate herself with him, consulting him about everything, from her daughters' education to her husband's proficiency at the mills, and her increasing familiarity with the Marston family who were considered landed gentry.

I was accustomed to Grandma's half-smile when I knew her thoughts were miles away but it was Aunt Myrtle who distantly informed Aunt Edith that Phillip Marston was hardly likely to marry a local girl, since he was destined to join the Royal Navy as soon as he was old enough.

'What has that got to do with it?' Aunt Edith demanded. 'There will be no girls where he's going and I should think he'll be glad to marry a well-connected local girl when the time is right. He chats to you Caroline, doesn't he, and Lady Marston's very fond of you.'

Caroline smiled complacently, while Aunt Myrtle looked sharply away, giving us all the benefit of her superior profile.

Even Grandma cautioned that since Caroline was only fourteen any talk of an engagement to anybody was far too previous.

Talk of Philip Marston joining the Navy gave Ralph the occasion to speak of his ambition to join the army, thus provoking one of the stormiest Sunday luncheons I had experienced.

When Bridie came in to clear away the dishes she took in

at once Grandfather's glowering face and the discomfort of the rest of them. As she reached the door she turned and catching my eye she smiled and I knew that Cook would get the full benefit of the scene when she reached the kitchen.

For the remainder of the afternoon the silence in the drawing room was oppressive. Grandfather sat with his head buried in the Sunday newspaper, while the rest of us lingered, looking miserable. Even Aunt Edith decided she had nothing to contribute, and only the clicking of Grandma's knitting needles could be heard above the spluttering logs in the grate.

Grandfather had said his piece, made his objections and opinions known and it was perfectly reasonable that we should all remain silent in order that we could deliberate on them. It was late in the afternoon when I heard voices in the hall and the next moment the door opened and my father was standing in the doorway with a smile on his face. With a cry of joy I rushed across the room and flung myself into his arms.

Into that silent room and that disgruntled group of people he brought a breath of fresh air, and suddenly Grandfather was smiling, the uncles were shaking his hand, Grandma was embracing him and crying with joy, and my cousins were eyeing with awe this tall khaki-clad figure who was smiling genially down on them, while I held on to his hand as though I would never let him go.

Chapter Two

What a change Father's presence brought to the house in the evening. Now Grandfather no longer talked incessantly about the mills and the workpeople. Father was not interested in cotton and they talked about the war and a great many other things far divorced from the cotton industry.

During the day we walked along the country lanes and across the fells and he introduced me to the beloved scenes of his childhood and the beauties to be found in the area. I discovered tarns and waterfalls, long sweeps of heather-clad moorland and cloud-shadowed Pennine hills.

After dinner I was happy to sit with my elders in the drawing room listening to their conversation and the click of Grandma's knitting needles.

My uncles never argued with Grandfather. They regarded him as being always right, even when they probably knew as much about cotton as he did, but Father opened my eyes to scenes of rat-infested trenches in Flanders, the sound of gunfire and death.

On his last evening Grandfather said brusquely, 'I can't think why your wife didn't decide to come home, Harry. It would have been better for the girl.'

'You seem to forget, Father, that to Elizabeth India is home. Her parents were married there and she was born there. Her father is serving in France but her mother is in poor health and is needing her at the moment. We both know that Amanda is very well cared for here with you. In any case, if there had been no war in Europe, we should have been in India and she would have been here in England to receive her education.'

'By the time she sees her mother, she'll have forgotten what she looks like,' Grandfather insisted.

Father smiled gently. 'Oh I don't think so. As soon as the war is over and the voyage from India is less hazardous I'm sure she will be coming to England to see you all.'

Sitting alone in the big cold room, staring dismally out of the window, I wept long bitter tears after Father left for France the next morning, and it was Bridie who came for me early in the afternoon, taking in my tear-stained face and expression of despair.

'Now come along with me Miss Amanda, Cook said you'd be unhappy this afternoon but there's tea and hot scones downstairs and your Grandma's out at her Red Cross meeting.'

Cook was equally brusque. 'You've been a very lucky girl to 'ave 'ad your father for these few days. Poor Jenny Alsop 'asn't seen 'er father for three years and no word from 'im. Now come along up to the table and I'll pour you a cup o' tea.'

'Who's Jenny Alsop?' I ventured.

'They lives at the first cottage on the road leadin' up to the moor. 'Er mother comes 'ere three mornin's a week to do some cleanin' and some o' the laundry. Joe Alsop, her father worked at Number One mill, Tackler 'e were.'

'How old is Jenny?'

'About your age.'

'Does she go to school?'

'That she does, but not your school. They can't afford such a luxury. She goes to St Joseph's church school in the town.'

'Does she ever come here with her mother?'

'Well of course. Would you like to meet her?'

'Oh yes I would, very much.'

I did not miss the warning glance that passed between Cook and Bridie but Cook said firmly, 'Why shouldn't she meet Jenny? She gets no invitations from 'er cousins, they couldn't care less 'ow she spends 'er time. And there's nothin' wrong wi' Jenny.'

Bridie didn't answer. Cook's word in the kitchen was law just as Grandfather's word was at the mills.

I had been allowed to take a week off school while my

18

father was at home and expected to be going back on Monday morning, but I was determined to see Jenny Alsop. I desperately needed a friend of my own age and although I had made some at school none of them lived within walking distance of Fairlawn.

When I went down to the kitchen on Friday afternoon Mrs Alsop was busy with Bridie, folding sheets, while Jenny sat at the table reading. Cook looked up and smiled and Jenny hastily laid her book aside and stared at me nervously.

'This is Miss Amanda, Jenny. I told ye 'er father's been on leave for a few days. 'Es in the army too. Now you two'll 'ave a lot to talk about I'm sure. Why don't ye take a walk up the road and get to know each other.'

'I 'ave to wait for mi mother,' Jenny prevaricated.

'Please Jenny, I'd like to walk up the road with you,' I insisted.

Jenny still hesitated: 'It's startin' to rain.'

'Then why don't we go up to the nursery. There's a fire up there and we could look at some of the books and talk.'

'Yes,' Cook insisted. 'Why don't ye both do that, and when yer mother's ready to leave Bridie'll come up for ye.'

Jenny was not proof against Cook's insistence and my pleas. She came reluctantly, glancing round nervously even though we used the back stairs and there was nobody in the house except the servants. In the nursery she looked around her with more interest and I poked some semblance of blaze into the fire and drew up two chairs for us to sit on.

Talking to Jenny Alsop was difficult. Brought up from childhood to regard local mill owners and their families as her betters, she was wary of me. So I was the one who talked and asked questions, to which she answered in whispers.

Bridie came in with a tray on which rested glasses of lemonade and a plate of small cakes and meeting her eyes I was aware that she understood how neither Jenny or I were feeling comfortable with each other.

After that day I was determined to persevere, even when I sensed Jenny was trying to avoid me. We were at different schools and when I arrived home in the afternoon she had already left with her mother or not arrived at all. On Saturdays when I was mostly alone I took to walking along the moorland road in the hope of meeting her and when I saw her in the cottage garden with several brothers and sisters I did not hesitate to lean over their garden gate with a bright smile on my face.

She came to me hesitantly and with her came two younger children, their eyes wide with curiosity.

'It's lovely out today Jenny,' I began. 'Can't we walk across the fell?'

'Mi mother's out shoppin'. I 'ave to take care of the children,' she said.

'They could come with us.'

'I 'ave to be 'ere when mi mother gets back.' That was the moment when she decided to be honest. 'Why do you want to be friends wi' me, Miss Amanda? I'm not your sort. Ye 'ave your own friends and yer cousins.'

'None of my schoolfriends live nearby, and I never see my cousins except on Sunday. Besides, they're all older than me, even Caroline, and they never invite me to go out with them. I get so lonely.'

Jenny remained doubtful. Her expression was doleful as she looked out across the fields. The little boy pulled on her skirts impatiently. 'I've told ye mother'll be 'ome soon,' she said sharply to him.

'Is your mother at Grandma's house?' I asked.

'No, she's at Doctor Atherton's this mornin'. She does too much, since Dad went away she's taken more and more and the children are missin' 'er. Perhaps we will walk up to the fell. It might keep 'em quiet.'

Gleefully the children ran ahead of us. In the main we walked in silence but it was a companionable silence and with encouragement from me she began to unbend. I discovered she had a wry sense of humour and her pale plain little face became suddenly pretty.

By the end of the afternoon I had her promise – somewhat ruefully – that we would spend Saturday afternoons together. 'Yer grandparents wouldn't like it Miss Amanda,' she said, and I was quick to say, 'Please don't call me Miss Amanda, Jenny. It makes me sound like some sort of schoolteacher. Call me Amanda.'

When I ran back along the lane towards Fairlawn that

afternoon I felt happier than I had felt for months. I had found a friend, somebody who would be there on the day I hated – Saturday – when I was mostly alone.

I had expected our friendship to go on for ever but Jenny informed me that when she was twelve she would be leaving school and going to work in one of the mills and it was possible she would be asked to work on Saturdays.

I stared at her in dismay. 'But you can't go into the mills, Jenny. Who'll look after the children when your mother's at work?'

'We've talked about that. She can take the children with her if they promise to behave. Anyway we need the money I'll be bringin' in and I'm not on mi own, a lot of us will be leavin' school and goin' into the mills.'

We walked in silence but I was remembering the flying shuttles and the horrendous noise, the young pale-faced girls sweeping dust along the aisles and from around the feet of the weavers.

'Don't you mind?' I asked her.

'Not really. What else is there for girls like me?'

On Sunday over lunch I listened to the conversation around the table with greater interest: Grandfather's usual gratification that the three mills were on fulltime and overtime; the uncles' assurances that under their respective management all was well, and Grandma's absorption with one committee after another.

Later when we moved into the drawing room for coffee my aunts talked about Masonic dinners and charitable works and my cousins talked about their clothes, the boys they had met and birthday parties. It was then that Aunt Myrtle said, 'We are having to give some thought to Ralph's seventeenth birthday. William thinks it is highly unlikely that he will be called up since he's due to go into a protected industry. After all, the mills are churning out work for the armed forces, Ralph is needed there.'

'Perhaps a birthday party isn't very appropriate at this time,' Grandma murmured.

'Well of course it is. We only have the one boy in the family, it would be awful to let it pass without some sort of celebration. I don't want the trouble of it at home, not that the house isn't large enough, but there will be a lot of guests and we thought somewhere like the town hall or perhaps the Masonic Hall with outside caterers.'

'I suppose you've made up a guest list?' Aunt Edith asked.

'Well yes, a tentative one.'

'I hope you're asking the Marstons. I'd like Caroline to get to know Phillip better.'

'Why Caroline? Surely Charlotte's the eldest?' Aunt Myrtle demanded.

'Because he was very taken with Caroline the last time they met. Phillip was home on leave and they looked so happy together. Even Lady Marston commented on it.'

'Well, naturally, we'll invite them,' Aunt Myrtle said tartly, 'but Phillip may not get leave for such a trivial occasion. There is a war on.'

'I'm only saying it's policy to invite them,' Aunt Edith said. 'We'll have to think about new dresses but heaven knows there's not much choice in the shops.'

'I'm having my dress made at Madame Geraldine's,' Cousin Sophie said proudly. 'I chose the material myself – pale cream satin with silk gardenias at the waist. Mummy's had the material for ages.'

'I don't want cream,' Caroline said sharply. 'I want pale pink or peach. Cream's nondescript.'

'It's also very sophisticated,' Sophie replied with some asperity.

Grandma smiled at me. 'We'll have to think about something for you Amanda. It will be your first party since you came here.'

'She's too young anyway,' Caroline said. 'She'll be the only eleven-year-old there.'

'I shall be twelve when Ralph's seventeen,' I snapped.

'Only just,' snapped back Caroline.

'There's something very wrong when twelve is too young for a party but not too young to go into the mills,' I said firmly.

'What do you know about girls going into the mills?' Aunt Edith demanded.

'I saw them there, and my friend Jenny Alsop is going to work in one of them in the summer when she leaves school.'

'Your friend Jenny Alsop,' Caroline said, 'Who's she?'

'Her mother works here some of the time and her father's in the army like mine. She's nice. I spend Saturday afternoons with her.'

Glances were exchanged and Aunt Myrtle said at last, 'She's hardly a fit companion for you Amanda. What's wrong with the girls you're at school with?'

'Nothing – they just don't live near here.'

'Well, I really think that in future you should spend your Saturdays with Sophie or your other cousins. If this girl goes to work at Dexter's it will be unseemly for her to be too friendly with the master's granddaughter.'

'I don't want to see my cousins, I want to stay with Jenny. My cousins never bothered about me before.'

Grandma and the aunts conferred; my cousins remained silent, which told me that they did not want me with them on Saturday afternoons. I didn't blame them, they had friends of their own age, it was obvious they didn't want a young cousin demanding their attention.

'I think we should leave matters alone,' Grandma said quietly. 'Once Jenny goes into work she won't be available on Saturday afternoon so Amanda will have to think of someone or something else. Now let's talk some more about Ralph's birthday party. Have you asked him what he would like?'

I received instructions from my cousins that I must be careful not to choose a party dress the same colour as theirs. That ruled out cream (chosen by Sophie), green (chosen by Charlotte) and peach (by Caroline).

With three sons Grandma had never been asked to shop for daughters and she wasn't much help. I desperately wanted pale blue because my hair was dark auburn and my eyes were blue, but Aunt Edith said auburn hair was good with yellow and so *yellow* it had to be.

Even Cook maintained that white or blue would have suited a young girl better, and on the day of the party Bridie helped me to dress, saying finally as she surveyed the finished result, 'You're pretty, Miss Amanda, a good thing too since that insipid primrose isn't for you.'

'I know Bridie, I hate it. I tried to tell Grandma I didn't like it but Aunt Edith was there and she said it was right for me.'

'Sure and she won't want anybody to look better than Miss Caroline. Just you wait 'till you're as old as her, she'll 'ave to watch out. It's you yerself who'll be the beauty in the family.'

Her words were designed to cheer me up which they did until I descended the marble steps in the town hall and saw the dazzling array of young girls in their pretty dresses. I was the youngest girl there. I sat miserably watching them dancing in the arms of Ralph's friends and went at last to sit on the stairs carrying with me a large plate of ice cream.

Nobody came to look for me and eventually a waiter came to take the empty plate away. I sat on, listening to the music and the laughter, and my eyes were hostile as they met the eyes of a tall young man who came to stare down at me with a smile on his face.

'Hello,' he said. 'What are you doing out here all alone?'

I didn't answer, after all what was I doing there all alone?

'Haven't you been dancing?'

'No, nobody asked me, not even Ralph.'

'I find that very remiss of him. Are you family or friend?'

'I'm family. He's my cousin.'

'So your father's Major Harry Dexter?'

'Yes.'

'I met him once when I was home from school during the holidays, I'd got a young horse and he went riding with me.'

Interested at last I eyed him over. He was handsome, with dark hair and grey eyes. His smile was entirely disarming and there was so much charm in it my hostility seemed to melt away.

'I don't suppose I'll see him again until the war's over. I wish he could have been here, my mother too.'

'Your mother isn't here?'

'No, she stayed on in India with my grandparents. I'm here to be educated but I'm going back to them one day.'

'I'm sure you are, I expect you're hoping to set India alight as I'm sure you will.'

'Are you one of Ralph's friends?'

For the first time I noticed that he was wearing naval uniform and seeing my surprise he said, 'I'm Phillip

Marston, I don't know Ralph very well but my parents are family friends.'

'Yes of course, I've heard about you, you're in the navy.' He smiled.

'I've heard my aunts and cousins talking about you. Did you have to get leave for Ralph's birthday party?'

'My ship saw some action and was damaged. At the moment she's in the shipyard at Barrow undergoing repairs, I'm due to rejoin her next week.'

'My cousin Caroline will be pleased about that.'

I saw his lips twitch with amusement and I hastened to say, 'Grandma and my aunts too. They all think you're very nice.'

He threw back his head and laughed delightedly. Then holding out his hand he said, 'Come along and dance with me and please tell me your name.'

'It's Amanda.'

'Well then Amanda, I hear they're playing a waltz. Will you dance it with me?'

'I'm not very good. I'm having dancing lessons at school but I'm probably not nearly as good as Caroline or Sophie.'

'I'm sure you are, but if you're not I too am a little out of practice.'

I was tall for my age but immediately we started to dance I was sure we were watched by every pair of eyes in the ballroom. I felt the silence, the unspoken amazement that the most eligible man in the room should have chosen to dance with a schoolgirl wearing a yellow dress that did her no favours.

During that dance I discovered that my feet had wings, that I had no difficulty whatsoever in following his steps and the melody filled my heart so that I wanted the waltz to go on for ever. He beamed down at me when it was over saying, 'You dance beautifully, Amanda. These young men don't know what they have been missing.'

Gallantly he escorted me back to the table where my grandparents and others in the family were sitting and when the music started again Caroline was there waiting for him to dance with her. For several minutes I watched them. He was smiling down at her, and she was chatting happily, they looked so much a pair as if they had laughed happily together a great many times and no doubt she was thanking him warmly for looking after her young cousin. At that moment Ralph invited me to dance.

I did not dance with Phillip Marston again that evening but thanks to him a great many other young men asked me, following Phillip Marston's lead.

Suddenly I felt carefree. I was young and alive and I could dance. Young men were smiling down at me with evident admiration and at the family table the uncles and aunts were witnessing the metamorphosis of their ugly duckling with some gratification.

I left the town hall with my grandparents in the early morning, calling out cheerful farewells to people I hadn't known before the party.

On Monday morning I would be a schoolgirl again but I had had a glimpse of what it could be like. The men and girls I had met that night would go on counting such events as highlights in their life but I was going to another life, the glamour of regimental balls in a country more exotic than any they would ever know.

I was too excited to sleep. I sat on the window seat looking out across the gardens, reliving the night before, and then suddenly my heart sank when I thought about Caroline walking arm in arm with Phillip Marston towards the car. He had been smiling down at her and as they reached us he had politely bid my grandparents goodnight, then smiling down at me he had said, 'You really did enjoy yourself after all Amanda?'

'Yes, I had a lovely time.'

'I rather think you broke the ice, Phillip. Until you danced with her she wasn't particularly enjoying herself were you, dear?' Grandma said.

Caroline's expression said it all. Condescension tempered with amusement, but my last memory was of the charm of Phillip's smile as he took my hand and said goodnight.

I'd laughed with my schoolfriends over their crushes on boys, feeling faintly superior that I was going on to better things, but I knew now what they had been talking about, that young love can be just as painful as anything that came after.

Chapter Three

The euphoria surrounding Ralph's seventeenth birthday did not last. Sunday lunchtime found Grandfather issuing his commands that Ralph should present himself at the mills promptly at seven-thirty on Monday morning and when Ralph looked at him in dismay he said shortly, 'You'll start at the bottom lad, you'll learn about weft and warp, cops and the way they're dyed and you'll learn how to tackle a loom.'

'Why can't I go into the office to be with my father?' Ralph demanded.

'You'll go on to the factory floor and learn to keep any eye on the weavers and winders. They'll have more respect for you later on if you know what you're talking about. I didn't start in the boardroom, I worked my way up to it and so will you.'

'The war isn't over yet. I could still be called up,' Ralph said darkly. I knew he was still hoping he would get into the army.

'Ours is a protected industry, we're working for the government.'

'Phillip Marston's in the navy and they're supposed to be gentry,' Ralph retorted.

'And that's what they are, gentry. They own land and breed horses and beef cattle. Their horses have gone to war and their cattle breeding is being supervised by men from the ministry. Young Phillip is better employed in the navy. You're different.'

'It wouldn't surprise me if Phillip didn't stay in the navy,'

Uncle Edwin said. 'His promotion has been pretty spectacular.'

'He told me he was loving it,' I said and was immediately wishing I had remained silent.

'What do you know about it?' Caroline demanded.

'He told me when we were dancing.'

'Goodness gracious, he only spoke to you for a few minutes and you know more than any of us,' she snapped.

'That wasn't very nice, Caroline,' Grandma said gently. 'Amanda was only expressing an opinion.'

Angrily Caroline looked down at her place and her sister Charlotte, who was sitting next to me, smiled. 'Because she's got a crush on Phillip she thinks nobody else should have anything to do with him,' she said vindictively. 'He'll probably stay in the navy and never come back to Belthorn.'

'You don't want him to come back because you're jealous,' Caroline said spitefully.

'Of course I'm not jealous,' Charlotte snapped. 'Why should I be?'

'Because he prefers me to you, that's why.'

'Girls girls,' Grandma said evenly. 'We can't have this over the dining table. You're far too young to be thinking seriously of Phillip Marston, Caroline, and, if indeed you are, then perhaps it's just as well he's serving in the navy.'

The sisters looked down at their plates, their faces red with embarrassment, and Aunt Edith said, 'They've always squabbled about their friends and their toys, it doesn't mean anything. I do think Phillip is taken with Caroline, but as you say, Caroline's only sixteen. There's plenty of time.'

'You danced with Phillip, didn't you Sophie? Did he say anything to you about staying on in the navy?'

'We didn't mention the navy,' Sophie said. 'We found plenty of other things to talk about.'

She smiled sweetly across the table at Caroline who glared at her in return and I for one was glad when Grandfather snapped, 'Tomorrow I want you to come with me to the mill, Ralph. You can meet some of the foremen – you'll need to ask their advice a good many times before you're competent enough to decide things for yourself.'

'Can I come with you?' I asked. Anything was better than

listening to the backchat between my cousins.

'There's nothing at the mills for you, Amanda. You'll be going back to India when you leave school,' Grandfather said firmly.

'I know, but I'd like to come.'

We drove to the mills in his big black car in silence.

I drove with grandfather to the mill at seven o'clock on Monday morning. It was too early for school and we waited in his office for Ralph and his father to arrive. Ralph's face was predictably sulky but nobody took any notice of the fact.

We followed my grandfather as he strode along the aisles, his eyes sweeping from left to right and as he passed some of the women acknowledged his presence by bobbing small curtsies while the others busied themselves at their looms in some degree of fear. The men touched their caps and Ralph muttered, 'This is what he likes. It's archaic.'

Halfway down one of the aisles I saw Jenny Alsop busily sweeping away the fluff. She looked fearful and a large red-faced woman snapped at her, 'Get from under mi feet, yer neither use nor an ornament.'

We were close enough for me to see Jenny's pale embarrassed face, and as we drew level the woman kicked Jenny's shovel away so that the lint scattered across the floor. Jenny burst into tears.

I went forward quickly and picked up the shovel, then I walked over to Jenny and handed it to her.

The weavers were all staring at me and now Ralph was picking up her brush and the large red-faced woman was glaring at me vindictively.

By this time Grandfather had joined us and stood looking down at the weeping girl and sensing immediately that there was trouble afoot.

'What goes on here?' he demanded.

The woman occupied herself at her loom and Jenny looked down miserably at the floor.

'Well?' he demanded.

'She's gettin' in mi way,' the woman snapped. 'I can't be doin' with her round mi feet.'

Shifting his gaze to the weaver on the next loom he said, 'Are you too complaining about the girl. If you are, she can get out.'

'The lass is right enough,' the woman answered. 'She's done nothin' wrong.'

'Well, get on with your work then,' he commanded.

Jenny looked up at me tremulously and smiling I said, 'I never seem to see you these days Jenny. I'll call one day when I know you're at home.'

Ralph stared at me in some surprise and I said quietly, 'This is my friend Jenny Alsop. Her mother does laundry at the house and some cleaning. Jenny and I used to walk across the fell together before she started work here.'

Ralph smiled down at her. 'Hello Jenny. We'll be workmates soon. I'll be a new boy.'

Her face was rosy with blushes and we looked up to see Grandfather waiting impatiently for us at the end of the aisle.

In later years when I looked back on that day it seemed strange that from such a small beginning so much that was unhappy was born. Why is it that so often the people we love when we are young are deemed so terribly wrong for us when we are mature?

On that day I had no hint of catastrophe when I walked home with Ralph in the late afternoon.

'That girl Jenny is rather pretty,' he remarked.

'Oh yes, I think so, but today she was afraid of that woman. You will keep an eye on her, won't you Ralph? Don't let that awful woman pick on her for nothing.'

'I'll look after her,' he assured me.

'You really don't want to work there, do you?'

'No. I shall hate ever minute of it.'

'Well of course you won't. One day the mills will be yours, you'll be in Grandfather's shoes. I know it's a long time off, but it will come.'

Cousin Sophie's twenty-first birthday and engagement were celebrated at the same party just before Christmas and the war had been over just over a month.

Flags were still flying throughout the town and Christmas lights shone out into the darkness from cottage windows, while a huge Christmas tree had been set up in the town hall square, the first for four long years.

Sophie's fiancé was Doctor Holleran's eldest son but he

had no aspirations to enter the medical profession; instead he was interested in politics and had been adopted as a potential Conservative candidate for the town of Brompton sixteen miles away. My first introduction to Jarvis Holleran was at their engagement party, and he was not at all the sort of young man I had thought Sophie would marry. For one thing he was rather short and plump, and he wore thick horn-rimmed spectacles which gave him an owlish look.

He had a lot to say for himself and Aunt Edith remarked snidely that he was pompous, but undoubtedly the right sort of material for Westminster. Aunt Edith was decidedly put out that Phillip Marston had elected to remain in the Royal Navy and since he was serving somewhere in the Far East he was unable to attend.

A crowd of people stood in the town hall square watching the guests arrive, mostly workers from the mills, and among them young women who stared morosely at expensively gowned women who had so much more than they were ever likely to have. I had a new dress for the occasion and this time I had been able to choose the colour – it was blue.

I danced with Ralph for much of the evening since he complained that most of the women were older than himself. There was an elaborate buffet but we sat on the stairs with plates piled high with food and Ralph grumbled, 'We don't want to sit with them. They're all trying to outdo one another. Besides, I'm the only one on the shop floor. The others have gone immediately into the boardroom.'

'They won't know as much about the business,' I said in an endeavour to placate him.

His expression was dismal, then suddenly it cleared and he said lightly, 'I've asked that friend of yours if she'd like to work in the mill office. She hates it on the mill floor.'

I stared at him, 'But Jenny said she would hate office work, she told me she wasn't clever at school.'

'She doesn't have to be. This is only a little office on the factory floor, not the main office block. It doesn't require much. She'll be making up parcels and writing labels, nothing too ambitious.'

'Has she accepted?'

'She's thinking about it. Some of those women are the pits,

31

loud-mouthed and spiteful. Some of them are decent but Jenny seems to fall foul of the others.'

'I wonder why that is?'

'Because she's young and pretty. I have to be very careful not to show favouritism since that day you told everybody she was your friend.'

'Don't you think you're showing favouritism by putting her in the mill office?'

'Perhaps. I'll survive. After all I am a Dexter.'

I was tempted to ask how well Jenny would survive but thought better of it. I saw Jenny very seldom now. Her father had not returned after the war and she made the excuse that she was too busy at home.

Government contracts were few and far between and I had to listen to Grandfather going on and on about short time and a reversal in his fortunes.

My father returned to India without coming home but both he and Mother were hoping to come to England for a few weeks' leave. They could take me back with them when I was seventeen. It seemed a lifetime away, and time passed in monotonous routine. One highlight might have been Charlotte's twenty-first birthday — but she declined to celebrate it with a traditional family party and opted for a small car and driving lessons instead.

Charlotte was spirited and independent. She professed that she was disinterested in the men her sister seemed to gather around her, but while Caroline was pretty, Charlotte was striking.

Aunt Edith expressed an opinion that Charlotte was too outspoken for her own good, whereas her younger sister was malleable and sweet-natured. Of the two I preferred Charlotte, since Caroline's malleability hid an often spiteful tongue which was reserved for those times when her elders were not there to hear it.

Six months after her party, Sophie was married in the parish church in Belthorn and along with my two other cousins, I was one of her bridesmaids. The church was full, since Sophie's fiancé was now a member of Parliament and in the congregation were politicians and civil servants, local dignitaries and cotton mill owners. Sophie looked radiant in white lace and we followed her down the aisle wearing identical pale-pink chiffon dresses. Ralph acted the part of groomsman in his first morning suit, and as we walked along the church path, I saw Jenny Alsop standing with her mother near the church door. I smiled at her, but she was not looking at me: her eyes were on my cousin Ralph and they were so full of hero-worship I worried about it all through the marriage ceremony.

Sophie's daughter Julia was born in the first year of their marriage and I attended my first christening.

I tried desperately hard to see Jenny during those few months after Sophie's wedding but she remained elusive, and when I said as much to Ralph he merely shrugged his shoulders saying, 'She's got other friends. Besides, what's the point? You'll be off to India one of these days.'

Grandfather brought home two Japanese gentlemen from Tokyo who were visiting the mills to learn about cotton. They were courteous and quiet although they spoke perfect English, and almost as soon as they had left they were followed by others from Hong Kong and Burma, Thailand and Sumatra, and if they did not stay with us they stayed at one of the uncles' houses.

In the meantime Grandfather complained about falling orders.

They came to learn about cotton, how to wind and weave, how to dye it and how to design it and they listened quietly with Eastern patience. Both grandfather and the uncles delighted in showing off their cleverness and invariably our visitors departed with gratitude. It never seemed to enter anybody's head that one day those countries who had sent them would be pricing us out of the market. That they could command slave labour to work in their cotton mills and we would be fighting strikes against a workforce demanding higher wages for the same kind of work.

I remember one day voicing my opinion on this, as they sat complimenting each other on the lessons they had been able to impart. That they should be interrupted by the youngest member of the family and with such seditious talk outraged

Grandfather. He fumed about it for days.

Cook complained that the master was cutting down. The family roasts became smaller, the cleaners fewer, hospitality dwindled, but he did purchase two expensive hunters and kept up his Masonic and Rotarian activities as well as his interest in horse-racing and hunting. On Sunday mornings after church we invariably went riding together across the fells and it was on these mornings that we came to know each other better.

It was on one such morning that we met Phillip Marston riding a chestnut horse across the same moorland fell. He raised his whip and with a smile elected to join us. There was a sharp east wind blowing, bringing tears to our eyes, and irritably Grandfather said after a while, 'I thought we'd ride up to the crags but I can't be doing with this wind, it's not good for my chest. I think I'll ride back. Are you coming with me Amanda?'

I stared at him doubtfully and Phillip said, 'Why don't we ride up to the crags Amanda, your horse is very fresh, he'd enjoy the exercise.'

'You two carry on then. She's a fair horsewoman Phillip. You'll find that out for yourself.'

It was unexpected praise which gave me a new confidence as we set off across the moor towards the tall stone crags at their summit.

Set almost like a Druid's circle, this natural rock formation offered some shelter from the wind. We both dismounted and stood looking out across the moors to the distant town, almost ethereal under a cloudy grey sky.

For a few minutes we said nothing. The ride had been exhilarating, leaving us breathless. The horses cropped the coarse moorland grass. Phillip was the first to break the silence.

'I thought you'd be going back to India. The war's been over for several years now.'

'My father has been serving in the hill country, as soon as he returns to Delhi he will get leave and they will come for me.'

'And when will that be?'

'In eight months.'

'Will you be glad?'

'I thought I would be. Just a few years ago I could hardly wait. Now I'm not so sure.'

'Why's that?'

'Well, I want to see my parents very much, but I was only eight when I left India. I've forgotten what it was like there.'

'I expect you'll soon remember. It could be very exciting for you.'

'Well yes. Mother writes about the regimental balls and the polo matches, but it isn't all like that I'm sure.'

'No, perhaps not.'

'Are you happy in the navy?'

'Oh yes, that's why I stayed on. I couldn't even begin to contemplate a life back here.'

'Don't your parents mind?'

'At first I think, but not now, they've become accustomed to the fact that my life is there, not here.'

'Suppose you marry, it could be very lonely for your wife.'

'Yes, but perhaps sailors' wives have to be a special breed and able to understand their loneliness.'

He smiled, and the charm of his smile once again made my foolish heart grow suddenly mature. I was thinking of Caroline, vain spoilt Caroline who wanted him and refused to think beyond him.

We rode back across the fell and now there was rain in the wind and Phillip insisted on riding back to the house with me. I knew that the family would be sitting down to afternoon tea and as he lifted me down from my horse I said, 'Would you like to come in for tea, the family are always here on Sunday.'

'Well, I'm hardly dressed for afternoon tea, the smell of horse won't go down very well. Make my excuses Amanda. I'm sure I shall see them some time during my leave, probably tomorrow – I'm taking Caroline out to dinner.'

His smile was warm, his handclasp firm but his words dispelled the joy I felt in being with him. As I bathed and changed into something more appropriate for the drawing room I felt furious with myself. He had been charming, kindly agreeing to ride with a young girl, but that was all. Caroline was the one he would be taking out to dinner, not just tomorrow but in those days when I would be a distant memory.

In the drawing room Caroline fixed me with a penetrating gaze. 'Didn't you bring Phillip in for tea then?' she asked.

'No. He said the smell of horse would not be acceptable.'

'Oh well, he's probably right. I shall see him tomorrow evening, anyway. He's taking me out to dinner.'

I didn't answer and Aunt Myrtle said, 'How long is he home for?'

'Two or three weeks I think, long enough for us to spend some time together,' Caroline answered.

I couldn't help myself saying, 'Don't you mind that he's stayed in the navy, he's home so seldom?'

'Well of course I'd rather have him home all the time, but I shall learn to cope. After all it's what Phillip wants isn't it?'

They were discussing Caroline's twenty-first birthday.

'I hope Phillip will get leave for that,' Aunt Edith said hopefully.

'And I hope Amanda's parents will be here,' Grandma said. 'Amanda will be nineteen and ready to return to India with them. It would be a real family party, Harry and his wife here, Caroline's birthday party and Amanda's farewell party.'

At that moment I hoped fervently that Phillip would not be on leave. I did not want to depart for India with memories of his smile, the charm of his voice and his hoped-for future with Caroline.

Chapter Four

It was the middle of January before my parents came to England. Deep snow lay across the Pennines driven by freezing winds but none of this mattered when my mother held me in her arms and I looked up into her gently smiling face. Unused to the cold and damp she had one cold after another and in spite of Grandfather's protests father seemed determined to return to India before his leave was up.

Neither of my aunts liked my mother. I became miserably aware that they thought her spoiled and with too many airs and graces. Since neither of them had lived in a hot climate it was ridiculous that they should be judging her.

Caroline was quick to say that it was quite unnecessary for us to have a joint party but for once Grandma was insistent.

'Goodness knows when we shall all be together again,' she said, and proceeded to send out invitations for a Friday evening at the beginning of March.

'I hope you've invited the Marstons,' Aunt Edith said. 'Caroline is hoping Phillip can get leave.'

'Well of course I've invited them, but Sir John's not been well. Though if he's not able to come, perhaps Phillip will escort his mother.'

'If his father continues to be ill perhaps he'll come out of the Navy sooner than expected,' Aunt Edith said hopefully. I looked at Caroline and saw her flush.

'I suppose you've brought clothes that will do for the party,' Aunt Myrtle said to my mother. 'Was it possible to buy anything decent in India?'

Mother smiled. 'We had a treasure who sewed for us and

getting clothes was never a problem before or after the war.'

They talked endlessly about their dresses and that night when Mother came into my room to wish me goodnight she said, 'We'll go into Manchester whenever the rain stops Amanda. Hopefully you'll be able to find something really nice there.'

Shopping with Mother was a far more exciting experience than shopping with Grandma had been. She loved the stores and time seemed to fly as we searched for what she described as the perfect gown.

We both agreed at last on a parchment satin which swept in long delicious folds to the floor, its only adornment chiffon roses of the same colour that formed a circle at my waist and fell to the hem of the gown. It was terribly expensive but Mother said, 'There will be a great many occasions for you to wear it in India dear, and in some respects the aunts are right, you'll see nothing like it there.'

In spite of the cold the city was crowded with shoppers and as we hurried with our parcels towards the train for Belthorn I felt the first faint stirrings of regret for what I would be leaving behind. I could have loved this cool green land and these dark hills under low-hung leaden skies, where dim moist fogs painted verdure on the rocky fells. For there were days when shafts of sunlight fell on far towers and dark old trees and hedge-bound meadows of green dreamed gently under skies as blue as a tropic sea.

I had lived many years in England, but now that they were ending there was regret and the shadow of a remembered pain. I had no doubt that one day I could come back, but would things be the same?

We waited on the station platform for the country train and when it came and the people came pouring out of the carriages there was laughter and expectancy in a night at the cinema or in one of the city's dance halls.

We elected to travel in the first compartment but as I looked along the platform I was amazed to see my cousin Ralph turning to help a girl out of the train, then as they started to walk towards us I saw it was Jenny.

Our eyes met and they both looked acutely embarrassed. Jenny's face was crimson but after a brief smile I joined my mother in the train while I watched them walking quickly along the platform to the barrier. I did not have long to wait before Ralph came up to Fairlawn to speak to me. It was early Sunday morning. We had only just finished breakfast, and we all stared in amazement as his head appeared round the door, and Grandma asked, 'Have you had breakfast Ralph? Are you on your own?'

'Yes, I walked up, I thought the exercise would do me good.'

'But it's raining, you must be wet through.'

'I've left my raincoat in the hall, I enjoyed the walk.'

I knew why he had come, and was aware of his impatience as we continued breakfast quite unconcerned by his sudden appearance. He sat in the window seat with the Sunday newspaper open on his knee, occasionally glancing across to the table. I smiled at him, wondering idly how he expected to get me on my own.

I need not have worried. As soon as the meal was over and Bridie came in to clear the table he called across, 'Have you still got that book on holidays in Scotland Amanda? I'd like to borrow it.'

I had never had a book on travels in Scotland and I smiled at him sweetly saying, 'If it's anywhere, Ralph, it will be upstairs in the nursery.'

He grinned. 'Will you find it for me?'

'You can hunt around for it yourself. Let me know if you can't find it.'

He glared, and Grandma said, 'I suggest you get it for him Amanda. He'll upset everything in the bookcase just like he used to do.'

We walked up the stairs together and he said when we reached the first landing, 'You know there isn't a book, I just wanted to talk to you.'

'I know, I've been expecting you.'

'It's about Jenny. It's not at all what you've been thinking.'

'How do you know what I've been thinking?'

'I know. We just travelled together, we both happened to be going into town on the same train.'

I looked at him and smiled and he had the grace to blush and look embarrassed.

'You seemed very attentive to her, whether it was coincidence or not.'

'Well, Jenny's a nice girl and I'd like her to think that I'm a gentleman.'

'Of course.'

'Come on, Amanda. You know what the family would say if they thought I was taking out one of the workpeople, the parents would be horrified and Grandfather'd probably sack her. People have been sacked for less.'

'That's archaic.'

'It's also a fact of life. Please Amanda, don't tell anybody. After all it was a one-off, there was nothing in it.'

'I don't know what bothers me the most, that you're merely flirting with her, or that I have to keep it to myself.'

'I like her.'

'Then why is it a one-off?'

'I've told you why. There is no way I'd be allowed to marry a girl like Jenny. She knows it and so do I.'

'I'm not going to say anything to anybody. There really was no need for you to leave home at the crack of dawn just to ask me to keep it to myself. I just think it will be awfully sad if Jenny falls in love with you while you're simply playing around.'

'Well of course she won't fall for me! She knows the score. Anyway thanks Amanda, you're a brick. What were you doing in Manchester anyway?'

'Shopping for my party dress. I don't suppose you'll be bringing Jenny to the party.'

'No such luck. I'm coming with the family and I'll be on my own most of the evening. How about the supper dance?'

'Thank you. They'll mostly be older than me too. I'll be glad of your company.'

Father had decided we would return to India just before Easter as he had a long leave, for he had taken none since returning to India after the war. I think those weeks were interminable to Mother. The weather was wet, cold and showing no signs of improving.

One morning after Grandma had noticed her pallor she said, 'It really is a pity you couldn't have come in the summertime Elizabeth. We could have shown you the countryside and you could have spent some time in the Lake District or at the coast.'

Mother smiled wanly while Grandfather merely looked at her with the utmost exasperation.

In the meantime Caroline displayed a great deal of interest in the dress I had chosen for the party but told me very little about hers.

Charlotte informed me that it was blue and had cost the earth. When I asked Charlotte about hers she grinned mischievously saying, 'I'm wearing the one I had for Ralph's do, after all I'm not out to capture the most eligible bachelor in the area. Caroline's set her stall out, Father's grumbling about the expense but Mother will have her way. She's set her heart on Phillip Marston.'

'He is coming then?'

'With his mother. His father has declined because he isn't too well.'

Since my parents' arrival I spent less time in the kitchen with Cook and Bridie but, even so, I noticed now that it was not always a good time to visit. If Mrs Alsop was there I was greeted with brief smiles and they seemed to have so much to do there was never time to chat.

I asked Mrs Alsop if Jenny was enjoying working in the mill office and she blushed to the roots of her hair and said, 'She doesn't talk about it Miss Amanda.'

I met Bridie one morning when she was tidying the dining room and she seemed anxious to be done with her task so that she didn't need to talk. There was only the two of us in the room so I said, 'We never seem to talk these days Bridie, I've been spending so much time with my parents.'

'Well of course ye 'ave Miss Amanda, and rightly so. You'll be leavin' 'ere soon, sure and ye'ave a lot to think about.'

'Does Cook mind that I haven't been into the kitchen much?'

'Gracious no, why should she be mindin'? She knows yer've better things to do with yer time.'

'I just wondered, she always seems so busy and not very welcoming these days.'

'Well I'm sure she doesn't mean to be. Cookin' for two

extra does make her busier and she's been asked to be more sparin' these days.'

'I know, that's because the mills are not so busy, Number Three mill is on short time.'

'That's so.'

'Is that why she's always whispering to Mrs Alsop? Is she afraid that Jenny might lose her job?'

'I'm sure she isn't, they do talk a lot together, I don't always know what they're talkin' about. My what a grand party it's goin' to be in March. Are ye lookin' forward to it Miss Amanda?'

'I suppose so.'

'Faith Miss Amanda ye should be livin' for it. It'll be the best party Belthorn's seen in years.'

'The workpeople who are laid off won't be too enthusiastic about it Bridie. They have very little money going in and here we are spending a fortune on a ball.'

'Don't worry about that, the good times'll come back, we've 'ad these ups and downs before.'

'I suppose so. Two weeks later I'll be on my way to Bombay.'

'That ye will luv, are you goin' to miss us?'

'I'll miss Grandma and you and Cook, I'll miss the snow and the life here, but I expect I'll be happy in India, my mother says after a few days it will feel as if I've never been away.'

Bridie smiled. 'Well I must get on now Miss Amanda, I'm runnin' late and ye know what Cook's like.'

March lived up to its reputation for rain and high winds and on the day of the party I stared out of the windows with dismay at the tossing trees and windswept fells. By early afternoon, however, the wind had abated and a pale watery sun shone out of a pale blue sky.

We stood in the hall waiting for Albert to bring the car round and the first real excitement got through to me. Grandma looked elegant in beige lace while Mother wore royal blue which complemented her fair hair and dark blue eyes. Grandfather looked very resplendent in full evening dress but it was Father in his dress uniform who really looked wonderful, and when I said as much to Mother she laughed saying, 'You'll see a great many handsome young men in uniform Amanda when we get back to India.'

I was unprepared for the crowds of people standing round in groups in the town hall square and lining the steps up to the town hall doors. It seemed that most of Belthorn had turned out to witness the Dexters and their guests arriving for the party, but I was aware that while some of them smiled others stared at us with grim hostility.

This was really Caroline's party – she was the one who had come of age. I was merely the girl who was leaving the area and hardly one of them.

The dress was admired and I did not lack for partners, indeed Ralph hissed at me, 'Don't forget you promised me the supper dance,' as I swept past him in the arms of a very presentable young man, who Grandma told me, was the younger son of another mill-owner.

Phillip Marston arrived with his mother, who was immediately pounced upon by Aunt Edith, who invited her to sit next to her, while Phillip, also in naval dress uniform, danced with Caroline.

'He's so handsome,' I remarked feelingly to Charlotte who simply laughed and said, 'It's the uniform.'

'He's good-looking without the uniform,' I retorted.

'Don't tell me you're besotted with him too,' she said. 'What a pity you're not a bit older. Caroline wouldn't have had all her own way.'

A short while after Aunt Myrtle invited three other people to sit at the family table, this time they were a man and woman accompanied by their daughter and were introduced as Mr and Mrs Carlisle and their daughter Rosemary. She was a little older than I and very pretty with dark hair and large brown eyes, and immediately Aunt Edith informed us that he was the new bank manager recently come to live in the area.

Minutes later Aunt Myrtle said in a whisper, 'I can't see Ralph anywhere Amanda. Do look around for him and ask him to join us.'

I hadn't seen him for some time and although I looked round the ballroom and the adjoining buffet room there was no sign of him. I wandered out on to the balcony that edged the stairs and there I saw him looking pensively through the window towards the square below.

He did not see me until I reached his side, then abruptly he turned away from the window with an embarrassed look.

'Your mother wants you to join her, she sent me to look for you,' I said, instantly aware of his impatient frown.

'Why, for heaven's sake?' he said sharply.

'I think she want you to meet someone, Rosemary, the bank manager's daughter, and her parents.'

I sensed his frustration as muttering to himself he turned away and headed for the ballroom. I stayed where I was looking out into the square. Rain was sweeping across the puddles and I was instantly aware of a solitary figure huddled under an umbrella staring at me, Jenny Alsop, and then almost immediately she had lowered her umbrella and was running across the square towards the streets beyond.

At that moment I had a feeling of the utmost foreboding. I was remembering Ralph's expression and the emotions that had chased themselves all too briefly across his face.

When I returned to the ballroom Ralph was already dancing with Rosemary while the family looked on approvingly. At that moment I was glad that in just over a week's time we would be leaving Belthorn.

We stood at last on the town hall steps waiting for Albert to bring the car round. Father had thought it was a ridiculous idea to ask Albert to drive us, as he could have driven us to the ball himself, but Grandfather had been adamant. 'We want to enjoy ourselves without thinking about the journey home, besides it's what I pay him for,' he had said.

I privately wondered what poor Albert had been doing while we had been at the ball with the rain beating down mercilessly and not a soul in sight down the rain-soaked streets.

While we were waiting Phillip Marston came across to speak to us while his mother waited under the awning with Aunt Edith and Caroline.

He smiled when Father explained why we were waiting, 'Mother insisted on her chauffeur even when I offered to drive the car myself,' Phillip said. 'I can't really think why.'

He looked down at me, 'You enjoyed yourself tonight, Amanda. You've grown up so much since the last time we met at a dance.'

I smiled. I hadn't grown up enough, but in the next moment he was saying to my father, 'You'll be off soon I hear?'

'Yes, in just over a week. How much of your leave is left?'

'A few days, I'll say my goodbyes now then and wish you all a safe journey back to India.'

We shook hands with him in turn before he rejoined his mother and in that moment a feeling of desolation overwhelmed me. It's a crush, I told myself, a silly schoolgirl crush that will end as quickly as it began. All girls have them, they don't mean anything, and one day there will be somebody else, more important, and I shall forget his smile and his voice.

Indeed the week that followed left me little time to think about anything except our imminent departure for India. We shopped for things that Mother said were impossible to find there, and she insisted that I visit the school I had attended since I came to live in England with presents for the headmistress and others who had been kind to me.

On the following Saturday morning Father and Grandfather set off together to some race-meeting or other and only the three of us sat down to lunch. At the end of the meal Bridie came to clear away and I could tell that she was nervous as she clattered the china on to a serving tray.

Whispering to Grandma and with an expression of acute embarrassment she said, 'Mrs Alsop wonders if she can 'ave a word, ma'am, after I've served coffee.'

'Mrs Alsop! I didn't think she came here on Saturdays.'

'Not normally, ma'am.'

'Oh dear, I hope there isn't trouble in the kitchen. Cook can be very abrasive at times, I do hope she hasn't said something to upset Mrs Alsop, and I really don't like to interfere.'

'It's got nothin' to do with Cook ma'am.'

'What is it Bridie?'

'I wouldn't be knowin' Ma'am. She's waitin' to know if you'll see 'er in the mornin' room.'

'Well yes, if it is so important. I'm due at the church hall at two and I really don't want to be late. Will you run down there Amanda and tell them I'll be there as soon as I can. I'll

45

see Mrs Alsop in about ten minutes Bridie. We'll have our coffee in here.'

I was glad to be leaving the house. Mrs Alsop had come about Jenny, I felt sure. With a murmured excuse I jumped up from the table and made for the door.

'You haven't finished your coffee,' Mother called out.

'I don't want any more. I'll go down to the church hall now Grandma.'

'Thank you dear. Oh I do hope Mrs Alsop isn't leaving. She's really quite a treasure and good servants are hard to come by. Perhaps she's got a fulltime job, I'm sure she needs the money since her husband didn't return after the war, she has two young children and her daughter can't be earning much in the mill.'

I was glad to escape. The church fête was well underway and waiting for the last of the local dignitaries to arrive. When I explained that Grandma would be a little late the vicar said, 'Well I do hope she won't mind if we open the fête without her, if she isn't here by two. Lady Marston is just arriving and the mayor is already here.'

'I'm sure she won't mind.'

'Well do explain things to her, Amanda. I'm sure she'll understand. We've worked very hard all morning so that Lady Marston could open the fête as soon as she arrived.'

One half of me wanted to remain in the church hall, the other felt compelled to return to the house. The vicar went forward to receive his honoured guests and I decided to go back. As I reached the road I saw Phillip Marston standing near his car and he smiled.

'Don't you fancy the fête then, Amanda?' he asked.

'Not really. I came to explain that Grandma might be a little late.'

'In that case I'll drive you home and bring your grandmother back if she's ready to come.'

He held the car door open for me and gratefully I sank back into its warmth.

He was disposed to make conversation.

'What will you remember most about England when you're basking in the Indian sunshine?' he asked.

'Probably the rain.'

46

He laughed. 'Not the spring, and primroses under the hedgerows. Not the sunlight lighting up those dark old hills? Not even the clamour of the cotton mills?'

'Oh yes I'll remember them, but most of all I'll remember the rain, there's so much of it.'

For a few minutes we drove in silence and then he surprised me by saying, 'You look worried Amanda. Is anything wrong?'

'No, I just hope Grandma can go to the fête. She was looking forward to it.'

He was staring at me intently and I was aware of my blushing face. I could not tell Phillip what I was worried about. I wished I did not feel so gauche with him. I wanted to laugh with him the way I had seen Caroline do. Perhaps to laugh and flirt a little but today was not the day for it.

He got out of the car and held the door open for me. 'I'll wait out here if you like Amanda. Tell your grandmother not to hurry, I have all the time in the world.'

I smiled. 'Thank you for the lift.'

'Not at all, and goodbye again.'

I entered the hall just in time to see Mrs Alsop leaving the morning room. She seemed upset and almost ran across the hall to the door leading to the kitchens. She was dabbing at her eyes and had to fumble with the door knob before she could open the door.

I looked up as Mother came out of the drawing room to gaze after her. When she saw me she beckoned me over, saying, 'I don't know what's wrong Amanda. Grandma will tell us I'm sure.'

'Is Grandma still in the morning room?'

'She must be. Perhaps we should go and find her.'

Grandma was sitting in front of the fire with her head in her hands and she was crying.

'Whatever is wrong?' Mother asked.

'Oh Elizabeth, it's too awful. I can't think what Edward will say, it will all have to be faced tomorrow when the family are together.'

'Shouldn't you be getting ready for the fête?' Mother asked.

'I can't possibly go. I'll have to ask you to go down there

again Amanda and tell the vicar that something has prevented me from going.'

'Phillip Marston is waiting outside to drive you there.'

'Then ask him to take you my dear. If Phillip asks any questions just tell him I'm unwell. No doubt he'll find out sometime or other. Everybody who knows us will find out.'

I stared at them both uncertainly and Mother said, 'Do as your grandmother asks Amanda. Stay at the fête if you would like to.'

I told Phillip Grandma was ill. He looked at me keenly and I'm not sure if he believed me or not. We drove back to the church hall and he said, 'Are you staying for a while Amanda?'

'No, I'd rather go home.'

'In that case I'll drive you. It's started raining. You've already told me how much you hate the rain.'

I made Grandma's excuses and ran back to the car where Phillip sat waiting for me. His face was pensive and we drove in silence. I believe he understood that I was in no mood for conversation. When we arrived he said with a little smile. 'This is our third goodbye Amanda, I always think the third time is the last time.'

'Yes. I'm so glad I met you. Grandma will write to us in India. I'm sure she'll write about you and people I've met here.'

'Well she won't be seeing much of me, I'll be at sea most of the time.'

'Oh but you'll come home on leave and you'll all meet up then.'

'You're sure about that, are you Amanda?'

I could not read the expression in his eyes, but the next moment he was saying, 'I'm not very sure about anything at the moment Amanda, I'm not even sure if I shall be able to remain in the Navy.'

'Why's that?'

'My father's a very sick man. If he dies I may have to rethink my life.'

With another brief smile he raised his hand in a farewell wave and drove away.

Chapter Five

I desperately wanted the evening meal to finish. Grandfather sat with a face like thunder while Grandma only picked at her food and constantly dabbed at her eyes. In answer to Father's questioning look Mother merely shook her head and after the meal was over, Grandfather stomped out of the room, slamming the door behind him.

Father said, 'What brought that on?'

Grandma burst into tears, but manlike he persisted, 'Has somebody died? What is the matter Mother?'

In a trembling voice she said, 'It's Ralph. It's terrible, there'll be such trouble tomorrow when they're all here.'

'Something gone wrong at the mill?'

'I wish it was that.'

'What then for heaven's sake?'

'He's got one of the mill girls in trouble – Jenny Alsop. Her mother does some work here.'

'Has he been to tell you?'

'No. Her mother's been to see me. The poor woman was distraught and I don't know what William and Myrtle are going to say.'

'So we can look forward to a family at war for most of tomorrow. I'm glad that we shall be leaving here early next week.'

'Oh Harry, I wish you were staying on. You know what your father's like. It won't just be tomorrow, it'll be every moment of every day until things are settled one way or another.'

'And how will they be settled?'

Again the tears fell down her cheeks as she murmured, 'How can I know? Adoption perhaps, if she keeps the baby he will have to support her of course. In any case it's the stigma, everybody will know.'

'What about marriage?'

She stared at him as if this was a prospect not to be contemplated.

'I can't think either William or Myrtle will agree to that. Ralph is a Dexter, one day he'll be the managing director of three large mills, and they have ambitions for him.'

'It's a great pity he didn't think about that when he dallied with one of the workforce.'

'Tell Bridie I don't want coffee, I think I shall go to bed although I'm quite sure I shan't be able to sleep.'

'It might be a good idea to drive over to the coast tomorrow Elizabeth, and leave the rest of them to sort things out,' Father said cautiously, but immediately Grandma said, 'No please, Harry, I'd rather you stayed.'

'I'm having nothing to do with this, Mother.'

'Well at least you're always logical and can be relied on to instil some sort of calm to the atmosphere.'

'I doubt that very much, Mother. Calmness with Myrtle and Edith hardly go together, Edith will gloat, Myrtle will have hysterics and we'll be wishing we were out of it.'

'But you'll be here Harry, and Elizabeth?'

Neither of my parents spoke, but Grandma left the room in the knowledge that they would be there for her. As for me I was dreading the next day. My parents and I sat in the drawing room that evening, Mother worked at her needle-point, I played chess with Father and after about an hour Grandfather came in and sat without speaking in front of the fire, a newspaper unopened on his knee, a glass of whisky on the small table near his chair.

His expression was morose but the affairs of the afternoon were ignored by all of us.

Around ten o'clock Mother said, 'I'll ask Cook if we can have tea Harry and then I think Amanda and I will go to bed.'

'No tea for me thanks, I'll join Father in a whisky and soda,' Father said, and looking at me questioningly Mother said, 'What about you Amanda?'

'No thank you Mother, I'll have a glass of water, I don't want tea.'

Aunt Edith and Uncle Edwin with their two daughters arrived first on Sunday morning. Aunt Edith as usual was complaining about the weather and the length of the vicar's sermon. Uncle Edwin appeared pensive and I immediately thought he might know about Ralph and had not told the others.

When Aunt Edith commented that the others were rather late he met my father's gaze with a worried frown which confirmed that I was right.

Aunt Edith, never mindful of atmosphere, prattled on, seemingly oblivious to Grandfather's glowering expression and Grandma's anxiety. At last we heard the sound of their car outside the house and her anxiety increased as her hands twisted and coiled the handkerchief on her lap.

Uncle William looked at his brothers and went to the cabinet to pour himself a glass of sherry. Aunt Myrtle was pale but dry-eyed. Normally she went on at length about Sophie and her little girl, but not this morning, and then Ralph was there, pale and obviously resigned to the trauma to come.

We sat down to dinner in silence, a silence that no doubt Bridie would report as soon as she arrived back in the kitchen.

'Everybody's very quiet this morning,' Aunt Edith said brightly. 'You've left me to do all the talking. We do miss Sophie, she was forever chattering on about something. Have you seen any more of Rosemary Carlisle Ralph, you looked very well together?'

Aunt Myrtle looked away sharply, Grandfather scowled and Ralph's face became a delicate crimson.

Now even Aunt Edith's expression grew doubtful as she gazed around the rest of us uncertainly and Caroline said, 'Everybody's so glum this morning, nobody's said a word about the ball.'

'There are more important things to think about than the ball,' Grandfather snapped, and that was the moment it began. Fixing Ralph with a stern look he snarled, 'And what

51

have you to say for yourself young man?'

Ralph evidently believed silence to be the better course to follow, but now everybody round the table was looking at him, and Aunt Edith's eyes were bright with anticipation.

'Had ye no more sense than to tangle with one of the work girls,' Grandfather demanded. 'And what do you intend to do about it?'

Ralph gazed down in silence at the tablecloth and Uncle William said testily, 'We have to talk about it, he knows that. Today. When the family are together.'

'Talking about it won't make it go away,' Grandfather said. 'She'll have it adopted I've no doubt, but it'll not be forgotten by them or the rest of the workforce. Have you spoken to the girl?'

'Of course,' Ralph muttered, finding his tongue at last.

'And . . .?'

'She won't have it adopted, that's the last thing she'll do.'

'And how does she propose to look after it? Her father was killed in the war and her mother has to work to look after the rest of them. Another baby in the family is something they don't want, the girl's wages are needed at home. I hope her mother and you have explained that to her.'

Ralph did not reply, and exasperatedly Grandfather turned to Uncle William. 'This'll not end here you know, they're a close-knit bunch on the factory floor, if you hurt one of them the rest of them limp so he's got to pay for what he's done. He'll be paying money for that child until it's an adult, it would be better to give her a lump sum now and have it adopted.'

'Like Ralph says Father, she is adamantly refusing to have the child adopted.'

'Then he'll have to give her money. She'll be a drain on him for years, and any girl he marries won't take kindly to him paying for another woman's child.'

'Does Rosemary Carlisle and her parents know?' Aunt Edith asked and was immediately shouted down by Grandfather who said, 'Forget about Rosemary Carlisle. She doesn't come into it and probably never will. Any decent young woman's going to think twice about Ralph in the next few years. Any money he earns will be spoken for.'

'If you'd let me go into the boardroom to be with my father I'd probably never have met Jenny,' Ralph said bitterly. 'I'm earning next to nothing on the shop floor and all I have to look forward to is some distant dream that might never happen.'

'It happened for some of my managers, it happened for me and for your father, they were prepared to work and wait for it, you want it all and you want it now. Well you've brought your pigs to a bonny market and now you have to pay for your sins. Find out how much money she's prepared to accept, either in a lump sum or every week till the child's old enough to work for itself.'

'I'm not giving her any money, at least not until I'm her husband. I intend to marry Jenny.'

The consternation might have been comical, had it not been so distressing.

'Ralph you can't marry that girl,' his mother cried. 'It wouldn't work, you've had a good education and you'll have absolutely nothing in common once the gloss has worn off.'

'We'll have the baby in common.' Ralph snapped.

'It's not enough.' She looked round the rest of us for support and it was Caroline who said, 'She'll be miserable Ralph, she'll never fit in. Your sister is married to a member of Parliament and then there's Phillip. What will the Marstons think about this?'

'You're not engaged to Phillip yet.'

'But I will be. Can you really think she'll ever be one of us?'

'I'm not asking any of you to come to the wedding, we'll get married quietly. The men and women on the shop floor will give us their blessing.'

'It'll be like Amanda marrying an Indian,' Caroline went on. 'It would never work would it, Uncle Harry?'

Ignoring the question Father said dryly, 'Shall I tell you what would have happened if a British soldier made an Indian girl pregnant? One night in some dark alley the girl's relatives would ambush him and he'd be found next morning with his throat cut. They would call that just retribution. We like to call ourselves civilised.'

Nobody spoke.

53

'This is your decision then,' Grandfather said at last, 'to marry this girl and set up house with her?'

'Yes, Grandfather.'

'And what do you expect the rest of us to do?'

'Get to know her. Jenny's a nice girl, you might even like her. Amanda does.'

All eyes were turned on me in surprise. 'You know her, Amanda?' Aunt Myrtle asked.

'Yes. She's pretty and she's nice. She's not stupid, she can educate herself if you'll give her a chance, and Ralph will be there for her.'

'There'll be no big wedding like Sophie had,' Aunt Myrtle said firmly. 'They will marry quietly. We'll buy a small house somewhere away from here, something better than she's accustomed to. Nobody's going to say your parents were ungenerous, and we'll do our best to get along with your wife and educate your child. I don't see that we can do any more.'

Aunt Edith made the most of the situation.

'Thank goodness my two girls know how to look after themselves. Charlotte isn't interested in anybody and Caroline knows what she wants, Ralph has been a complete fool.'

'It might work out better than any of you think,' Father said.

'Oh, Harry, of course it won't. Myrtle will never like her, and she'll simply never fit in. Suppose they want to visit you in India. Will you welcome them?'

'I hope we wouldn't be unkind enough to forget that they are family. India is riddled with the caste system that calls people untouchables. It's nice to think that we are a little more charitable.'

His eyes met mine, and in them I read doubt and uncertainty. Were we really any different, not if this family was anything to go by?

Later that afternoon Father and I went riding on the fells and as we stood our horses on the crest of the hill looking out across the lonely moorland towards the distant town I sensed his sadness. This was the countryside he grew up in, the world he had exchanged for something infinitely more exciting and exotic, but at that moment I knew he was remembering his boyhood.

54

Tarns sparkling silver in the sunlight, purple heather in autumn, gorse in spring, rivers gurgling between stones, swollen by winter rains and mist hanging low on the Pennine hills.

His memories were happier than mine. I might only remember rain on cobbled squares and the pitiless stupidity of family pride.

'Just another few days,' he said at last. 'Will you be sorry, Amanda?'

I shook my head.

'Won't you miss it at all?'

'Some of it. I made some friends at school, and I'll miss Grandma. I'll miss Cook and Bridie and I'll miss Ralph — he's the nicest of my cousins.'

'In spite of his fall from grace?'

'Yes, of course. Will they come to like her do you think? Oh surely, when the baby's born they will?'

'I wouldn't bank on it, love.'

'That would be so cruel.'

'Yes, but maybe she won't mind. Perhaps she will never like them, in which case she won't miss them.'

That was a prospect I hadn't imagined, now I saw its possibility.

Neither of us seemed to have any wish to ride back and instead we carried on to the summit of Rushmere Fell from where we could look down on the parkland surrounding Marston Hall, the Marston's family home.

'I suppose Phillip's gone back to his ship,' I mused thoughtfully.

'Probably,' Father agreed. 'Perhaps his days in the navy are numbered. I doubt if his father will ever be well again.'

'But he so loves the navy. It doesn't seem fair.'

'As you get older, my dear, you will discover that life is very often unfair. Lady Marston can't possibly manage the estate if her husband dies and one day it will be Phillip's. The responsibility for its well-being will also be his.'

'Couldn't Lady Marston get a good manager to look after it?'

'Perhaps, but I doubt if that's the answer. If the estate was mine I'd want to look after it myself.'

'Have you never been sorry that you didn't go into cotton with Grandfather and the uncles?' I asked curiously.

'Never. But, then, it's a very different situation from the Marston's.'

'Caroline will love being Lady Marston.'

He smiled. 'You think it's so imminent, do you?'

'Caroline thinks so and she always gets her way.'

'Oh well, like you say, Amanda, Caroline will take to the title like a duck to water. She's the one who won't take kindly to little Jenny Alsop.'

'Phillip isn't like that, he'll be kind to Jenny if none of the others are.'

'You like him, don't you Amanda? But not too well, I hope.'

'I think he's nice.'

'So it isn't a crush?'

'A very small one perhaps.'

'Then, it's just as well that our days here are numbered.'

Afternoon tea was over by the time we arrived home and we made our apologies for being absent. There was still an air of gloom and doom about the house. Aunt Myrtle sat pale and silent with her head averted from the rest of us. Ralph sat staring morosely out of the window and Grandfather and Uncle Edwin were playing snooker in the billiard room.

Grandmother and Aunt Edith were discussing knitting patterns while Caroline read a book. There was no sign of Mother and Charlotte, and Grandma said they had gone for a walk.

Promptly, at half past five, Aunt Myrtle rose to her feet saying, 'Go and find your father, Ralph. It's time to go home.'

'Well, we can't go till Charlotte gets back,' Aunt Edith said. 'I suppose we'll all be here next Sunday as usual?'

'Well, we shan't be here,' Father said. 'We're leaving on Friday.'

'Oh yes, of course, I'd forgotten. Does that mean we'll be having a get-together before you leave?'

Father was quick to say, 'Oh, I don't think so. We shall have a lot of packing to do. I'm afraid, Edith, today will have to serve as our farewell dinner.'

56

'Perhaps one day one of the girls might like to visit you in India? It will probably be Charlotte. I rather think other things are in store for Caroline.'

'If Charlotte decides to come, she will be made very welcome.'

At that moment the door opened and Mother and Charlotte came in, their faces rosy from the keen wind blowing across the fells. 'Did I hear my name?' Charlotte said.

'I was saying you might like to visit your cousin in India one day.'

'I might. It would be a change from here.'

'I wish you were more interested in the things we enjoy doing, Charlotte,' her mother said crossly. 'You don't like this and you don't like that. None of the young men appeals to you and heaven knows we've tried to see to it that you meet the right sort of boys.'

'I don't like them because they're all the same. Caroline's snaffling the only decent one around.'

'And you wouldn't be his type,' Caroline hissed.

Aunt Edith giggled. 'You see what we have to put up with. Perhaps a visit to India might be a good thing.'

'So that Uncle Harry could line up a string of eligible officers for me to choose from, you mean? I promise Uncle Harry that won't be the reason I shall be visiting you in India.'

'Come along William,' Aunt Myrtle called out with some asperity, 'Do hurry up both of you, I want to go home.'

I went with my parents to the door to wave them goodbye and while they stood chatting I managed to speak to Ralph.

'I do hope everything goes well for you Ralph. I'll be thinking about you. Couldn't you drop me a line to let me know if everything is all right.'

'Oh, it will be. Grandma'll be writing to let you know about the wedding and the baby. They'll get used to the idea of Jenny and me being together.'

'I do hope so.'

'It could be years before we meet again, Amanda. I don't suppose you'll be in any hurry to come back.'

'Why do you say that?'

'Well, you've never really been one of us, have you? I'd be

the same in India, neither fish nor fowl. Father said your father was always different, never had any time for cotton or the fact that the family owned three mills.'

'No, I don't suppose he did, and Mother could never settle here if ever they come back to England.'

'So, like I said, it could be years or never again.'

I threw my arms around his neck and kissed him. I believed he was speaking nothing but the truth. These next few days would be the last I would see of the rolling fells and the brooding hills, the last I would see of mill chimneys, or hear the clatter of clogs on cobbled streets, and at that moment I was dismally aware of a certain sadness and a vague feeling of remembered pain.

Chapter Six

The last twelve years had crawled all too slowly but the next four days seemed to flash by in an instant. We shopped for things we would need on the voyage and visited friends Father had known in his youth, and we packed.

Two days before we left I went into the kitchen to see Cook and Bridie. As usual Cook was at the kitchen table rolling pastry, Bridie at the sink preparing vegetables for our evening meal. They smiled at me warmly and Cook said, 'I knew you'd come to see us afore ye left Miss Amanda, I said as much, didn't I, Bridie? I expect yer all packed up and ready for off.'

'We're getting there,' I said.

'Well come and sit at the table and Bridie'll put the kettle on. I wonder 'ow long it'll be afore we see ye again?'

Scones were produced and the tea was made. Bridie pulled a chair up to the table and started to pour the tea while Cook said with a sly smile. 'I thowt the sergeant might 'ave bin round this morning, but I expect there's time yet.'

I looked up with interest and Cook said, 'Sergeant Wilson. He 'as a habit o' walking round to see that everything's locked up and safe last thing at night and 'e's taken to callin' for a cup o' tea in the mornin'. It's Bridie 'e comes to see, but she'll 'ave none of it.'

Bridie had blushed to the roots of her hair but mercilessly Cook went on. 'I've bin tellin' 'er she could do a lot worse for 'erself. 'E's got a nice little 'ouse and 'e's got his eye on a business when 'e retires from the force.'

'Do you like him, Bridie?' I asked, and with an embar-

59

rassed smile she said, 'Faith and 'e doesn't come round here for me Miss Amanda, 'e comes for a warm and a cup of tea. Sure and his wife's only bin dead two years, I don't think he's thinkin' about gettin' married again.'

'Well of course 'e is,' Cook said adamantly. 'A man needs somebody to look after 'im and 'is wife was a nosy bossy woman if ever there was one.'

'Has he invited you out?' I asked Bridie.

'No 'e 'as not, nor will he. It's Cook arranging everybody's lives.'

'And I'm never far wrong, am I? Wasn't it me that said there'd be trouble after I saw Master Ralph and young Jenny Alsop together in the lane and wasn't it me who told Mrs Alsop to see the mistress as soon as she knew 'ow far it'd gone?'

There was an embarrassed silence, so that the sound of the kitchen clock seemed exceptionally loud, and Bridie looked down at her plate as if it had suddenly become special. At last Cook said, 'And what d'you think about yer cousin Ralph, Miss Amanda, what's more, what do the family think about 'im wantin' to marry 'er?'

'What do you think, Cook?' I asked her pointedly.

'Well I'll say this for 'im, 'e's actin' proper and not shiftin' 'is duty, but I'm not sure it'll work. I think there was a better solution.'

'What sort of solution?'

'Money. One day she could 'ave married a man in 'er own walk of life, somebody she could 'ave bin 'appy with.'

'Don't you think she'll be happy with my cousin?'

''E's a Dexter and one day 'e'll be the big man at the mills. Will she fit in? Will she get along wi' that sister of 'is and the rest o' the family? Will any of 'em take to 'er?'

'My Grandma will be kind to her.'

'That she will and it's my guess she'll be the only one who will. Jenny's mother's explained all this to her, but all she says is that she'll 'ave Ralph. She'll go to evenin' classes and learn elocution. 'Ow she's goin' to do all that wi' a babby to look after, I don't know, and it's my guess she'll do none o' them things.'

'But they're in love with each other,' I ventured.

'Eh, luv, there's times when luv isn't enough, there's more things dividin' 'em than unitin' 'em. It might be all right for a time, but in the long run I has mi doubts.'

At that moment there was a knock on the outside door and Bridie got up to answer it. She returned, her face warm with blushes, followed by the tall figure of Sergeant Wilson, who, when he saw me, looked momentarily disconcerted, but Cook was quick to reassure him and introduce me to him.

Bridie busied herself brewing a fresh pot of tea and Cook pushed the large plate of scones forward, telling him to help himself.

He smiled at me. 'I've seen ye on the fell riding your horse, miss, ye'll not be able to take him to India with ye.'

'No.'

'And yer'll not be missin' the mill chimneys and the rain?'

I laughed. 'I'll never forget the rain, even in summer we never quite knew how long the sunshine would last.'

He shook his head dismally. 'That's right. I'm a Yorkshire man miself and on our side o' the Pennines it were always colder, but this side was damp, I could never quite make up mi mind which was the worst.'

I got to my feet saying, 'Well perhaps I should be getting back to the packing now.'

'Don't you be leavin' on my account, Miss Amanda.'

I stood up and embraced Cook and Bridie, then shook hands with the sergeant, and left.

Grandma was sitting alone in front of the fire when I returned to the drawing room – my parents were visiting our neighbours. She looked up and smiled at me and I said, 'I've been saying goodbye to Cook and Bridie. I thought there might not be time tomorrow.'

'I'm going to miss you, Amanda. I used to worry about you. Somehow or other you never seemed part of the life here. I always had the feeling that you were like a bird of passage, alighting for a little while before moving on.'

'Isn't that exactly how it was, Grandma? I was never meant to stay here.'

'Perhaps dear.'

'Will you write to me Grandma? I shall so want to know

about Ralph and Jenny, and the baby when it comes. I do want them to be happy.'

'Yes I know, and so do I, but one can't help worrying about them. I'm sure Jenny is a very nice girl, but their upbringing has been very different. She could so easily be hurt and he will have to be very tolerant. I'm not sure how either of them will cope.'

She stared pensively into the fire and there was nothing I could say to ease her anxiety. Tomorrow would be my last day in England and there was so much gloom in the atmosphere I was glad. It was worse when Grandfather was present as he covered his disappointment in Ralph with long bouts of silence, his expression one of angry depression.

His moods were reflected in Grandma's silences and occasional tearfilled eyes, and the rest of the family had stayed away, leaving us to spend our remaining days surrounded by the misery Ralph had created.

As soon as we were on the boat going out to Bombay, my life changed. In Lancashire I had been unimportant; now, for the first time, I seemed to have a life of my own. The family had been kind to me, but I had never felt one of them. Cotton was their king. It had meant nothing to me.

Here on board I was a serving officer's only daughter. I was young and pretty – or so I was told by a string of young officers who squabbled with each other to dance with me. By the time we reached Bombay I had a list of addresses all over India and the Far East of boys I had promised to write to, boys who promised to look me up whenever their service took them to Delhi where Father was stationed at Headquarters.

Mother told me he could be moved around at any moment, but I really didn't mind. For years at school I had been hearing about India, the Jewel in the Crown, the exotic land which was part of our empire, and although my childhood memories of it had faded I was now going back to it.

For two nights we stayed at the Bombay Hotel, the most prestigious hotel in the city, and I had my first taste of British ambience and native depression.

There were laws and good roads, British standards in a

land made up of so many different cultures, and a soaring population. My first night in Bombay taught me a lesson that was never to leave me.

With one of my dancing partners I wandered out into the gardens. Lights from a myriad of chandeliers streamed out across the gardens and scents perfume of jasmine and oleander were strong on the air. A gentle breeze stirred the trees.

Other couples sauntered in the gardens, men in dress uniform, women in pretty gowns, and my escort talked about his regiment, the Royal Engineers and his service in Madras.

'What a pity we're going in opposite directions tomorrow,' he said boyishly.

'Perhaps you'll get service in Delhi one of these days,' I said placatingly.

'Perhaps. One never really knows with the army. I have your address, if there's any chance I'll let you know.'

'Oh yes, that would be nice. Unfortunately my father could be moved any day, like you said, one never really knows with the army.'

He laughed. 'You're beginning to sound like a long-established Memsahib already.'

By this time we had reached the main entrance gates, where a fountain played in the centre of a vast courtyard, and for the first time I could see, beyond the gates, a throng of people standing outside staring through the railings. Some of them smiled and waved to us, others stared back in angry silence, hostility alive in every dark face. My delight in the evening fled. Seeing my expression, my companion said, 'Don't let it get to you, Amanda, it's always there under the surface: resentment, anger, envy. They refuse to see the good we've done for India and feel only resentment that we're here.'

I had always felt such pride in our empire; after all we were such a tiny island, and yet the British flag flew bravely over so much of the world. Now for the first time something less than pride troubled me.

When we returned to the ballroom and my partner went off in search of drinks, I conveyed something of my worry to Mother who sat chatting with another lady, and before

Mother could say a word, the other woman said, 'My dear, you simply haven't to worry about things like that. They didn't have to come to see what was happening here. They could have stayed away if it makes them miserable. And where would they be without us? At each other's throats.'

'Are there any Indian people at the ball?' I asked her.

'This isn't their sort of thing. When you get to Delhi you'll see Indian native rulers at a great many of the functions, the ordinary people would not be invited into their homes or to their tiger hunts or polo matches.'

In Delhi life was different. Here was imperialism at its most profound, and the westernised part of Delhi was magnificent with its wide boulevards and public buildings. Our bungalow was a joy with its shaded gardens and cool beautiful rooms.

We celebrated Father's promotion to lieutenant colonel surrounded by our friends at the Officers' Club. Toasts were drunk, speeches were made and then we sat out under spreading chestnut trees on green lawns to watch Father's regiment beat another regiment on the polo field. Men in uniform or pristine white attire chatted to women in pretty hats and dresses, there was the sound of voices and laughter, a gay warm civilised world where native servants, urbane and turbaned, served drinks and pampered polo ponies gambolled under a tropic sun.

Mill chimneys and rain lashing down on Pennine hills seemed far away from those sunlit lawns, and yet I waited anxiously for letters to arrive from England.

I did not expect to hear from my cousins and Grandma was notably a bad correspondent, but at last her letter came to inform us that Ralph and Jenny had been married quietly and had gone to live in a small semi-detached house Uncle William had bought for them on the outskirts of the town.

Since their marriage the rest of the family had seen little of them and the baby was expected at the end of July.

Ralph's sister Sophie was expecting her second child in August so there would be two young babies in the family. The fact that Jenny's baby had been included in the family cheered me a little.

Grandma's next letter came in September to tell us that

Jenny had given birth to a daughter, Alice, and Sophie had had a baby boy, Colin.

Sir John Marston had died at the end of August and it was now expected that Sir Phillip would be leaving the navy to take up his responsibilities at home. Of course it might not be for some little while, but Caroline was delighted as it meant she would see much more of him.

Charlotte was concerned with Red Cross charities and had engineered a visit to Africa where she was working with deprived African children. Aunt Edith was predictably outraged by her decision, saying charity began at home and she would probably contact cholera or some other disgusting tropical disease.

When Father read the letters his expression was noticeably cynical but Mother was troubled by another problem. Her parents had elected to stay in Lahore after Grandfather's retirement from the army and we were due to visit them. Now they had decided to go back to England since Grandfather was unwell and Grandmother's health had been declining for years.

I went to Lahore with Mother to help them pack their belongings, and there was so much sadness in their leaving. They loved India and were reluctant to leave, and I had seen so little of them. Now they were going out of my life almost as soon as I had come back to theirs.

I loved them. Grandfather was a kind gentle man who had time for me, and in those few days before they left they made me feel I had never been away. I loved Lahore with its wide, exquisite streets and white marble buildings, redolent with its ancient past. When we left Lahore, I had a nostalgic feeling that one day I would go back.

The ball at the Viceroy's palace was the highlight of British life in Delhi. Women talked of nothing else: the gowns they would wear, the notables they expected to meet, the intrigue in exalted circles. And I had a new dress: white chiffon and silk gardenias.

'Perhaps it would be a good idea if you invited one of your junior officers to join us,' Mother said on the morning of the ball. But, immediately, Father said, 'I don't think so, Elizabeth. Amanda may not like him overmuch and he'd feel committed to staying with us. She'll not lack for dancing partners, I'm sure.' On the evening of the ball when I was dressed and waiting for them on the balcony of our bungalow, he looked down at me smiling.

'You're beautiful, Amanda, auburn hair and gardenias. I'm very proud of you, my dear.'

It was of such occasions that dreams are made. The ornate ballroom was filled with officers in dress uniform and beautifully dressed women; a regimental band played for dancing.

My dance card was filled quickly with friends of my father and my parents smiled when I looked across the room rather sadly to where a group of young officers laughed and joked together.

'Don't worry,' Father laughed. 'If you meet some young gallant you find irresistible I'm sure one of us would willingly step aside.'

My dance with Major Cathcart came to an abrupt end in front of the group of young officers and he wiped his brow with his handkerchief, smiling at me ruefully.

'I was never a dancer, Amanda,' he said, 'but one has to do one's bit.'

Indeed his prowess in the ballroom would have done credit to the drill ground and as the music started up again one of the young officers stepped forward and invited me to dance.

When he realised that it was merely an encore of the last dance he apologised and immediately Major Cathcart said, 'You go ahead, young feller, after my display she'll be glad of the change.'

The young officer looked down at me with an engaging smile and, after Major Cathcart, waltzing with him was bliss. He was tall and handsome, with piercing blue eyes and fair hair and his smile was so warm it was not difficult to respond to it whole-heartedly. When the dance was over we stood for a moment at the edge of the ballroom and he said, 'I hope we can dance together again. Have you room for me on your dance card?'

I handed it to him and he looked down at it uncertainly.

'Gracious me, it's already full. Two dances with the colonel, I am in salubrious company.'

'He's my father,' I said with a smile.

'He'll think I'm a bit of a bounder to chase after his daughter, I'm afraid.'

'He'll be happy that I'm having such a good time.'

'So you will dance with me again?'

'Yes, of course. I was dancing with Major Cathcart before the supper dance, I'm sure he'll be glad to know I've found another partner. He was only being chivalrous. This is my first regimental ball.'

'Mine too. We only got here from Madras yesterday.'

'My name's Amanda Dexter.'

'Gosh, how remiss of me. I'm Anthony St Clare.'

'Lieutenant St Clare?'

'Yes. My promotion came through just before we left Madras.'

At that moment my next partner came to claim me and was smiling down at me. Lieutenant St Clare said, 'I shall look forward to the supper dance Miss Dexter.'

When I eventually waltzed with my father he said, 'I suppose you and Cathcart will be joining us in the supper room, but I knew from the twinkle in his eye that Major Cathcart had already told him that somebody considerably younger had taken his place.'

'He's very nice,' I assured him.

'I'm sure he is. Four of them came in yesterday, which one is your dancing partner?'

'Lieutenant Anthony St Clare.'

'Brigadier Jameison's nephew. I believe he brought the boy up, or at least acted as his guardian. Apparently both his parents died young.'

'He's awfully handsome.'

'You'll meet a lot of handsome young officers, my dear, don't get carried away too soon.'

But as we talked together in a corner of the ornate supper room it was easy to respond to his charm, to the young open face with its embracing smile and the ease with which he talked about his life and family.

He told me his father had been killed on service in Africa during the Boer War and when Anthony was only a few months old. Only weeks after his father's death the war in Africa was over and of course Anthony could not remember

67

his father, or very little of his mother who died three years later in a riding accident.

His mother's brother who was serving in the Indian Army became his guardian but, because he was a bachelor, Anthony had been left in England in the care of a succession of nannies and later, kindly housemasters at Marlborough College where he went to school.

I felt saddened by the story of his early life, but Anthony was not a sad person. He had risen above his early deprivation with the help of friends and a sunny disposition that was there for me to see.

At the end of the supper interval I promised to meet him next day at the polo grounds and for the rest of the evening I didn't mind that I was marched up and down with military precision, only that across the room his eyes smiled at me and there was promise of so much more.

It was so easy to fall in love in that exotic land where the sun shone out of a cloudless sky and spice-laden breezes swept across cool green lawns and in a city that the British had adorned and embellished in the name of empire.

Of course there were instances of unrest, quickly quelled, and infamous treachery in several provinces, but they were largely the antics of small groups of trouble causers well know to the authorities and quickly brought to justice.

In Delhi there was pageantry and colour, and India's darker side was concealed under wraps of civilised normality. Letters from England were few, since only Grandma wrote and only occasionally. I, however, wrote to her regularly and I told her about Anthony.

Anthony who spent every free moment with me, who made me feel loved and wanted and in my letters I enthused about the charm of his smile, his tenderness and how very much in love with each other we were.

We had been in India for eighteen months when we received an invitation to the wedding of my cousin Caroline to Sir Phillip Marston, and Father remarked wryly, 'Of course they won't expect us to attend. It's simply a polite gesture and we shall be expected to send them a wedding present.' In the end he sent them a substantial cheque and one evening Anthony said, 'You're very quiet tonight, Amanda.

Is something wrong?'

'Not really. My cousin Caroline is getting married to a man who is far too nice for her.'

'And that bothers you, does it?'

'A little.'

'A man you like rather too well, perhaps?'

'I did like him. I had a bit of a crush of him, but of course I was far too young, and I'm over it now.'

'Promise?'

'Absolutely. Now I've met you.'

Chapter Seven

It was so easy to forget the years in England when I had waited, often impatiently, for what I thought of as my destiny.

Here I was in this magical city, young and in love – how magical the phrase. We were the people of the Roaring Twenties, with the war well behind us and peace and sovereignty to look forward to. Flushed with pride in an empire upon which the sun never set, and belonging to a generation that chose to ignore the signs of resentment and hostility in many quarters, we felt we had no reason to care. How many proud empires had felt it before us?

My parents felt I was too young to marry and insisted that I wait until I was twenty-one, but youth is impatient and Anthony swept me off my feet with his laughter, his charm and the love I saw shining in his eyes, eyes a bit bluer than English skies.

We were surrounded by men and girls living life to the full, young men who danced divinely, played polo with reckless flair and who looked unbelievably romantic in splendid uniforms.

Soberly, my father tried to tell me that life would have its sterner side, that in many parts of India there was danger and that as a serving officer Anthony could not expect to remain in Delhi but must encounter service elsewhere. I didn't care. Wherever he was sent I would be with him. We would make our home in Calcutta, Madras or Bangalore, it would not matter, Anthony would do his duty and come home to me.

Resigned to the fact that we wanted to marry my parents gave their reluctant permission, not because they did not love

Anthony but because we refused to look beyond the here and now.

We were married at the English church in Delhi on a golden morning at the beginning of September surrounded by well-wishers and attended by a bevy of bridesmaids and young officers acting as ushers and best man. This office was performed by Anthony's friend Captain Malcolm Baxter. I remember that a great many of my friends were in love with him, but he did not single one of them out and I asked Anthony if there was some other girl at home.

He seemed a little disconcerted by my question but there was so much going on on that day the question passed and I forgot about it. We took the overnight train north to Rawalpindi and then rode onward on horseback to Kashmir.

I had my first glance of the Himalayas rising through the morning mist, snow-capped and omnipotent. For long ecstatic days we either lazed on our comfortable houseboat on the lake or rode our mules along the foothill paths. It was a time of enchantment, a time to look back on when the sterner things of life brought my dancing feet down to earth. It was a time of joy and youth and love, and it was a time to hold close to my heart when the world became a colder, sadder place.

We had three rapturous weeks before returning to Delhi, where we stayed on with my parents. Then Anthony received his posting for service in Lahore. I was delighted. I remembered it from my visit to Grandfather. It had been a city of Sikh kings and Mogul emperors and each culture had left Lahore the richer. Now we were merely exchanging the beauty of Delhi for the beauties of Lahore, and not even father's restrained warning that we were going into a more dangerous part of India troubled my blissful heart.

It was one morning soon after our return to Delhi when I was packing our suitcases for all we would need in our new home that the houseboy came to tell me that I had a visitor.

'Who is it?' I asked him, hoping that it was a woman friend who might conceivably help me with my packing.

'It is Captain Baxter, memsahib.'

'Very well, tell him I'm coming.'

I wondered why he should come to the bungalow when

Anthony was out and a feeling of anxiety washed over me. Had there been some sort of accident, was Anthony hurt?

I found him in the living room looking through the window, and he turned with a smile as I entered the room. Something of my anxiety must have been apparent because he was quick to reassure me.

'Nothing's wrong, Amanda,' he said with a smile, 'I have something to tell you. I haven't seen Anthony, I'd like you to tell him.'

I stared at him in some surprise. It seemed incongruous to me that Anthony's friend should be asking me to tell my husband something he had not told him himself.

'I don't think he'll be too surprised,' he said. 'I have decided to marry Hadassah. My friends have known about her for some time. They've all done their best to dissuade me and I know they mean well but I know how I feel about her, how she feels about me.'

'Hadassah, Malcolm, but who is she? Where does she live? I don't know her?'

'Of course not. None of my friends or their wives know her, my brother officers only know of her.'

'Tell me about her. Please sit down, would you like coffee or something cold?'

'I'm due at HQ in a little while, Amanda. Something cold would be nice.'

'Gin?'

'Thank you.'

He did not speak while the houseboy poured the drinks but returned to the window where he seemed lost in thought. Taking the drink from me he said, 'Perhaps I should have told Anthony, but he's tied up most of the morning. I wanted you both to know before you left for Lahore.'

'But you're going to Lahore too?'

'I know, but not immediately, in a few weeks I think.'

'I see.'

'You don't see about Hadassah, Amanda.'

'No. Why haven't I met her if she lives in Delhi?'

'You haven't met her, because her father's Indian, a stationmaster with a Scottish wife. Hadassah doesn't exactly mingle in our class-ridden society.'

72

There was bitterness in his voice, his expression entirely cynical. I waited for him to go on.

'Her mother came out here as nanny to me and my sister. My father was in the diplomatic service. She didn't know anybody in India and was left much to herself to make friends wherever she could find them and she met Hadassah's father. When she left my mother's service and Mother discovered the friendship she ordered her to go home, said she would pay her passage and compensate her for loss of earnings, but instead she stayed on in India and married Anwar Bashir.

'I know Hadassah's parents, he's a decent hard-working man, a good husband and affectionate father, she's a nice level-headed Scots woman, totally unconcerned with the anomalies of British life here.'

'And Hadassah?'

'She's beautiful and intelligent and I'm very much in love with her. It will be difficult for us in Lahore, or anywhere else in India for that matter. I shall be invited to functions. She will not. If I insist on taking her she will be snubbed unmercifully. The men can be expected to be reasonably charitable, their wives not. One day it will change, it has to, but the time is not yet and I have come to ask if you will receive her, Amanda. Anthony and I have been friends a very long time – we were at Marlborough together. I joined the army before he did, but he followed me here and we were pretty inseparable. It might be stretching our friendship a bit too far to ask you to be kind to Hadassah, but I felt I had to talk to you, Amanda, to see how you felt. If you think you should stay aloof from us I shall understand.'

'Oh, Malcolm, of course I can't stay aloof, nor will Anthony want me to. Of course I'll receive Hadassah in Lahore. When will you marry?'

'Very quietly by special licence.'

'Does it have to be like that?'

'I'm afraid so. My commanding officer has already told me I'm a bloody fool and I expect he's not the only one thinking it.'

'Anthony will want to be your best man, Malcolm, I'm sure of it. We shall both come to your wedding.'

'No Amanda. It would antagonise too many people. This is my crusade, I don't want to drag anybody else into it. Besides, you're leaving for Lahore in two days' time.'

'But you'll bring her to meet us before we go.'

'This is your parents's house, Amanda. I doubt if your father will agree to it.'

'Please Malcolm, I'll talk to my father.'

'Well, perhaps, if we called round for a short time one evening when you and Anthony are here alone.'

'Gracious me, that's terrible. This is Hadassah's country, we're the ones who don't really belong here.'

'There speaks a girl who is just recently out from home without the years of experience that life in India can inflict on us.'

I sat on the verandah for a long time after he had left, gazing out across the gardens, gardens where jasmine tumbled across the rockeries and its scent lay heavy on the early evening air.

I had had my first lesson on barriers dividing man from man, invisible barriers that so many could not pass. Oh those invisible barriers of manners, speech and colour born of arrogance, ignorance and folly that one day we would be asked to pay for.

I was still sitting there when I heard the sound of the latch on the wicker gate and Anthony was striding along the path lifting up his hand to wave to me.

'All alone,' he greeted me, 'your parents not back yet?'

'No. I had a visitor, Anthony, Malcolm Baxter.'

I saw his expression change and suddenly it became wary.

'He came to see you, Amanda?' he said softly.

'You know why he came, don't you Anthony?'

'They're all talking about it at HQ. I wasn't sure if it was true or not. They say he's decided to marry Hadassah Bashir.'

'Anthony, Malcolm is your friend, don't you know? He was upset and anxious, surely you must know something about it, how it started and why it's such a terrible thing for him to do?'

'It was when Malcolm came back here, he discovered that his old nanny was living in Delhi and he'd been very fond of her. His mother was a busy socialite and had precious little time for her children, their nanny had supplied the love and care they never got from her. Malcolm made it his business to look Mrs Bashir up and he met her daughter Hadassah. You know the rest.'

'Have you met her?'

'Yes. She's beautiful and intelligent. She teaches school to Indian children in the city and she's proud and independent. It's not enough Amanda, they'll crucify them both.'

'But why if she's all the things you say she is?'

'Because she's Eurasian, that forbidden mixture of European and Asian ancestry that is frowned upon by the west and hated in the east.'

'I've told Malcolm that we will receive them in Lahore.'

His expression was dubious and the cry was torn out of me, 'Anthony, how can we not invite your best friend and his wife into our home, it would be monstrous?'

'Yes, it would be monstrous, and you, my dear, will incur the wrath of every friend you have made. They'll find it hard to believe that you can approve of Malcolm's choice of wife and the evening will be a disaster.'

'Then we'll simply invite Malcolm and Hadassah and not bother about the others.'

'And you think they won't know?'

'I shan't very much care.'

He put his arms around me and drew me into his embrace. 'Oh, my darling, I do so admire your courage but don't say I didn't warn you. Your father knows about Malcolm. I'm sure he'll give you the same warnings I've given you.'

'I asked Malcolm to bring Hadassah here one evening. Perhaps I should have mentioned it to my parents first?'

'Did he accept?'

'He said they might.'

'When he's had time to think about it I rather think he'll change his mind, out of respect for your parents and Hadassah.'

'I don't understand all this,' I cried. 'Here it's the colour of somebody's skin; in England it was the size of their pockets. My cousin has married a girl who worked in the family mill and the family were horrified, here if you're a native, you're unacceptable.'

'In England it's snobbery, Amanda, here it's simply different cultures, different habits and customs.'

'And different colour,' I murmured.

'That too. It will be a monumental task to overcome years of prejudice, and I doubt very much if it will happen during our time in India.'

The arrival of my parents brought our conversation to an end and neither of us spoke of the matter to them; it was as though we silently agreed to keep matters to ourselves until Malcolm decided to visit us or stay away.

I did not sleep well that night. For what seemed an eternity I lay sleepless, staring up at the tracery of palm fronds on the ceiling, listening to the soft murmur of the breeze as it swept across the garden. When I did sleep I dreamed about Jenny Alsop, that she was locked inside the mill while a crowd of screaming men and women waited for her outside armed with kitchen brooms and other weapons. I could feel her terror, see her wide frightened eyes, hear her screams, and I was helpless as if steel bands had been placed around my arms.

Over breakfast Father commented on my pallor and Mother said anxiously, 'You'll find life in Lahore much less demanding dear, and your feet haven't stopped dancing since you arrived in Delhi. Anthony will be kept busy in Lahore and you may not have so much time for socialising.'

Father smiled. 'Oh I think she'll manage that. When did you stop socialising my dear? It didn't matter where we were, Calcutta, Madras, Amritsar.'

'I'd prefer to forget about Amritsar, darling,' Mother said feelingly. 'My parents were there when General Dyer fired into a crowd of unarmed people protesting against anti-sedition laws. Four hundred protesters were killed and it will take them a long time to forgive us for it. I'm glad you're going to Lahore Amanda, I wouldn't have been as happy to see you going to Amritsar.'

Across the table my eyes met Anthony's. Since I came back to India I had known only her beauty and her sunshine, the excitement of regimental balls and glamorous uniforms, now I was learning a little of her sadness and the cruelty that man inflicted upon man.

76

Father was saying, 'There is a beautiful temple in Amritsar, Amanda, the Golden Temple with its upper walls lined with beaten gold. It is the spiritual centre of India's Sikh religion.'

Dryly Anthony said, 'It would be amazing if there was not conflict in India with the Sikhs, the Hindus and the Moslems. We do not do too bad a job of maintaining law and order.'

His words were a reproof against any disturbing thoughts I had about the British role in India.

The officers and men of Anthony's regiment moved out to Lahore two days later and their wives followed two days after that. Anthony had told me that we were to occupy a bungalow vacated by an officer and his wife who had lived there for three years, and after his arrival he would go there to see if everything was ready for our arrival. There would be a houseboy, and there was a garden, so much we had been told.

I stood with the other wives on the station platform in Delhi waiting for the train to carry us northward into the Punjab and on that hot dusty afternoon I recognised for the first time that from this day onward I would see the real India and the meaning of what life would be as the wife of a serving soldier.

The platform was crowded with Europeans as well as a conglomeration of Indian, Sikh and Moslem travellers. There were natives surrounded by crates of chickens, goats and market produce and I knew from experience that if there was not room on the train they would clamber on to the roof and cling to the doors. It promised to be a full train, and as I was staring around me Mrs Lewisham the adjutant's wife joined me. She was a nice woman with a motherly appearance from her silver hair to her plump matronly form and she smiled encouragingly.

'This is still new to you Amanda, don't worry, I rather think you'll like Lahore.'

'Yes, I wanted to see it again.'

'You're expecting it to be like Delhi?'

'No, my father assured me that it was not.'

'No. The men will see real service. There are military posts dotted about the Punjab and as far as the frontier. In the weeks to come, Amanda, I think you will realise that life is real and earnest.'

'That's why we're here Mrs Lewisham. My parents warned me, at least perhaps I'm better prepared than so many of them.'

'Of course. Have you seen Malcolm Baxter over the last few days? I think they'll be joining us in about three weeks.'

'He came to see me one evening but Anthony was out. I thought he might have come back with Hadassah but they didn't come.'

Her face was pensive, and the words were dragged from me. 'You don't approve do you, Mrs Lewisham?'

'It's not a case of approving or disapproving, Amanda. I don't know the girl personally. I've only ever seen her, but prejudice is very real here and the young man has a career to make. She could ruin it for him.'

'Wouldn't that be terribly unfair?'

'Yes, but one has to be realistic. East is still east and the west is still the west. Personally, I don't think we're ready yet for mixed marriages and in Hadassah's case there is as much resentment from her father's people as there is from the British here. I would like to think it would work out for them but I'm very afraid.'

'Will you receive them?'

'It will be very difficult and I hope he will not ask it. That sounds terrible but Malcolm chose to ignore all the advice he was given. He will expect to pay the penalty.'

'You mean that none of them will receive them?'

'Not a single one of them will wish to create a precedent.'

'But if just one of us did, don't you think that would open the door to others?'

'And you are thinking that you might, Amanda?'

I didn't answer her, and she continued to stare along the platform, then suddenly taking hold of my hand she said, 'There is Hadassah going towards her father's house. She will have to walk along the path there.'

I saw a slender girl in a beige cotton skirt and silk blouse walking quickly towards us. Her black hair was caught back from her face in a bright orange-coloured scarf and as she drew near us I saw that she was beautiful, exotically so, but as her eyes swept over us they were filled with hostility. Proudly she looked away and at that moment I felt terribly ashamed that the smile froze on my lips.

'She hates us,' I breathed softly.

'Hadassah was born in this country and has experience of what it is like to be Eurasian. Her father's family has ostracised them because her mother comes from the west, and the British have ignored them because a Scots woman had the temerity to marry a native. There are a good many years of deep-seated hatred buried in that young woman's psyche.'

'Then how can she love Malcolm, how can she ever marry him?'

'Hatred and love my dear are very strange bedfellows. It never ceases to amaze me how one can feed upon the other.'

We were saved from further discussion on the subject by the arrival of the train and immediately those sitting on the platform leapt to their feet and made for the train, only to be beaten back by the military police making room for the Europeans waiting to board her.

It filled me with amazement that in only a very short time the platform was deserted and that, by fair means or foul, all that crowd had managed to find room on the train. I could hear their chattering, hear the noise from their birds and animals, but of the men and women there was not a sight.

Chapter Eight

The adjutant's wife stood smiling at us as we descended from the train with our new luggage, our tennis rackets and picnic hampers, a bevy of young wives arriving in a strange city with so much hope.

For the first time in my life I would have a bungalow of my own and my own servant; my husband would come home to meals and long cosy evenings together. Looking back I can see now how naïve she must have found us.

As I stood on the pavement looking at the bungalow through the garden my spirits soared. It was a pretty building and the gardens had obviously been lovingly tended by its last occupants. As I struggled with the latch on the wicker gate a young native boy came running across the lawn, his face wreathed in smiles, calling out, 'Welcome, welcome, Rajiv will open gate.'

I smiled at him warmly and waited while he collected my luggage, then he beckoned me to walk before him into the house. I had known what it would be like: wicker furniture and blinds shading the windows, brass hanging lamps and softly shaded rugs on the floor, satin cushions against the wicker and low tables for drinks and books as well as several side lamps.

On one table stood a large oriental vase filled with jasmine. Throwing open the far door Rajiv announced, 'Bedrooms memsahib,' and holding up two fingers and with a wide smile on his face, 'Two.'

'Thank you Rajiv, I would really like a cup of tea before I start to unpack.'

'Yes yes, kettle boiled, I make it now. First I leave luggage in bedrooms.'

While Rajiv made the tea I familiarised myself with the bedrooms, one master bedroom and one much smaller; through the bedroom window I could see the verandah and the lawn shaded by leafy trees.

The sound of a gong brought a smile to my lips so I shrugged off my light travelling coat and returned to the living room where Rajiv had placed a silver tray containing a teapot, cup and saucer and milk and sugar. He hurried in again carrying a plate of English tea biscuits, and placed it on the table with much aplomb, a delighted smile at his own inspiration in providing them.

'Thank you Rajiv,' I said. 'Do you know what time Lieutenant St Clare will be home?'

He shrugged his shoulders and shook his head. 'He come, he go. It is army, memsahib.'

I smiled. 'I suppose so.'

'I make meal at seven o'clock. If he not come, you eat alone.'

'Thank you Rajiv.'

'Do you live in the bungalow Rajiv?'

'I have room in garden, see there, memsahib, wicker house in corner of garden.'

'And is that room all right when the rains come?'

He laughed. 'Yes yes lady. I live there many years, rain-proof.'

'Did you work for the people who were here before?'

'For five years. Nice people, Captain Jarvis and his lady.'

'Five years! But you're very young Rajiv.'

'I sixteen.'

'Then you were only eleven when you came to work for them?'

He grinned. 'That right, Memsahib. I come with older brother, now he works somewhere else but I stayed. I liked it here.'

'I'm sure we shall get along very well together. I shall need your advice about a great many things.'

'Advice?'

'Why yes. I do not know Lahore at all.'

81

'It very beautiful city, but the memsahib will learn about it from many friends and from the Sahib St Clare. Is tea to your liking lady?'

'Yes thank you Rajiv.'

It did not take long to finish unpacking and familiarise myself with the layout of the bungalow, then I went into the garden. I had fallen in love with eastern gardens in Delhi where jasmine ran rampant across the stones and exotic trees screened the houses from the roads.

I remembered how in England twilight crept gently across frozen fields and misted hills, but here in India darkness came suddenly after a blazing sunset.

Rajiv informed me that dinner was ready, but still Anthony had not arrived home and when I hesitated he smiled gently, 'You eat, memsahib, many times the Memsahib Jarvis waited and had to eat alone. This is . . .'

'I know Rajiv, this is army. Very well I'll eat now, you needn't wait for my husband. I'll look after him.'

So I ate the food Rajiv put in front of me and had to admit that he was an excellent cook. He cleared away noiselessly after bringing in coffee and I heard him humming cheerfully in the kitchen before he reappeared to say 'All is finished now, memsahib. Rajiv will go now and return for breakfast.'

'Thank you Rajiv.'

It was as quiet as the grave. No sounds came from the street, and the sporting magazines on the table were hardly to my taste. I wondered how Mrs Jarvis had amused herself during her husband's absence. I longed for a gramophone but there was none. The clock on the table ticked increasingly loudly, or so I imagined.

Why couldn't Anthony have left me a message to say he would be late? Why was there nobody to tell me anything, and who were my neighbours?

As the hours passed I grew sick with worry. I longed to rush out into the road in search of a friendly face who might reassure me, but sternly I told myself that it would not be British to do such a thing. I was an army wife and should never forget it.

I lay for hours unsleeping, leaping up at the slightest sound, but in spite of my anxiety weariness overcame me and eventually I slept. It was the morning sun that woke me, and for a moment I stared up at the ceiling before its unfamiliarity brought anxiety back to me, and grabbing my robe I thrust my feet into my slippers and hurried towards the door.

The house was silent and as I opened the living room door I stared with dismay at Anthony fast asleep in one of the chairs. He was still wearing his uniform and had evidently sat down with a cup of coffee which remained stone cold on the table. Silently I moved across the room to draw back the drapes and glancing at my watch I saw that it was just after six o'clock.

I picked up the coffee cup and went into the kitchen to empty it, then searched for tea or coffee in the cupboards. I was still searching when the door opened and Rajiv came in, a broad smile on his face, whispering, 'Sahib home, now Rajiv make breakfast.'

'My husband's still asleep, perhaps we should let him sleep on.' I suggested.

Rajiv gave his familiar shrug. 'He smell cooking, he wake up.'

Anthony was still sleeping soundly so I bathed and dressed and already from the kitchen came the smell of cooking and the clattering of crockery. When I reentered the living room Anthony was rubbing the sleep from his eyes, smiling at me ruefully before saying, 'What a rotten homecoming for you Amanda. I really meant to be here, to have everything perfect for you, but we had to go up to Chikarti. They're being harassed by tribesmen and a show of strength was needed.'

'Did anything happen to your men?'

'No. We knew they were there. You could feel eyes boring into the backs of your heads but there was nothing to be seen. A unit from Rawalpindi arrived with a few casualties but it meant that we were released to get back here.'

I stared at him doubtfully, and he gave me a lovable boyish grin. 'Don't worry darling,' he said. 'You'll get used to this sort of thing, it's part and parcel of why we're here.'

'I know, this is army. Rajiv reminded me twice yesterday.'

'He's a good lad. We seem to have landed on our feet here darling.'

For weeks I echoed that sentiment. It was not Delhi but it

was a good imitation. There was tennis and polo, garden parties on cool green lawns and gatherings in the officers' mess. My two ball gowns were aired at two regimental balls, and it was then for the first time I beheld the splendour of the maharajahs who had once ruled India. Their power had gone under British rule but their style was undiminished as they arrived with a retinue of servants all richly attired in magnificent silks and wearing fabulous jewellery.

We were entertained by Indian dancers performing their ancient patterned dances, their wrists and anklets adorned with bangles covered with tiny silver bells. Their beautiful faces and slender sinuous bodies enthralled me as they danced with hands and head as well as feet. The insistent drum beat entered into my soul. I became a part of this vibrant colourful scene. Anthony took hold of my hand and squeezed it, whispering, 'This really is something, isn't it Amanda.'

It was in Lahore where I saw splendidly adorned elephants striding majestically along the city streets, palanquins draped in shimmering silks carried on long poles by luxuriously adorned servants.

'They like to put on a show of this sort of thing,' Anthony said. 'It reminds them that they are a conquered nation and it reminds us that we should not be too complacent.'

In my quiet moments I thought I would never understand. They served under the British flag, side by side with the British and Anthony said they were the bravest soldiers he had every known, and yet under it all there was something that caused me unease. Anthony said it was the mingling of Hindu and Moslem, together with the Sikhs who were proud and warlike and again and again I asked myself how was it possible to govern a country where so many conflicting beliefs warred against each other.

I knew that Malcolm Baxter and his wife had been in Lahore for several weeks but they did not come to any soirées or formal gatherings. Malcolm played polo but went back to his home immediately the match was over, and all I got from him was a distant wave of his hand and a smile.

I speculated on how Hadassah spent her days. They were living in a bungalow some distance from ours and Mrs

Lewisham told me she spent her time shopping in the bazaars, although they did have a houseboy. When I mentioned them to Anthony he simply said Malcolm knew the score, and perhaps it was better this way.

The heat was intense and the hot wind swept from Karachi across the plains. I longed for a few days' respite so that we could travel north to the hill country or to some other district where the rains had made the land green.

There was always something that prevented us going, and now Anthony was moving out again to the frontier with a contingent of men: they were to buy horses from the local tribesmen. It was a yearly event, and not one I believed to cause me any anxiety.

'When I get back, we really will make that effort to go north to Kashmir,' he said. 'But I do have some good news for you darling.'

'What sort of good news can you possibly have?'

'My promotion came through. You're now looking at Captain Anthony St Clare.'

He was so thrilled I was ashamed that I couldn't be more delighted, but promotion meant added responsibility and I was seeing less and less of him.

'Who's going with you to the frontier?' I asked him.

'Malcolm. I'm rather glad really, we've done a great many things together, I couldn't have wished for anyone better.'

I watched him go, turning to wave to me from the garden gate, and after he had gone I stood in the doorway for a long time. I had the strangest feeling that he was walking out of my life.

Bad news is not broken by tactful words, and long before they were spoken, my heart was filled with a terrible despair. Our days together had been so pitifully few. Those who have lived together many years learn to read each other's minds: vanities and tempers, virtues, hopes and fears. It seemed to me that in those first few days all I could remember of Anthony was his warm smile and the sunlight gleaming on his fair head.

People were very kind to me. They came with reassuring words that I was young and time was a great healer, that one day all this would be behind me and I would learn to live again, but their words passed over my head – unreal platitudes. They came with gifts of fruit and flowers, so many flowers the house was filled with them, but still I was unable to ask questions and it was the adjutant's wife saying sadly, 'I feel I should go to see Hadassah but I doubt if she will see me.'

'Hadassah?' I echoed stupidly.

'Oh my dear, didn't you know? Malcolm was killed as well as Anthony, along with two of the men and a Punjabi soldier.'

'I can't believe it. Anthony said there was no danger.'

'There's always danger. A rogue tribesman, a group of bandits.'

'They left them there?'

'They had to bury them there. It was impossible to bring them back in all this heat. It is practice to bury them as quickly as possible. Leave the bungalow Amanda, come and stay with us until you decide to leave.'

The bungalow would, in any case, be needed for Anthony's replacement.

But before I packed and went to stay with the adjutant's wife, I knew what I had to do. Later that afternoon I went to see Hadassah.

Their bungalow was much like ours, but as I walked up the path I was aware that a houseboy was busy carrying out suitcases and paper parcels which he left lining the path. I paused uncertainly and the boy stared at me curiously before returning to the house.

It was obvious that Hadassah was leaving, and I remained poised on the path, unsure of my welcome. The boy came out and walking towards me he said, 'My lady is leaving, memsahib, she is very busy.'

'Please ask her to spare me a few moments. Tell her it is Mrs St Clare.'

He bowed and returned to the house and I waited. Oh, surely, she would not refuse to see me, not now when tragedy had made us sisters under the skin.

Again I waited and then the door opened and she stood there, and with something like shock I realised she was wearing native dress, a dark blue sari with a long silk scarf covering her hair. I had thought her beautiful in her European attire, but today she had deliberately made herself different, and the long look that passed between us left me with nothing to say.

It was Hadassah who broke the silence.

'You have come to tell me that you're sorry for me because my husband is dead. The feeling is mutual.'

The words were unvarnished by sentimentality or even sorrow and it was the bluntness of them that made my eyes fill with tears. More than all the words of sympathy they brought home to me the agony of loss, the emptiness of a world suddenly grown cold. The tears rolled unchecked down my cheeks, and I saw her expression change from hostility to compassion and understanding.

'I've been ungracious,' she said. 'You don't deserve it, you've done me no harm. Perhaps in some other time we could have been friends you and I, but the time isn't now.'

'Hadassah, I'd like to be your friend, you more than anybody else.'

She smiled, and the sadness of her smile made the tears start afresh.

'You won't be staying here in Lahore, you'll be returning to Delhi and become a part of British life there, soirées and garden parties, women's gossip over tiffin. I too shall be returning to Delhi, but my life will be very different.'

'But you are a British officer's widow, why should it be different?'

She smiled, the saddest smile I had ever seen.

'It was different before I married Malcolm. I am Eurasian, the product of a union between east and west and distrusted by both sides. Many times I told Malcolm that I would not marry him because I knew what marriage to me would be like for him. He tried very hard not to show it, on those evenings when there were functions. Had he had a British wife he would have been welcomed, but with me . . .'

'It's so wrong Hadassah. This is your country.'

'It's my father's country, not my mother's.'

'But didn't your mother become Indian when she married your father?'

'Only on paper. Do you know what my mother talks about

when we are alone? The heather-clad braes of Scotland and the lonely lochs. She has been married to my father for twenty-two years but she speaks hardly any Hindi and she reads either her bible or Kipling. Do you know how Kipling described us? Your new-caught, sullen peoples, half-devil and half-child.'

'You think Kipling was wrong?'

'No. Those silent, sullen people have murdered my husband and yours.'

We stared at each other in silence, an Englishwoman and a woman who was half Indian, neither of us able to step forward and reach out our arms to bridge the gap. It was Hadassah who broke the silence by saying, 'It's late. I still have much to do. When will you return to Delhi?'

'Within the next few days.'

'And you're staying at the bungalow alone?'

'No. I'm going to stay with the adjutant and his wife.'

The cynicism in her smile said it all. We had both lost our men but only I had been invited into their home.

'Shall I see you in Delhi Hadassah?' I asked her.

'Perhaps, around the city, in the bazaars, but then you are unlikely to be visiting the bazaars. Thank you for coming to see me. It was kindness that prompted your visit and kindness is not something to despise. I wish you well Amanda.'

That should have been the moment when I stepped forward and put my arms around her, but her proud expression and her stiff unyielding stance deterred me. Instead I smiled and turned away.

Chapter Nine

Life in Delhi did not pick up its pattern. My parents were supportive and overkind. It was the sympathy and words of comfort I could not face, and I knew that wherever I went they would be there. Instead, I worked on my needlepoint and pottered around the garden and it was left to Mother to try to amuse me with all the current scandals, for, invariably, there were some.

It was a warm golden morning and Mother had tried unsuccessfully to persuade me to attend a charity garden party at the Viceroy's residence.

'Darling, it's been almost four months now since Anthony was killed. You should think of getting back into harness,' she encouraged.

'I will, Mother, but not at a function like this, something smaller perhaps. Everybody will be there this morning and I just can't face their well-meaning platitudes.'

She smiled sadly and left me alone.

I wasn't miserable. Inside I was coming alive, but what was alive? I was twenty-two years old, a widow, feeding desperately on the memories of my all too brief marriage to Anthony. I was young, pretty and I was rich. Anthony had been a rich man, even though I had not known of it, and both my parents and I had been amazed when his uncle's solicitor wrote to disclose the contents of his Will.

Anthony's uncle wrote to me. He lived alone in Devon, and pressed me to visit him, if I decided to leave India or take a holiday, and I promised I would, should I ever return to England. Mrs Lewisham visited us often and she informed us that Hadassah had returned to teaching children, and that she had handed a large of amount of money which Malcolm had left her to the local Brahman to be spent for the benefit of local people.

'He'll take her money but she won't be made to feel one of them,' Mrs Lewisham said. 'In his eyes she is neither fish nor fowl. She should have moved away and kept the money for herself. No doubt she has made provision for her parents, but giving money to the Brahman isn't the answer.'

'Where would she go to if she left here?' I asked sharply. 'She only knows India. Surely it's better for her to be here with her parents than alone in some far-off place?'

'Perhaps,' she answered. 'The longer I stay here the less I understand.'

Left to my own devices on the morning of the garden party I picked up a magazine Mother had brought in the day before. It was filled with the usual gossip about upper-crust England, the clothes they were wearing, the functions they were attending and one or two pithy novels of little or no interest.

I looked up in surprise at the sound of a woman's voice outside in the garden and the next moment our houseboy appeared gesticulating wildly and saying, 'Memsahib arrived, much luggage.'

Luggage! We had no plans to receive visitors bringing luggage so I jumped to my feet and followed him out into the garden. I stared with dismay at the sight of several travelling cases standing on the garden path together with tennis rackets and a large round hat box. The houseboy looked at me in round-eyed surprise and I hurried to the gate to see a girl struggling with another suitcase and a taxicab driving away.

She turned round and grinned at me, and I stared back at my cousin Charlotte, a picture of fashionably dressed England from her neat shingled head to her high-heeled shoes.

'Grandma said I should have written instead of simply arriving, but I couldn't risk you saying it wasn't convenient. I so desperately wanted to come here,' she said brightly.

'I thought you were in Africa.'

'Gracious no, that finished ages ago, but I have itchy feet, I couldn't settle at home listening to Mother's trivia. I got

Dad to give me some money, after all I've been nowhere near as expensive as Caroline, I felt they owed me something.'

Together with the houseboy we struggled with the luggage and inside the bungalow she looked round appreciatively.

'I imagined it would be like this, cool shuttered rooms and wicker, silk cushions and oriental rugs. Oh I'm so looking forward to being here.'

'How long are you intending staying Charlotte?'

'Hardly welcoming Amanda, but understandable. It rests with you.'

'With me?'

'That's right. We were all terribly sorry to hear about your husband and I started to think about you here in Delhi, unhappy and lonely and what we could do to help you to get over it.'

'Only time will help me to get over it, Charlotte.'

'Well of course, but time doesn't simply mean sitting here on your own and waiting for tomorrow. Time means filling every day with something worthwhile.'

I smiled. 'And what is worthwhile? My mother is at a garden party at the Viceroy's residence this morning and I was invited, I didn't want to go.'

'I'm not thinking about garden parties or things like that, I'm thinking about seeing something of the world. There are so many things I want to see. I say, I'm dying for a cup of tea, can't we talk over that.'

'Of course. Do sit down Charlotte, we'll see to the luggage later.'

When I went into the kitchen, the houseboy was already busy setting out a tray with a plate of tiny almond cakes.

'How grand,' Charlotte enthused, when I had given Jamil directions on preparing Charlotte's room, and we were sitting drinking our tea. 'To be addressed as memsahib and that deferential bow. Oh, I'm really going to love being here. I really roughed it in Africa, the heat, the dust and the flies. I hated the injections against cholera and malaria but the natives were dying off like flies. It was an experience, this is going to be different.'

'You mean the garden parties and the balls, the polo matches and the soirées?'

'Not at all. Oh, I'll probably not mind sampling a few of them but what I really want is to see the east, the real east.'

'I thought you'd had enough of heat, dust and flies?'

'But this will be different Amanda. Africa was a great leveller. I was the one with an expensive education, but I knew nothing about nursing or caring for the sick, the old or children. I'd had absolutely no experience of anything like that so I was the general dog's body. I was never any good at school, never academic that is, but I did absorb one or two things.'

'And they were?'

'I wanted to travel the Silk Road from Samarkand into China and see the dawn coming up like thunder on the road to Mandalay. I wanted to look out at the roof of the world from Nepal and see the paddles chunking across Victoria Harbour in Hong Kong. I wanted to see the Jewel in the Crown. This is my jumping-off place.'

'Charlotte, be practical. How do you propose to do all this alone. This is still a man's world, and what about money? You're talking about a great deal of money.'

'I know. Father was not ungenerous and we needn't stay among the fleshpots.'

'We!'

'Why yes, you and me. Don't you want to see the roof of the world?'

'I've already seen it.'

'Or the Great Wall of China, or the Road to Mandalay.'

'Charlotte, it isn't possible.'

'Well of course it is. What will you do if you stay here? You'll go back to being a daughter of the Regiment and in time there'll be another handsome young officer upholding the White Man's Burden and leaving his bones to rot in some foreign field. I'm sorry I shouldn't have said that, but it's true Amanda. If that's what you want you can come back to it, but you can live a little before you do.'

'Tell me about the family Charlotte. I can't take in all the rest just now.'

'Well, Grandma's well, a little more forgetful and Grandfather's as quarrelsome and self-opinionated as ever. The mills are losing orders; most of the work is coming out here to the east. I do remember you once said it was shortsighted to train the people from the east and you were laughed down and told not to be a silly little girl.

'Lady Marston is enchanted with being Lady Marston and Sophie is wallowing in being an MP's wife. She has two children.'

'And Phillip?'

'He left the navy soon after his father died. I've only seen him once since I got back from Africa, I suppose they're happy enough. One would never really know from Phillip.'

'Ralph and Jenny?'

'I suppose they're all right.'

'Don't you know?'

'Well I wasn't home long. I only saw Ralph for a few minutes in the town one day. The parents still go to Grandma's on Sunday but the others visit when they can. Sophie's busy with her children and Caroline, the lady of the manor, often has other fish to fry.'

'You don't much like her, do you?'

'She's my sister, but we never really got on. She was always the pretty one, the one Mother liked to dress up in pretty things, the ladylike one. I was always a tomboy. I played with the boys and climbed trees, I hated sitting in town cafés, drinking China tea on Saturday afternoons, and I never seemed to like the boys Mother expected me to like.

'My sister's wedding was the event of the year. Sophie and I were her bridesmaids and there were four little girls who got in everybody's way all morning. Phillip was predictably handsome and Caroline was beautiful. The entire town turned out for it and stood around while she placed her flowers on the War Memorial. They're still talking about it in Belthorn, and now, of course, she's the chairwoman on a multitude of committees, and when prominent people visit the town she vies with Sophie for attention.'

'Did you never see Jenny?'

'No. I told Ralph I would call but he didn't seem to think it was a good idea. He said he might not be in and Jenny didn't like entertaining.'

'And their little girl?'

'Alice? I've never seen her. Caroline says she's a plain little thing, but Grandma has her to stay and keeps her fitted out

93

with clothes I feel sure.'

'Don't you find it all very sad?'

'I suppose so. They have a small semi in the town but I've never been there. Ralph's parents bought it for them and furnished it, there wasn't much more they could do.'

'They could have tried to like her?'

'That's the hardest thing of all when they were so terribly disappointed. But let's not talk about the family. Can't we talk about us, when we can start and where we want to go?'

'Charlotte, I don't even know if I'm coming. It's a hare-brained scheme, don't you think? My father will probably be the first to say so.'

'You can always say you're old enough to please yourself, you've been a married woman, however briefly, and you have to admit it's preferable to the alternative.'

'I'm not so sure.'

'You can afford it.'

'How do you know?'

'Your parents would help, besides I don't suppose Anthony left you with a pittance.'

'Serving officers don't amass fortunes.'

'On the other hand, most of them have private incomes. You could afford to travel, couldn't you Amanda?'

'Yes I could afford it. I'm doubting my courage and the recklessness of it. I do know something about the dangers of travelling anywhere in this part of the world, a little of the unrest. When you talk to my father you'll find he will try to talk you out of such a venture.'

'He won't succeed Amanda. It's been my dream since I was a young girl, it was my dream when I asked my father for money.'

'It might not be enough.'

'I'm quite prepared to sponge off you Amanda.'

I laughed, suddenly realising that it was the first time I had really laughed for weeks. There was something so wholesome and audacious about Charlotte, something that my father would respond to and as I helped her to unpack her suitcases I said, 'Surely you're not thinking you'll need all this luggage on your travels. There's enough stuff here to take you round the world and in some degree of affluence.'

'I brought a couple of evening dresses in the hope that I might need them here, but, if your mother doesn't mind, what I don't need on our travels I can leave here until we get back.'

'I notice you keep on saying we.'

'That's because I know you'll come with me.'

'Why did I never get to know you better in England? None of you made me exactly welcome, except Ralph that is.'

'I never got along with my sister or Sophie. I thought you'd be like them so I never really tried. Come to think of it I never really got along with Ralph or any of them.'

I was remembering Charlotte, the little girl who stood in her sister's shadow, taciturn, defiant, quick with snide remarks and rapid judgements, yet strangely alone and vulnerable. I could not reconcile the Charlotte I remembered with this sophisticated and attractive woman who was tossing things out of a suitcase and scattering them across the bed.

'I'm sorry the room's so small Charlotte,' I found myself apologising. 'It's only a spare room and I don't think it's ever been used before. I could suggest that the bed is taken into my room which is quite large.'

'Gracious, it's luxury to what I've been accustomed to in Africa. We either slept in tents or under the stars round a camp fire to keep away the wild animals. I had to be content with a sleeping-bag of sorts and a tin bath at the end of the compound.'

'Did you tell your mother all this?'

She threw back her head and laughed. 'I took great delight in telling my mother all that. You have no idea how much my mother used to annoy me. She was always so grateful that she'd actually married into the Dexter family she felt she constantly had to keep her end up. My mother was a terrible snob, and there was always that terrible rivalry between her and Aunt Myrtle. I think my mother was secretly delighted when Ralph fell from grace – she said it served Aunt Myrtle right for being so superior.'

'I don't think I'll ever forget that Sunday when Ralph said he would marry Jenny.'

'I know, if he'd announced that he was going to marry a woman from darkest Africa they couldn't have been more shocked.'

'I wrote to Jenny once or twice after I got here but she never replied, perhaps she's not a good correspondent.'

'Perhaps not, and there was a certain amount of bitterness all to do with the class system I expect. I don't suppose you have it out here.'

One day I would tell her about the class system in India with its history of untouchables and when religion and class divided people as well as colour. Charlotte would find out for herself.

She sat on the bed and looked at me. 'Forget the clothes for a minute Amanda. Tell me about Anthony.'

'What do you want to know?'

'If he was nice, handsome, kind. If you were very much in love with him, but not how much it hurts.'

'Yes he was nice and handsome. He had bright blue eyes and fair hair, and his smile lit up the day. He'd just received promotion to captain and he was thrilled by it. We were going to celebrate when he got back from the frontier.'

'And were you very much in love with him?' she prompted.

'Yes. Who wouldn't have been? He was gallant and he was kind, we had a lot in common and we laughed together. I shall never forget him.'

'Well of course not, but you won't always be remembering him Amanda. The hurt goes, time alters many things.'

'How would you know?'

'I don't know, I only know what I've heard, but you have to help yourself. You have to re-enter the land of the living, because Anthony has gone and he isn't coming back Amanda. You owe it to him to go on and do the best you can.'

'You speak with a great deal of logic Charlotte, prompted I'm sure by your wish to have me travel the world with you. It's something I have to think very seriously about.'

My parents received Charlotte warmly but their views on her proposed journey with me as companion were received more reservedly. Mother was outrightly against it, Father was amused at her enthusiasm. She talked of nothing else and all their attempts to tell her the dangers we might be facing the more persuasive she became.

Both the adjutant and his wife were dismayed by the

prospect, as were a great many other people in our circle, but nothing deterred Charlotte, and now it was Charlotte who insisted we accept invitations to dine out, and attend many of the functions where neither of us lacked escorts.

Complacently Mother said, 'Let's hope she finds a nice young man to settle down with, somebody who'll make her forget these hare-brained schemes.' But although she met a great many nice young men none of them had the power to halt her dreams.

On those nights when we stayed home she sat with Father, pouring over maps. He humoured her, explaining how it was possible for her to see many of the things she wanted to see.

'Forget Samarkand and the Silk Road for now,' he advised her. 'Under Russia there's been considerable unrest there and much of it still lingers on. With the British in Burma you shouldn't have any trouble and Siam is a possibility. From Singapore you can take a steamer to Hong Kong and that should be enough to be going on with.'

'How about Japan and China?'

'My dear girl, you'll be so weary of travelling when you reach Hong Kong, I can only think you'll be desperate to get back.'

She didn't argue with him but she didn't believe him either, and one morning when Father and I were alone he said, 'Are you sure you want to do this trip with Charlotte, Amanda, she's a bit of a harum-scarum and she doesn't really know what she's letting herself in for.'

For several minutes I was thoughtful but then I said seriously, 'I think it would be good for me. People have been very kind, but I don't want to pick up the pieces here as though Anthony had never existed. I'd like to get away for a while. This could be the opportunity I'm looking for.'

'You could have gone home to England Amanda, seen your grandparents and Anthony's uncle.'

'No, I wasn't ready for them. I want to be somewhere where nobody ever knew me or Anthony. I don't want people to feel protective towards me all the time, or that I'm something of a curio because they think I'm too young to be a widow. I really think I want to take this journey with Charlotte. She's fun and we get along.'

'She's also a bit of a loose cannon.'

'She might seem that way, but she can't surely have forgotten that her mother is still looking over her shoulder.'

'From a very long distance my dear.'

I laughed. Charlotte's mother would have no power to sway her daughter either one way or the other and in any case it was very doubtful that Aunt Edith would have any conception of the Golden Road to Samarkand or the Road to Mandalay.

With Father's help we made our plans and we spent hours discussing what we would need for our travels. Father insisted that we stay in decent hotels, saying that after all we were young Englishwomen and he appeared with lists of the best hotels in wherever we were heading for.

Doubtfully Charlotte said, 'I hope my money's going to spin out, I'd rather thought we'd be doing this trip on the cheap.'

'Have you forgotten that you said you wouldn't be ashamed to sponge off me.'

'No, but I wasn't thinking of sponging on you for this amount of money.'

'Let me worry about it, Charlotte. Father's right, we can't stay just anywhere, two young women on their own might be frowned on even in the best places.'

'Only out of envy.'

'I'm not too sure.'

Father was adamant that we kept to the beaten tracks. Men were the people who climbed mountains and explored unknown territories. Men could carry guns and defend themselves, women were merely meant to be pretty and ornamental, and much as Charlotte scoffed at this idea the more serious he became about it.

In the end we allowed him to arrange our journey as far as Calcutta and onward into Burma, then on to Hong Kong.

Charlotte complained that she really wanted to see the roof of the world from Nepal but he placated her by saying when we returned to India he would arrange a holiday for us in Kashmir. I wasn't too sure I wanted to revisit Kashmir with all its memories of Anthony, but it served to pacify Charlotte for the moment.

Chapter Ten

Charlotte was an entertaining companion. Filled with excitement about everything she saw from the exotic temples to the ramshackle bullock carts we encountered on our passage from India to Burma.

In Mandalay we walked for miles around its mass of pagodas carved with the texts of Buddhist scriptures and we climbed Mandalay hill with its magnificent views over the city. On that night when we returned to our hotel, weary but ecstatic, I realised for the first time that I had not thought of Anthony all day.

That was also the night when I became aware of considerable animosity from a British major and his wife sitting at the next table in the dining room. Charlotte and I had been enthusiastically discussing the events of the day but when I looked up I was aware of his frowning face and his wife's obvious disapproval. Charlotte later informed me that he had accosted her in the hotel lobby and told her in quite condemning tones that it was unfitting for two young Englishwomen to be travelling unescorted in Burma.

Charlotte had derived great pleasure from telling him that I was the daughter of a superior officer and the widow of another officer and that our travels had been strictly planned and we knew how to conduct ourselves.

The following morning they were rather more friendly, bidding us good morning before leaving their table.

I would like to have stayed longer in Mandalay but my father had so meticulously planned our route and arranged accommodation for us it was impossible, so after four days in the city we boarded the train for Rangoon and found to our annoyance that the major and his wife were travelling on the same train and in the same compartment.

To confirm what my cousin had told him, he questioned me about my father's regiment as well as my husband's and I learned that he was a staff officer serving in Burma and had only been in the country two months.

His wife hated it – the climate, the country and its people – and the longer we talked the more doubtful I became about the suitability of those who carried the white man's burden.

'Of course,' she said confidently, 'we don't mix with the natives, so perhaps it's wrong of me to be so scathing, but one has to keep up certain standards I think.'

'Are you staying in Rangoon?' the major asked.

'For two or three days before we go on to Bangkok.'

'Be very careful in Bangkok. The place is riddled with prostitution and Siam is not a British province.'

Charlotte's eyes were raised heavenwards and it was left to me to thank him for his solicitude and the hope that we might be left in peace for the remainder of our journey.

We loved Rangoon with its enormous Shwe Dagon Pagoda dominating the city, shimmering with the thin sheets of gold that covered it in the evening sunlight. Here were rubies and jade, gold and silver and exquisite silks and satins, and here were the royal lakes on whose shores the country's elite had built their villas.

We had only a few days to explore Rangoon but we promised ourselves that we would return for much longer on our way back. It was here too where Charlotte promised herself she would buy a ruby if she had any money left.

We both fell in love with the city of Bangkok sprawling besides the Chao Phraya river, a place of klongs or canals, temples, monasteries and the exquisite glory of the royal palace. Here we stood in the company of a party of American tourists adorned with garlands of flowers to kneel in the presence of the reclining Buddha before following them on bare feet to view the Emerald Buddha fashioned in translucent jasper and the Golden Buddha covered in more than five tons of gold.

The Americans showed their admiration for two British

girls travelling alone but they too had covered a great many miles and we were happy to swap experiences.

We learned later that they were staying in our hotel and we met up with them again that evening where we watched a group of Siamese dancers performing their graceful dances across a room lined with spectators, their long slender hands and tapering nails resembling birds as they postured and posed before us.

We were still in bed the following morning when we heard the American party leaving for yet another step on their journey home. They had been so weary and as I turned over and went to sleep I felt grateful for the fact that we were able to journey in a more leisurely fashion through these exotic lands.

While we were in Bangkok the rains came and we were confined to the hotel for several days until it eased and then when we did journey out we found the people living in houses built on stilts in the river. Along the banks saffron-clad monks stood in prayer while the smiling good humour of the ordinary people seemed undiminished by poverty or rainwater.

After Bangkok Singapore seemed almost too pristine, and Charlotte's one desire as we left Raffles Hotel was to board the ramshackle steamer for Hong Kong. She had still not bought her ruby but she had accumulated a collection of jade buddhas, necklaces made from cowrie shells and several closionné bracelets. I had listened to her haggling with street vendors, their smiling good humour and Charlotte's persistence followed by her delight on acquiring some quite ridiculous trophy.

'What will you do with them all when you get home?' I asked her.

'Tell my mother that they are priceless, in which case she'll wear them in front of all her friends, and please don't dare tell her anything any different.'

'So you do intend to go home one day?'

'I suppose so. I've nowhere else to go and I can't live on fresh air for ever.'

'So you're either going to get a job or get married?'

'What sort of work am I suited for? I suppose I could get a

101

job in Father's office, but all I wold be fit for is making the office tea. The men in the offices wouldn't exactly welcome me with open arms and the man I might marry doesn't really exist, at least I've never even remotely found him.'

'Describe him to me, what sort of a man must he be?'

'I don't honestly know, except somebody different from the sort of man I've met up to now. I was terribly smitten with Phillip Marston but he had to be for Caroline.'

'I didn't realise that.'

'Well of course not. Nobody did. He was in the navy so we didn't actually see much of him, and then when he left the navy, Mother pushed Caroline for all she was worth and I got away.'

I didn't say a word about my crush on Phillip. It had all been a long time ago and both Charlotte and I had lost out.

It was late afternoon when we sailed into Victoria Harbour amid a conglomeration of junks, and ferries plying between Hong Kong Island and Kowloon, and several large stately passenger liners anchored there. There was excitement in the crowded streets and blazing lights, at floating banners strung across narrow alleyways and as we crossed from Hong Kong on the ferry to our hotel on Kowloon the lights from a multitude of windows reflected in the dark waters. We were tired and excited. We were also reminding ourselves that this was the final stage of the journey my father had planned for us, after Hong Kong we would be heading back to Delhi.

While we unpacked in our bedroom at the Peninsular Hotel Charlotte echoed my thoughts by saying, 'I can't believe that after Hong Kong we'll be heading back. I still haven't seen the roof of the world or the Silk Road from Samarkand, we still haven't been into China.'

When I didn't answer she went on, 'Don't you want to go on Amanda, China, Japan?'

'You've been on a voyage of discovery Charlotte, I've been running away.'

'But you don't need to run away now, you can't go on mourning for Anthony for ever. There will be somebody else.'

'As you say. Some other young officer I might meet at some regimental ball or on the polo ground.'

'Perhaps. He'll be no worse for that.'

'Only that the pattern will be the same.'

'The pattern will be the same for me if I go home to England. The people at the golf club and the tennis club, Mother's bridge parties and Grandma's every Sunday, where I'll be bored to tears listening to Grandpa's grouse about the mills and trade in general. I can't go home to all that, Amanda. At least in India there'll be something different.'

'But it's not really our life is it, Charlotte? We're birds of passage, the only reality is home leave.'

'I suppose your parents will go home to England when his service in India is finished.'

'Yes, I'm sure they will. England is home after all.'

I wandered out on to the balcony where the music from the hotel ballroom drifted along the empty terrace and from where I could hear the hum of conversation and laughter.

Home to England, what would it entail and where would it be? I couldn't think that my parents would wish to live in the north but I had never heard them discuss it. As I stood with the cool breeze fanning my cheeks and the scent of hibiscus all around me I was dismally aware of the uncertainty of life.

Anthony had never talked much about our future. His concerns were his service in the army, India, the Sudan, Burma; retirement was something in the far distant future. For my father it must surely be different. He had seen years of service in India; on the other hand there were men considerably older than he still serving in India. It would all depend on his promotion, I supposed.

Behind me, in the room, Charlotte was humming a tune, and, turning to her I saw that she was wearing one of her prettiest dresses. Seeing me smile, she said, 'I think we should dress up tonight. Isn't that dance music we can hear?'

'There may not be anybody to dance with.'

'Well, even if there isn't we can still look as if we're having a good time. What are you going to wear?'

'I haven't thought about it, but as you're all dressed up I suppose I must find something.'

'Wear that blue thing, you always looked lovely in that.'

The blue chiffon had been Anthony's favourite, and as I looked in the mirror I thought about his eyes smiling down

103

into mine as we had danced in the ballroom in Lahore. He had looked so handsome in his dress uniform and we had been so happy that night, it seemed incredible that I should be wearing the same dress in a hotel bedroom in Hong Kong in the company of my cousin Charlotte. That night in Lahore I had never giving a thought to Charlotte, or any of them, not even Phillip, who had once been the centre of my universe.

As I fastened the double row of pearls around my throat, Charlotte came to stand in the doorway. She was smiling as she slid her hand into an intricately carved jade bracelet.

'I'm sure I'll find my ruby here in Hong Kong. Did you see those avenues of shops here in the hotel?'

'They looked very expensive, I doubt if you'll be able to afford to buy a ruby from one of them.'

'Oh well, there are the bazaars. I'll bet they're open all night and there'll be so many of them. Tomorrow I'm going to start looking in earnest. Are you ready?'

We were the only two girls dining alone in the vast dining room and we were looked at with some degree of curiosity. Pukka sahibs and their ladies inclined their heads graciously, richly attired orientals spared us barely a passing glance, and Charlotte murmured, 'You're right Amanda. There won't be anybody to dance with.'

Our attention was drawn to a tall thin man crossing the room, followed by a small oriental servant who pulled out his chair for him, and placed a rug over his knees before leaving him alone. Immediately he was surrounded by waiters and Charlotte whispered, 'I wonder who he is. He looks like a Chinese Mandarin.'

His looks were arresting. High cheekbones and arched eyebrows, smooth black hair and a complexion the colour of aging ivory. I thought his features more Mongolian than Chinese but Charlotte would have none of it. 'He must be a Mandarin at least. Oh, I wonder what part of China he comes from?'

I had reckoned without the curiosity of my ebullient cousin. Next morning she told me that she had seen her Mandarin climbing into his white Rolls Royce in front of the hotel as she was leaving in search of her ruby.

'I smiled and said good morning to him,' she laughed, 'and

do you know he smiled back and replied to me in English. Now that I've broken the ice, I can speak to him over dinner.'

When he did not appear for dinner she said petulantly, 'I wonder if he's left the hotel? Oh, I do hope not – he was the most interesting person I've seen on all our travels. I wonder if he isn't well, his servant was very attentive and anxious to see that he was kept warm. Do you suppose he's already left?'

'Charlotte I haven't any idea.'

We lingered at the table after most of the other guests had left and still her Mandarin failed to appear and in the end she said 'I suppose we have to go, we're almost the last.'

Her good spirits were restored the following morning when we passed him sitting at his table reading his newspaper. Charlotte bade him a bright good morning and he answered, raising his head to smile. Hazarding a guess at his age I thought he was probably around forty. His features were aristocratic with that strange immobility peculiar to eastern races. He was wearing a long-fitting robe in cream Shantung which seemed to add to his height, and its graceful folds added to Charlotte's conviction that he was Chinese and of some consequence.

'I wish we could talk to him,' she said. 'Amanda you're a daughter of the White Raj – surely you can dream up some sort of conversation?'

'Certainly not,' I said adamantly.

So we continued to nod and smile at each other, and once I saw the gleam of amusement in his narrow slanting eyes as Charlotte went out of her way to pass his table.

It was several days later when I was sitting alone on the terrace, looking out across the harbour towards Victoria Hill. A mist hung across its summit and as always between Kowloon and Hong Kong island the water was alive with traffic of all descriptions from decrepit junks to opulent ships.

My book lay idle on the table in front of me. No book had the power to obliterate the vitality of the scene before me and until he spoke to me I had no awareness of the man and his servant passing my chair to go to the next table.

He bowed courteously, said good morning and moved on.

He was attired in western dress. Cream Shantung jacket and elegant cream trousers and as he sat down again the servant spread a rug across his knees, and seeing me watching he said, 'My servant is attentive, I am recuperating from an illness.'

'I'm sorry. I hope you're feeling better,' I replied.

'Thank you, yes.'

His English accent was perfect, too perfect. It was not the accent of an educated Englishman but rather that of a man expertly taught and I did not think English was his native tongue.

At that moment Charlotte came hurrying along the terrace, her pretty face alive with excitement, and for once she seemed more anxious to speak to me than greet our next-door neighbour.

'Amanda, I really think I've found what I was looking for,' she began. 'A shop in one of the bazaars. Oh, he has the most beautiful stones but there was this one dark red ruby. I didn't decide there and then, I told him I'd go back with my cousin. You will come with me, won't you?'

'Yes, of course, but I don't know anything about rubies.'

'I told him I couldn't afford the price he wanted, so he'll reduce it. Perhaps he'll reduce it more if there are two of us.'

For the first time Charlotte noticed the man at the next table and blushed furiously when she realised he must have heard our conversation.

He smiled. 'Pardon me,' he said softly. 'I heard your conversation and ask you to be cautious when buying from the local bazaars. It could be that the ruby is *bona fide,* but there are better ways of buying stones than at the bazaars.'

'They're too expensive in the hotel shops,' Charlotte said.

'Yes, of course. But I can give you the address of a man who mines them in the area of Aberdeen Harbour. I will give you a note, present this to him and he will not attempt to overcharge you.'

'Thank you, you're very kind.'

'Two English ladies can hardly be expected to be experienced in buying jewellery in this part of Asia.'

'We have come from Delhi where my cousin's father is in the Indian Army.' Charlotte explained unnecessarily.

He graciously inclined his head and bowed, making no comment, and hurriedly I said, 'We are English, however, and unused to buying jewellery in Hong Kong.'

'Here in the Far East if you wish to buy jewellery, jade or ivory, it is better to seek advice before doing so.'

'I'm sure you're right.' I murmured, and unabashed Charlotte said, 'Are you from China? I've been telling my cousin that you must be, but she didn't agree with me.'

'I had not realised that I was the subject of so much curiosity, madam.'

'Oh, please forgive me. I am sorry. It wasn't that at all but all this is so new to me and I'm curious about everything and everybody. I'm on a journey I've wanted to do for a great long time. I can still hardly believe it's happened.'

'And have you seen everything you want to see?'

'Not everything. I wanted to travel the Silk Road from Samarkand into China. I wanted to see the roof of the world and now I want to go on into China and on to Japan. Unfortunately, we're going home at the end of the month.'

'And home is?'

'For Amanda home is Delhi, for me England.'

'Without seeing all of your dream.'

'Yes. That just about sums it up.'

'Tomorrow, if you are agreeable, I will place myself and my car at your disposal and we will drive to Aberdeen Harbour where you can look at rubies. Forget the ruby you saw in the bazaar.'

We thanked him warmly and once again when he smiled I was aware of the smooth ivory skin stretched tight across his delicate high cheekbones and the inscrutability of his dark eyes.

Charlotte was ecstatic, until I reminded her that he had not disclosed whether he was Chinese or where exactly he was from.

'He's Chinese and a Mandarin. I've always known. Don't you find him terribly attractive?'

'My mind doesn't stretch beyond Englishmen, Charlotte.'

'Well, of course not. Englishmen in uniform with a stiff upper lip and bristling with British Raj authority. I can't wait for tomorrow to come and I'm going to find out all about

107

him, where exactly he comes from and where he's going to. Think about it, a journey in that beautiful white Rolls and rubies at the end of it.'

'I hope you've got enough money.'

'Just take plenty with you, Amanda, I might have to sub.'

He did not appear that evening in the dining room much to Charlotte's disappointment but I was relieved. I knew she would not have hesitated to join him and ask questions.

Instead, we were joined by a man and his wife from Texas who were undoubtedly curious as to why two young Englishwomen should be staying alone in Hong Kong and Mrs Bernstein was as eager to ask questions of us as Charlotte had been to question her Mandarin.

'I saw you talking to the foreign gentleman this morning on the terrace,' Mrs Bernstein said. 'He's very striking to look at, I wonder where he comes from?'

'From China I'm sure,' Charlotte said stoutly. 'I think he's probably a Mandarin.'

'Do you really think so? He speaks very good English.'

'My cousin doesn't agree with me,' Charlotte said. 'He's obviously very well educated, he's definitely somebody.'

'I don't think he's Chinese, not pure-bred Chinese,' Mr Bernstein said. 'He looks more Mongolian to me. He's evidently rich, seen the Rolls Royce he has and his servant dancing attention.'

Charlotte didn't answer. The fact that her Mandarin might be Mongolian or some other race hadn't occurred to her and it needed thinking about.

Charlotte was always the one to linger in bed while I was up and encouraging her to rise. Not the next morning, however. She was already dressed and standing on the balcony while I was luxuriating in bed.

I stared at the bedside clock. It was only seven and breakfast was two hours away, but when she came closer I saw that she was dressed in her prettiest skirt and silk blouse.

'You look very nice,' I said.

'Well, of course. One has to do justice to a white Rolls Royce.'

'And a Chinese Mandarin.'

'That too.'

108

'Remember Kipling, Charlotte. "East is East, and West is West."'

'Kipling's old hat, Amanda.'

'He wasn't old hat in India. Anthony's best friend married a Eurasian girl and they were ostracised for it.'

'Did she care?'

'She cared for him.'

'My Mandarin wouldn't care, he wouldn't be interested. With all his money he wouldn't need to care.'

'Come down to earth, Charlotte. This morning is a morning to look at rubies, not a day to tilt your hat at windmills. In a few days we'll be going back to Delhi and he'll be going home to Peking or wherever he's come from, beneath the Wall of China or the outskirts of Mongolia. His world and yours are miles and centuries apart.'

'You know what's wrong with you, Amanda? India and marriage have taken all the romance out of your life. You're regimented. Look at you, you're beautiful, far more beautiful than I am, and you have a figure to drive men mad. You're rich and I've seen men looking at you, wanting to know you better, so why is it me who craves for adventure and is unafraid of what the future holds?'

'Perhaps because when I was unafraid catastrophe seemed more terrible.'

'Well, this morning, we're going to forget about catastrophe and embrace life before it's too late.'

Chapter Eleven

It would appear our host had changed his mind about the dealer in Aberdeen Harbour when instead we drove through the New Territories towards Lantau where the white Rolls Royce commanded considerable attention from the people working in the long low paddy fields surrounded by steeply sloping hills.

There was nothing remotely pretty about the landscape as the car ran along the narrow road rutted after the rainy season and the windows became covered with a fine dust so that it was difficult to see through them.

At last we came to the coast and were staring out at a multitude of tiny islands, the largest of which we were told was Lantau. Here we left the car for a small boat in which two elderly Chinese men were sitting and after a short conversation in Chinese the two oarsmen rowed out.

Indeed our journey had not prepared us for the beauty and tranquillity of the island of Lantau, with its fine sandy beaches and dramatic mountains. Our host took us to visit the Po Lin Buddhist monastery and we marvelled at the largest outdoor statue of the Buddha we had ever seen. Disdaining a guide he led us himself through the gardens explaining as we went the many twists and turns of religious life and looking at Charlotte's rapt expression I knew that she was completely enchanted with the low charm of his voice.

We ate lunch at a small restaurant he appeared familiar with, and while I watched his long tapering fingers helping us to beautifully cooked sea bass and fresh tender vegetables I too felt that we were being entertained by some Chinese

Mandarin of ancient lineage.

When he left us to pay the bill Charlotte whispered, 'He speaks fluent Chinese, it must be his native tongue.'

After lunch he took us to a single storey building hidden from the road by a massive rock where we were welcomed by a smiling man in a heavily embroidered silk coat, who could easily have been a Mandarin.

He was tall and very thin, and on his narrow head he wore a small embroidered silk skull cap. Slanting eyes and a long curled moustache over thin lips that showed a row of yellowing ivory teeth when he smiled convinced me, but his deference towards our companion reassured me that he must be a man of some consequence and was known to the Chinaman.

We were totally unprepared for the enchantment that followed. His premises were an Aladdin's cave of jewels, silks, jade, ivory and rose quartz.

Exquisitely carved figures were everywhere. Dragons in every pose, stylised Chinese horses and Buddhas, figurines of men and women working in the fields, all carved from ivory or jade, and pictures of lotus blossoms exquisitely embroidered on the finest of silk. These were the things that occupied my attention while Charlotte went to look at the jewels: vast trays of rubies, sapphires and emeralds and I could hear her squeals of delight.

I selected a book filled with pictures of oriental embroidery and a small jade horse resting on a carved ebony stand, then I wandered into the next room where Charlotte stood surrounded by trays of precious stones. When I joined her she looked up with a broad smile, saying, 'What do you think of these, Amanda? I can't make up my mind between them.'

I looked at the stones she had laid aside, three rubies, and two emeralds, all of them incredibly beautiful and not too ostentatious. I had thought when confronted with so many she would chose unwisely but the Chinaman said softly, 'I have explained that it is not necessarily the largest stones which are the most valuable,' and my heart sank.

'Help me, Amanda, which would you choose?' she urged.

'I'd rather you chose it for yourself, Charlotte, but you have been saying you wanted a ruby.'

'I have, haven't I, then it had better be a ruby. This one I think.'

She picked up the ruby and laid it in the palm of her hand where it sparkled and throbbed with every colour of red from vermilion to deep and tragic crimson.

'Is it to be a ring or a pendant?' I asked her.

'I'll think about that later. Nobody will ever give me a ring more beautiful than this one. Caroline had a beautiful engagement ring but she'll be pea-green with envy when she sees this one.'

'Oh, Charlotte,' I said laughing. 'Surely, that isn't why you want it?'

All the time the two men had been watching her with some amusement, now she looked up at our guide saying, 'I haven't asked him for the price, I might not be able to afford it.'

'I will bargain with him,' he said. 'And you Miss Amanda, what have you got there?'

I passed over the articles I had selected and he raised his eyes in surprise at the book.

'This is an unusual thing for an English lady to select,' he said. 'Are you fond of embroidery?'

'Not really, I'm not very good at it, but I loved the designs and the colours. I don't really know why I chose it. The horse is lovely, I think.'

'Yes, the jade is very fine, and the workmanship.'

He went away to speak to the Chinaman, coming back after only a few minutes to tell us the price of the things I had chosen and I was surprised at the figure.

'Are you really sure? I had thought they would be far more expensive.'

He shook his head. 'I am known here. I have bought many things here over the years. That is the price he is asking. And now the ruby, Miss Charlotte.'

I was astonished at the price of the ruby and felt immediately convinced that he was willingly subsidising the purchase of it. Charlotte too seemed unsure as she handed over her money, and when he had gone away to pay she whispered, 'I can't believe it, Amanda. I was so sure it would be double the price.'

112

We stared at each other doubtfully before looking away quickly when he rejoined us.

The journey back to Kowloon was taken largely in silence. Our host seemed reflective and we were feeling some concern that we had not paid enough for the things we had chosen. It was only when we stepped out of his car at the Peninsular Hotel that he said with a grave smile, 'I must ask you to forgive my silence on the journey back but I have not been well, this time at the Peninsular is to help me recuperate. This evening I shall rest in my room.'

We were both quick to thank him for taking us to Lantau and offering our apologies for a day he had found tiring.

'No no, I enjoyed it,' he was quick to say. 'Tomorrow I will feel refreshed.'

He bowed and as he climbed the shallow marble steps up to the terrace his servant was hurrying down to meet him.

If our guide felt refreshed the next day I did not. I had been feeling faint over breakfast and Charlotte said anxiously, 'You're awfully pale, Amanda. Aren't you well?'

I felt sick and unable to eat anything, and was dismally aware of the hum of voices around me and that the sound was at one time a thunder in my ears and then a whisper. I was unsure if I could walk out of the room without fainting and Charlotte's look of alarm confirmed the fact that I was decidedly ill.

I learned later that I was assisted out of my chair and across the room, and I remember very little of the journey to our room and how I got into bed. A doctor was called and a fever was diagnosed. I was instructed to stay in bed for a few days and then to take it easy for another week as the heat and humidity would do little for me.

In the first few days I was aware of people flitting in and out of the room and Charlotte's anxious face bending over me from time to time. After that I recovered quickly, even though Charlotte insisted I obey the doctor and sit out on the terrace instead of going out of the room. I was young and strong. I was hungry for life and did not want to spend what was left of my time in Hong Kong sitting alone on the terrace, whatever Charlotte might say, but Charlotte was conspicuous by her absence for most of the time and after a few days I made up my mind to get dressed and look for her.

A good many of our fellow guests paused to ask if I was feeling better and although I searched around the hotel corridors where the shops were situated and the terraces outside and gardens there was no sign of my cousin or our companion to Lantau.

The white Rolls Royce was missing from its accustomed place outside the hotel and by this time I was glad to sit out on the terrace with a cool refreshing drink.

I was still sitting there when the white car returned and I smiled at the sight of Charlotte stepping out daintily on to the road, waiting for her companion to join her before ascending the steps to the terrace above. They were almost upon me when she saw me and I was immediately aware of her blushing face and her embarrassment.

'Amanda, you're up and about,' she cried. 'Are you better? You really shouldn't have come down here alone.'

'I am better Charlotte. I was rather fed up with being an invalid.'

I smiled at her companion who bowed gravely before stating his intention of returning to his room where he had letters to write. 'I shall no doubt see you both at dinner. I am pleased that you are feeling well again,' he said.

'We've been to Aberdeen,' Charlotte explained, taking the chair opposite mine. 'Tell me you like it.'

She reached inside her handbag and handed over a small silk purse which I opened and pulled out a gold chain on which hung the ruby mounted in gold. It lay in the palm of my hand sparkling in the sunlight and looking up I saw that her eyes were watching me anxiously.

'It's beautiful, Charlotte. Did you have enough money?'

'Yes, it was very reasonable.'

Why didn't I believe her? Why did I have the sudden feeling that there was more that she wasn't telling me?

I handed the purse to her and watched her slipping it back into her bag.

'When are you going to wear it?' I asked her. 'For Caroline's benefit I'm sure.'

She didn't speak and yet I was still aware of her embarrassment. There was no reason for it, after all it was

114

unimportant that she had been to Aberdeen Harbour with a man who had been courteous to both of us. During my illness she had probably been very lonely, he had been kind to her and yet there was that distance between us.

'I hope our friend is feeling better,' I said. 'It seems so awful to call him our friend but I don't know his name.'

'It's Sanjay Ramirez Khan, and he isn't Chinese.'

'And he isn't a mandarin.'

She smiled. 'I'm afraid not. He's Mongolian with some Chinese and some Indian. He has homes in China and different parts of Mongolia. He's very rich.'

'I can believe that.'

'He has a house in Samarkand.'

'And Samarkand is where you want to go, Charlotte. I expect you've learned a lot about it from your friend.'

'Yes.'

There it was again, the terseness of her reply, the sudden rush of colour into her face and the way she looked away towards the hills above Hong Kong island.

'How long is he staying here?'

'Two more weeks at the most.'

'So, he'll be leaving about the same time as ourselves. My indisposition has kept us here longer than we intended, Charlotte, but perhaps we should now think of getting back. I'll write to my father tomorrow and tell him we're returning soon.'

She didn't speak.

'Will you be sorry the holiday is almost over?' I asked her.

She jumped to her feet suddenly, and then she was running quickly across the terrace and I was left staring after her in dismay.

I felt her remoteness again in our bedroom before we went down to dinner. Normally Charlotte could chat about anything that came into her head but on this evening her thoughts seemed far away, either that, or she was unhappy that we were returning to India when there was so much more she wanted to see.

I wasn't short of money and Charlotte had borrowed small amounts from me from time to time. I didn't mind, nor did I want her to return it, but neither did I think either of us had sufficient money to extend our holiday any further.

Charlotte enjoyed her food but this evening she pushed it around her plate and I had to ask, 'Aren't you enjoying dinner, Charlotte?'

'I'm not really very hungry.'

'But you usually have such a good appetite and the duck is lovely. I do hope you haven't caught my bug.'

She smiled. 'No, of course I haven't. When will you write to your father?'

'I thought after dinner. Will you go into the ballroom or on to the terrace?'

'On to the terrace I think.'

'I'll join you there, Charlotte. It's a view I shall remember as long as I live.'

Her smile was pensive as she turned away and walked towards the wide glass doors which opened out on to the terrace.

As I left the dining room I saw that our Mongolian friend was taking his seat at his table and for some inexplicable reason I was glad I did not have to pass him on my way out.

I told my parents that we were nearing the end of our holiday and would be heading home during the next few days. I told them we intended to return through Singapore and Burma, crossing the Bay of Bengal to Calcutta for the last stage of our journey.

It seemed to me that with that letter home all that was left for us was to pack and prepare for our return.

There was no sign of Charlotte on the terrace but I did not think she could be far away. It was a soft moonlight night when starlight and the lights from a thousand high buildings shone into the black waters of Victoria Harbour and when only the ferries seemed to stir in the stillness as they plied between Kowloon and the island.

The streets of Hong Kong and Kowloon would be seething with people, the tramcars on the island filled with sightseers and everywhere there would be that strange mingling of east and west, each separate race oblivious of the other's tastes and pleasures.

People drifted out on to the terrace to stand looking across the water. I knew a great many of them by sight and seeing

116

me alone several of them paused to chat. I was even invited to dance by a very presentable young officer in the Hong Kong police.

'Your friend not with you then?' he said.

'She's my cousin actually. She's around somewhere.'

'I've seen her around the district with the foreign chap with the Rolls Royce.'

'Mr Sanjay Khan.'

'Oh, you know him?'

'Only as a guest here.'

'People talk, you know. He's as rich as Croesus, has to be with a car like that, a servant constantly in attendance and estates here, there and everywhere.'

'How do you know?'

'Well, not from him obviously. He's a pleasant enough chap but keeps himself to himself. That's why it was rather surprising to see him with an English girl.'

'My cousin asked his advice about certain things she was shopping for.'

'I see.'

The dance came to an end and disposed to chat he said, 'How long are you staying in Kowloon?'

'We're leaving in a few days.'

'Home to England?'

'No, to Delhi. My parents live there.'

'Live there!'

'My father's in the army.'

'I see. Major Bingham's returning to India within the next few days, he's the one with the delicate wife. He's going back to Calcutta. She's going home to England.'

'I don't think I've met them.'

'There they are at the table near the window.'

I had seen them around. A pale pretty woman who sat out on the terrace with a rug draped around her knees and a tall military looking man who fetched and carried for her day after day. Drinks and newspapers, fly whisks and toilet water. Totally lost in the humidity and turmoil of the Middle East, Charlotte had stated emphatically.

I declined my dancing partner's invitation to join him in the bar saying I must look for Charlotte but when I returned to the terrace there was still no sign of her.

I was sitting there, when Major Bingham came along and stood for a while, thoughtfully smoking a cigarette, and I guessed his wife had probably retired for the night.

He smiled and wished me good night as he passed my chair and I realised I was feeling anxious and not a little annoyed. I felt conspicuously alone sitting by myself, so I decided to go up to our room and start to pack one of my suitcases.

Indeed I had almost finished when Charlotte came back.

She took in at a glance the open suitcase and open drawers and staring about her in dismay said, 'Why are you packing tonight, Amanda?' You're not leaving in the morning?'

'No, it was something to do. I looked for you on the terrace Charlotte, and I got rather tired of waiting alone.'

She sat down heavily on her bed, her pretty face troubled, her eyes refusing to meet mine and in some exasperation I said, 'Charlotte what is it, something's wrong, I've sensed it all evening. I know you don't want to go home but our money isn't elastic. We have to think about the cost of the journey home.'

She jumped to her feet and started to pace about the room until out of sheer desperation I cried, 'Charlotte, for heaven's sake, sit down and talk to me. I've written to my parents to tell them we're leaving in the next few days, you must realise it's inevitable.'

She glared at me mutinously for several seconds before saying stolidly, 'Amanda, I'm not going back with you.'

I stared at her stupidly before sinking on to the edge of my bed.

'I'm sorry, Amanda. You've been an absolute brick these few weeks and I've loved ever single minute of it. My not going back has nothing to do with you. It's just that I've nothing to go back for.'

'You mean you don't want to go home to England?'

'Or to India. Amanda, they're your parents in India, they'll welcome you with open arms but there's nothing for me in India. There's certainly nothing for me in England except the sort of life you were thrilled to be getting rid of years ago. My mother's a silly snobbish woman who bores me to death.

'I've nothing in common with my sister or my cousins and I can't face listening to them going on day after day about Sophie's husband's success in the political world and Caroline's fitness to be Lady Marston. It's silly and false and I don't have to go home to listen to it.'

'What do you intend to do then? You can't stay here, you won't have the money. One can live in reduced circumstances in England but not out here in the Far East if you happen to be English.'

'Before we embarked on this journey I told you what I wanted to see. The world. Thanks to you I've seen more than I ever dreamed of but there's still an awful lot left. I still want to see the roof of the world and travel the Silk Road from China to Samarkand.'

'Charlotte, I don't think I dare ask you how you intend to accomplish these wishes.'

'I'm sorry he's not a mandarin, but he's the next best thing. He's charming, very handsome too in an eastern sort of way, and he is rich. He can show me all the things I've only dreamed about and one thing's for sure, he isn't after my money.'

'What's in it for him, Charlotte?'

'I can't tell you that. He hasn't asked for anything beyond my company. I'm not so naïve as to believe that he's doing this solely out of the goodness of his heart, I'm pretty sure it will have to be paid for in one form or another, but that's something I'll face when I come to it. I'm twenty-six years old and I've never been in love. I've never had a lover and I've never even thought about the sort of man he'd be. I've never even thought that it might be a tall brooding eastern gentleman with Mongolian and Chinese ancestry. All I know is that we're going north together in his beautiful white Rolls Royce to his home in Samarkand.'

'He could be married. Have you thought of that?'

'He could have a harem, some of them do, don't they?'

'What shall I tell my father? What will he tell your parents?'

'My dear Amanda, I don't give a toss. I'm not afraid. He's charming, cultured and civilised. I don't care that he's an oriental, that he's east and I'm west.'

I knew that whatever I might have said she would have ignored it. Charlotte had made up her mind and I had to accept it.

'When will you go?' I asked her.

'Within the next few days. Sanjay has business in Peking and is anxious to get home.'

The sound of his name sounded incongruous on her tongue and she smiled at the doubts in my expression.

'We shan't leave until you've left, Amanda. I want to wave you off and I want you to embrace me and wish me all the happiness in the world. I don't deserve it but I'm not going into this without a million anxieties.'

Chapter Twelve

Three days later, I boarded the small steamship for Singapore, in the company of a few British passengers and a conglomeration of other nationalities.

Charlotte had tearfully embraced me, as I stood sad-eyed and doubtful on the quayside, and Sanjay had clasped my hand, and given a stiff bow.

The day before he had joined me as I strolled through the hotel gardens, on my way back from buying last-minute gifts for my parents.

His manner had been grave, his expression urbane, as he said, 'You are leaving in the morning Amanda?'

'Yes.'

'Charlotte will not change her mind and leave with you. It may well be that Samarkand will disappoint her. The reality is often less wonderful than our imaginings.'

I smiled.

'I ask you not to be concerned about your cousin. She will be taken care of, we are not uncivilised in Samarkand.'

'I'm sure you are not, but, even so, I am concerned. She's going to a different culture in a strange land, and if you'll forgive me saying so, with a man about whom we know very little.'

It was his turn to smile.

'I give you my word that Charlotte will be safe and cared for. She may well wish to return in a very short time, in which case I will make the necessary arrangements. If she does not wish to return I will try to make her life in Samarkand as wonderful as she imagines it to be.'

'Shall I see you tomorrow?'

'But of course. I will accompany Charlotte to the steamer with you.'

A long look passed between us and neither his eyes nor mine flinched, then with his customary bow he turned and walked away.

Now, they stood together on the crowded quayside, a tall Oriental and a pretty Englishwoman, an incongruous couple, he in his long robe, she in her silk dress and large straw hat. I was unaware of who was standing next to me until an English voice said, 'Your friend not travelling with you then?'

I turned to see Major Bingham regarding me with a smile.

'No, she's going on to China.'

'Alone?'

'No, with Mr Kahn.'

'The devil she is.'

'I beg your pardon.'

'No, I beg yours. I shouldn't have said that, but most people would say there is some sort of danger in a journey of that magnitude and with so obvious a foreigner.'

I knew he was right,so why did I feel so terribly angry? This was prejudice, the same sort of prejudice that I had experienced with Hadassah and Malcolm, and seeing the anger in my expression he said quickly, 'You're right to be angry, it's none of my business. Please forgive me.'

He turned quickly and walked away leaving me suddenly contrite. He had said what any other Englishman might have said at that time, or if they hadn't said it they would most certainly have thought it, and irritation with Charlotte grew. She had behaved irresponsibly, uncaring that I was travelling home alone, while she embarked on a hazardous journey with a man she hardly knew. But as the steamer slipped gently away into the stream of water traffic in the harbour, I was aware of both her arms waving farewell while her escort stood in dignified silence beside her.

That evening as I entered the small dining room I saw that Major Bingham was sitting alone at a small table near the wall and I asked if he would mind if I joined him.

Gallantly he rose to his feet to pull out a chair for me.

122

Thanking him I smiled, and he said 'I take it I'm forgiven then for my crass remarks this afternoon?'

'Yes of course, and they weren't crass, they were opinions I expressed to my cousin and to myself as soon as I knew what she was planning to do. Nothing I said would make her change her mind.'

'She's your cousin then, a young lady not to be moved by logic or common sense?'

'I'm afraid not. Charlotte always knew what she wanted, you would have to understand something of her background to appreciate her motives now. Has your wife returned to England Major Bingham?'

'Yes.'

For several seconds he stared down at the table top, then making up his mind to be more forthcoming he said, 'It's a funny thing but we met out here in the Far East. I was serving in Madras, her father was in the police force in Hong Kong and we met when I came here on leave. You'd have thought the climate wouldn't have been any trouble to her but soon after we were married she had one illness after another, typhoid, hepatitis. Since then we've met every two years for a month's leave, either in Hong Kong or Singapore, then she goes home to Warwickshire and I stay on in India.'

'How long will that last?'

'I've another five years before I can get out of it.'

'Then you'll go home to England?'

'Yes, but what I'll do there I can't imagine. I've been in the army too long, I know very little else.'

'But your wife will be happy?'

'I hope so. You don't need to answer this question if you don't want to, but does your cousin intend to marry her Mongolian?'

'I don't know. She calls him her mandarin.'

He laughed. 'A very rich mandarin from all appearances. Money hides a multitude of sins.'

'I'm sure you're right, but in this case I don't think money was the criterion. It was something more, something inexplicable.'

He asked no further questions on the subject of Charlotte and as the days passed and the little ship sailed on towards

123

Singapore we learned a lot about each other as people do who are thrown together in alien situations for a little time before they go their separate ways.

We were journeying together to Calcutta so it was inevitable that in Singapore we boarded the same steamer to take us to Rangoon where Major Bingham left me in the comfort of my hotel while he went to make enquiries about the next stage of our journey, by train through Burma.

When he had not returned in time for dinner I began to feel anxious. Accidents happened on the streets of Rangoon, Englishmen were robbed and threatened and one look at his troubled face when he finally arrived confirmed my anxieties.

'It's not good news Amanda,' he said quickly. 'They've had torrential rains and part of the track is washed away and won't be repaired from some time. It's either staying here until they've managed it, or looking for some other means of getting to Calcutta.'

I stared at him in dismay. The hotel was expensive and I had no wish to be short of money in a strange country, but what other means were available?

'There's a sea journey across the Bay of Bengal, but it won't be a luxurious crossing. The Chinese boats that make it can't hold a candle to that little bucket we sailed in from Hong Kong to Singapore.'

'What do you think we should do?'

'Well, I have to get back before my leave's up and who knows how long it's going to be before the railtrack is in operation. I think we should cut our losses and look for a steamer. Will you leave it to me?'

'Yes, of course, I'd be grateful.'

'Don't expect too much Amanda. It could be the most horrendous experience of your young life.'

I realised three days later that his words had been no exaggeration. The small steamer was a rust-burdened wreck and it's Chinese crew a bunch of sullen individuals commanded by a captain who walked about the deck with a whip in one hand and a whisky bottle in the other.

Every meal was rice, served up in what looked like unwashed bowls, so I confined my eating to mangoes and small leathery oranges. Rain fell from leaden skies and the sea around us heaved in a solid black mass and yet the humid nights were so hot I could not sleep as I lay on top of my bunk listening to the rain pattering on the deck and the ravings of the captain as he belaboured his hapless crew.

'How can he ever keep his job?' I complained to Major Bingham.

He thought my question very funny.

'My dear girl, who is he answerable to? He probably owns the ship and underpays his crew. In Calcutta they'll probably jump ship and he'll have to find others. He's got our money, he'll spend it on booze and sail off when he's a mind to.'

There were six British passengers, two Australians and an American. We kept very close to each other, fancying that we would all be robbed or murdered if we didn't, and none of us could quite believe the shoreline of Calcutta when we saw it through a golden haze of sunlight several days later.

Even unperturbable Major Bingham heaved a sigh of relief.

'We've made it Amanda,' he said with a smile. 'I have to admit there were days and nights when I doubted it.'

'Oh, me too,' I murmured. 'I can't thank you enough for all your kindness.'

'I've been very glad of your company my dear, and now you're off to Delhi, are you glad to be home?'

'For many things, it isn't really home, is it, for any of us?'

'I suppose not. Will you go back to England?'

'That isn't home either. My future is something I have to think about very carefully.'

He accompanied me to the station and saw me on the train along with my luggage, and stood on the platform until the train pulled out of the station. We would probably never meet again and yet he had been one of the best friends I had ever had. It was then for the first time in weeks I thought about Charlotte.

Where was she at this moment and had it all been worthwhile? Would I ever see her again and if I did how difficult would it be?

I thought about the excitement we had both felt at our first sight of the Ganges and the plains of Bengal. I thought about the magical afternoon we had stood in awe before the exquisite Taj Mahal and Charlotte had clapped her hands with glee at seeing the names on railway platforms, Agra, Cawnpore, Benares.

I was remembering Sanjay Khan's aloof immobile expression. The correct dignity of his bow, his expressionless ebony eyes. How would he regard Charlotte's enthusiasm and wild excitement, when he showed her the Great Wall of China and the Golden Road to Samarkand?

Major Bingham had wanted to inform my father that I was on this train, but I had said I would prefer to surprise them. I did not want them to meet me at the station and see their amazement that Charlotte was not with me.

An attentive attendant came to make up my bunk and bring me a tray laden with fragrant Assam tea and lemon, and that first night I slept soundly with the knowledge that ahead of me lay some 800 miles before we reached Delhi.

It was early morning two days later when I stepped from the train in Delhi and looked around me at the familiar station. A group of soldiers had alighted further up the train and walking towards me were two Catholic priests in their long black garments. I looked curiously at Hadassah's house at the end of the platform, realising immediately that something was different. There were no flowers in the little plots around the house, which Hadassah's mother tended religiously every day.

I was just looking for a porter, when I saw my father walking towards me, wearing his white trench coat, because the rain had followed me across the Bengal plain and was sweeping dismally along the station platform.

Meeting my amazed gaze, he said with a smile, 'Your friend Major Bingham telephoned to say you were on this train and that you were alone.'

'I asked him not to tell you. I knew Mother would be worried if she thought I was travelling alone.'

'I'm very glad he told me. Your mother is in England, in Devon. Your grandmother has had a stroke. She's recovering slowly but your mother will be away for a few weeks I'm afraid.'

'Oh dear, poor Granny, I am sorry.'

'And I'm more concerned about that unreliable little

baggage who has gone off into the blue to leave you to come home alone.'

'I'll tell you all about that later.'

He didn't press the subject but as we passed the station house I said, 'It's the first time I've seen it without flowers in the borders.'

'Mrs Bashir looked after the garden. Unfortunately she died a few weeks ago.'

So many things had happened in my absence, now I was thinking about Hadassah, who had lost a husband and a mother in such a short space of time.

We drove to the bungalow in silence. Delhi was coming to life and the driving rain impeded our progress, as did the people hurrying along the streets. I was remembering the rain in the north of England and thinking it was a great leveller. Delhi looked no more prepossessing than Manchester had looked when the rain danced on the pavements and obscured the distant hills.

The houseboy helped Father bring in my luggage and was quick to produce coffee.

'I'll get out of these travelling clothes,' I said hurriedly. 'They're feeling rather damp.'

When I returned to the living room I saw that Father had poured out the coffee and, as he handed me a cup, he said, 'Now, young lady, I want the full story of why Charlotte isn't with you. Bingham didn't elaborate, he simply said he thought I should know you were on your way home, and alone.'

I told him briefly and watching his astonishment I realised there was no way I could have minimised the tale.

'You mean she's actually gone off into the blue with this Mongolian or whatever he is?'

'Yes. He's very cultured, and he's very rich. She was fascinated by him from the moment they met. He told me he would care for her and see that she was safe.'

'Is he married?'

'I don't know.'

'Is it the man himself, or the excuse to see more of the world that has tempted her?'

'Both I think.'

'I've never heard of anything more irresponsible. English women don't do that sort of thing. What am I going to tell her father?'

'You can only tell him the truth.'

'And that won't be good enough, I can tell you. Why couldn't she come back with you and then go home to England? She's a good home to return to and generous parents. Her mother will have hysterics.'

'Charlotte is accustomed to living in a dangerous environment. She lived in Africa and she wasn't exactly cosseted there.'

'Are you sticking up for her, Amanda?'

'She didn't want to go home. There's nothing for Charlotte at home in England, just as there was never anything for me there. In many ways I understood her.'

'Oh, you did, did you? I can't think that her parents will be so accommodating. Why was there nothing for Charlotte in England?'

'Aunt Edith was a terrible social climber and everything had to be for Caroline. Charlotte was always the odd one out. I never really got to know her.'

'Your not knowing each other very well didn't prevent her bludgeoning you to take a very expensive trip largely at our expense. She'll get a piece of my mind if ever I see her again.'

'No, please Father, I'd rather you didn't. We had a wonderful time, she was fun to be with and we were good friends. I'm very afraid for her but I do understand her. I think we should forget about it and hope that she's happy. I hope we do see her again. She's the only relative who has taken the trouble to keep in touch.'

'And we both know why that is, don't we?'

I didn't speak. I understood his anger, but it could not undo what had happened and it could not reach Charlotte.

'It's awfully quiet without Mother. You must be hating it.'

'Yes, well, it couldn't be helped. So now, young lady, you'll have to take her place and accompany me to the functions she would have gone to. You made a lot of excuses not to go to them before you went away and we understood, but now my dear you have to rebuild your life without

Anthony. I think you'll find that people are very kind, they understand it will be difficult for you.'

So, in the weeks that followed, I emerged from my chrysalis to re-enter the world of Delhi society as a daughter of the regiment.

People were kind but it did not take me long to realise that I was not the young eager girl who had danced the night away in Anthony's arms. Widowhood had given me a grown-up sophistication that somehow or other set me apart from the other young women who were finding their feet in an adult world and falling in love.

To them I was a girl who had been in love and the man I loved had gone. I was not one of them because they did not want reminding that what had happened to me could happen to any one of them. I had had my chance, now it was their turn. Consequently the men who invited me to dance and watch them play polo were older men, obsessed with their careers. Dancing with the colonel's daughter aided their ambitions.

Now it was friends of my father who asked me to dance, bluff, hearty, kind-hearted men whose wives encouraged them to be kind to me, and in those few months before my mother returned, I began to feel that my youth had gone for ever, even though I was only twenty-three years old.

We heard nothing from Charlotte. I made excuses for her, saying she was probably in some quite outlandish place and post was difficult, but Father said it was nothing of the kind. This was not the Dark Ages, he said, it was 1929.

We did, however, receive a long, angry letter from her father who accused me of deserting her, that I should have gone on into China with her, instead of leaving her to go off with some quite impossible heathen, and he would hold my father to account for her well being.

'But it isn't fair,' I cried after reading it.

'Of course it isn't fair, but he doesn't know anything about life out here. It's the sort of stance I expected him to take. She is his daughter after all.'

'Are you going to reply to it?'

'Perhaps when he's had a chance to simmer down. In the meantime I've got a few feelers out to find out as much as I possibly can about Mr Sanjay Ramirez Khan.'

'But he lives in Mongolia or some other inaccessible place.'

'Once they were inaccessible, now they are not. I have contacts who will do what they can.'

So we had to contain our patience until someone could bring us news of Charlotte's whereabouts.

It was one Sunday morning as I was walking alone from the church that I saw Hadassah walking towards me, holding a little girl by the hand. We both paused and she would have walked on with a brief smile had I not said 'Hadassah, I was sorry to hear about your mother. It must have been quite sudden.'

She walked back to me. 'Yes it was. She had a heart attack.'

'I thought there was something different when I missed the flowers in the borders around the house. Your mother was so proud of them.'

'Yes, she loved flowers.'

'There is just you and your father now?'

'Yes. This is one of my pupils, her mother is ill and I'm looking after her this morning.'

'I would like you to visit me at the bungalow Hadassah, or perhaps I could visit you.'

'My father would not like it, he would not think it proper,' she said stiffly.

'Then please come to my home. My father is out tomorrow evening if you would rather come when I am alone.'

She stared at me with her dark questioning eyes and I felt she was about to make some excuse. Instead, however, she bowed her head, saying stiffly, 'Very well, I will come after school is over, for a short time if you are agreeable.'

'Oh, I'm so glad. Stay as long as you want, it doesn't have to be for a short time.'

She smiled briefly before pulling the child gently away. Only the child looked back to see me standing where they had left me.

Chapter Thirteen

My father was attending the silver wedding of two of his friends and although I had been invited I made an excuse not to go. He made no comment when I said Hadassah was coming to see me, I had always made it very clear to my parents that I wanted her to come and that I was unconcerned with the opinions of others.

Hadassah arrived in late afternoon, in the ramshackle old car I had seen her driving around the streets of Delhi. She was wearing a beige cotton skirt and cream blouse and a beige silk scarf tied back her long black hair. I was waiting for her on the balcony and as she walked along the garden path that skirted the lawn I thought again how beautiful she was. It was a sultry exotic beauty that even colourless western dress failed to disguise and as she came to sit in the chair next to mine she smiled, a smile that lit up her dark eyes and curved her ruby-red lips.

'It's nice here in the garden,' she said. 'I have often wished we had a garden but all we had were my mother's borders.'

'They always looked very colourful.'

'Yes, they were her joy. When I came back to Delhi I missed our garden in Lahore. It was the first I had ever known.'

She did not say it in a complaining voice but simply as a matter of fact.

I rang the bell on the small table in front of us and immediately one of the houseboys came to enquire if I wanted tea. He looked at Hadassah curiously and I was instantly aware of his resentment. He was prepared to wait on me, he was very

131

unsure that he should be expected to wait on Hadassah, and as I ordered tea and he walked away, she smiled. 'He does not approve of your guest Amanda.'

'We must mend his ways then.'

'I doubt if it will be you who mends his ways Amanda, prejudice of one sort or another will only go when India belongs to her people and when our own fate is about our necks.'

Hadassah's dream seemed an impossible one to me at that time however ardently she believed in it. I decided it was time to change the subject, so I said, 'Did your mother never want to go back to Scotland to visit her family?'

'She talked to me about Scotland a lot when I was a little girl. She talked about the lochs and the braes, the glens and the heather and she showed me pictures. I desperately wanted to go there but we didn't have that kind of money and in the end she stopped talking about it.

'It took my mother a long time to see the prejudices we were surrounded with and in the end she knew we would be subjected to those same prejudices in Scotland. How could she expect her stiff-necked, hide-bound sisters and their families to accept one of their clan who had married outside her faith and colour. Can you begin to imagine me besides those fair-skinned Scottish cousins?'

'What is your future going to be, Hadassah?'

'A teacher at my school has asked my father for my hand in marriage. He's a good man, my father likes him and is pressing me to accept him.'

'But what about you?'

'At one time I would have had no choice. My father would have arranged a marriage for me, but because I married an English officer he feels he is no longer able to do this without my full consent. He also feels that this might be my only chance.'

'Why should he feel that?'

'Because I am Eurasian and a widow, the widow of an Englishman.'

'It's too complicated for me.'

She smiled. 'Will you ever marry again Amanda?'

'How can I say?'

'Perhaps, when you go home to England, there will be somebody for you.'

'You seem very sure that I shall go home to England.'

'But of course. Don't they all go home eventually?'

She stayed until the lamps were lit and as their glow filled the shrubbery dragonflies flitted among the blossoms, their wings iridescent and strangely ethereal.

I walked with her to the gate and waited there until the sound of her car's engine died away.

I felt unsettled by her visit, by the story of her life and the thought that she may soon marry a man chosen by her father. She had seen nothing untoward in this, merely a sort of good fortune that there might be a future for her in the role of his wife.

Several evenings after Hadassah's visit my father brought home a guest for dinner. He was Major Donaldson recently returned from service in Rawalpindi and now serving as a staff officer in Delhi. He was a little older than the young officers finding their feet in Colonial Service, and he was rather shy – but charming.

We got along and he began by inviting me to watch him play polo and then to several dances in the officers' mess. Knowing glances were exchanged between our friends and acquaintances but although I enjoyed Alan's company he evoked no feelings of passion in me. He was nice, a courteous escort and a charming friend, nothing more.

I knew that he was soon harbouring romantic ideas about me but I was not yet ready to take advantage of them and I began to feel pressurised into a relationship I did not want.

When he invited me to the ball at the Viceroy's residence, Mother said, 'Tongues are wagging Amanda, are you ready for this?'

'No, I'm not. I like him enormously Mother, but if he wants something more from me at this moment I would have to say no.'

'He's very eligible. He has an excellent family background and your father and I like him immensely.'

'I know. I like him too, but liking isn't enough, Mother.'

Two weeks before the ball a parcel arrived for me and as the houseboy placed it on the table I stared at it in some surprise. I had no idea why anybody should be sending me a present for no apparent reason.

The parcel had been expertly wrapped but there was no indication on the wrapping paper of who it had come from, nor was there a letter on top of the tissue-wrapped inner bundle.

Very carefully I used the scissors to open the ends and Mother asked anxiously 'What is it, Amanda? Can't you see inside?'

I tore away the wrapping paper and we both stood back in amazement at the roll of delicate silk in colours that glowed and flamed as perfect as the feathers of a peacock.

I took it up and held it against me so that the silk unravelled and fell to the floor in beautiful shimmering folds and our eyes met in astonishment. Mother said, 'There must be a letter Amanda, something to tell you where it has come from.'

There was nothing except the postmark smudged and difficult to read, but as we pored over it together, Mother gasped, 'Bukhara, Amanda. It must be from Charlotte.'

There was nothing else, and in some exasperation I cried, 'Oh why couldn't she have sent me a letter. This is so beautiful, I need to thank her for it, but how can I when I don't know where she is.'

'I'm sure she doesn't want you to write to her,' Mother said. 'But she's obviously feeling a little guilty about what she did to you. You must take it to Mrs Fielding, she's marvellous with the clothes she's run up for me. It will make you the most beautiful ball gown, you'll see nothing like it here.'

She was right. The gown was beautiful and throughout the evening people were remarking on it and asking where I had managed to buy such a thing. Admiration was evident in Alan's eyes as we danced, and on our way to the supper room Mrs Lewisham whispered, 'He's besotted with you Amanda and no wonder in that dress.'

In other years I thought of Alan Donaldson as one of the nicest men I had ever known. He made no demands and was anxious to give me all the space I craved to recover from Anthony.

I wasn't fair. I had in fact recovered from Anthony a long time ago. I had loved him, with a young, earnest puppy love, anxious to get out into the mainstream of life, but I was not ready to commit myself to what marriage really meant. Years and years of army life my mother had endured without complaint – its dangers, its traumas and its dedication.

I was not ready for that now. I had never understood its full implication with Anthony, I had been too young, but I understood it now and as the months passed I began to fret about it in case it was inevitable.

Hadassah married her Indian schoolteacher and I sent her a wedding present and wished her well. Hadassah had obeyed her father out of a sense of duty. Hadassah and I were two very different people.

It was one evening when Alan had invited me to an informal function at the officers' club that I realised I would have to be honest with him. I declined to attend the function even though my parents were to be there and I made a rather lame excuse that I had a bad headache.

I mooned about the house wishing I'd gone, surprised when half way through the evening the houseboy announced that Major Donaldson wished to see me.

I felt trapped, but one look at his face made me see that decision-time had arrived. He came straight to the point, his grey eyes looking calmly into mine, his entire stance resolute even when his first words took me my surprise.

'Amanda, I've come to tell you that I'm moving out within the next few weeks. Being a staff officer isn't my scene, it never was.'

'Where are you going?'

'I'm going to Lahore with the Twenty-ninth. I know Lahore has unhappy associations for you but I'd like you to come with me as my wife. You must know how I feel about you. I thought it was too soon but this posting alters matters considerably.'

'But you were happy to be a staff officer. You said you'd seen enough of the other stuff to last you a lifetime.'

'I know. I was wrong.'

'Why does it have to be Lahore?'

'Why does it have to be anywhere, my dear? You shouldn't

135

need to ask me that.'

And he was right. I had been conditioned all my life that the army had to be obeyed, everything else came as a secondary issue. Even before I had had time to think about it I heard my voice saying, 'I couldn't go to Lahore Alan, anywhere but Lahore.'

I knew as soon as I had said it that it was a lie. It was merely an excuse.

I hated the disappointment in his face, and in my heart the feeling of betrayal.

'You mean you don't care for me enough Amanda?' he said gently.

'I think you might have discussed it with me first.'

It wasn't true. If he'd discussed it with me from here to eternity it wouldn't have mattered.

'Perhaps we should think about it Amanda.'

'No Alan.'

'Because it's Lahore?'

'Alan I like you more than any man I know, I wish it could have been more, but I'm not even sure if I can feel love for anybody again.'

'I'm prepared to wait Amanda, give you more time to get over Anthony.'

'I am over him Alan. There are whole days when I don't think about him, but I remember what it's like to fall in love. I'm not ready for the love that comes with the years and perhaps never really comes at all. I'm sorry Alan. I'm so very fond of you and I do wish you well.'

For what seemed eternity we sat without speaking until he looked up with a brief smile saying, 'Well I suppose that's that. I'd better get back to the hop. Your father told me to come around, he'll be waiting to see what progress I made.'

The weeks that followed that meeting were difficult. People speculated about why Alan and I no longer were seen together. My parents were very disappointed but after that first evening never referred to it, and only Mrs Lewisham, who was an inveterate gossip, said feelingly, 'What has happened between you and Alan Donaldson Amanda? You were so right for each other and it was obvious he was head over heels in love with you.'

When I didn't reply but continued to look embarrassed she said, 'Don't mind me dear, you know what a nosy parker I am, but is it because he's going to Lahore? I know Lahore has very unhappy associations for you.'

'I don't want to go back there Mrs Lewisham, but it's not entirely that. Perhaps I need to get away from the army.'

'Well, of course, you don't mean that. It's Lahore and memories of Anthony that's doing it. Perhaps it's too soon.'

'I don't think so. It's four years since Anthony died, Hadassah has married again.'

It seemed incredible at that moment that Anthony had been dead four years. I had not counted the days or the months or the years, they had come and gone and only now when I had had the courage to put those years into words did they become reality. For several minutes we stared at each other in silence then she said gently, 'That's different my dear. Hadassah is Eurasian and lucky to have found a respectable Indian to marry her. I expect her father pushed it for all he was worth.'

'I happen to think it could be true.'

'Well, even if you're right, nothing like that troubled you. You're British, beautiful and rich. We all thought how lucky you were to have Alan Donaldson, and we can't really understand what you're thinking about to turn him down.'

'But it has nothing to do with anybody outside Alan and myself Mrs Lewisham. People should really be encouraged to mind their own business.'

'My dear, we're a small community in an alien world, allow us to gossip a little. It doesn't have to be malicious.'

'But a great deal of it is, isn't it, Mrs Lewisham?'

'Perhaps. You are thinking about Hadassah and Malcolm?'

'Yes. They loved each other and were happy together. Why couldn't people simply accept it and let them get on with their lives?'

'Perhaps because we're not ready for it yet, Amanda. Gossip about you was different, kinder. We wanted you to find happiness again. Now we simply think you've tossed it aside.'

'I can't love to order.'

'No, perhaps not. But you have to think about the rest of

your life my dear. Will you be content to spend it with your parents as if you'd never been away?'

I stared at her mutely. I'd never given it much thought, I'd simply been content to go on from day to day without looking too closely into the future, and seeing my stark expression she said gently, 'Forgive me Amanda, I'm an old busybody about something that's none of my business. I'm very fond of you, and your parents, but I spoke out of turn.'

'No you didn't, and you're right. I've given it very little thought. Now you've made me realise that I must think about it and move on. Where, I'm not exactly sure, but I don't think marriage for the sake of it is the answer.'

'It's surprising how well it works sometimes, my dear.'

'I'm sure it does, but not for me. I'm very fond of Alan, I hope we can continue to be friends. In any case we shan't see very much of each other when he leaves for Lahore.'

'I hope Lahore wasn't the problem.'

'No. I didn't love him enough, if I had, the Arctic Circle would have posed no problem.'

I believed that Mrs Lewisham would in all probability repeat our conversation to whoever was interested and it really didn't matter.

So how did the years go?

Hadassah and I became better friends. She introduced me to her brightest pupils and I helped them with their English. I followed less and less the pursuits attended by other Englishwomen and I became something of an eccentric. My parents left me alone to get on with my life and there must have been times when I disappointed them sorely.

I was not unhappy, I was in limbo.

I travelled whenever it was possible, from Delhi to Bombay and on to Mysore, across India to Madras and on to Singapore, then I sailed back to Ceylon in a disreputable steamer that reminded me of the one I had sailed in from Rangoon to Calcutta. The captain was not a drunkard but he was a tyrant and the screams of his unfortunate crew could be heard the length and breadth of the ship.

When I returned home it was to learn that Alan Donaldson had visited us and that he was engaged to be married to a nursing sister he had met in Lahore where she had nursed him through a bout of dysentery.

I met him on the street just before he returned to Lahore and from the look in his eyes as he gazed down into mine I felt very unsure that he should be getting married at all. Alan Donaldson still had feelings for me, and when I wished him well his smile haunted me for days by its sadness.

I received another large parcel from Charlotte, this time from China's region of Shantung. It was packed with reams of exquisite silk Shantung from delicate pale turquoise to cream and again there was no letter, simply an ornamental card bearing the writing 'Enjoy'.

Then, one day, out of the blue, I decided to go home to England to visit my grandparents in Devon and Anthony's uncle, and then go on to visit the other grandparents in the north. In some annoyance, I said to my father, 'I want Charlotte to know that I intend to go home to England. How can I tell her, I don't know where she is?'

His reply was entirely logical. 'Well, she's travelling around and can obviously afford to spend money on expensive presents. I suggest you write to her care of Mr Sanjay Ramiriz Khan, Samarkand. If he's as well known and rich as we think he is then I'm sure the letter will reach either Mr Khan or Charlotte. Either way you should receive some response.'

It was not an easy letter to write. I told her a little of the years since we last met and I told her I was returning to England where I would see her parents. I asked her to write to me and tell me what had happened to her so that I could put their minds at rest. Weeks passed without any reply.

I had almost given up hope when another parcel arrived from Bukhara and this time within the parcel was a white envelope simply addressed 'Amanda'.

I did not even open the tissue wrapped enclosure I was too anxious to read her letter, and there were several pages of it written in Charlotte's small spidery writing.

She hoped that I had liked the silks and that they had helped set fire to Delhi's social scene. She was surprised that I had not remarried. 'What are the young officers in Delhi thinking about?' and she went on at length about her travels.

She had walked along the Great Wall of China and almost

died from heat and exertion. She had seen the roof of the world from the Forbidden City and travelled the Silk Road from Samarkand into China, often with disappointment but the experience had only succeeded in making her want more of the same.

She was surprised that I had decided to return to England and if I discovered that her family were concerned about her I could tell them she was living in Central Asia with a man who was one third Russian, one third Mongolian and one third Chinese, and, before her mother had a Canary fit, they were married. Not a western ceremony, but apparently legal.

She went on to discuss the temples and the paddy fields, their servants and their expectations for more travel, and it was only at the very end of her letter that she said, 'If my mother by this time is fainting with despair, please tell her he is a millionaire several times over. I may never see any of them again but she will conceivably dine out on it for the rest of her life.'

I put the letter down and stared at it. I need not have spent a single minute worrying about Charlotte, she was a survivor and not once in her long epistle had she mentioned my journey home from Hong Kong alone.

The tissue-wrapped parcel contained more silk, but this time more vibrant silk that only an eastern culture could have produced.

'Take it to England with you,' Mother advised. 'You'll find somebody there who will make it up for you.'

'Why don't you have it Mother. You'll be attending considerably more functions than I shall.'

'I've enough clothes darling, you must have it. Charlotte meant it for you.'

I had spent my childhood and young girlhood in England but I knew very little about the country itself. In wartime we had not been able to travel about and when the war was over all we seemed to know was the north country and the coasts of Lancashire and Yorkshire.

Devon would be a new place to me and on the morning I boarded the ship that was to take me to England I looked back at the bustling harbour of Bombay with something akin to fear.

This was India and reality, England was somewhere we called home but wasn't. Home was something that should be welcoming and remembered with joy. I had no such memories. Home was Grandfather's truculence over the dining table and the aunts vying with one another for attention. Home was talk of cotton and mill chimneys, clogs on cobbled pavements and rain, so much rain.

I fell in love with Devon from that first morning when I looked out of my bedroom window at a shining blue sea and rocks the colour of old mahogany. I grew to love the impossibly high hedgerows adorned with wild flowers, and the gentle hills topped with rugged rocks. It was a gentle and romantic land and I loved the old stone house covered with virginia creeper and the gardens that ran down to the cliff top.

My grandparents received me ecstatically into their way of life – of dog shows and church bazaars, cattle shows and Evensong – and when they entertained as they frequently did, their guests were elderly, kindly people with similar tastes to their own and I quickly discovered that a great many of them had a history connected with India and the White Raj.

Grandfather's golfing friend was a retired brigadier who had served in Burma and Calcutta, and Granny's friends on the church committees had mostly seen service abroad with their husbands or as nursing sisters.

They made me very welcome and encouraged me to stay with them as long as I liked, but I had promised my father that I would visit my other grandparents in the north of England and it was a promise I had to keep.

It was with some trepidation that I telephoned Anthony's Uncle who lived about twenty miles away with the idea of visiting him while I was in the area. I need not have been troubled. His voice was warm and welcoming and sitting over afternoon tea in the large beautiful garden I felt I had known him always.

He showed me pictures of Anthony's childhood and in Anthony's old bedroom on one wall was a long school portrait of Anthony with his fellow pupils at Marlborough College. I found him in the centre of the second row, and the smile on that young boy's face brought the treacherous tears into my eyes. Then at the end of the next row I saw Malcolm and the appalling finality of death was brought painfully close.

I parted from him at the garden gate and for a long moment he held my hand in his saying, 'Don't live with the past Amanda, let it go. You're a very lovely young woman, a very rich young woman, and when I go you'll have more. I've nobody else to leave it to.'

I allowed the warm beautiful summer to drift by and it was already Autumn. I could not put off my visit north any longer, as my memories of cold dreary winters were still with me, and at the end of September I made up my mind to visit them for a few weeks and return to Devon in time for Christmas.

'Perhaps you should write and tell them you're coming,' Granny advised.

'They're sure to be at home. I never remember them going anywhere, particularly in September.'

'Things may have changed dear,' she insisted. 'The war was on when you lived there. They'll now have more time for travelling about.'

I did not take her advice but decided to arrive unannounced.

Book Two

Chapter Fourteen

I got out of the taxi and stood for a moment, gazing up at the house before I turned to pay him.

'It's a fine house,' he said with a smile. 'Mi father used to bring me up 'ere when I were a lad, just to look at the 'ouses and the folk wi' their 'orses. Will ye be stayin' long, miss?'

'I don't know. Just a few weeks perhaps.'

'I'll give ye mi card, just in case.'

'Thank you.'

As I walked up the steps toward the terrace and the front door an old man who had been pruning one of the shrubs touched his hat and smiled at me, eyeing my luggage curiously.

I could feel his eyes on me while I stood at the front door pulling the bell rope and he called out to me, 'The rope's broken, miss. I should try the knocker or the bell button.'

I smiled and thanked him and he watched while I pushed the bell button – an innovation since I was last at Fairlawn. A young housemaid opened the door.

'Is Mrs Dexter in?' I asked her.

'No miss. She's visitin'.'

'Oh well, I'll bring in my luggage and leave it in the hall. I really should have written to tell them I was arriving today. She'll be in later?'

'About five miss. She didn't say she was expectin' visitors to stay.'

'No, of course not.'

I looked up towards the stairs where a young girl stood staring at me.

She seemed about ten or eleven, and if her face had been less sulky she would have been pretty.

I smiled and said 'Hello, who are you?'

'Who are you?' was her answer and there was no smile in return.

'I'm Amanda St Clare. Mr and Mrs Dexter are my grandparents.'

'I don't know you.'

'And I don't know you, so why not tell me who you are.'

'I'm Julia Holleran. My father's a member of Parliament.'

'So you're Sophie's daughter?'

'Do you know my mother?'

'Yes, she's my cousin. I also know your father but not very well. I was one of their bridesmaids when they married.'

'You're the one who went out to India. I've seen your photograph in Mummy's wedding album.'

I smiled.

'You're older than the photograph.'

'Yes. It was eleven years since that picture was taken.'

By this time she had walked down the stairs and was standing gazing down at my luggage.

'Are you staying here then?' she asked.

'For a little while.'

'Grandma didn't say anybody was staying.'

'No. I didn't write to tell her, perhaps I should have done.'

'Well of course. Mummy always writes to tell her when we are visiting.'

'Are your parents visiting as well as you?'

'No. They're in America. Daddy had to go on business and Mummy's gone with him. They go away a lot. I always stay here when they're away.'

'I see. You and I will have to get to know one another then. Do you ride?'

'Sometimes. I don't much care for it.'

'What do you care for Julia?'

'I go to dancing classes and I like tennis.'

'That's nice.'

Meanwhile the housemaid was looking at my luggage with some dismay and I said, 'When I lived in this house I slept in the room overlooking the lawns at the back. We called it the

146

rose room, perhaps you could put my luggage in there for the time being.'

'That's my room,' Julia said sharply.

'Oh, I'm sorry. Then perhaps we can leave it here in the hall until I know which room I am to occupy.'

'I'll put it upstairs in the room at the front of the house miss. I'm sure you'll be wantin' to freshen up after your journey,' the maid said with a wry smile.

I picked up my small valise while she picked up the larger one and as we walked upstairs I could feel Julia's eyes boring into my back. In the room itself there was a double bed covered with a chintz cover to match the curtains and dark mahogany furniture.

'If you're to stay in 'ere miss I'll be sure to air the bed,' the maid said. 'It's not been slept in since I came 'ere. Visitors don't stay 'ere these days, they just comes for the visits.'

'I see. What's your name?'

'Polly Maxton, miss. I've worked 'ere now for three years.'

'When I was here the housemaid was called Bridie and the cook was Mrs Eltham. Whatever happened to them?'

'Well, Mrs Eltham lives in the village. Got a little stone cottage she 'as, near the church. She's a big bug at Saint Andrew's.'

'I'm sure she is, and Bridie?'

'I 'eard she'd married a retired police sergeant and they live nearer the town, got a newspaper business they 'ave.'

'I must look them up, I spent a lot of time with cook and Bridie. Who's the cook now then?'

'There's only me lives in. Mrs Roberts comes every mornin' about ten and Mrs Johnson comes to 'elp with the cleanin'.'

'I suppose the family come on Sundays.'

'Only the older people. Miss Julia's parents are often away. 'Er father's a junior minister and in the school 'olidays Mrs Dexter's saddled wi' Miss Julia.'

I grinned at her and she blushed furiously. 'I shouldn't 'ave said she were saddled with 'er miss. I'm sure Mrs Dexter looks forward to 'avin' the young lady.'

'Poor Grandma's been saddled with a great many people I'm sure. One of them was me for ten years.'

As I wandered through the rooms of the house, it was as though I had left it only days before: the carpets and upholstery were exactly the same, as well as the rich walnut and mahogany furniture which at one time had spoken of wealth and standing.

There were still the ebony tables topped with great vases and bowls. Still the bronze figures of Roman gladiators and horses, still the stags' heads in the hall and the marble fireplaces with their brass fire tongs and coal scuttles.

A rather dejected castor-oil plant stood in the centre of the dining-room table and over the sideboard still hung Grandfather's pride and joy, a dark oil painting of a Scottish loch with its heather-clad hills and roaming deer, and on the grand piano were the family photographs. My father resplendent in his dress uniform and wedding groups showing me pushed firmly in front because I had been the smallest at Sophie's wedding.

On the wall overlooking the garden where the light fell on it hung a portrait of Caroline, in a white satin gown with feathers in her hair and a feather fan across her lap: obviously an official portrait of the gown she wore when she was presented at court. Her proud lovely face had been captured to perfection and I was still staring at it when the door opened and Polly came in with a tray containing tea and biscuits.

Seeing me standing in front of the portrait she said proudly, 'That's Lady Marston miss. Isn't it beautiful?'

'Yes indeed it is. Does she come here often?'

'Now and then miss, but she's a very busy lady, she sits on a lot of committees and she's been made a JP.'

After Polly had left me and I had drunk my tea, I stared for a long time through the windows at the mist-laden moors and the steady downpour of rain. I thought about Devon where the rain seemed to lie on the wind and fell gently on the red earth, and the torrential monsoons in India which were forgotten quickly in the newborn heat of the sun.

Polly came into the drawing room just before five, carrying a newly filled coal scuttle, and made up the fire.

'These autumn evenin's are cold,' she said. 'The master doesn't like 'em lit too early in September, but the day's miserable and the mistress might feel the cold when she gets in.'

'I suggest you're something of a treasure Polly,' I said smiling.

She blushed. 'Well I'm 'appy enough 'ere. There's precious little work these days. I'm lucky to 'ave found a decent job, the mills are on short time.'

'Why's that?'

She stared at me. 'Well, miss, the orders aren't comin' in. It's gone from bad to worse since the war ended. Mi dad says the mills were boomin' durin' the war when they were makin' uniforms for the armed forces, but all that's gone now miss, and if ye buys anythin' at the market it were made in Hong Kong or somewhere else in the Far East.'

I nodded. I was thinking of the little girls in Siam working throughout the night in cramped conditions, living together in dormitories and receiving small reward for their labours. I remembered my warning to Grandfather. He had been predictably scornful – and angry. They had gone on entertaining men from the Far East, instructing them in the whys and wherefores, and the eastern gentlemen had smiled and bowed and my grandfather and uncles had congratulated themselves that they were educating the heathens and performing Christian duties.

'I think that's the mistress coming,' Polly was saying. 'She's allus back for five wherever she's been.'

I went out into the hall and stood in the doorway watching my grandmother getting out of the car. She had been driving it herself and I thought it remarkable that Grandfather had allowed her to learn to drive.

She looked towards the house and in those first few moments I knew she didn't recognise me. Then she smiled, and I rushed across the rain-sodden forecourt to embrace her.

'How wonderful Amanda. Why didn't you write so that somebody could have been here to welcome you?'

'I wanted to surprise you.'

'When did you arrive in England then?'

'I've been staying with my other grandparents in Devon for a few weeks.'

'Well, I hope you're in no hurry to return to India. Amanda

149

dear, we were all so terribly sorry to hear about your husband. It was quite terrible and you're far to young to be a widow.'

'Yes, I suppose I am. You would have liked Anthony, Grandma.'

'I'm sure I would. Did Polly give you something to eat?'

'She looked after me very well.'

'And you've met Julia. She's here until her parents get back from America. I don't suppose she put herself out to entertain you. She's a withdrawn child, likes being by herself. I can never get close to her. Perhaps you'll make an effort.'

'I'll try.'

'I don't suppose your grandfather's back yet. I really don't know why he feels the need to go down to the mills every day. He doesn't think they can get along without him and the mills are not busy these days. Your uncles and Ralph are very competent.'

'I'm looking forward to seeing them all again.'

'Well they come on Sundays, the older ones that is. I can't remember the last time I saw Ralph, it must have been long before Easter and Sophie's always either in London or abroad.'

'And Caroline?'

'Oh, she comes when the spirit moves her. Phillip often rides over and he makes excuses for her. I don't know where Charlotte is, her mother always changes the subject when I mention her.'

'What about Jenny?'

'Jenny?'

'Ralph's wife, and her little girl Grandma?'

'Oh yes Jenny, and Alice. I've asked Jenny to call whenever she comes to see her mother but she never does. We've never really got to know Jenny and it's a long time since Ralph brought Alice over.'

'But they're happy I hope?'

'One hopes so. It's difficult to know when we never see them and Myrtle changes the subject whenever I ask about them.'

'How long have you been driving?'

150

'Since Albert retired. Grandfather's never taken to driving, so I learned to drive. Needless to say your grandfather doesn't like driving with me.' She paused for a moment. 'We still have Major, your grandfather's hunter, you know. The only time he gets ridden these days is when Phillip comes around and invites him to take the horse on to the fells.'

'Phillip was always kind, Grandma.'

'Well of course, and there are times when I think Caroline could do more for us. Still, the young have their own lives to lead. I shall telephone round and tell them you've arrived, so perhaps they'll all come to dinner on Sunday for old time's sake.'

On Sunday the aunts and uncles came for lunch. Caroline and Ralph made excuses.

Grandfather I had found as brusque as ever. He sat with his face buried in his newspaper, or gazing into the fire, a large whisky and soda on the small table beside his chair, his thoughts far away.

When we sat down to lunch that Sunday I felt as though I had never been away, that I was still living in limbo, waiting for the time when my father would come to spirit me away. That I had never been away, never married Anthony, never known anything beyond the family sitting stoically round the dining table.

The uncles had hardly changed at all. A little less hair perhaps, a little greyer, but that was all. Aunt Edith had put on considerable weight and she had had her hair dyed dark auburn. She wore high-heeled court shoes and an expensive dress, while Aunt Myrtle remained thin, her aristocratic hawk-like face a little more lined, her hair a little greyer, still wearing tweeds and twin sets.

Politely they asked about my parents and expressed their condolences about Anthony's death. After that, it was as though we had met yesterday. Julia sat between Aunt Edith and Grandma, taking no part in the conversation and replying in monosyllables when she was spoken to.

As always, the two aunts vied with each other as to the importance of their respective daughters and just once across the table my eyes met Julia's and she grinned. After that I warmed to her considerably.

151

It was only much later when Aunt Edith found me alone in the conservatory that the subject of Charlotte arose.

'I want to know about Charlotte, Amanda. I can't believe that she'd simply go off and marry some foreigner and live in some country we'd never heard of. Did you quarrel? How could you possibly allow her to go off on her own into a strange country with a complete stranger?'

'I couldn't stop her, Aunt Edith. Charlotte had made up her mind what she wanted and she did leave me to travel back to India without her.'

'Then you must have quarrelled. That wasn't like Charlotte at all, and who is this man she's supposed to have married?'

'I sent you her letter, Aunt Edith.'

'I'm asking you about him, Amanda. What sort of man is he? Is he a gentleman? He can't possibly be Chinese.'

'Not entirely. I believe he's one third Mongolian, one third Chinese and one third Russian.'

She stared at me blankly for several minutes before snapping, 'Did you meet him?'

'Yes, I met in Hong Kong.'

'What's he like?'

'You mean what does he look like or what sort of man is he?'

'Both.'

'He's tall and slender. Oriental-looking but strangely handsome. I thought he was cultured, educated and rich.'

'Rich?'

'I would imagine so. He was travelling with an oriental servant and in a white Rolls Royce. Charlotte was considerably impressed with his Rolls Royce. She thought he must be a Chinese mandarin at least.'

My remarks were malicious but she was making them so. Her every word was an accusation that I had let Charlotte down.

'Where is she living?'

'Her letter came from Samarkand.'

'Where on earth is that? In China?'

'No Aunt Edith. It's a very ancient city north of the Afghan border. It was Charlotte's dream to go there. It stands on the old Silk Road into China.'

'Are you inferring that she simply married this man to get to a place she wanted to go to?'

'No Aunt Edith. I'm sure Charlotte wouldn't do something as stupid as that. She was attracted to him from the first moment she saw him. When has there ever been a time when any of you could influence Charlotte either one way or the other? There was nothing I could do, nothing I could say.'

'She has never written to us. How often did she write to you?'

'Just once, the letter I sent you.'

'Nothing else?'

'She sent me several parcels containing silk and Shantung. There was no letter with any of them.'

'Because she's unhappy, made a mistake and won't admit to it.'

'You don't know that. The letter she did write doesn't say she's unhappy.'

'I'd like to give her a piece of my mind. I certainly don't dine out on her misdemeanours. I don't want a Chinese son-in-law and I don't want to talk about a daughter of mine living in some God-forsaken place like Samarkand.'

'Aunt Edith, Samarkand was a beautiful cultured city while we were still living in the Dark Ages.'

'You would say that, wouldn't you. Always hankering after going back to India with your parents. You never settled here Amanda, and I really think you had a hand in persuading Charlotte to do this stupid thing.'

'You must think what you like, Aunt Edith. Write to my father about it. He was furious with Charlotte and furious that you were blaming me. At least Caroline has fulfilled all your ambitions for her.'

'And more. She's Lady Marston, a magistrate, presented at Court and the chairwoman of a great many important committees.'

'She doesn't have children?'

'They're in no hurry. Gracious I hope Charlotte doesn't have children. I want no half-caste's among my grand-children.'

Bristling with annoyance she swept out of the conservatory. For the first time, I really understood Charlotte's desire to stay as far away from her mother as she possibly could.

Charlotte had been right. There had been nothing for her here, only stagnation and a desperate longing to be someone else somewhere else.

I quickly realised that Aunt Myrtle's questions about Charlotte were prompted out of a singular sort of triumph that Charlotte had let the side down whereas Sophie had enhanced it.

For that reason it gave me a great deal of satisfaction to dwell on Sanjay Khan's culture as well as his wealth, which had the satisfaction of wiping some of the disdain off her face.

We had afternoon tea in the drawing room as always and I listened to the uncles and Grandfather discussing the mills, and Grandfather's antagonism to Ralph who seemed to be spending rather more time on the golf course than in the board-room, I turned away thinking that nothing had changed.

'What are you going to do with your time Amanda?' Uncle Edwin asked.

'I'm looking around for a car and I'll probably ride a little, that is if Grandfather will allow me to ride Major.'

I looked at him enquiringly, but he merely shrugged his shoulders with the remark, 'Ride him all you want to, he needs the exercise.'

'You intend staying some time then?' Uncle Edwin remarked.

'I really haven't made any plans. I might walk down to the mills one day and take a look around.'

'You'll find nothin' to interest you there,' Grandfather snapped. 'Nothing only short time and idleness.'

The silence after the last remark was oppressive, and looking through the window I could see Julia walking in the garden with Benjie, Grandma's Lakeland terrier. I grabbed a trenchcoat from the hall wardrobe and I let myself out through the conservatory door.

Chapter Fifteen

'How about a walk on the fells,' I said to Julia.

'It's wet underfoot.'

'I always found that if the lawns were wet the fells were dry. We can keep to the paths if you like, besides Benjie would like it up there.'

'All right. Perhaps they'll have gone when we get back.'

Her last remark was offered so hopefully I couldn't help but smile, and for once she smiled back, a smile that lit up her face and made her seem so much prettier.

'You don't like it when the family come?' I asked her.

'Not much. Aunt Edith's always going on and on about Aunt Caroline and then Granny starts about Mummy. It's so boring.'

'It was ever thus.'

'Did you hate it too?'

'Some of it. What do you do about school when you spend so much time here, Julia?'

'I have permission to go to Miss Ralston's in the town. I'm here for two weeks, then, when I leave I shall go back to my school in London.'

'I hadn't realised you went to school in London, I thought you would go somewhere in your father's constituency.'

'No, they spend more time in London than anywhere else. They only come up here when they have to.'

'Have you friends at school?'

'Some.' She paused. 'I feel like a parcel being handed around all the time.'

'I'm sure Grandma doesn't think of you like that.'

'I feel like that.'

'Would you like to go riding with me one day?'

'We only have Major.'

'I'm sure we could borrow a horse from the riding stables. I know there are some at the bottom of the fell.'

'I'm not very good.'

'One gets better with practice.'

'I could go to the mills with you. I've never been there and the girls at school are always asking me what the cotton mills are like. Could I come with you before I go back to London?'

'Yes of course, why not.'

She grinned. 'Uncle Ralph wouldn't like to see me, I'm sure.'

'Whyever not?'

'I've seen him on the golf course with one of Aunt Caroline's friends.'

'Well, men and women do play golf together, there's nothing very strange in that.'

I looked down at her blushing face, strangely sly, and she was quick to say, 'Oh I know they play golf, but I've seen him with her in the town too. She's pretty. Aunt Jenny's not pretty and she's so old-fashioned. It's not because they haven't got any money, she just doesn't have any idea.'

'I don't think you should speak about your Aunt Jenny like that Julia.'

'I don't really know her very well, she never comes to anything we have. I don't think he should be with Daphne Browne though, I don't like her. Mummy says she cultivates Aunt Caroline because she's married into the gentry and Aunt Caroline can't see it.'

I stared down at this strange child who suddenly seemed too worldly. A lonely child who listened to too much gossip and had opinions which were far too adult. I hadn't like what she told me about Ralph and Jenny.

We hadn't been walking very far when Julia suddenly said, 'I think I want to go back now, it's cold on the fell and I have a good book I want to finish.'

So we retraced our steps and I realised I would not have to look to Julia for company. The dog Benjie was a far better proposition.

'When are we likely to be seeing Sophie again?' Aunt Edith asked, when we were gathered round the fire.

'Well I don't see much of her. We all know how she's placed.'

'That's the way it is with Caroline,' Aunt Edith said. 'She's away on a conference this weekend, somewhere in the Lakes.'

'Isn't Phillip with her then?'

'No, he's visiting friends in Derbyshire. I don't say too much but since she was on this committee and the other they seem to spend less and less time together,' Aunt Edith complained.

'I've heard talk,' Aunt Myrtle said. 'She should have children, I'm sure Phillip wants a boy to carry on the name.'

'Oh Myrtle, that really is old hat. He has plenty of cousins with children and after her miscarriage Caroline was really very depressed and miserable. I think she's afraid to try again in case the same thing happens.'

'You mean she doesn't intend to have any?'

'I mean we don't talk about it.'

'I wonder what Phillip's mother thinks about it?'

'Well we hardly ever see her in these parts, she's happy enough living with her sister in Shrewsbury.'

Promptly at six Uncle William consulted his watch and declared it was time to be heading for home. Dusk was creeping across the fells. At any moment I expected to see Ralph come into the room carrying the outdoor clothing and Charlotte and Caroline squabbling as to who should sit in the front seat of the car.

'Will you all be coming next Sunday as usual?' Grandma asked and Uncle Edwin said, 'Of course, Mother. You know we always keep Sunday specially for you and Father.'

'Do remind Caroline and Sophie when you see them that Amanda is here and hoping to see them.'

'Well, yes, of course, Mother, I'm sure they'll get around to seeing her when it's convenient.'

'Will you be at the mill tomorrow, Father?' Uncle William asked. 'I don't know why you bother to come down every day. After all, you're supposed to be retired.'

'I like to keep an eye on things,' Grandfather snapped.

'Well, things do tick over without you. There are three of

157

us to look after them.'

Grandma said, 'I'd like to see Ralph one of these days Edwin. Ask him to call round with his wife and little girl. Tell him that Amanda is here.'

Next day was fine and bright with sunshine. Grandfather set off for the mills at half past eight.

'Would you like me to drive you to the mill?' Grandma asked gently. 'Or Amanda could drive you.'

'I want no woman driving me,' he snapped. 'Besides it does me good to walk. Young folk don't walk enough.'

We watched him striding through the garden, a tall slim upright figure, in country tweeds and carrying a rolled umbrella.

'He's so stubborn,' Grandma complained. 'He'll never retire. He'll go down to those mills as long as they're there.'

Major stood looking over his stable door, expectancy in his eyes, and as I stroked his soft muzzle he nudged my shoulder gently. I was busy saddling him up when I heard the clip-clopping of a horse across the cobbled yard, and looking round I saw that it was Phillip.

There was something else that had not changed. I looked up into his face and the old magic was there. I was a young girl again, sitting on the steps outside the ballroom.

In those first few moments I felt gauche and stupid, willing my heart not to flutter, my cheeks to stay pale, my voice to remain wilfully calm, but reason paid little heed to emotions that surfaced too easily.

He jumped down from his horse and came to take my hand, kissing my cheek briefly before saying, 'You've hardly changed at all Amanda, a little taller perhaps, a little more grown up, but if I'd seen you in the street I would have recognised you instantly.'

'That's only the outer me Phillip,' I murmured.

'You mean the inner you is far more complicated?'

'I'm afraid so.'

'I was very sad to hear about Anthony, Amanda,' and for the first time I realised he was the only one of my northern relatives who had given him a name. It had always been 'your husband'.

158

'You must miss him terribly,' he said.

'Yes, I did miss him terribly, but it's some time ago now. One doesn't forget but one doesn't remember it all the time.'

'No. I suppose not. Would you like to ride across the fells,we have a lot to talk about and it's a nice day.'

So he helped me on to Major's back and together we set off over the fells towards the distant ring of crags that had once been our favourite place.

At the summit we dismounted and leaving our horses to crop the short moorland grass, we went to sit on some rocks, and once again it was yesterday.

What did we talk about that morning sitting on the Pennine hill overlooking the distant town? My years in India and my brief and fated marriage. My parents and my father's promotions, my weeks in Devon and the state of trade in the cotton mills below us. What we did not talk about was Phillip and his marriage to my cousin. We spoke of what life had done to me, not of what it had done to Phillip.

It was only later in the day when I was alone staring into the fire that I realised not once had he mentioned Caroline or his marriage; it was as if great shutters had come down on his life since the last time we had met: shutters hiding too much that was unpleasant, or too much that was sacred to himself and his marriage?

I believed in the first reason, perhaps because that was what I wanted to believe.

When I told Grandma that I had ridden across the fell with Phillip she said evenly, 'That was nice Amanda, and nice for Phillip to ride over to see you. Did he mention Caroline at all?'

I had to admit that he had not and I was suddenly aware of the shadow of doubt that fell across her face. Grandma was worried about her family, I felt sure, but loyally she would say nothing.

'What are you going to do with yourself this afternoon?' she asked brightly. 'I have to go to a meeting down at the church, I really do get very involved and every year I say I'll do less and less but I never do.'

'The more you do the more they will expect you to do, Grandma.'

159

'I know, but we're missing Lady Marston. She was a tower of strength. She went away to live with her sister, when Caroline moved into the hall.'

'Didn't Caroline take her place?'

'Not on the church committee my dear. I hardly think it's glamorous enough for Caroline.'

As if she instantly regretted this disclosure she said quickly, 'I shouldn't really expect if of her. After all, they are all considerably older than Caroline, and she has so many other committees that interest her more. You haven't said what you intend to do with yourself while I'm away?'

'I thought I might go down to the mills and take a look round there.'

When she seemed doubtful I said with a little smile, 'I know Grandfather won't be pleased but I'm curious, besides I'd like to see Ralph, if Mohammed won't come to the mountain the mountain will have to go to Mohammed.'

'Didn't you tell Julia she could go to the mills with you?'

'Another day Grandma. This afternoon I thought I would go alone.'

'Tomorrow Amanda, we'll visit some of my friends in the area, they are all wanting to meet you again. I do hope you'll stay for a while now that you're here, at least until Christmas is over.'

'Christmas is months away, Grandma.'

'I know dear, but you'll be amazed how quickly the weeks fly by.'

I would not stay until Christmas. Indeed, I had already made up my mind that I would not linger too long where I was likely to meet Phillip. The wound was still raw, the pain too intense.

Grandma elected to saunter down to the church later so she instructed me to take the car and try to persuade Grandfather to drive home with me later in the afternoon.

'You may not manage it my dear,' she said with a smile. 'He hates to think that women are driving cars these days. He lives in the past when women were seen but seldom heard.'

I left the car in the old mill yard and climbed the familiar stone steps to the first floor. I stood in the vast room staring round at the empty looms in amazement. Once the noise had

160

been a crescendo in my ears, in a world filled with sound where women mouthed words at each other across the aisles and I had stood in awed amazement.

A light burned in a small mill office at the end of one of the aisles and I walked towards it aware that my high heels were making the only sound in that arena of silence.

Two men were sitting at a long table drinking tea from pint pots and they both looked up with surprise as I made my entrance. I recognised one of them as a tackler who had been employed at Dexter's since boyhood and he recognised me instantly, smiling broadly and saying, 'Miss Amanda, so yer've come back to Lancashire then?'

I smiled. 'How are you Mr Broadbent? I'm glad to see you're still here.'

'And this is Joe Grimshaw,' he said indicating his companion. 'This is Miss Amanda Dexter Joe, 'er as went out to join 'er father i' foreign parts. Have ye come back fer good miss?'

'No, just a visit.'

'Then yer'll 'ave noticed a big change fro' the last time yer were 'ere?'

'Where are all the people and the noise?'

'There's no people without orders and no noise without people Miss Amanda.'

'You mean there's no work at all?'

'Not since the last order were completed for a place in South Africa. There's a bit o' work in the weavin' shed through there but the weavers in 'ere 'ave been laid off for six weeks now and no sign of any new orders.'

He confirmed my worst fears.

'We can't compete in price wi' the Far East. They works for slave labour. They probably lives on rice and precious little else and they can afford to sell their goods for a tenth of ours. Didn't we allus know this might 'appen?'

'Then why didn't the factory owners see it Mr Broadbent?'

'You tell me, miss. They used to come round the looms wi' yer uncles and yer grandfather askin' their questions and smilin' at our replies. Allus so polite they were wi' their bowin' and scrapin', then they went back to wherever they'd come from thinkin' what fools we all were.'

161

'I agree with you Mr Broadbent.'

'Why did we never see it? 'Ow could we let it 'appen?'

'But are the finished products as good as ours?'

'Probably not, but when my missus buys em on the market she doesn't compare 'em, she only compares the price she's paying for 'em.'

'What do you find to do all day?'

'Precious little. I'm on three days a week fro' next Monday.'

'And Joe?'

'I'm laid off Miss.'

'Is there nothing to be done?'

'We could pray for a miracle, miss. Some new ideas. They're weavin' gingham and the old designs and we gets orders fro' some o' the old sources, 'ow long they'll continue is anybody's guess.'

'Are my uncles and Mr Ralph here?'

'Well I've seen the old man wi' Mr William this mornin', I've not seen either Mr Edwin or Mr Ralph. Maybe they're out lookin' for orders.'

'I'll try the office then. Try not to worry too much Mr Broadbent, I'm sure things will pick up.'

He smiled ruefully. 'They'd pick up if there was another war, but none of us wants that do we Miss Amanda. Mind yerself on them steep steps in them 'igh 'eels. I'm allus tellin' mi daughter she'll break 'er neck one o' these days wearing 'eels like that.'

I smiled as I made my exit, and once more the sound of my heels reverberated across the flagged floor as I made my way to the stairs.

The general offices of William Dexter and Sons Ltd were a palatial building set apart from the mill and across the mill yard. There was a lofty downstairs hall and steps ascending up from it to the realms above. The steps were richly carpeted in Turkey Red Axminster as was the hall above and at the head of the hall hung a large portrait in oils of my grandfather looking considerably younger: a handsome man wearing a morning suit and sporting a white carnation in his button hole. The half smile on his face oozed prosperity and self-satisfaction. I looked around at other portraits. Uncle William and Uncle Edwin wearing dark lounge suits and Ralph wearing an unfamiliar moustache and striped blazer.

I decided to ring the push button bell on a small counter near a window labelled Reception, and immediately it opened and a girl was enquiring 'Yes Miss?'

'Could I please see either Mr William or Mr Edwin Dexter?'

'I'm not sure they're in miss. Who shall I say is callin'?'

'Mrs St Clare.'

The name meant nothing to her.

'What is it about miss? They don't usually see anybody without an appointment.'

'Perhaps you could tell them their niece has called to see them.'

My name produced some alacrity and in seconds she was knocking on the door of the private office and was ushering me in.

Uncle William sat behind the huge mahogany desk with Uncle Edwin sitting on a chair in front of him and my grandfather standing staring through the window. They all three looked up when I was announced and Uncle Edwin came forward with a smile saying, 'So here you are Amanda, I thought you were joking when you said you wanted to come down to the mill.'

'Why no, Uncle Edwin, why should you think that?'

'Well, young ladies don't usually find any interest here, neither of my daughters did and Caroline still doesn't. Did you come straight up here?'

'No, I went to the mill office first.'

'Then you'd find it quiet, with no weavers and no work,' Grandfather snapped.

'Yes. I'm sorry. It will recover surely?'

'We hope so,' Uncle William said grimly.

'I was hoping to see Ralph here.'

'He's upstairs in the second weaving shed, hopefully doing some work for once,' Grandfather snapped. 'You can sit here and wait for him, your uncles and me are talking business but that's today's paper on the desk there, and I'll ask the girl to bring some tea in for you.'

I had already seen the daily newspaper and I didn't particularly want tea, but it was evident he didn't expect me to show any interest in the business they were discussing.

Instead I said, 'I'll take a look round for Ralph, Grandfather. I don't want tea and you'll get along much better without me. I won't take Ralph away from whatever he's doing, I promise.'

'It doesn't take much to make him forget what he's doing,' Grandfather said, taking his place from across Uncle William's desk, so that I was glad to escape, quickly forgotten, as the drone of their voices followed me out.

Chapter Sixteen

As I walked up the steep stone stairs towards the floor above Mr Broadbent's domain, I could hear the sound of machinery, but nothing like as profound as it had once been. Only half the looms in the vast room were in use and as I walked between the aisles to the small office ahead I could see that they were weaving gingham and checks, the sort of material I had worn as a child.

There were two men in the office, a tall thin man with receding hair and my cousin Ralph, a plumper Ralph wearing a small dark moustache which made him look older. He grinned at me across the room before getting up from his seat to embrace me.

He held me away from him and looked closely at my face before saying, 'You were always a beauty Amanda, I say as much to Caroline when I want to get at her. Nice to see you.'

'Thank you, it's nice to see you. I wasn't sure whether to look for you here or at the golf club.'

He grinned. 'I suppose Grandfather tells you that's where I spend most of my time?'

'Something like that.'

'Well, I see no point in sitting around here with nothing to do.'

'But they are working up here this morning.'

'Yes, but we're getting to the end of the orders and others are slow at coming in.'

'Won't gingham always be in fashion?'

'I suppose so, but they produce it cheaper in the Far East.'

'Surely, you remember the day I told Grandfather that one

165

day they'd beat us at our own game, and he slammed me down so hard I never said another word?'

'I remember. When did he ever listen to one of us.'

'How's Jenny and your little girl?'

'Well she's not such a little girl now Amanda, she'll be ten soon. They're all right.'

'All right!'

'Well yes. What else did you want me to say?'

'I expected you to say that they were well and happy, and that you would invite me to visit.'

For a few moments he looked acutely embarrassed, then with a smile he said, 'I was sorry I couldn't get up to see you with the rest of the family yesterday Amanda, but I couldn't really let my partner down at the last minute. I knew we'd get around to each other pretty soon.'

'What's happening on the floors above?'

'Not very much. We're doing some block printing for curtaining and upholstery. Hopefully it might take off but they're old designs and people are looking for something new.'

'I'd like to take a look Ralph.'

He stared at me. 'Why this sudden interest in the mills Amanda? I thought this was to be a short visit.'

'It is, but I'd still like to see what it's all about.'

'Come on then, but I can assure you whatever is going on here will bore you to tears. Have you seen my father this morning?'

'Yes, I went into the office block, but I didn't linger. I felt I was intruding. Is this where you usually work?'

'Well no. I am allowed to put my nose in the board room now and I have my own office there but I prefer it here.'

'I remember when you hated it. You expected to be put in the board room on your first morning.'

'I know. Here, I don't get asked questions about the whys and the wherefores. Here, I don't have to account for my time, leisure or otherwise.'

As we left the room I smiled at his companion, even though Ralph had not introduced us, and as we passed through the room towards the stairs, a great many of the weavers stared at me curiously. It had been over ten years

166

since I had walked through the mills and if they still worked for Dexters it was doubtful if they remembered me.

'Are all the mills on short time?' I asked Ralph curiously.

'Yes. Number two mill is completely at a standstill, but they are doing a bit of experimenting in number one mill – block printing. Trying out new designs for cretonnes and damasks. Of course, they're not really new designs, merely copies of old designs.'

'Like what for instance?'

'Well, florals, paisleys, garlands. We could do with some new designers but Grandfather believes that old and tested patterns do best. You know what he's like, hates anything new and will adamantly refuse to modernise. In some ways I agree with him. Whatever we produce they'll copy it in the Far East.'

'That's terrible. We taught them their trade. I've seen what they can do in the Far East, their designs are as stereotyped as ours unless you can lay your hands on more expensive and traditional ones.'

He nodded, but my mind was busy with the beautiful silks Charlotte had sent. Those patterns had never been seen in the shops and bazaars I had had access to. They were designs of old Asia, old Imperial China and later as we stood watching the block printing of hackneyed designs on linen and damask a new and frightening ambition was born in me.

When we returned to the office we met Grandfather coming out and frowning darkly at us he said, 'Seen all you want to then?'

'For the moment Grandfather.'

'We've lost that order from Grimshaws,' he snapped, turning his angry gaze on Ralph.

'Well of course, it was what I expected.'

'Then perhaps you can tell me why we've lost it?'

'We're too expensive. Lostocks undercut us, and they're not even likely to get it. The order can be shipped in.'

We watched Grandfather striding down the road, anger in every step.

I needed somebody to help me and advise me. I would get no assistance from Grandfather and Ralph and the uncles were completely overpowered by him. I had to believe in my

167

dream and I needed somebody else to tell me it was possible.

There was only one person who would help me, but asking Phillip would bring him too close to me, an ally, a partner even, and I could not ask Phillip to range himself with me against the family.

My thoughts were filled with too many tantalising questions that afternoon as I walked back to the house through a fine drizzle of rain. I had reached the bottom of the hill when a loud voice called out, 'It is Miss Amanda, isn't it? I 'eard you'd come back, I was 'oping you'd visit me.'

I turned quickly to find Cook, Mrs Eltham standing under her umbrella staring at me from the front garden of a small stone cottage.

I smiled and walked across the road to join her. 'How are you Mrs Eltham? I had every intention of coming to see you!'

'Well, come along in now and 'ave a cup of tea. There's no hurry to get 'ome, is there? It's a long time afore dinner.'

So I followed her into her little parlour and while she made tea I looked around me with interest. It was cosy with chenille curtains at the windows and a bright-red curly rug on the floor in front of the fireplace. On the mantelpiece were ornaments in brass and copper and on the top of a walnut bureau were photographs of the Dexter family including wedding photographs of both Sophie and Caroline. There was a snapshot of me in a pale pink dress with a pink ribbon in my hair and another of Ralph with a small cocker spaniel and Sophie wearing school uniform and pigtails.

I was still looking at them when she bustled in with a tray and with a broad smile on her face she said, 'I likes to keep them up there and folks likes to look at them when they come to see me. After all, this town was built around Dexter's. There were others o' course but Dexter's came first. I sees your grandmother at the church and we allus 'as a chat. She's a nice lady, well respected, she were a pleasure to work for.'

'Yes, I'm sure she was, Mrs Eltham.'

'Nay, call mi Cook, most people still do.'

'Do you see Bridie at all?'

'She comes to see me and I call to see 'er when I'm in the town. Didn't I aullus say she could do a lot worse than marry

168

that policeman. They're happy and they 'ave a nice little business.'

'I'm glad.'

'She'd be glad to see you Miss Amanda.'

'I'll call when I'm in the town.'

' 'Ave ye come back for good then? We were all that sorry to 'ear about your young 'usband. I wouldn't blame ye if ye didn't feel ye could go on livin' out there after what happened to 'im.'

'I don't know how long I shall be staying here, Cook.'

'I expect they all turned out to see ye last Sunday.'

'The aunts and uncles came, and Julia is staying with us at the moment.'

'Ye mean Caroline and Ralph didn't come?'

'Caroline was away for the weekend and Ralph was playing golf.'

'Oh ay, 'e's a great one for the golf course, and I can't tell ye the last time we saw Caroline in church. Her mother-in-law was a pillar of strength there, but it's not fancy enough for her ladyship.'

When I didn't speak she said, 'I shouldn't be sayin' anythin' but ye can't stop people talkin' can ye? So ye 'aven't seen either of 'em?'

'I've seem Ralph this morning at the mill.'

'Hmmm,' she murmured.

'Do you see Jenny at all? I would like to call to see her but Ralph didn't seem to think it was a good idea, he made all sorts of excuses, that she went to her mother's, that she'd be shopping. How is Jenny?'

She was so long in answering my question that I began to wish I hadn't asked it, then just when I was about to change the subject she said, 'Jenny's mother doesn't see much of 'er. She doesn't come this way at all and I very rarely see 'er in the town. There's all sorts o' talk ye know.'

'What sort of talk?'

'About 'is philanderin', 'er dowdiness and young Alice in the middle of it all. I doubt if that child's ever been near Fairlawn since she were little more than a baby, and the house looks uncared for even if they 'ave moved into somethin' bigger.'

'I didn't know they'd moved, where are they now then?'

'In one o' them detached 'ouses near the park, the one on the corner. I allus thinks the 'ouse looks unlived in except when ye sees Mister Ralph's Riley standin' in the drive, and that isn't offen I can tell ye.'

I thought it time to change the subject so I said, 'My cousin's told me I might get a decent car where he buys his. I might go there tomorrow.'

'Ay, that'll be Bridge's at the crossroads. They only do Rileys unless ye wants a used car.'

'Well, we'll see. Thanks for the tea, Cook, your scones were always so good.'

She beamed.

At the front door, she said, 'Well, it's stopped rainin'. I expect ye missed the rain in India Miss Amanda?'

'Oh we got rain, we got torrents of it, but we always knew when it was the rainy season. Here it just never knows when to stop.'

'I hopes ye'll call again.'

'Of course.'

'I hopes you'll go to see Jenny, give 'er a good talkin' to. Ye were friends once, she'll not 'ave forgotten.'

Her talk about Jenny had upset me and all the way up the hill I thought about it. There were so many undercurrents I did not understand, most of all my grandmother's silences.

I was met in the hall by Julia glaring at me angrily.

'You said when you went to the mill I could go with you,' she accused. 'Why did you go without me?'

'Well you were at school. We can go again one day.'

'I'm going home at the weekend.'

'Are your parents coming for you?'

'No. My grandmother will put me on the train and one of them will meet me in London. They'll only just have got back from America so they'll both be too busy to think about me.'

I felt a sudden rush of pity for this child who was too much alone. She reminded me of myself at that age, left in an alien world with people I couldn't relate to. On reflection there had really only been Grandma and Ralph, I'd gone to India after the war without really getting close to any of the others.

170

'Have you got a lot of homework?' I asked her.

'Some.'

'Well, it's a nice day, how about a long walk to work up an appetite before dinner? We could take Benjie.'

'No thanks. I don't feel like walking. When are you going to the mill again?'

'Perhaps on Thursday. You can get off the bus there and I'll be waiting for you.'

Slightly placated she turned without another word and walked up the stairs.

I found Grandma in the conservatory watering her plants. She looked up with a bright smile. 'Did you see Ralph at the mill Amanda?'

'Yes. He showed me the room where they were doing some block printing for curtains and chair covers. It was very interesting, but he doesn't seem to think anything would sell very well.'

She smiled but offered no comment. Whenever the mill was mentioned at Fairlawn I seemed to be met with a wall of silence.

Throughout the week, whenever the opportunity presented itself, Julia reminded me that I had promised to meet her at the mill, so on Thursday after lunch I set off on foot.

Ralph was not expected, they informed me at the office, so we wandered up to the second floor where the block printing took place.

We stood watching while the two men working at the large tables painted the designs etched on the huge sheets of damask, patterns I had known all my life – of roses and traceries of leaves, gentle English patterns that had covered English furniture and English windows for centuries – and while we watched I thought about the exquisite designs in the book I had bought in Lantau and the silks Charlotte had sent me from Samarkand.

'Can *any* designs be printed on damask or linen?' I asked one of the men.

'Yes, miss, but we'd need a good pattern-maker, somebody who understands his job.'

'How long have you been doing these designs?'

'As long as I can remember, and my father afore me.'

'One would think people would be getting fed up with them.'

'Maybe they are, miss, but there aren't any others.'

In spite of her insistence that she visit the mill Julia was singularly bored with it all. She complained about the noise and when I explained that it was nothing compared to the war years she shook her head in disbelief.

It took her less than half an hour to see all she wanted and then she was urging me to leave. As we walked up to the house she said, 'I don't suppose Uncle Ralph is here?'

'No. He's away on business.'

'He's with that Daphne woman. I saw her in his car going to the golf club.'

'Did he see you?'

'Yes I made sure he saw me, I waved to him.'

She grinned at me, uncontrite. We continued our walk in silence and I wondered what sort of tales she would be recounting to her parents when she arrived home.

On Friday morning Aunt Myrtle came for her and Grandma and I stood at the door to see them drive away.

After she'd left Grandma said, 'She'll be back again soon. It's very unsettling for her education, a few months in London, a few weeks here. I've talked about it but nobody listens.'

Later in the morning I decided to visit the garage Ralph had told me about to look for a car.

I had my own ideas of what I wanted. Something reliable and not too ostentatious. I did not want to be seen driving a car that would command too much attention through a town where unemployment was rife. After all I was a Dexter.

The salesmen quickly realised I was not to be pushed into buying one of their grandiose models, when I insisted on a smaller Riley which was a used model but had very little mileage on the clock. I made arrangements to collect it at the beginning of the following week and then I decided it was time to see Jenny.

By the time I left the garage it was mid-afternoon and there was a fair walk ahead of me before I reached the park. Her street was lined with large double fronted houses with neat front gardens and larger back ones. I recognised Jenny's house immediately from Cook's description – she was right – compared to the others it did look singularly uncared for. It needed a new coat of paint everywhere and the lawns needed cutting. The concrete path up to the front door was broken in several places and the brass door knocker was sadly in need of a polish.

In spite of my echoing knock, there was no response. I stood back to look up at the windows. The house had a dejected air. I was turning away when a neighbour who had been weeding her garden called out, 'Haven't seen her go out. Have you looked round the back?'

'You think she might be there?'

She shrugged her shoulders. 'It's possible. Alice will be home from school soon after four, she has a key.'

The back of the house was no more salubrious than the front. A rusted swing stood in the midst of a long uncared for lawn; some of the shrubs were in flower, but looked straggly and neglected.

I knocked on the back door but there was no reply, so I took a look through the kitchen at a sink piled high with dirty crockery.

'Perhaps she isn't well,' the neighbour suggested, as I was leaving.

'Would you know if she were ill?' I asked.

She looked embarrassed. 'Not really, she keeps herself to herself. We don't really neighbour. If I see Mr Dexter I could tell him they've had a visitor, who shall I say called?'

'Perhaps I'll wait for Alice, it's almost four.'

'Yes, that might be a good idea. She's a nice little girl.'

I waited by the front door, and it was not long before I heard schoolchildren running across the road, so I walked back towards the gate.

They were walking and running in groups along the road, happy and laughing, in their school blazers and panama hats. Then, behind the others, I saw a little girl walking alone, her eyes on the ground, and somehow, instinctively, I knew that this was Alice.

Chapter Seventeen

She stared at me uncertainly, a plain little girl with Jenny's dark brown hair and eyes. I opened the gate for her and smiled.

'It's Alice, isn't it?' I ventured.

'Yes. Have you come to see Mummy?'

'Yes, but I can't make anybody hear me. Is she at home?'

'I think so. Sometimes she goes to sleep in the afternoon. I have a key. Does she know you're coming?'

'No, I wanted to surprise her.'

'Are you selling something?' she enquired.

'No. I'm your Daddy's cousin, Amanda.'

Her eyes opened wide as she paused on the path to stare at me. 'Daddy hasn't got a cousin called Amanda. There's Caroline, she lives at the big house on the other side of the river, and there's Charlotte, she's abroad somewhere.'

'Well, I was abroad too, until recently. Now I'm here and wanting to see all my relatives again. Did you say you had a key?'

'Yes.'

Her entire demeanour was one of uncertainty, of not knowing if she should allow this strange woman into her house, and another uncertainty of what we should find there.

I followed her up the path and on the step she turned round to say, 'Why don't you come back when my Daddy's at home?'

'I made a special effort to come this afternoon Alice. Suppose you open the door and go inside. The lady next door seems very curious.'

'She's always always watching us.'

'She's doing her garden, Alice.'

'That's so she can watch. She's always in the garden.'

The door was open at last and I followed Alice into a rather dark hallway. A hallstand had a tarnished gold-framed mirror and on a small table a vase filled with faded flowers.

I felt the child's anxiety, and I felt an overwhelming pity that Alice should have to cope with a situation like this. Looking at me doubtfully she said, 'Perhaps you should wait here while I see if Mummy is still asleep.'

'It's all right, Alice. Your mother and I are old friends. I think she will be glad to see me.'

The room we entered was a large one, overlooking the front of the house and Jenny was fast asleep on the sofa in front of the fireplace. The fire had burned low and it was chilly. In front of her was a small table and the first thing I noticed was the empty glass and a half empty bottle of whisky. I watched Alice shake her mother gently, but Jenny was drunk to the world and in response to Alice's tear-filled gaze, I said briskly, 'If you'll show me where to find things, Alice, I'll make coffee, nice black coffee that will soon bring you mother round.'

'She's not well, she's never been like this before,' she said, so why didn't I believe her?

The kitchen which I had seen through the back window was indeed in a mess. Unwashed dishes, untidy worktops, but Alice produced coffee and I said gently, 'What are you having to eat Alice, are you hungry?'

'Not really, there'll be tinned things in the cupboards.'

She said it disinterestedly, adding, 'Perhaps we should see to Mummy first.'

'Why don't you walk down to the shops around the corner. The fruit bowl is empty, so I'll give you some money so that you can choose what you would like.'

When she seemed reluctant, I insisted. 'I'll look after your mother Jenny, you'll see, she'll be perfectly well when you get back.'

'There's some money underneath the fruit bowl, I can take that,' she prevaricated.

'No Alice, take this. I'd like to buy your fruit,' I said

pressing two pound notes into her hand. 'Don't be afraid to spend it all, I'm sure you'll find some lovely things to buy.'

I heard the sound of the front door closing behind her while I set about making coffee. I felt angry, with Jenny, with Ralph and with whatever circumstances had led to this. When I tried to rouse her she moaned in protest, but I persisted until she opened her eyes and peered at me sleepily and without recognition.

'Come along Jenny,' I coaxed her. 'I've made coffee and Alice has gone to the shops for fruit.'

The bottle of whisky and the glass had been removed from the table by Alice before she had gone out, and she looked down with bleary eyes at the tray I had placed on the empty table.

'Don't want coffee,' she murmured.

'Oh yes you do,' I insisted holding the cup to her lips. It was strong black coffee which she was soon drinking noisily so that it ran down her chin and dribbled on to the front of her dress.

'Feeling better?' I asked her.

She nodded, and I poured out another cup which she was now capable of holding herself. I watched the coffee disappear, and when I asked if she would like more, she shook her head slowly. For several minutes we sat in silence, then raising her head, she said, 'Who are you, where's Alice?'

'Alice has gone to the shops Jenny. Don't you recognise me? Surely I haven't changed all that much?'

She opened her eyes wider and stared at me, then with a little moan she put her head in her hands and sobbed convulsively.

'I'm sorry Amanda, I'm so sorry,' she said, over and over until I said briskly, 'Don't worry Jenny, you don't want Alice to see you crying do you? She'll wonder what I've been doing to you.'

'Did Ralph ask you to come?' she asked.

'No. He doesn't know I'm here. Jenny, there's something terribly wrong. Why are you so unhappy, why are you doing this?'

Her expression was mutinous, until she dissolved into tears

176

and sobbed uncontrollably. I sat beside her in embarrassed silence, until Alice returned.

Putting her bag of fruit on the floor, she rushed over to her mother and put her arms round her, looking at me accusingly 'You've made Mummy cry. Why have you made her cry?'

I didn't answer and Jenny said plaintively, 'Go out and play for a while Alice. I'll call you in when Amanda's gone.'

She went reluctantly, staring back at me with an attitude that cautioned me to be careful, and we remained silent until we heard the door close behind her.

'I hate myself for doing this to Alice.' Jenny said at last. 'Every day I tell myself that I mustn't drink, but I get so lonely and this way I don't have to think so deeply.'

'Why? Don't you have friends in the town, and what about your mother and sisters? Don't they come to see you?'

'My mother's angry that I drink. She's told me she'll come back when I've stopped drinking and my sisters' never come near us. I don't go to them for the same reasons.'

'And Ralph?'

'Oh he knows I drink. He's lost patience but it crept on me so slowly I was hardly aware of it. Now he spends most of his time at the golf club when he's not at the mills, and there's probably some other woman.'

'Do you really know that, Jenny?'

'I wouldn't blame him. I'm no good as a wife and not much better as a mother. Look at the house, it's a mess. Every day I say I'll do something about it but every day I lose interest. People were right when they said Ralph should never have married me, but I did try Amanda, at first I really did try.'

'I'm sure you did jenny. When did it start to go wrong?'

'I felt like a fish out of water. I was suddenly a Dexter and at first we went every Sunday to Grandfather Dexter with the others. I couldn't talk to Lady Caroline and I had nothing in common with Ralph's sister and her husband. Ralph's father was nice enough but his mother was distant and Aunt Edith used to look me up and down and watched every morsel of food I put into my mouth.'

'Don't you think you probably imagined most of it Jenny?'

'No I didn't. We were invited to Caroline's wedding and I hated every moment of it. My clothes weren't right, only

Grandma and Sir Phillip took the trouble to speak to me. Even Ralph told me to make an effort but I just couldn't. I just wanted to come home.'

'I think Grandma is rather hurt that she never sees Alice. She's called to see you several times but she says you're always out.'

'I stood in the window to see who was calling, I didn't open the door.'

'Whyever not?'

'Because I thought she'd called to see why we never visited, and I didn't want to visit. When I married Ralph I went for elocution lessons, I went to a proper hairdresser and bought some new clothes, but I really didn't have much idea, and they were never the right clothes. They were always too flashy and frilly.'

'One day we'll go into the city and have lunch Jenny. I'll go with you to choose a new outfit, something I know Ralph will like. What do you say to that?'

'I can't remember the last time I went into the city. It wouldn't be any fun for you, Amanda. You tried years ago to make friends with me and I didn't make it easy for you. I really haven't changed you know.'

'All the same, we're going to do this, and now how about your evening meal, can I do anything?'

'No. I'll do it. I ought to do something and the kitchen's a right mess. I'll tidy it up and get our meal going before I call Alice in.'

'I'm picking up a car next week Jenny, so I'll call round again, and next time we'll have a nice long chat and make arrangements to go into the city.'

She gave me a bleak smile that promised little, but she came to the front door to see me off and stood there while I left the gate. There was no sign of Alice in the road as I walked briskly towards the bus stop and I imagined she had found friends to play with.

All the way back to Fairlawn my mind was obsessed with thoughts of Jenny and her problems. I knew only too well how the rest of the family could make her feel inferior. They had tried it with me but it hadn't worked. But, after all, I had been a Dexter and able to hold my own.

When I told my grandparents over the evening meal that I had visited Jenny Grandma merely said, 'Did you find her in then? I never have yet.'

'Well, I arrived almost at the same time as Alice arrived home from school.'

'How is Alice? She's the one great grandchild I never see.'

'She's a very nice little girl, good with her mother and a great help around the house.'

'I really would like to see her.'

'I'm taking Jenny into the city one day. I'll tell her to bring Alice to see you.'

'Ralph should bring them. Was he at the mill?'

'Not this morning.'

'Not he. He'd be on the golf course,' Grandfather said, entering the conversation for the first time.

'I was watching the man block-printing on damask, Grandfather. It was fascinating. What a pity they have no new designs.'

'What is there to pity about that? Those designs are well tried and tested. They're English traditional designs the English like.'

'I saw beautiful designs in the Far East, Grandfather, dragons and butterflies, lotus blossoms and hibiscus in the most wonderful colours you've ever seen, printed on silk and cotton. If they can do it in the Far East why can't we?'

He glared at me. 'Because, young lady, this is Great Britain, and we don't need the Far East to sell us their designs. It's bad enough that they're selling cotton in Lancashire.'

'What did you expect, Grandfather, when you had them over here to train them, to show them how to weave it and what to make with it? They're not stupid, they're very enterprising and hard-working. They work for slave wages. They don't expect our living standards, and now they've priced Lancashire cotton out of the market.'

I was oblivious to Grandma's warning looks and Grandfather's red, blustering frown. I felt it and I had to say it. Somebody had to tell him where he'd gone wrong. It seemed that I was to be the only one who dared.

'I heard that sort of talk from you when you were knee-high to a grasshopper,' he growled. 'I don't take that sort of talk from my sons, I'll not take it from a girl, who knows nothing about cotton or the Lancashire mills. If you don't like what's going on there, I'm forbidding you to go down there, putting silly ideas into young Ralph's head, I've no doubt, as well as anybody else who's listening, instead of getting on with what I'm paying them for.'

'I haven't said anything to anybody, Grandfather. I thought I'd talk to you first.'

'And I'm not listening. If you're not happy with life as we live it, then it might be a good idea if ye went back to India where apparently they do things better than we do.'

I didn't say that, and I've never inferred it.'

'You've inferred it today!'

'And you haven't really been listening to me, Grandfather. I care about Dexters, and I care about the poor people who have no work to go to. You should listen to whatever help you can get.'

He answered by pushing back his chair and rising to his feet.

'And I'm not listening today, young lady. I'm going into my study for a bit of peace and I don't want this sort of conversation ever again. This is my house and I should be able to say what I want in it and expect some respect.'

'I've not been disrespectful, Grandfather. I only wanted to tell you about something you know nothing about and which I thought might interest you.'

'Well, it doesn't, so we'll have no more of it. Tell the servant I'll have my coffee in the study, where I can get a bit of peace.'

With that he stamped out of the room, leaving me angry and frustrated and Grandma, who hated discord of any kind, looking decidedly troubled.

'He's so blinkered,' I fumed. 'He never listens to anybody and why won't he admit that times are changing and we all need new ideas?'

'You're arguing with him about his life's work Amanda. He doesn't know anything else, and Dexters are a long standing family firm. Those mills in the town should tell you how successful they've been.'

'Oh they do, Grandma, but they're not successful at the moment, are they? And they could be again with a bit of acumen and imagination.'

'Your grandfather won't change Amanda, so I really do think you're flogging a dead horse, my dear.'

I remained silent, but the thoughts were buzzing around in my head, and the time had come when I had to talk to somebody who would listen and tell me there was sense in my feelings.

It had to be Ralph, but Ralph was as afraid of Grandfather as his father was. There was Phillip, but Phillip knew nothing about cotton. Did that really matter? After all, what did I know about the working of a cotton mill, and yet I could see the possibilities of new designs, new ideas in place of old outworn ones.

I would not approach Phillip, but perhaps if we rode together on Sunday morning I could talk to him.

I was glad that Grandfather absented himself from the house on Saturday to go racing with some friends.

Grandma grumbled. 'It's a cold day and they'll be standing out in the wind until the last race. Tomorrow he'll have a cold and we'll all have to listen to him moaning about it. I don't know if Phillip will expect him to ride, perhaps I should telephone him today to tell him not to come.'

'I wouldn't, Grandma. You don't really know if Grandfather will catch a cold. If he doesn't want to go riding I could go instead.'

'Yes, of course, dear. Why didn't I think of that?'

When Grandfather returned home, predictably complaining about the cold, he went to bed early, with a hot toddy, and as he left the room Grandma said, 'Will you want to go riding in the morning, or can Amanda go instead?'

'I don't think I shall go. See what Phillip thinks about your hare-brained scheme for changing things at the mills. I think he'll tell you to leave well alone.'

'Phillip isn't interested in cotton, dear,' Grandma said. 'I'm sure they'll find other things to talk about.'

He snorted and left us alone.

'You've made him very angry, Amanda. Never once in all our married life have I discussed the workings of the mills with

181

him, and I don't think your aunts have discussed cotton with you uncles. We're Dexter wives, content to enjoy the status, without interfering in what we don't think concerned us.'

It was the first time she had ever chastised me but I felt compelled to say, 'I'm sorry if I've offended you, Grandma, but I am not a Dexter wife, I am a Dexter daughter. I hate seeing the industry my great grandfather built up going wrong.'

'Don't you think your grandfather and your uncles feel the same way? If orders are not coming in, there's very little they can do, Amanda.'

'They can try something new.'

'The other cotton mills are suffering in exactly the way ours are. How is it that you come along and suddenly think you can change everything? Your father hated the mills, you've not been brought up in them like the rest of us, so why should you think you might be the one to transform everything?'

'Grandma, I don't know. I had an idea, if nobody will listen to me, how can I tell if it's any good?'

She shook her head sadly, then thinking it was time to change the subject she said, 'When are you picking your new car up?'

'Monday morning.'

'Perhaps we could go out somewhere, visit friends, drive to the coast. I never drive any distance, only to the shops and the church, and it would be nice to go somewhere when somebody else is doing the driving.'

'We'll go somewhere on Monday afternoon. Think about where you would like to go.'

I was still in my bedroom when I saw Phillip riding up to the house on Sunday morning. It was just before eight, and I hurried into my riding habit, and was leaving the house by the back door as he arrived at the stables.

He smiled. 'So you're to be my companion this morning, Amanda,' he said.

'Yes. Grandfather caught a cold at the race meeting. You don't mind Phillip?'

'Not at all. He never wants to stay out long and our horses are in need of the exercise.'

182

We rode in silence but I was racking my brains as to how I could raise the topic which was uppermost in my mind. I was wishing I could think of him as a friend and ignore the deeper feelings that tortured me each time we met.

I jumped down from my horse before he could assist me and then we were walking across the short springy grass towards the crags which had been our favourite place throughout the years.

From the villages below came the sound of church bells and we looked across the fell to the distant town and its forest of mill chimneys, misted and ethereal in the early morning sunlight.

In fact it was Phillip who brought up the question of the mills.

Chapter Eighteen

'I wonder why your grandfather feels compelled to go down to the mills every day,' he began. 'It must be depressing for him.'

'I've been there twice. So many of the looms are empty and I remember those corridors crowded with people and noise. Do you ever go into the mills Phillip?'

'No. That doesn't mean I'm uninterested. This town and a great many others were built around cotton, it was our mainstay and it seemed as if it would be as permanent as these hills.'

'When I was a little girl I tried one day to tell Grandfather he shouldn't be entertaining people from the Far East, that one day they'd be better at it than us, but he wouldn't listen. He was very angry.'

Phillip laughed. 'I don't know whether you were foolhardy or brave, Amanda. A girl in a man's world, particularly a girl whose father had turned his back on cotton years before.'

'I know. Neither Grandfather nor my uncles will listen to me, I thought Ralph might, but now I'm not so sure.'

'What is it you want them to hear?'

In a rush, I told him about the block printing on damask, the old-fashioned designs of roses and leaves, and I told him about Charlotte's silks and the book I had bought in Landau.

'If they can print those old designs, why can't they print my designs, why are they so afraid to learn anything new? You're going to laugh at me, Phillip, tell me I've been talking nonsense, but the sight of those empty looms and the despair on so many faces on the streets has made me long to help them. Do you think I'm being stupid?'

He didn't answer me immediately. Instead he stared into the distance and I was aware of his profile and the companionable warmth of his body sitting next to mine. At last he turned his head and there was no derision in his eyes, only the awakening of interest. My spirits soared.

'I would like to see those designs, Amanda.'

'I would like to show them to you, but I couldn't do that in Grandfather's house. There would be too much curiosity, and how could I explain?'

'No. I see what you mean. Then why don't you bring them up to the hall. It's time we had you for dinner. Caroline should have been in touch before now. It really has been very remiss of her.'

'I'm not sure that I want Caroline to see my designs.'

'Why not? You think she might tell the others and cause a family confrontation?'

'I think she might, or she would be scathing.'

'Was that how she was when you were a little girl here?'

'Sometimes.'

'Very well then. We'll look at them when she's out. I know that next Thursday she's going off for a few days on one of the committees I've lost track of, we could have dinner and look at the designs. Where did the silks come from by the way?'

'Charlotte sent them to me.'

His eyes were filled with amusement as he said, 'It would be very interesting if Charlotte's silks could make an impact in the future of Dexters, particularly as the rest of the family have decided it is wrong even to mention her name. I remind Caroline every now and again that she is after all her sister and has been condemned without a hearing.'

I smiled. 'Charlotte wouldn't care, Phillip. She had no interest in coming back here. I think Charlotte got the measure of the family a long time ago.'

'I hardly got to know her. Did you like her?'

I had to think about it. I had liked her, she had been different, a sort of free spirit, a girl not to be moved, by art or flattery, from whatever she had set her heart on, but I had understood why she had decided to stay away from her family. I was suddenly aware that Phillip was watching me closely and I said hurriedly, 'Oh yes, I did like Charlotte. I enjoyed my holiday with her.'

'And you understood why she went off with an Eastern gentleman and married him. Was it escape, Amanda, or love?'

'I think it was both. I know she admired him, something in him attracted her. I'm not sure whether it was his culture, the fact that he was more exotic than other men she had met, or if she simply wanted to show the rest of us that she was different. I hope she's happy, but her letter told me very little. I'm not even sure why she sent the silks. I had one of them made up into a dinner gown. It was the sensation of the evening.'

He laughed. Then he was asking, 'Do you miss your husband terribly Amanda? Your marriage was very short-lived.'

'There are days when I can't really think that I've been married at all – we had so little time together. But there are times when I remember him but, strangely, as a friend rather than a husband. He was sweet and tender, he had a lovely boyish smile that lit up his face and he was fun and gentle to be with.'

'There's been nobody else?'

'No. Oh, there were men who would like to have got to know me better but the pattern of life would have been the same and I didn't want it.'

'You're young and beautiful, Amanda. One day there will be somebody else.'

I didn't answer him. How was it possible to tell the man I loved that I could ever fall in love with somebody else, and Phillip was saying, 'Perhaps we should think of riding back. The family will be gathering for Sunday lunch.'

When I pulled a face, he laughed. 'I can see you're not looking forward to it,' he said. 'Shall we say seven o'clock on Thursday evening. Will it be difficult for you, what will you tell your grandmother?'

'That you've invited me for dinner.'

'Won't she think that a little strange, if she knows Caroline isn't at home? You can't tell her about the designs.'

'You mean it's not very circumspect of us to be dining alone?'

'Your grandmother might think so.'

'Let me think about that, Phillip. We are family, and Caroline had been very remiss in not inviting me to dinner. I've been living back at Fairlawn for two weeks and I haven't set eyes on her.'

'You would be surprised how many days go by without my setting eyes on her myself, Amanda. Concern has been expressed by your grandmother with regard to the state of our marriage.'

'I didn't know.'

'People have to talk about something. I shall look forward to seeing you on Thursday, Amanda.'

We mounted our horses and galloped back across the fell until the house was in sight. Then Phillip left me to ride back to the hall. From the garden wall I watched the big black horse jumping the hedges effortlessly and then he was suddenly lost to sight behind the slope of the hill.

The family had gathered. My two uncles had their heads buried in the Sunday newspapers while Grandma and the aunts looked at photographs of Sophie and her husband in America, their son Colin in his school uniform, and a studio portrait of Julia looking suddenly far more grown up than her ten years.

The talk was all of America and all they had seen and Aunt Edith looked decidedly put out that she had nothing of her own with which to interrupt the flow.

'I hear you've been riding with Phillip?' she said at the first lull in the conversation.

'Yes. Grandfather didn't feel well enough to ride this morning.'

'I wish Caroline had taken to riding. Her father and I wanted to buy her a pony but she wasn't interested. Neither was Charlotte.'

'Charlotte rode quite well, Aunt Edith.'

'Well, she probably learned to ride in one of those God-forsaken places she went to. She never wanted a pony.'

Aunt Myrtle decided to stir the embers by saying, 'Sophie and Jarvis do like the same sort of things, I'm glad about that, it makes for a far happier marriage than two people going their own way.'

'Are you meaning that Caroline and Phillip go their own way?' Aunt Edith demanded.

'Well, they seem to. Phillip likes horses, Caroline doesn't. Phillip spends time on the estate and at the hall, Caroline spends a great deal of time away – all those committees she serves on, they take her all over the place.'

'I think it's highly commendable that she does so much for charity, and she is a magistrate, that's very time-consuming,' Aunt Edith said firmly.

'Yes, but aren't husbands important too?'

Aunt Edith's expression was decidedly hostile and Grandma was watching them with a worried frown. At that moment, however, Grandfather arrived and she asked anxiously, 'Are you feeling better dear?'

He nodded and went to his chair beside the fire, and Uncle William said, 'We're sending troops to the Middle East, there's trouble. There could be some orders for tropical cotton in it.'

Grandfather snorted. 'I've stopped looking for miracles. There's always trouble somewhere, but the orders aren't coming in.'

'Can we have our lunch without talking about the mills,' Grandma said. 'You know how it always upsets your father and things are not going to get better overnight.'

'No, I don't want to discuss the mills today, I've had enough this week listening to my granddaughter telling me what I should do without my Sunday lunch being spoiled.'

'Why, what has Amanda been saying?' Aunt Edith demanded.

'I've told you I don't want to discuss it,' he snapped and stomped out of the room.

My instinct was to get away, to leave this house of mixed emotions and envies, to leave this area with its smokeless mill chimneys and the constant harking back to past prosperity and ever-constant yearning for times that were gone.

And then there was Phillip. Marriage to Anthony and ten years' absence had not obliterated that old punishing

188

attraction I felt for him. If I stayed, there was only hurt and disillusionment waiting for me, and there had already been too many hurts.

For the rest of the week I thought how I could telephone him and politely cancel our dinner engagement, but in the end I knew I would not do it.

I collected my new car on Monday morning and was leaving the garage when I saw Ralph getting out of his car round the corner. He had not seen me but I felt I had to talk to him about Jenny.

He smiled and waved as I walked towards him. All the same there was an embarrassed look on his face: he was not looking forward to a confrontation. His tone was breezy, however, as he called out, 'Got your car then? Nice model. I thought you'd have gone for the open tourer though.'

'You can't be serious, when do we ever get to put the roof down in this part of the country.'

He grinned. 'So what are you doing now that you've got it?'

'I'm taking Grandma visiting this afternoon, and I promised one day to take Jenny into town. Did she tell you?'

'She might have said something about it.'

'She did tell you I called to see her?'

'Alice told me. She said a lady had called who said she was my cousin, but she didn't believe her. There's no reason why she should, the cousins never visited, although she does know who they are, but not you.'

'I'm worried about Jenny, Ralph. She's unhappy, she's unhappy with the family, with her life, with you. Why aren't you more supportive?'

'You've been out of our lives for over ten years, Amanda, so please don't come along and tell us where we've gone wrong. I've heard about the cotton episode from Father, and now it's my turn with Jenny. It hasn't exactly been easy for me, Amanda.'

'But it was worse for Jenny. You could have helped her more. Your parents could have got involved. They never see her, or Alice. Do you ever take her to visit them. Do you ever take her anywhere?'

His face was mutinous.

189

'She resents them. She says they make her feel gauche and stupid. Caroline invited us to a ball up at the hall but she wanted to go home half way through the evening, because she said her dress was all wrong. Nobody else had said anything.'

'Oh, Ralph, you wouldn't see it if they had, but Jenny would see it. You're forgetting that I've been a part of them all when I was growing up here. I'm a Dexter but there were times when they made me feel an interloper. Caroline in particular is very good at that.'

The sulky, hurt, little-boy-lost expression on his face was known to me but I didn't know the answer. It was a marriage that should never have been, and they were now two people soldiering on because of their child yet totally opposed to each other. It was no use blaming Ralph. He did not have the power to rebuild broken bridges, recapture lost dreams. They were two people life and circumstances had torn apart, both of them floundering in water that was too deep.

We stared at each other sorrowfully, and as I turned away he said, 'Leave it alone, Amanda. See Jenny and take her out, if you feel you must, but don't expect miracles. It's gone on too long and we can't put anything back. We've thought about divorce, but the Dexters don't divorce, they cover up their disagreements and disenchantments with bravado and hope nobody'll notice. You've only got to look at me and Jenny, and Caroline and Phillip.'

'Caroline and Phillip!'

'Heavens yes. Living their separate lives, going their separate ways. She enjoys being Lady Marston, queening it over her charities, revelling in the limelight, being gracious and condescending to those she thinks of as lesser mortals, and Phillip is bored by her, cynical about her. Don't you go riding together, haven't you guessed?'

'No, and I'm sure you're wrong.'

'If you stay here long enough, you'll find all the skeletons in our cupboard. You've only been here just over two weeks, and you've found out that the Dexter empire is on the slide, that my marriage is a sham and so is Caroline's. While we're on the subject, I might as well tell you that my father's had a mistress for years. My mother knows about it but she's a

Dexter and she's staying a Dexter. It's no wonder that our grandparents are tetchy and that Grandma's constantly in a brown study.'

'At least your sister seems happy.'

He grinned. 'Oh well, Jarvis's a political animal. He bores the pants off me and I don't seem to know Sophie any more. Think about Julia, that girl's a zombie. She wouldn't be like that if she was happy.'

'Are you telling me all this to detract from your own shortcomings?'

'No, you're right. I do have a girlfriend, I've had her for years, nothing will come of it.'

'But it makes your wife unhappy.'

'I doubt if she'd care.'

Ralph's depiction of the family's fortunes depressed me utterly. This was a family of some prominence to the town, a family who went to church and involved itself in local events, a family who employed a great many people, pillars of local society. Now they were being pointed at as less than perfect, a family torn apart by disloyalty and broken faith.

After I had left the car on the drive and was walking up to the house I thought back to when we were children, riding our ponies in the country lanes below the fells, squabbling in the nursery about books and toys, sitting in the drawing room listening to music and the talk of our elders. When had it all started to go so wrong?

Grandma came out to view the car and give it her approval, then over lunch she laid down a programme for the afternoon. Visiting old friends and putting flowers on the family grave. It would have been so easy to suggest that we visit Jenny, but I did not know what we would find if we went there, and I had to save my grandmother from a scene such as I had witnessed.

It started to rain as we left the house, light rain that merely speckled the car windows and had almost stopped by the time we entered the churchyard. We encountered the vicar walking along one of the paths, his cassock flapping around his ankles. He greeted me warmly, telling me that he remembered me well and had been sorry to hear about my husband's tragic death in India.

191

'Sir Phillip's here,' he informed us. 'The church needs a fair bit of restoration so I've been showing him around. He's kindly offered to help us. Of course, I do wish Lady Marston was more interested, but she has many calls on her time.'

Grandmother merely nodded without comment, and he allowed us to go on our way.

As we drove away, I stole a quick look at her face, preoccupied, sad, but she said nothing about the vicar's remarks. She would never divulge any of her problems to me or anybody else, they were locked away in her heart and I had no means of knowing what it would take to release them. She would greet her friends smiling, urbane and carefree.

That evening I telephoned Jenny to say I would call for her next morning and we would go shopping in the city. She did not sound enthusiastic, saying she wasn't sure about Alice nor about Ralph.

She had told me that Alice had her lunch at school and arrived home about four in the afternoon, and I knew that Ralph never lunched at home, so I was adamant about the shopping expedition. In the end I told her I would call for her at nine-thirty and we would lunch together in town.

I guessed that the coat she was wearing she had had some considerable time. It was dark-brown tweed, unfashionably short and her felt hat was one that my grandmother might have worn.

She made no comment about the new car and conversation was minimal, with me doing most of the talking. As we neared the city limits she said, 'Are you going to buy something new?'

'Possibly, and I hope you are too.'

'There's nothing I need. I don't go out much.'

'Well, we'll look around. I'm sure you'll find something you feel you can't live without.'

We went to the best shops and I bought several things but when I persuaded Jenny to look for something she was disinterested. She did look at dresses for Alice, explaining that she needed something new for the Christmas party at school.

'Do you go to the party Jenny?'

'No, it's only for the schoolchildren.'

'Do you do anything at Christmas?'

192

'Well no. There's the golf club dinner but I can't really leave Alice alone in the house, she's far too young.'

'You could get somebody to stay with her, your mother perhaps.'

Her face set in mutinous lines but she did not answer me.

She seemed uncomfortable in the dining room of the hotel I selected for lunch. She picked at her food and in the end I said desperately, 'Aren't you very hungry Jenny?'

'I don't like this sort of place, I'd rather have a teashop, something smaller.'

'I'm sorry. I thought I was treating you to something special.'

'There's no need for you to treat me at all, Amanda. I don't like the city. It's too big and too noisy.'

'I'm sorry,' I said again. It seemed so ridiculous that I felt the need to apologise for something that had been meant to be enjoyable.

'Do you want to look for a dress for Alice, or would you rather go home?'

'Well, we're here now. We might as well buy her something.'

I did not suggest a shop where children's clothes were the best because they were expensive. Instead I allowed her to choose a store she was familiar with and where she selected a dark green velvet dress which I thought would do very little for Alice, but which she seemed to like.

As we walked back to the car I had a sudden brainwave, suggesting that we should try to get our hair done and it would be my treat.

'I always have the same hairdresser nearer home,' she prevaricated.

'Well, I do need to have mine done. Please Jenny, I shall hate you having to wait for me. Why not have yours done at the same time?'

She had pretty hair, but it was worn too long and untidy. The girl attending to her asked if she might be allowed to cut it, but Jenny was adamant that she liked it long, it suited her, and her daughter would be horrified if she had it cut.

I was happy with mine, Jenny considerably less so even when I assured her that she looked pretty and younger. There was nothing to be done now except go home and the relief on her face when I stopped the car outside her front door was evident.

'Would you like to come in and have a cup of tea?' she asked as she got out of the car.

'No thank you, Jenny, not this afternoon. We must do this again, perhaps we could take Grandma with us.'

The look of panic was all too evident.

'I'd rather not if you don't mind, Amanda. I really don't like the shops and I hardly know Mrs Dexter.'

'If you don't meet her, you'll never get to know her. You would like her. She's really very nice.'

'I'm sure she is, but here's Alice. We've just got back in time. Perhaps I'll see you before you go back to India.'

I felt like laughing. My efforts to give Jenny a day out had been disastrous, but the urgency in getting me back to India was very apparent.

Chapter Nineteen

I should have been able to tell Grandma the truth; instead I only told her half the truth.

I couldn't tell her that Phillip had invited me to discuss what could be done to utilise my Eastern designs as alternatives to those the Dexter mills had used for many years, nor could I tell her that I would be dining with Phillip alone because Caroline would be away.

She smiled, well pleased that I had been invited to the hall saying, 'I'm so glad dear. I've been thinking that Caroline could have put herself out a little to welcome you back. Are you to be their only guest?'

'I think so, Grandma.'

'Well, put on your prettiest dress my dear. Caroline is always in the height of fashion and she must spend a fortune on clothes. Phillip is far too generous. He spoils her dreadfully.'

When I didn't reply, she said more doubtfully, 'There's so much talk in the town that they go their separate ways. Nothing has been said in my hearing, but Myrtle tells me. Sophie hears so much around the constituency, after all, the Marstons are local gentry for miles around, and people will talk about them when they've nothing else to do.'

'Yes, I'm sure they do.'

'If you sense there's something wrong up there, I do hope you'll tell me, Amanda. If there's something for me to worry about, I'd rather it be something concrete than mere hearsay.'

I dressed carefully in a navy blue silk dress I particularly liked, a dress that complemented the three strands of pearls around my throat and the pearl earrings that had been a Christmas present from Anthony. Grandma smiled at me, well pleased with my appearance, saying, 'You look very nice dear. I always think something quite simple like the gown you are wearing is nicer than something flamboyant. You didn't tell me what Jenny bought when you went into the city.'

'She bought a dress for Alice. She said she didn't need anything.'

'Was it a nice dress?'

'Yes, quite nice.'

'I always send them a cheque for Christmas, and I often wonder what they buy with it. Ralph never tells me.'

I didn't want to talk about Jenny, it was too painful and I didn't want her to ask questions about them. I felt that she worried a great deal about her family and kept most of her worries to herself.

It was almost dark when I drove along the narrow country lanes towards Ellesmere Hall. The sunset had been glorious and now in the west the sky was still a bright glowing red, turning the crumbling autumn leaves into a scarlet ribbon on the grass verge. In India I had forgotten the long country twilights that linger on long after the sun disappeared. Now I could see the large imposing house with its tall chimneys and graceful terraces etched against the smouldering sky.

I felt strangely nervous, like a schoolgirl at her first dance, and, as I walked up the shallow steps towards the front door, I was aware of my heart fluttering nervously. I clenched my hand on the small bag I was carrying in an effort to still its trembling.

A darkly clad manservant opened the door for me, smiling as he took my coat, and the next moment Phillip was striding across the hall to greet me, a warm smile on his face, his hands outstretched.

'We're dining in one of the small rooms at the side of the house,' he informed me. 'It's less formal and much cosier. We'll have a glass of sherry before dinner, in here, Amanda.'

He held the door open for me and stood aside so that I could pass in front of him. The room we entered was large and beautifully furnished but very little registered, and I felt that Phillip was aware of my nervousness when he said, 'This was my mother's favourite room. Caroline has gone to town on the rest of the house, I'll show you round after dinner. You've never been here before, have you, Amanda?'

'No. I used to sit on the fell and look at it. All I ever knew of the hall was from Caroline.'

'Well yes. She and her mother were constant visitors.'

His voice was bland so I could not tell if it was merely a statement or an aspersion.

I sat on the long sofa in front of the fire while he went to pour the sherry, then he came to sit beside me asking, 'I see you've brought the designs. We'll take a look at them now before dinner and talk about them again afterwards.'

I watched him turning the pages of the book I had bought in Lantau before handling the silks I had received from Charlotte, and I watched his expression. Eyes that could change from gravity to amusement, a mouth that could enchant me with its smile, yet lips that could grow suddenly serious when gravity was necessary.

Now it was very evident that he was interested in my patterns and looking up with a smile he said, 'I can see what you mean, Amanda. These are very beautiful. I can see why you think they can be useful. Come along, we'll have dinner and then we'll talk about them.'

We ate in a small dining room. As I took my place at table, I said softly, 'I could get lost in this place, it's overwhelming. Didn't Caroline find it so?'

He smiled. 'Caroline finds it very much to her taste, in spite of the fact that she spends very little time in it.'

The meal was exquisitely cooked and presented, and after a while I lost my anxiety and was able to respond to his efforts to put me at ease. We talked about India and my travels with Charlotte, we talked about horses and his love of sailing. We did not talk about Dexter's, neither the mills nor the family. After we had eaten he said, 'We'll take a look around the house now, Amanda, and have our coffee later, so that we can look at the silks again.'

I stared round the large drawing room, aware that Phillip was watching my expression with some amusement. Dexter's traditional chintzes hung at the large windows and covered

197

the chairs and sofas. They were patterns I had known all my life, softly coloured leaves and roses, pretty against the pale peach plain carpet, and looking at Phillip I said, 'Have you always had Dexter's chintzes in here?'

'No. I gave Caroline a free hand after my mother left the house. She didn't like the velvets my mother liked and these were all a wedding present from her father, as well as those in the rest of the house.'

I didn't comment, and I did not think he expected me to. They would not have been my choice. After all, I had grown up with them at Fairlawn. I was remembering Caroline's taste as a girl, pretty pastels and frills, flower-trimmed hats and fancy shoes, and then I found myself looking at her portrait at the head of the first flight of stairs, a large painted version of the photograph at my grandparent's house.

Pale blond hair and white osprey feathers, a white satin gown showing delicate shoulders, and her light blue eyes looking out calmly from a face of refined beauty.

'She looks very beautiful,' I commented.

'Yes. She enjoyed every moment of that evening.'

'Did she sit for the portrait?'

'Yes, but photographs were taken also. Doesn't your grandmother have one?'

'Yes, I expect all the family do.'

'I didn't see one at Ralph's house.'

'Probably not.'

He had turned away and was walking down the steps and I had no means of knowing if he agreed that Caroline was right to see little of Ralph and his family. I had to find out.

We were back in the room he had first shown me into and where a maidservant was serving us coffee. When she had left us alone I said, 'There are velvet curtains in this room, I take it Caroline had nothing to do with the furnishings in here?'

'No. As I said, this was my mother's favourite room, and here I drew the line as to how it should be left.'

'Why did you say "probably not" when I said I hadn't seen a photograph of Caroline in Ralph's house?'

'She doesn't visit them and they don't visit us.'

'And you agree with that?'

'No. I think it's deplorable. I insisted that she invite them to the ball she gave last Christmas, but they left halfway through the evening.'

'Why was that, do you think?'

'I think Ralph's wife felt very much out of her depth and Caroline could have made an effort to make her feel welcome. I'm not sure if the marriage could have worked, perhaps in the first instance, but now I think it's too late. Have you seen Jenny?'

So I told him about the shopping expedition and the afternoon Alice and I found her with the empty bottle of whisky.

'I'm so desperately sorry for both Jenny and Ralph,' I said, 'but I'm sorry for Alice. It's all too much for a child of ten to face.'

His expression was sad and reflective but I sensed that it was a sadness not wholly concerned with my cousin and his family problems, it was something else, something deeper and more personal, but in the next moment he was saying brightly, 'Come and sit near the fire, and we'll talk about your designs. I have something to tell you that might interest you.'

I stared at him in surprise, and he took his seat beside me, laying the silks and the pattern book on the small table in front of us.

'I have it on good authority, Amanda, that your grandfather and uncles are thinking of selling Number Three mill. That's the smallest of the four, the last to be built.'

'They don't think trade will recover, then?'

'Perhaps not to the same extent. Most of the mills will combine into one large syndicate, the smaller mills will go to the wall.'

'Can they hope to sell it?'

'Well, it's evident that new industries have to be found if the town is not to become a ghost town. New ideas have to spring up. The cotton industry will survive but on a lesser level than before, and perhaps something new, but equally as sound will take its place.'

'Who do you suppose would be interested in buying Number Three mill?'

'They've had one or two offers, I believe. The paper industry, wholesale food, I don't think any of them have been accepted as yet.'

I was thinking about Number Three mill standing on the banks of the river, small and compact, and close to the sports field used by the employees and the cricket pavilion. Phillip was watching me intently and with a little smile he said, 'What are you thinking, Amanda, that it could be an ideal place for you to begin a new enterprise?'

'Grandfather would never sell it to me, even if it was a possibility.'

'Probably not, but he needn't know. The solicitors have it in hand and I could make enquiries for you.'

I was tremendously intrigued. My own business with my ideas, but where would I find the workpeople and would I have enough money to finance it? I could not steal my uncles' employees for something as untried and unorthodox as the designs in front of me which were so completely different from those the Dexters had used for years.

As if he read my thoughts Phillip said, 'You're unsure how it could be done, Amanda, but you would need advice from people who know the trade. A great many people will be thrown out of work. It's conceivable that you could lure them into working for you.'

'They'd never allow it.'

'You're an adult, Amanda. If you wanted to go ahead with it they couldn't stop you.'

'But all I know are these. I don't know anything about cotton.'

'How do you think anybody starts in business? They have the great idea, and they learn. How do you think your great grandfather started? How do you think he acquired four mills? He started small and it grew. You can do the same, Amanda.'

'None of the family will help me, not even Ralph. His father wouldn't let me him.'

'You say none of the family, Amanda.'

'Yes. I mean it.'

'Aren't I family, even though I only married into it?'

'You would help me Phillip? What would Caroline say?'

'I know nothing about cotton, Amanda, but I do have considerable knowledge of the financial market, and I know people who would answer your questions. You will need a great deal of advice, a good solicitor and an even better accountant, and I don't think we need trouble ourselves about any reaction from Caroline.'

'How do I start?'

'Leave it with me. I'll put out feelers regarding what you might expect to pay for the mill, what sort of machinery you will need and where an experienced workforce are likely to come from. As soon as I have something concrete to go on, I'll contact you, the sooner we get things moving the better.'

I was afraid and I was excited, but I was no longer alone. Phillip was the bulwark I needed to lean on, but as I drove back to Fairlawn I thought for the first time about my feelings for him. I loved him, I needed him and I was being catapulted into a situation fraught with danger. I was not out to steal my cousin's husband and yet I was very aware that Phillip was not happy in his marriage and how easily needs can turn into love.

I was glad that my grandparents were in bed when I let myself into the house. I went immediately to my bedroom but it was many hours before I slept.

Grandma was eager to question me about the evening before, I said it had been a very pleasant occasion, the hall was beautiful, and we had talked about all sorts of things. Before she could ask any more questions, I said brightly, 'I think I'll drive down to the mills this morning. I found them really interesting and I've only just scratched the surface.'

'Your grandfather doesn't like you down there, Amanda.'

'I don't see why. I *am* a Dexter. Isn't it natural for me to be interested in the family concern?'

'None of the other girls were interested. Your grandfather thinks you'll very soon be returning to India where you'll quickly forget the way of life here.'

'I've no plans to return to India, Grandma. In any case my father may decide to retire and I can't think that they'll spend their retirement in India.'

'Well, I wouldn't go into the office, if I were you. He's down there now, so I think it would be better if you looked at one of the other mills.'

I had every intention of doing just that.

My first feeling was one of acute disappointment. The gates and doors of Number Three mill were firmly closed. Weeds grew in the garden surrounding the building and the small stream that flowed underneath the stone bridge appeared sluggish and contaminated with rubbish.

I looked up at the windows of the three storeys and asked myself what sort of industry was likely to be interested in it. Phillip had said offers had been made, but I was beginning to realise that my knowledge of industry was negligible: all I had was a dream, and there were so many problems ranged against me.

I wandered disconsolately round the perimeter of the mill, startled when a voice cried out, 'What are you doing here, Amanda?' It was Ralph getting out of his car on the road in front of the gates.

'I was passing and wondered why the gates were locked. What's happening here?'

'It's up for sale.'

'That means Dexter's will be down to three.'

'That's right, and those three will probably be part of a combine, the survival of the fittest.'

'Will you be able to sell it, do you think?'

He shrugged his shoulders. 'It's possible. There've been one or two tentative enquiries.'

'Who would want to buy a cotton mill?'

'Well, one enquiry came from a warehouse, the other from a firm of upholsterers. We're waiting to see if there are any better offers of course, but you know Grandfather. When he gets a bee in his bonnet he wants to get on with it.'

'Are you going into the mill?'

'No. I was just driving past when I spotted you. I hear you dined at the hall last night. Grandma told Mother you'd been invited.'

'Ralph, what's going to happen to you if the mills are integrated into a combine?'

'Never mind me, how about your invitation to the hall? I know for a fact that Caroline was away.'

'Yes, but I haven't told Grandma.'

He grinned. 'So it was a pleasant tête-à-tête with the lord

of the manor in his wife's absence, something you felt obliged to keep to yourself?'

'I'd never set foot in the hall, Phillip was kind enough to show me around. I don't want you reading anything else into it, there wasn't anything.'

'I wouldn't blame him if there was. Caroline was lucky to get him, she'll be lucky to keep him if she continues to act the way she does.'

'What do you mean? She doesn't play around.'

'No, I don't think she does, but she's always lording it over some function or other. She enjoys the position not the commitment.'

'Perhaps Phillip doesn't mind?'

'No, but isn't that when it becomes dangerous?'

'Well, your own marriage isn't exactly flawless.'

'No, but I wasn't offered the same incentives as Caroline's been offered. Hers was supposed to be a marriage made in heaven, mine was flawed from the outset.'

'Perhaps neither you nor Caroline tried hard enough?'

'Perhaps, and now it's too late. Watch your step Amanda. You're walking on thin ice.'

'Well, if I can't get in here to take a look round, I'll have to think of something else to do.'

'Why do you want to look around anyway? Why are you suddenly so interested in cotton?'

'I have to be interested in something, perhaps it's in my blood.'

'The old man isn't amused, so I'll not be telling him I've seen you around here.'

'Perhaps I'll call on Jenny.'

He stared down at me seriously. 'Amanda, you're flogging a dead horse with Jenny. There have been many times when she's hurt me, she could hurt you.'

'How?'

'She didn't enjoy the shopping trip, Amanda. She hopes you won't ask her again. She doesn't like visitors who arrive unannounced. She doesn't like members of my family, period. Why subject yourself to apathy of that sort?'

'There has to be a reason why she feels that way.'

'If there is, I stopped asking myself about it a long time

ago. You could try for ever to get through to Jenny, and don't think that I haven't, but in the end you won't succeed, and in the end you could be the one who gets hurt.'

So I parted from Ralph and drove up the country road until I came to a wide grass verge where I could leave the car and climb the stile leading up to the fell.

Storm clouds scudded across an autumn sky and I was glad of the sheepskin coat I had placed in the back of the car. Buffeted by the wind I scrambled across the moorland grass until I could look down on the hall, astonished that my footsteps had taken me there without thinking where I was going.

Was this what was happening to my life? That I was blindly travelling onwards like a leaf tossed in the wind, without direction unaware of the dangers that might be ahead.

Chapter Twenty

Why did I always feel so superfluous when the family came on Sundays? All talk of the cotton industry was shelved until the men stayed on at the dining table after the women had left, and at the table the talk was of family matters or some sort of scandal within the community.

I did not have long to wait for Aunt Myrtle to raise the matter of my dinner with Phillip.

'Did you enjoy dining at the hall last Thursday?' she asked.

'Yes, thank you, Aunt Myrtle. It was very pleasant.'

'Not at all boring?'

'No, why?'

'I just thought with Caroline being away, you and Phillip might not have had much to talk about. But then of course, you go riding together, so I expect you've got to know one another.'

'Did Phillip invite you?' Aunt Edith snapped.

'Yes, Aunt Edith.'

'Did he know Caroline would be away?'

'I assume so. Is it important?'

'I would have thought it more congenial if she'd been there.'

'Oh I don't know. Phillip is a very interesting person. He made me feel at home, and I've been here over three weeks now, Aunt Edith, and I haven't seen Caroline at all.'

'That's because she's a very busy woman. She'll get round to you eventually.'

'Waiting for Caroline is like waiting for Christmas,' Aunt

Myrtle said. 'We know it's coming, we simply have to be patient.'

'What's that supposed to mean Myrtle? How many months is it since we've seen Sophie? She simply parks her daughter here and disappears into the blue.'

'She also happens to be very busy, Edith.'

'I hope you're not inferring that Caroline does nothing. Look at the charities she sponsors, look at her magisterial work as well as all her social engagements.'

'People talk,' was all Aunt Myrtle allowed herself to say.

'Then they've nothing else to do with their time and a great deal of it is pure jealousy. Girls who were at school with Caroline and their mothers, people who are envious of her position and her style. Don't tell me you listen to their tittle-tattle, Myrtle.'

'When it's repeated often enough one can't very well avoid listening to it. Now if they get wind that Amanda went there alone, it will give the gossips something more to talk about.'

It was Uncle William who brought the conversation to an end, by telling his wife to drop the subject.

Aunt Edith rose to her feet and swept out of the room, followed by Aunt Myrtle and Grandma. I felt like a piece of furniture, and ornament, to be discussed and enlarged upon, but something that was not expected to answer back or explain.

The worried look was back on Grandma's face, the look I had seen so many times.

I had done nothing wrong, so why should I feel so guilty. The guilt lay in my heart and foolishly I told myself that so long as it stayed there there was no danger.

The silence was oppressive. It was a condemnation and an accusation, and unable to stand it any longer I jumped to my feet 'I think I'll go out for a walk. I'll take Benjie,' I said.

She looked up with a little smile. 'That will be nice Amanda, he could do with a walk.'

I had reached the door when she said, 'I'm sure your aunts didn't mean to be unkind. And there has been talk about the state of Caroline's marriage. Lady Marston was always here, you see. She did just as much work for charity and her work on the Bench, but she loved and comforted her husband, she was with him, he was always her main concern.'

'Why are you saying this to me, Granny?'

'Because unhappiness makes people vulnerable and you're a very pretty woman. Caroline isn't unhappy, she is too self-centred to realise what she is doing, but Phillip is a gentle sensitive man. You could be that shoulder for him to cry on.'

'Phillip is advising me on a business venture, Granny, and we like riding together. Business is all we have discussed, that and my marriage which ended too soon.'

'I'm glad dear. For all our sakes, please keep it like that.'

There was so much resentment in my heart as I trudged with Benjie through the damp November mist, and when I returned to the house I was delighted that their cars had gone.

There was no sign of Grandfather and Grandma sat in the drawing room playing Viennese Operetta on the gramophone. While she listened, I wrote letters. When the record finished she looked up with a sad smile saying, 'I hope you won't mention any of this afternoon's gossip to Phillip, Amanda.'

'I've no intention of discussing his marriage with him at all, and I'm sure he won't wish to talk about it to me.'

'I never thought it was right. Both Edith and his mother pushed it. When his father died he left the navy to manage things here. His mother wanted to get away to be with her sister and Caroline was never away from the place. She was the sweet gentle girl he could talk to, always ready to listen and encourage, always looking her best, and she is very beautiful, I'm sure he believed he was in love with her. Personally, I think Caroline has only ever loved herself.'

'Caroline is your granddaughter, Granny. Doesn't it bother you that you should think about her in this way?'

'It bothers me a great deal. I have talked to her, but she laughs it off, tells me I'm an old worrier and that she and Phillip are very happy. Perhaps I'm being silly and there really is nothing wrong.'

'I have to go into town in the morning, Granny. Is there anything you want from the shops?'

'If I think of something I'll tell you. Where are you going?'

'Well I have an appointment to see a solicitor about something and I thought I might call round to see Jenny.'

'Yes dear, that would be nice. Do ask her to call round to

see me and bring Alice. She doesn't seem to want to come but if she knows you're here she might make the effort.'

'I'll do what I can. Ralph should bring her, I can't think why he doesn't.'

'I hope nothing's wrong Amanda, seeing your solicitor I mean?'

'No, Granny. A business matter, that's all.'

The solicitor was Phillip's, I had no one of own. He was urbane and smiling, affording me old-fashioned courtesy and a cup of excellent coffee.

'You're the one member of the Dexter family I haven't actually met,' he said.

'I wasn't aware that you were Grandfather's solicitor too, Mr Scotson.'

'No, I'm not. I've met your family at certain functions in the town and at Sir Phillip's house.'

'I see.'

'Sir Phillip told me it was a business venture you were interested in.'

'Yes. I want some advice on purchasing my family's Number Three mill. I believe it's for sale and that there have been one or two offers to buy it.'

His look of surprise was very apparent.

'And why would a granddaughter of Mr Dexter wish to buy a mill he so evidently wishes to dispose of?'

He listened without interruption while I told him about the oriental designs and how I thought they could be utilised and when I had finished he said seriously, 'It's a considerable undertaking, Mrs St Clare. You would need work people who know what they are about, machinery, printing expertise. Have you had any thoughts on how you would get them?'

'A great many of the Dexter workforce will be made redundant. Surely some of them would be glad to find alternative employment? There will be looms for sale and other machinery that I would need. Surely members of the family will help me.'

'Could you rely on them to help you?'

I was uncertain. I would receive no encouragement from my grandfather, who would be horrified at the very thought of my venturing into an industry he had spent his life in and

I had not, and my uncles were very much under his thumb. Ralph was a possibility, but Ralph had changed: he had too many pressures surrounding him.

He was watching me shrewdly, recognising my insecurity and the doubts chasing around in my mind. With a little smile he said gently, 'I can see that you're unsure about a great many things. Sir Phillip thinks you have something going for you, but he has never concerned himself with the cotton industry. You would need the loyalty of the men and women you would want to work for you, but I have no doubt if the will is strong enough you could find them.'

'Who are the people wanting to buy the mill, Mr Scotson?'

'I've heard there are one or two wholesale furniture people who're thinking in terms of taking over the mills as a warehouse. Another interest is from a haulage firm who merely wish to purchase the lower floor and surrounding land.'

'Have either of these offers been accepted?'

'I believe not.'

'Do you know if that's because the offers are too low?'

'They're hoping something better will turn up.'

'Would you make an offer on my behalf, and offer a further five per cent in excess of the highest offer they have received. You have my permission to exceed this sum, Mr Scotson.'

'So you've made up your mind?'

'Yes. I believe in this venture. Now I have to shop around and find people who know considerably more about it than I do.'

'I must say I admire your courage, but we do have to be logical about matters. Are you quite sure you can afford to take on an enterprise such as this, Mrs St Clare? And what do you suppose the family will say about it?'

'My husband left me very well provided for. I had no idea when I married him that he was a rich man, we never discussed money but he was always generous and I supposed he had some sort of private income. It was only after he died that I was made to realise that he had been a rich man. He was an only son, his parents were killed in an accident and all their money went to Anthony. I can assure you Mr Scotson I can afford to embark upon this enterprise, as for my family, I doubt if many of them will be speaking to me at the end of the day. I shall be encroaching on what they consider to be a man's world. Neither my grandmother nor my aunts have ever concerned themselves with the mills, but are merely content to live well on the money they make. But times have changed. Cotton is no longer King in Lancashire, but none of them have any idea on how things can be changed. Perhaps some of my great grandfather's spirit lives on in me I can't bear the thought of all those people being thrown out of work. I want to do something if I can.'

'Sir Phillip told me you were a very unusual woman, Mrs St Clare. He said you would surprise me. A very beautiful young woman who has spent many years away from Lancashire and its cotton industry and who comes back to us with a burning desire to bring it back to life. Believe me, Mrs St Clare you're unique.'

'You are not a Lancastrian, Mr Scotson?'

'No. I come from Yorkshire. I know more about woollen mills than cotton mills, and I must tell you that neither of my sisters were remotely interested in rescuing the woollen industry when it faltered from time to time.'

'Perhaps it's because I haven't anything else of importance to do.'

'I shall watch your progress with considerable interest Mrs St Clare and I shall take much pleasure from informing Sir Phillip that everything he said about you I found to be true.'

It was after twelve when I left the solicitor's office so I decided to defer my visit to Jenny until the afternoon. I drove towards the centre of town, but I was half way down the street when the car started to veer wildly. I stopped and got out only to find I had a flat tyre.

The garage where I had bought it was only round the corner, and they assured me they could fix it by two. In the meantime, there was nothing I could do but to lunch in town and look at the shops.

It was years since I had really taken a good look round. I remembered that my grandmother liked to take tea at the Royal George in the main shopping street, so I headed for there. The reception was filled with men attending a Rotary lunch, and as I was about to enter the dining room I was hailed by a voice saying, 'I thought it was you Amanda. Have you decided to lunch here?'

Phillip was smiling down at me and once again I cursed my wretched heart that it should beat so swiftly and that I could not avoid the warm blood flooding my cheeks.

'I've had a puncture. I had to leave my car at the garage so there wasn't time to go home.'

'Well they do a very decent lunch here. I'm at the rotary luncheon. We finish around two so I'll drive you back for your car.'

'It doesn't mater, Phillip. I'll look at the shops and walk there.'

'I think you'll find the service slow, Amanda, particularly on rotary lunch day. I'll look round for you anyway.'

I smiled my thanks and moved into the restaurant.

Phillip was right, the service was slow and by the time I walked back into the foyer, the Rotarians were already leaving and I saw Phillip chatting to another man near the cigarette counter. He raised his hand and smiled, and after a brief word the other man left him and Phillip came to join me.

He smiled. 'Enjoy your lunch?'

'Yes thank you.'

'The car's just round the corner.'

'You really needn't trouble, Phillip. It's only a short walk to the garage.'

Without answering he put his hand under my elbow and propelled me through the door.

The car mechanic was apologetic when he showed me the ruined tyre.

'It's beyond repair miss. Nail's gone right through the rim. You'll be needin' a new un,' he said.

'How long will it take?'

'We'll 'ave to send round to the tyre warehouse at the edge o' town. The lad's out wi' the van at the moment, so it'll be nigh on four o'clock afore we can get one. Can you call in later?'

By this time Phillip had joined us. 'There's no problem, Amanda,' he said, 'I can drive you round to Ralph's house, do my business in town and pick you up later.'

That was it: even small circumstances were throwing us together now.

It was almost three when we reached Jenny's house, and as he brought the car to a standstill, Phillip said, 'Would you like me to come in with you Amanda, I feel we should all make an effort to get to know Jenny, even at this late stage?'

'I'd rather you didn't. She would be embarrassed. She's so easily embarrassed.'

'Then I'll wait in the car until I'm sure she's letting you in.'

In the room on the right of the front door the long curtains were still drawn, and although I knocked on the door there was no response. I walked round to the back as I had done before and looked through the kitchen window. Again my eyes were met with a sink piled high with breakfast dishes and the tablecloth still lay on the small kitchen table under several items of china.

I knocked on the back door so loudly that the woman who had been in her garden next door put her head over the fence.

'Is Mrs Dexter expecting you Miss? I haven't seen her all morning.'

'She doesn't know I am calling today. Would you know if she's gone out?'

'Oh, I wouldn't think so. Perhaps she's having a lie-down.'

Phillip raised his eyebrows as I got into his car. 'Nobody at home?' he said.

'I don't know Phillip. Oh, this is a dreadful house. It never looks lived in, the curtains are still drawn and the breakfast things are in the sink. You carry on, I'll take a walk in the park and wait for Alice.'

'You have to get back for your car at four. We'll drive around for a while and come back later.'

'I thought you had business in town?'

'Nothing that can't wait until another day. We'll drive up on to the fell and I'll show you where I used to play when I was a boy.'

How innocent it was that drive in the damp grey of November afternoon. From the crags that topped the fell we could look down on the town below at some chimneys that smoked and others that stood out sharp and clean against the autumn sky. We sat without speaking and once I looked at his face, at a profile beautiful and almost remote, before he turned his eyes away from the hills and looked down at me. We stared at each other in silence, but it was a silence pregnant with unspoken perplexities and the words were dragged from me, 'Phillip I think perhaps we should go back.'

'Yes. Perhaps you're right,' he murmured.

We did not seem to have been up on the fell very long and I was surprised to hear the church bell tolling four when we reached the perimeter of the park. There were children running along the road now and a crowd of young mothers holding their children by the hand. I could hear their laughter and their chattering voices and my eyes searched for Alice among them, then I saw her running along the road, her coat flying in the wind, her dark hair lank and heavy in the shower of rain.

'There's Alice,' I cried. 'What's she doing on the road, she must have lost her key.'

We caught up with her at the corner and Phillip stopped the car before we reached her so that I could get out.

'Alice,' I called. 'Where are you going, isn't your mother in?'

She turned to stare at me and the stark misery in her face made me suddenly afraid. 'Alice what is it?' I asked again.

'It's Mummy, I can't wake her up. She's fallen on the floor.'

By this time Phillip had joined us and then he was lifting her into the back of the car and I was sitting beside him while he reversed and drove back towards the house.

She had left the front door standing wide so that the tiled vestibule and inner glass door was wet with rain and she was running ahead of us into the house.

I had had this feeling once before when I saw Anthony walk out of my life, that alien feeling of despair that heralded disaster, and I was kneeling on the rug in front of the embers of a dying fire looking down on Jenny's pale face smoothed of every care, no longer vulnerable, no longer afraid. Jenny was dead.

I was suddenly aware of Alice screaming in Phillip's arms and I rose to my feet to take her away from him.

I had to drag her into the other room and Phillip added

coals to the fire and drew back the curtains. She was sobbing incoherently, clutching at my coat, her face anguished, and I held her close and tried to comfort her.

'I'll telephone for an ambulance,' Phillip was saying. 'We have to get her doctor here. Do you know who he is, Alice?'

'Mummy's dead, Mummy's dead' was all Alice could say in reply.

I did not hear the knock on the door, but then the neighbour was there, her eyes wide with astonishment, her expression shocked bewilderment.

'I saw Alice run along the road,' she said. 'I had no idea there was anything wrong. Has anything happened?'

'Mrs Dexter has had an accident,' Phillip said shortly. 'We need to get her doctor.'

'That will be Doctor Crossland, his practice is on the corner there.'

'Then I'll go for him,' Phillip said. 'Could I ask you to invite Mrs St Clare and Alice into your home until after he's been here?'

'Yes, of course, I'll make us a cup of tea. Does Mr Dexter know?'

'Not yet. We'll try to get in touch with him as soon as possible.'

Alice and I went with her, sitting in front of her blazing fire in a room of similar proportions to the one we had left, but with all the evidence of being lived in, and Alice sipped her tea wrapped in her silent miserable world, and I sat with my ears trained to the noises on the street and the sudden clanging of an ambulance bell.

Less than half an hour later the house next door was locked up, Jenny had been taken away by the ambulance, and the doctor had signed her death certificate. Alice and I sat in Phillip's car driving up the hill towards Grandfather's house, and Phillip was saying steadily, 'I'll drive you down for your car in the morning Amanda. You can telephone the garage to tell them you'll pick it up then.'

To say that there was consternation at Fairlawn is an understatement. The doctor came and Alice was put to bed with something to help her sleep and Phillip and I had the task of telling my grandparents all that had happened during the afternoon.

It was singularly unimportant that Granny should ask after he had gone, 'How did Phillip come to be with you at Jenny's house, Amanda?' and when I looked into her eyes in utter amazement, all I was aware of was the worried frown I was becoming accustomed to.

Jenny Dexter might be dead, her daughter distraught, but at that moment the only thing that registered in my grandmother's mind was the fact that Phillip and I had been together. Death was a positive thing, the threat of infidelity and the scandal it aroused far more potent.

Chapter Twenty-One

It was almost eight, and the family were gathering. Alice was tucked up in bed and sedated, and we sat in the large dining room around the huge table that had been the scene of so many family occasions.

At its head sat Grandfather, and at the other end Grandma. I stared dismally at the shining polished walnut until I could stand it no longer and went to the window to look out at the rainy night.

The headlights of the first car to arrive lit up the long drive. The spreading puddles and dripping conifers, the beeches tossing their branches from which the summer leaves had all but fled, and then two figures left the car and came running towards the house, sheltering under an umbrella that seemed too fragile in the driving wind: Aunt Edith and Uncle Edwin, their faces registering bewilderment. I could feel Aunt Edith's eyes boring into my back, but after a brief nod I turned back to the window. Another car arrived: I could hear Aunt Myrtle's voice saying, 'I suppose we're in the dining room. My feet are wet, I've just stepped in a puddle.'

Her words seemed incongruously funny, even though I had never felt less like laughing. Her daughter-in-law was dead and her grand-daughter oblivious to her loss; why should the stepping into a puddle be significant?

Aunt Myrtle and Uncle William took their places at the table. The room was oppressive with their silence, and then there were other headlights sweeping up the drive and again two figures left the car and ran into the house. In the next moment I was staring into my cousin Caroline's eyes for the first time since my return to England, and she came immediately across saying 'What a terrible occasion this is, Amanda. I had hoped to see you in far happier circumstances. I was going to arrange a family gathering at the hall, but this really has put the kibosh on it.'

Phillip, standing behind her, merely smiled and then we moved back to the table to sit with the others.

'Is Ralph intending to join us?' Grandfather asked shortly.

'He's been in London all day. I don't suppose he knows what has happened yet,' his father said.

'Well, it's on the front page of the local paper. "Ralph Dexter's wife found dead this afternoon in her home by her daughter and Sir Phillip Marston", after which follows a summary of the family, most of it inaccurate and meaningless.'

'Did it mention Amanda?' Aunt Edith asked.

'No. I doubt if the newspaper is aware that Mrs St Clare is a Dexter. They'll make more of that in a future edition I should think.'

'Really Grandfather,' Caroline said airily. 'Why should they make anything of it at all?'

I was aware of the look that passed between Caroline and her mother and I was aware of the cynicism in Phillip's eyes. Granny was saying, 'Alice is absolutely distraught. The doctor has sedated her so that she could sleep, but I shall have to face her in the morning. How will Ralph be able to cope without his wife? The child will need somebody to see to her meals and be there when she gets home from school.'

'He'll have to get a housekeeper,' Aunt Myrtle said sharply. 'Other widowers have had to do it, look at Doctor Chambers. His wife left him with two little boys to bring up and he coped remarkably well. He got a splendid woman to look after them until they were old enough to go away to school.'

'That would be the answer of course,' Uncle William said. 'Alice should go away to boarding school. She'll be well taken care of during the holidays.'

'Particularly if Ralph gets married again,' Caroline said slyly.

'Hardly a suitable suggestion at this particular time,' Phillip added.

'Nor a particularly kind one,' Aunt Myrtle said acidly.

Outside, an approaching car could be heard and Uncle William said, 'This must be Ralph, he's evidently been informed.'

Ralph's face was pale and strained and I was forcibly reminded of that time when he had told the family he intended to marry Jenny. Then his expression had been determined and ready to face them all; tonight it was the face of a man bewildered by circumstances, and I felt an overwhelming feeling of pity for him when he asked, 'Is Alice here?'

'She's upstairs in bed, dear,' Granny said. 'We called in the doctor and he's given her something to help her sleep, the poor child was devastated.'

'Did you get the message in London?' his father asked.

'No, I'd probably already left. A policemen was waiting for me at the station. I left my bag at home and called in to see the woman next door, she told me some of the details. You found her Amanda, you and Phillip?'

'Yes,' I murmured.

'Good thing Philip was with you, it must have been terrible.'

'Yes. Alice was with us too, it was terrible for her.'

'And now we've got to think about where we go from here,' his mother said. 'There'll be the inquest and the funeral. After that you have to think about what you're going to do about Alice.'

'Do about her?' Ralph said sharply.

'Well yes. You're a businessman and she's a schoolgirl. You can't leave her to get her own meals when you're at the office and out of town, you'll need to get a decent house-keeper, we've all got to put our heads together and think how we're going to find one.'

'We've talked about boarding school,' Aunt Edith said quickly. 'That would seem to be the best solution, I know she'll get long holidays but we can all face those when we come to them. I expect we'll all do our bit.'

'Alice is my problem, Aunt Edith. I'll look after Alice.'

'You can say that now, Ralph,' his mother said, 'but you'll find it's not as easy as you think. She's eleven years old, quite the wrong time to cope with the loss of her mother.'

I noticed for the first time that Ralph was still wearing his overcoat and that it was spotted with rain. I felt sorry for him. It was enough to cope with the loss of his wife without the entire family questioning him on something that could not be resolved immediately.

Jumping to my feet I said, 'I'll make coffee, you look starved Ralph. I expect you could do with something hot.'

'Oh yes, please, Amanda,' Granny said. 'I've given the maid the evening off. I felt it was better that way.'

It was a relief to go into the kitchen and face something as normal as making coffee and I had not been there long before Caroline joined me, perching on the corner of the kitchen table. I knew she had not come to help, but merely to satisfy her curiosity about a great many things.

'You were lucky to have Phillip with you this morning, Amanda. How did you come to meet up with him?'

I explained briefly, and somewhat mollified she said, 'Of course Phillip's a rock in a crisis, I wonder what Ralph will do?'

'He'll find something I'm sure.'

'Well Daphne Browne's no solution. She's already run the gauntlet of two failed marriages and if she's looking for a third it won't be a widower with a daughter like Alice.'

'Don't you think it's a little obscene to be talking about Ralph marrying anybody tonight. Don't you credit him with more sense than marrying your friend?'

'Who told you she was my friend?'

'Sophie's daughter.'

'That little brat is far too old for her age. Actually, she's not a particular friend, simply an acquaintance from one of my charities.'

'The coffee's ready. Perhaps you'll help me carry it in.'

'Of course, but why don't we drink ours in here? I don't think I can cope with all the trauma in the dining room.'

'Don't you think we should be showing an interest in why we're all gathered here?'

'Leave it to me. I'll explain that we really have a lot of catching up to do.'

I knew exactly what she meant, our conversation would be one she could repeat to her mother in the morning, but curiosity made me accede to her request. We served the coffee and Caroline said airily, 'Amanda and I are going to drink ours in the kitchen. We have a lot to talk about.'

'What's more important than the reason we're gathered here?' Grandfather said tartly.

Putting an arm round his neck and holding her face against his she said, 'Don't be so grumpy, darling. I have to ask Amanda about my sister and there are enough of you here to talk about Jenny without us. Phillip will tell me later everything you've talked about.'

We sat at the kitchen table and it didn't take her long to launch into questions most people would have regarded as entirely personal.

'What sort of marriage did you have Amanda? Were you in love with your husband?'

'Of course. We had a good marriage, it was terrible that it had to be so brief.'

'Was he good looking? Was he nice?'

'Yes, to both questions.'

'And has there been anybody since?'

'No.'

'But there will be, darling.' She was staring at me analytically. 'You're very beautiful and I do think foreign travel gives a woman a certain air. I asked Phillip what you were like now, and he said you were very intelligent and attractive. I don't want you to see too much of him darling.'

'You don't sound very sure of him.'

'Oh, but I am. Because we don't live in each others' pockets is no reason for him to succumb to temptation.'

'If I didn't know you better, Caroline, I might construe your remarks as offensive, as it is I merely regard them as the sort of curiosity you displayed throughout our childhood.'

'You understood me very well, Amanda. You knew not to touch my books or my dolls, now I'm warning you not to spend too much time with my husband. More coffee darling?'

She filled up my cup and hers and in the next breath said, 'Tell me about Charlotte, whatever possessed her to go off to Outer Mongolia with some heathen Mongolian she hardly knew?'

220

'Why were you so surprised? Charlotte never conformed, she was always different.'

'I know. Off she went to central Africa to work in some malaria-ridden community with savages, then just when we thought she'd got all that nonsense out of her system she disappeared again to the Far East and next thing we knew she was married to some heathen and living in some God-forsaken place in Central Asia.'

'You're assuming an awful lot, Caroline.'

'Well, Charlotte hasn't even had the grace to tell us herself, we only knew from your father.'

'My father didn't tell you she had married a heathen and was living in some God-forsaken place.'

'Well he must have inferred it. My father was furious.'

'The man your sister has married was cultured, singularly handsome and extremely rich, and Samarkand is a very old and beautiful city. Rich in architecture and prosperous before we were even heard of.'

'When you say he's rich, how rich?'

'I don't know. All I do know is that he was cultured, highly intelligent and much travelled.'

'I'm impressed, but why doesn't she write to us? Will she ever come to visit, do you think?'

'I've no idea. Perhaps one day.'

'I wonder how long this wretched meeting is going on, I have to do my stint on the Bench in the morning I don't want to be here half the night.'

When I didn't answer she said testily, 'Whatever possessed Jenny to do such a dreadful thing? She was a disaster right from the very beginning and we did try. I invited them to a ball at the hall one Christmas and she wanted to leave halfway through, she said her dress wasn't right, and people were staring at her.'

'What was wrong with her dress?'

'Well, nothing, I suppose, but she could have worn it for one of the mill hops, not a ball at our place. I'm sure nobody commented, and in any case Ralph should have advised her on the right sort of thing to wear. She never came at Christmas to any of us. Ralph went to his mother's and took Alice when she was very small, but even that fizzled out.'

221

'I'll collect the coffee cups,' I said rising to my feet.

'I'll come with you. I do hope by this time everybody's ready to go home. Heavens, there's the funeral to come, all the town will be out and the press will be there in full force. Did you say you had to collect your car in the morning?'

'Yes.'

'Well I'll pick you up on my way to the Court. Phillip said he'd promised to take you, now he needn't bother.'

In the dining room they sat around the table in morose silence. Phillip was standing at the window staring out into the gloom and he turned as we entered the room.

'I think we can leave now,' he said. 'There's nothing to be done tonight and events will have to take their course. I'll pick you up in the morning to take you for your car, Amanda.'

'There's no need darling,' Caroline said with a smile. 'I've already promised to call for Amanda on my way into town.'

I did not miss the look of self-satisfaction on Aunt Edith's face as mother and daughter exchanged glances, Granny's worried frown and Phillip's cynical expression.

It soon became apparent that Ralph was staying the night rather than returning to the house and as I washed up the coffee cups he came to sit in the kitchen. His face was a mask of misery but I could not tell if it was for Jenny or himself. Certainly his life had changed beyond recognition and I was reluctant to break the silence.

I was putting away the cups and saucers, when he said, 'Why on earth did she do it, Amanda? I'll admit we hadn't a lot going for us, but I did try to include her in what I thought she might enjoy. She used to like the cinema but then she fell out with that, said she didn't like any of the films these days. She wouldn't go to the theatre, said only snobs went there, and she wouldn't set foot in the golf club for the same reason.

'People tried to be nice to her, but she never responded. She was a loner, Amanda, and she blamed it on me and my family. We're not blameless, right from the beginning she was out on a limb and I should have known it would have been like that.'

'Didn't she have any friends from her girlhood?'

222

'Not really. They thought she didn't want them when she married into the Dexter family, so they stayed away from her. She must have been lonely, and I suppose I lost patience with her instead of trying harder. What do I do about Alice? I can't take her back to that house where she found her mother.'

'You'll have a better idea when you've spoken to Alice.'

'And I'm dreading it. I could move house, I'm not tying my life to bricks and mortar and I never liked the place. It was Jenny's choice but heaven knows she never even tried to make it a home.'

'Where you ever in it, Ralph?'

'Not as often as I should have been, but there was no incentive. Let's face it Amanda, we'd grown apart. Our values had changed and she refused to grow with me. I worked hard to give her a good standard of life but at the end of the day there had to be something more than going home and staring at each other across the room.'

'Why don't you have a drink and take a couple of aspirins to help you to sleep? Nothing else can be done tonight, you can sort things out later.'

'I suppose so.'

We left the kitchen together and Ralph went into the dining room to pour himself a drink and I waited for him to join me on the stairs.

'Thank you for what you did for Alice, Amanda. I must remember to thank Phillip, it was fortunate you were together.'

When I didn't answer he said softly, 'Is anything going on there Amanda?'

'You're as bad as the rest of them Ralph. We met by accident. We've gone riding together and he's advising me on a business enterprise. If you can make anything out of that, you're welcome.'

'And you're a shade too touchy, my girl.'

'What do you expect?'

'Well, whatever it is, you have my blessing. I can't stand Caroline, never could, and she really doesn't deserve him. She's a bossy, selfish do-gooder to everybody except her husband and one day she'll get her come-uppance and nobody will be surprised.'

223

'If you need me to look after Alice tomorrow, Ralph, I'll be back as soon as I get my car. You only have to ask.'

'Thanks Amanda.'

He put his arms around me outside my bedroom door and for several minutes held me so close I could feel the beating of his heart. Then he released me and I could see that his eyes were filled with tears.

It was only the beginning. There would be more tears, more heart-searching before Jenny was laid to rest, and afterwards would be the rebuilding of a life, the coming to terms with change, memories that would not die when time had eased so much of the pain.

The inquest was a formality. Mrs Dexter had been suffering from depression for some time, which resulted in suicide while the balance of her mind was disturbed. And then the crowds in the square and reporters and cameramen were running everywhere.

As we left the courtroom I saw Jenny's mother in the company of two young women I presumed were Jenny's sisters. They hurried across the square with heads bent against the wind, and if some looked at us with sympathetic eyes others looked on surlily with condemnation.

I watched Ralph shouldering his way through a crowd of reporters, his face flushed and angry as they badgered him with questions, and then we were driving back to the house and between Granny and me Alice sat pale-faced and tearless, staring straight ahead.

In the days since we found her mother I had tried hard to make friends with her but I had been unsuccessful. She remained distant, apathetic, spending most of the time in her room staring through the window.

She was hardly eating anything and I determined that afternoon that I would take her afternoon tea to her room myself to see if I could encourage her to eat.

As soon as we arrived home she ran upstairs without a backward glance and Granny said, 'Perhaps when Sophie's daughter comes here, they'll be able to get along together.'

Personally I thought it was a forlorn hope. Julia wasn't exactly the easiest person to get to know and I secretly hoped her visit wasn't imminent.

As I had expected, I found Alice sitting on the window seat, staring out through the window. She did not turn her head when I entered, so I pulled up a table, deposited the tray and sat down beside her. 'I've come to eat afternoon tea with you, Alice,' I said brightly, 'I thought we might have a chat about school and the things you like to do.'

I poured out the tea and pushed the cup and saucer towards her.

'There are scones and jam,' I said, 'and there's a vanilla sandwich, one of your favourites I think.'

Without answering she took a scone and crumbled it on her plate, then after a few minutes she pushed the plate away, and I said anxiously, 'Alice, you must eat, it's worrying us all. Somewhere in heaven your mother will be very unhappy that you are behaving like this.'

'I don't like being here, I want to go home.' she said stolidly.

'There's nobody at home, Alice, your father's staying here.'

'But we will be going home, won't we? This isn't our home.'

'You have to give your father time to make arrangements, Alice. This is just as terrible for him as it is for you. Don't make it worse for him by refusing to eat.'

She stared at me for several minutes in silence, then she reached out for her place and started to eat the scone.

Chapter Twenty-Two

Jenny's funeral was a condemnation of all that was happening in the cotton industry: the unemployment, the poverty and the betrayal. It was us and them. They forgot the years of affluence; they failed to understand that they were living in a country where standards of living were high compared to those in third world countries, which were now producing the goods.

None of these people standing in groups by the cemetery gates or along the paths had seen the sweat shops in distant Thailand and Indonesia. Children living in ill-lit dormitory shacks, abandoned by their families and working in shifts day and night, paid only a pittance and poorly fed on bowls of rice.

As we walked between them their animosity was evident. We were being blamed for Jenny's death: we were the enemy. They stared unashamedly at me because none of them really remembered me. Phillip was accorded the respect due to him as a member of a family outside the industry, the one person who had had no hand in its downfall, and Caroline stood close to him, no doubt relieved that she was no longer a Dexter.

Mist hung low across the graves and narrow paths and the wind echoed eerily through bare branches. Alice stood close to her father clutching a small posy of flowers and on the other side of the open grave Jenny's mother and sisters stood pale-faced and shivering in the cold November morning.

Grandma's face appeared pale and pinched and I found myself thinking that she didn't deserve this. She was a good woman. She'd tried, all her life, to help those less fortunate than herself and she would have been kind to Jenny if Jenny had only met her half way. After the committal I saw her go forward to speak to Jenny's mother and then we were walking towards the waiting cars and along the paths a few people stepped forward to offer their sympathy. Not all, it seems, was lost.

I felt a hand touch mine as I was about to step into the car and when I turned round I found Bridie and Cook sad and tearful.

'We're so sorry,' Bridie said softly. 'We're sorry for your grandmother and Mister Ralph.'

'Thank you, I'll tell my grandmother that I spoke with you.'

'Will you be goin' back to India soon, Miss Amanda?'

'I don't think so. I'll call in to see both of you when I can.'

When was I going back to India? It seemed an age since I had given India a thought and now going back there seemed too remote. As I sat in the front seat of the car taking us back to Fairlawn I thought about India with a sense of something irretrievably lost, her sunshine and her pageantry, my parents and the memory of Anthony smiling down at me as we waltzed together in the ballroom of the viceroy's palace. It had been a fairy tale, another life, another dimension; now I was facing reality and something had to happen quickly. I needed to speak to Phillip, but that was something that might prove difficult.

It was while we were eating a buffet lunch that had been laid out for us at Fairlawn, that Philip came to speak to me.

'We have to talk soon, Amanda, about your plans for the mill. Offers are coming in for it, and you will need to start things moving if you intend to carry on.'

'I was hoping I might talk to you soon, Phillip. It isn't going to be easy.'

He smiled grimly. 'No. Not with Caroline's mother watching us like an indignant vulture.'

'I feel I shouldn't trouble you. Perhaps your solicitor is all I need.'

'He's an excellent man, Amanda. I'll make an appointment to see him during the week. We can both be there. I really think that's the best plan.'

227

'If you're sure.'

'I am. I'll ask him to write to you stating which day he will see you, and I will arrange to be present.'

He was about to turn away when Caroline joined us. Her pretty face was petulant as she looked around the room.

'How soon before we can make an excuse to leave Phillip?' she asked him. 'I hate it in here, I can still smell all those wreaths and we've had nothing but gloom and doom for days. It's dragged on so.'

'If you're ready to leave, we can go after we've spoken to your grandparents and Ralph.'

'Well yes, do let us do that then. You must come to visit us at the hall, Amanda. I'll be in touch, one evening when I've nothing much on.'

'One evening when you're free, Amanda,' Phillip added dryly.

'Amanda's free most evenings, aren't you darling,' Caroline trilled. 'I'm the one who's burdened with your mother's lame ducks. Come along, Phillip, I can see Granny standing alone, this is our chance.'

From the window I watched them driving away and Ralph standing beside me said, 'I suppose she couldn't wait to get away. I've arranged for Alice to go back to school next Monday. Our daily woman's promised to be there when she gets home from school soon after four. She can have her lunch at school.'

'Alice could be spending a lot of time alone,' I said unhappily. 'You are often away from home. You go out in the evenings and there's the golf club. I don't suppose you intend to give anything up, you need interests too, Ralph.'

'I know. If this doesn't work then I shall have to think about a girls' boarding school. There are several in the area, Sophie would know of a good one, she put feelers out about Julia before they decided to place her in a school near London.'

I wasn't sure how Alice would take to boarding school. Jenny had always been against it, but I knew the cruelty young girls could be capable of. Sophie and her husband had not attended the funeral: an MP's duties taking precedence. And Sophie was entertaining important guests from America.

Long-standing family friends had been invited to the

funeral and as I moved among them I could not help but be aware of the feeling of despair that hung over the gathering.

It had not been like that at Anthony's funeral. Sadness yes, but Anthony had been a serving soldier and death was something men like him had lived with. This was different, this was the deliberate taking of life by a young woman who could have had so much to live for, and the sight of Alice bewildered and vulnerable reached out to all of us.

In the morning she would be returning with her father to their own home, and her thoughts must be constantly on that untidy room and the body of her mother lying motionless on the floor.

I felt I had to get out of the house, and although it was drizzling I donned a trenchcoat and headscarf, and let myself out through the conservatory door.

The drizzle felt cold and sharp against my face and my feet splashed in the puddles along the path. It did not seem to matter as I climbed the hill behind the house that led upwards to the fell, and even as I reached the stile I was aware of a solitary horseman riding along the rim of the hill and disappearing behind the crags. I tramped on until the path came to a sudden end and only the moorland grass lay before me and the mist-laden moor.

I was about to turn back when I heard the sound of a horse's hooves coming towards me and then the rider reappeared out of the fog. He pulled his horse up sharply when he saw me.

'You're soaked through, why are you out in the rain?' Phillip said, and I smiled.

'Why are you out in the rain?' I answered.

He smiled. 'A sudden need to get some fresh air, even if it is a miserable November day.'

'That's how I felt too.'

'Are there still people at the house?'

'Yes, and likely to remain some time I think.'

'There's no shelter up here, Amanda. you should go back before you catch cold.'

I nodded, and he rode alongside me as I walked back along the lane. I could smell the steam rising from the horse's body and as we reached the gate where he would have to leave me to return to the hall across the fell I looked up at him. His eyes were sombre in a face that had haunted my girlhood and still had the power to stir my foolish heart, and in the next moment he jumped down from his horse and came towards me. For what seemed an eternity we stared at each other in silence, then he reached out his hands and took my rain-soaked body into his arms.

There was peace in his embrace and sudden warmth. My head rested against his shoulder and he was stroking my hair from which the scarf had blown away in the wind. Through a mist of rain I looked up into his face and then his lips were on mine and we were clinging together in a kiss that stole every logical thought, every tangible dream.

'Why did you come back into my life?' he murmured against my hair.

'Phillip, I want you to love me, I know it's wrong, terribly wrong, but I can't help it. I loved you before I went away, I wanted you then, but I was too young and there was Caroline.'

'I think I must have loved you too, Amanda. I always wished that Caroline was like you. I saw something in you, then, that I wanted. Why did you go away? If you'd stayed we might have discovered each other sooner.'

Neither of us thought about what might come after, there was only that brief moment in the wet misery of the day and then after one more embrace he was riding away from me across the fell and I was stumbling down the hill towards the house.

Grandma was crossing the hall when I entered it and she stared at me in amazement.

'Where have you been, Amanda? You're drenched. Surely you didn't go walking on such a day?'

I was shivering, and before I could answer she said sharply, 'Go upstairs immediately and change into some dry clothes. All we need is you in bed with pneumonia. Try to hurry, Amanda, people are ready to leave.'

There was no time to think about the afternoon's events as I hurried out of my damp clothes, towelled my damp body and changed. I ran down stairs in time to see our guests before they went to their cars, one or two of them staring at

230

me curiously, no doubt wondering where I had been and why I had changed my apparel.

Ralph looked at me curiously, asking, 'Where did you get to?'

'I went for a walk.'

'In the rain?'

'Well of course. I haven't melted.'

'Well, I can think of better ways of consoling myself than tramping on the fell in this weather.'

'I feel better for it.'

'Oh well, everybody to his or her own taste.'

I felt better because Philip had kissed me. His eyes had said so much more than his words, words were something that had to come later, but what would they say? Where would we go from here?

Only the family were left: Aunt Edith reading the cards and letters of condolence and Uncle Edwin and Uncle William standing at the window staring out into the dusk. Grandfather sat with a glass of whisky in his favourite chair and Aunt Myrtle was talking earnestly to Ralph, no doubt about Alice.

'There was a lot of antagonism around the cemetery this morning,' Uncle William remarked. 'A lot of it had to do with the short time the mills are on, and they were remembering that Jenny's father had worked with them. She was one of them, we were the opposition.'

'They'll forget their antagonism when they remember which side their bread's buttered,' Grandfather said acidly. 'We're the ones who're going to decide who we keep and who are going.'

'Have you reached a decision about Number Three mill?' Uncle William asked.

'Not yet. I've had five or six offers, one of them from an unknown source, offering to pay a good deal more than the others.'

'Unknown, you say. Didn't the solicitor give you any idea?'

'No. Since then I've had another offer from an engineering firm and they seem pretty keen to buy it. We'll wait and see what our unknown hopeful feels about that.'

231

'Well the sooner we sell the better. We can spend that money on improvements to the other mills.'

'We're not in this on our own,' Grandfather said, 'we're a combine, we do things together or not at all.'

'Well of course, but they don't all have our resources.'

'We pay equal shares. Neither one of us paying more than the other. I don't intend to plough everything I own into the business, particularly now when the Far East is stealing our trade.'

Across the room his eyes met mine, and sarcastically he said, 'Isn't this usually where my granddaughter tells me it's our own fault, that we shouldn't have been so ready to teach them our business.'

'What does Amanda know about cotton?' Aunt Edith snapped.

'Exactly,' Grandfather agreed.

Now was not the time to argue, that would come later. But I was dismally aware of the powerful opposition I would face and how far would Phillip be able to help me?

They were talking about Alice.

'I still think she should go to boarding school,' Aunt Myrtle was saying. 'It would do the girl a power of good, improve her personality, help to erase all these last painful memories.'

'I'll play it one day at a time, Mother,' Ralph said firmly.

'It could be that Alice will be happier at home. She's a lot like her mother and Jenny hated anything new and different in her life.'

'And I think she should be weaned off her mother's likes and dislikes. Alice must change, we don't want her going the same way as her mother, do we?'

'With respect, Mother none of you really took the trouble to get to know Jenny, or Alice either for that matter.'

'That's unfair, Ralph,' Aunt Edith said stoutly. 'Look at the ball Caroline gave and she wanted to leave halfway through the evening. Look at your grandmother's constant invitations to Sunday lunch, she came twice and never again. You knew her, Amanda, before you went out to India. Did she ever write to you? Did she ever send you a picture of her little girl?'

'I never expected Jenny to write to me, Aunt Edith. She was always a shy girl. She told me she wasn't good at writing letters.'

'One makes an effort sometimes to do the thing one hates,' Aunt Myrtle said stonily.

'Jenny's gone, Mother. Isn't it time we stopped discussing her failings and concentrated on what we can all do for my daughter.'

'Well, I'm willing to have her one day a week for tea and some time during the school holidays, and her grandmother will be pleased if you join us here every Sunday for lunch. I'm sure your Aunt Edith and Uncle Edwin will have her, and Amanda will take her out whenever it's possible, isn't that right everybody?'

Everybody agreed that they would do their bit and Aunt Edith said, 'I think we should be getting home, there's nothing else to be sorted out today. I'll ask Caroline to invite Alice round for tea. She's a very busy woman but there will be a day when she's nothing much on, and it will do Alice no harm to let her friends see that Sir Philip and Lady Marston are entertaining her.'

My eyes met Ralph's across the room and I had the utmost impulse to dissolve into laughter.

They had gone and the house settled back into normality. Grandfather read his evening newspaper then dozed in his chair. Granny occupied herself with her needlework and Ralph and I played gin rummy. Promptly at nine Polly came in to ask if she should take Miss Alice a glass of milk up to her room.

'I'll take it, Polly,' I said. 'I asked her to join us down here but she preferred to sit in her room and read.'

'I've stoked up the fire Mrs St Clare, it's nice and warm in there.'

'I'll go up and have a word with her,' Ralph said. 'I asked her to come down here too but she didn't want to.'

After he had gone out Granny shook her head dismally, 'I wonder if any of us will ever be able to get close to Alice,' she said sadly.

'It's early days yet, Granny, I'll see to her milk. Is there anything you and Grandfather want from the kitchen?'

'Not just now, dear, you see to Alice.'

Alice had had her bath and was in bed. She looked remarkably like Jenny the first time I had seen her with her dark curly hair tied back from her well scrubbed face, her dark brown gentle eyes. The pages of a book lay open on the bedcovers but she was not reading. She looked up as I entered the room but there was no smile of welcome.

'I've brought you some milk, Alice. Is that all right or would you have preferred hot chocolate?'

'Milk's all right.'

'I've brought the tin of biscuits, you can help yourself. Is it a good book?'

'It's all right.'

'You don't sound very sure.'

'We're going home tomorrow. I'm glad we're going home.'

'Yes, I know you are, Alice. I'll call and see you and I'll take you out in the car one day if you'd like to come.'

'I have to go to school.'

'Of course, but you won't be at school all the time.'

When she remained silent I asked, 'You do have friends at school don't you, Alice?'

'Some.'

'Friends who would invite you to their homes and you could invite them back?'

'Not really. Mummy was always resting and they stopped asking me around.'

A wave of pity washed over me for this strange child who had had adult responsibility forced upon her before she was ready for it.

With more optimism than I believed in I said, 'I'm sure your friends will all rally round now, Alice, and one day if you like I'll take you all out to the cinema or to a theatre.'

She stared at me curiously before saying, 'My mummy once told me about you. She said you were nicer than the others but you'd gone away. Why did you go away?'

'I went to India to be with my parents, then I got married out there. India was home to me for many years.'

'What happened to your husband?'

'He was killed doing his job. For a long time I was very sad

234

but I had to come to terms with it, pick up the pieces and get on with my life. That's something you will have to do, Alice.'

'How did you do it?'

'I went back to my parents, started going to balls and polo matches again, all the things I'd done with Anthony, and then Charlotte came and we went on a long journey together. Did you never meet Charlotte?'

'I've heard of her. She never came to see us but I think I met her once at Grandma Dexter's. Wasn't she the one who went off to Africa?'

'That's Charlotte.'

'Lady Marston's sister.'

'Yes.'

'Daddy said I must call them Aunt Caroline and Aunt Charlotte but I never have. Aunt Sophie's my real aunt, isn't she?'

'Yes, she's your father's sister.'

'The girls at school had aunts and uncles and they were always around, mine never were.'

'Well your Aunt Sophie lives in London most of the time and your Aunt Caroline is a very busy woman.'

'She came to the school on speech day, she's a governor. I told the girls Lady Marston was my aunt but they didn't believe me.'

'Why didn't they believe you?'

'Because I went up to speak to her and she just stared at me, then she smiled and turned away. They must have asked around because they knew I'd been telling the truth but when she didn't speak to me they said it was because she didn't like me.'

How cruel children could be. When did they learn to be kind and supportive, why did it give them so much pleasure to be hurtful?

'Shall I put out the light, Alice, or are you going to read a little when you've finished your milk?'

'I'll put the light out.'

'Very well then. I'll see you in the morning before you go home.'

She didn't smile in answer to mine, she watched me walk towards the door where I turned to say goodnight. I knew it would take me a long time to forget the sad expression on her pretty face, the expression of a bewildered child with too many memories and precious little faith in the future.

Chapter Twenty-Three

On the day of my appointment with Phillip's solicitor I was relieved to find him waiting for me in the foyer.

'Are you quite certain this is what you want Amanda?' he asked.

'Yes. I've thought about it and I'm quite sure.'

'No turning back, no afterthoughts about taking too much on?'

'No. I have to make it work.'

'Well come along then, we'll see how much it's going to cost you.'

I knew it was going to cost much more than money: I had to face the antagonism of my grandfather and my two uncles, I had to make them see that I wasn't overriding them, thinking I could do things better. It was merely a hope I had that something could be salvaged, that something new could put life back into a small part of the industry.

We learned from the solicitor about the offers that had been made for the mill and that my grandfather and uncles were seriously considering the last offer from an engineering firm.

'They want the entire mill, not just the ground floor as so many of the other offers have bid for. Your grandfather thinks they should up their price and they probably will, but that's something that needs to be gone into when they know there's competition for the mill.'

'Whatever they offer I'll pay more.' I insisted.

'You're so sure it can be successful, Mrs St Clare?' the solicitor asked.

'I'm not sure. No. I'm hopeful.'

'You think you can find the machinery and the workpeople?'

'When I've talked to my family I hope I can persuade them to be on my side, that they'll help me with the machinery and put me in touch with the workpeople.'

'What do you think about all this, Sir Phillip?'

'I've seen her designs and they're very beautiful. I'm less sure about her family's reaction. But I have faith in Amanda, I think she can pull it off.'

'Are you ready to hear the amount offered by the engineering firm?' Mr Scotson asked, and I knew from his tone that it would surprise me.

Indeed it was double what I had envisaged, and for the first time I began to have doubts about what I was hoping to take on. I was a rich woman, but I would be risking a great deal of money. If the venture failed what would I have at the end?

My family would not come to my rescue, indeed they were more likely to say they had told me it wouldn't work, and was I really prepared to bankrupt myself for a cause only I believed in? I was aware that Philip was looking at me thoughtfully, watching the doubts cross my face, seeing the indecision, and when I turned to him appealingly, he said quietly, 'If you want help financially, Amanda, I can give it, but I know nothing about cotton, nothing about printing. You would be totally on your own. Only you can decide whether the idea is feasible.'

'You can think about if for a few days Mrs St Clare, that is all,' the solicitor said. 'Your grandfather is becoming impatient, I really do think he wants to get things finalised.'

Both men looked at me intently but neither pressed me. I would get no help from the Dexters, and I would accept none from Phillip. This was something I had to do on my own. If I sank I would have to live with it, if I swam, it would all have been worthwhile.

'Offer the Dexters ten per cent more than the last offer, but only if it is accepted at once,' I said firmly. 'If he prefers to wait to see if there's a better one forthcoming, you have my permission to withdraw mine.'

It was done. I had thrown down the gauntlet now. Only time would tell if I had made the right decision. As we

238

walked out into the chill November day, Phillip said, 'We need to talk about this Amanda, obviously as quickly as possible. Have you any suggestions?'

'I would be glad of any help you can give me about the workforce.'

'Well, employees of Dexter's are tenants on my land, I can find out whether they are to be thrown on the scrap heap and if they would work for you.' He smiled, 'I'm a very considerate landlord Amanda, they'll talk to me.'

'I'm sure the family will be furious if I accept help from you,' I answered him ruefully.

'Your family have nothing to do with what I do, Amanda. If I wish to help you, I will, and, believe me my girl, you're going to need every bit of help you can get.'

He stood looking down at me, as a friend, a benefactor, a man I could ask advice from, but in my heart at that moment was the memory of his eyes, his lips that smiled before they crushed against mine. There was nothing of that man now in the friendly, polite stranger gazing down at me encouragingly.

'Now, when can we talk this through, Amanda? One evening perhaps for dinner, or lunch if you would prefer.'

I didn't answer him immediately. I was being watched, so how would it be possible for us to meet without angering the watchers, and what about Caroline? Phillip might not care what the family said or thought, but I was the one facing their anger and condemnation.

'When I know that Grandfather has accepted my offer, I'll face them, then after that I'll be glad of your help Phillip.'

'If that's what you want, Amanda.'

'It is. And there will be absolutely no reason why Caroline can't be present when we meet. She'll probably wish to anyway.'

His face was impersonal. I could not tell if he was hurt by my decision or indifferent as he politely shook my hand saying, 'I'll hope to hear from you when you've sorted yourself out, Amanda. Please don't be afraid to get in touch.'

He was the first to drive out of the car park with a brief wave of his hand and the hurt was so intense I could have wept.

I returned home to see an unfamiliar car in the drive, the hallway cluttered with suitcases. Before I could enter the living room, Julia came running downstairs, rather more animated than I had hitherto seen her.

'I wondered if you'd still be here,' she greeted me.

I smiled. 'How long are you here for this time?'

'A month. Mummy and Daddy are going to the Far East. You can tell them all about it, can't you, you've lived there.'

'Are your parents here?'

'Yes, they're in the living room with Great Granny and Grandpa. They're staying here until Monday morning. Granny's organising a family get-together for Sunday. Mummy says it will be just like she remembers it when she was a little girl.'

My heart sank. The last thing I wanted was a family party on the day I intended to drop my bombshell to Grandfather and the uncles.

Sophie was plumper than I remembered her, a matronly figure in navy blue, heavy georgette and wearing several rows of pearls round her neck. She came forward to greet me, kissing my cheek before she took stock of me: 'You look very well, Amanda. You're very thin, but then I have put a little weight on myself. I suppose it was the climate in the Far East, it might help me to lose a little.'

Her husband came forward and shook my hand. If I had seen him outside the house I doubt I would have recognised him. He too had put on weight but it gave him a sense of importance: successful politician with a safe seat and an assured future, unless the unthinkable happened in some forthcoming election.

Granny was in high good humour. 'We're having an old-fashioned family get-together on Sunday lunchtime, Amanda, and I'm not prepared to accept excuses. Everybody has been invited to give Sophie and Jarvis a good send-off, I want Ralph to come and bring Alice. She should get to know Julia, and I've told Caroline I don't want any excuses from her.'

There would be two people missing from the family party, Charlotte and Jenny. While Jenny's absence would evoke a sense of tragedy, Charlotte's might well give rise to a devious sense of malice.

In the few days before Sunday we listened to Jarvis holding forth on a great many matters connected with the Far East, and after one lengthy debate he suddenly said, 'I have been going on a bit, haven't I. I was forgetting that you know the Far East better than most of us. What was it like out there, the poverty I mean, and the squalor?'

'Is that all you are expecting to find Jarvis? If it is, your eyes will see little of the splendour and the beauty.'

'We're spending very little time in India, so there won't be much opportunity to see the Jewel in the Crown. We're going on to Indonesia and Hong Kong, Malaysia too. I can assure you it won't be all temples and palaces.'

'Then you must make up your own mind about the Far East. You *will* see poverty and seediness, but you should not close your mind to other things. That would be a terrible mistake.'

'What about Charlotte?' Sophie put in quickly. 'Does anybody hear from her, what sort of a life will she be living?'

Granny shook her head sadly and I kept silent.

'We could have found time to visit her if she'd kept in touch; as it is we don't know where she's living. We're not going anywhere near Samarkand, isn't that where she was going to?'

'That is where she was living when she wrote to me,' I said.

'This is a trade delegation we're embarked upon,' Jarvis said. 'If she hears something about it, there's no reason why she can't meet up with us in Hong Kong or some other civilised place.'

'What do you think, Amanda?' Sophie asked.

'You're talking about great distances, I really don't know where Charlotte is likely to be.'

Inwardly I thought that Charlotte would have little interest in being anywhere near Sophie and her husband and the days leading up to Sunday only served to reassure me that I was right in this assumption.

Jarvis Holleran was a bore with the inflated opinion that he was running the country single-handed. He talked politics all the time and not even Grandfather nodding in his chair and the look of glassy inattention of Grandma's face had the power to stop him.

241

Over the years Sophie had learned the ability to switch off, and it was left to me to say either yes or no and nod in the appropriate places.

One evening I caught Julia grinning at me wickedly from her place at the table and later she said, 'Daddy's a terrible bore about politics, he goes on and on all the time.'

'Perhaps he doesn't know anything else.'

'He doesn't think there is anything else. Will Alice be coming here on Sunday?'

'Yes, I hope so.'

'I don't know her. I never met her. Why did her mother commit suicide?'

'I don't think we should talk about it, Julia, and we mustn't talk about it to Alice, it would be very unkind.'

'Granny Dexter says she might be going away to boarding school.'

'I didn't know.'

'Mummy says it's the best thing for her. Uncle Ralph is far too busy to cope.'

From Julia's conversation I gathered that Alice's future had been well and truly discussed in Uncle William's household but I doubted if Alice's thoughts on the matter had counted.

On Sunday morning the household was astir early and Grandma was happily flitting in and out of the kitchen to assure herself that everything was going to plan. It was a family gathering similar to those I remembered from my childhood. Only now the children had grown up and no longer arrived with their parents.

Sophie greeted her mother and father with great affection and I wondered why they didn't stay with them instead of staying with my grandparents. It soon became clear when Aunt Myrtle said, 'The decorators haven't finished yet, the entire house is upset.'

Aunt Edith and Uncle Edwin were next to arrive, and after a quick glance round the room Aunt Edith said, 'Caroline is coming I hope, I told her not to be late.'

'They're here now,' Uncle William said from his place at the window. 'Ralph and Alice are here too. That's the family complete I think.'

Caroline and Sophie greeted each other effusively and I was amused when Caroline trilled, 'Darling, you've put on a little weight, you'll have to bant like mad to get rid of it.'

'It's all those political dinners. How do you manage to stay so slim?'

'Oh, I watch what I eat. One has to, you know. The social whirl is death to one's figure.'

'Amanda never puts an ounce on,' Ralph said with a smile in my direction. 'She's as youthful and beautiful as she always was.'

Neither Caroline or Sophie commented, although I knew his words had been designed to annoy them. Ralph had always had the unfortunate ability to say the wrong thing at the wrong time.

I handed glasses of sherry around the guests and Phillip accepted his with a smile, before turning away to resume his conversation with Grandfather.

The food tasted of nothing and once Grandmother said, 'You're not eating very much, Amanda. Is everything all right?'

'Yes of course. I'm not really hungry.'

'That's the reason you're so thin, Amanda, you're afraid to eat,' Caroline said sweetly.

Alice and Julia sat together at the other end of the table. Unsurprisingly they had little to say to one another. Alice had all her mother's diffidence and Julia was abrasive and had already formed the opinion that her cousin was hopeless.

I was nervous and as the talk went on over the table I was rehearsing in my minds the words I would say later. Once I caught Phillip's eyes upon me across the table and he smiled. I knew that he was aware of my anxiety but I was wishing it was a normal Sunday with just my grandfather and two uncles present.

The meal was over at last and Granny was the first to rise to her feet saying, 'We'll have our coffee in the drawing room. This is the time the men talk nothing but business.'

The women drifted away but, turning to Phillip, Caroline said, 'You won't forget that I have to meet the show committee at Mrs Ancliffe's this afternoon, darling.'

'Really,' her mother said sharply. 'Surely you could have

put them off for one afternoon. They could have managed without you.'

'Not really Mother, I'm the chairwoman.'

'Well, you could have tried. If you're late they'll have to go along without you.'

'I don't intend to be late. I'm noted for my punctuality.'

Today is not the right day, I was telling myself. Tomorrow I'll go down to the mills and speak to them in the office. Granny was urging Julia and Alice to get to know each other, that they might even take a walk in the garden if they wrapped up warmly, but Aunt Myrtle said sharply, 'They can chat in the morning room. It's far too cold to go outside.'

I was still sitting at the table and looking at me curiously Granny said, 'Are you coming dear? I'm sure you're not interested in men's talk.'

I rose to my feet and turned to leave the table when Phillip said softly, 'You're leaving us Amanda?'

I stared at him, seeing the encouragement in his smile, and then was it really my voice saying, 'I need to speak to you Grandfather.'

He looked at me with an impatient frown, 'Not now girl, your uncles and I have urgent business to attend to. I know it's not of much interest to Jarvis and Phillip, but we're to give an answer tomorrow. Today's the only time we've got.'

I knew that the answer he had to give was to my offer and tomorrow was the deadline for it. Today was my last chance to tell him the offer for the Number Three mill had come from me.

I sat down at the table and by this time I was aware of their eyes staring at me in various degrees of surprise, impatience and annoyance.

Grandfather said sharply, 'Well then, get it over quickly and then go and join the others.'

'Grandfather, I know that you want to discuss an offer you have had for Number Three mill, and I have to tell you that the offer comes from me. I want to buy it.'

If I had said I wanted to set fire to it, their astonishment could not have been more profound. Only Phillip's face remained serene.

Grandfather's face was red with anger, the rest of them

incredulous, and there was truculence in his voice as he shouted at me, 'What in heaven's name do you want the mill for? Some hare-brained scheme that makes you think you can do better than any of us? Don't you think I've had enough of you telling me we've been doing things wrong, that suddenly you can come back from India to tell us how to run things, now you're setting up in competition, are you?'

'No Grandfather, that isn't my idea at all.'

'Well, you're not interested in buying the mill to do anything for us, you're only interested in furthering your own crackpot ideas.'

'I don't happen to think they are crackpot. I think they can work, and I think they can work for Dexter's. You're getting rid of a lot of workpeople. I think I could find some of them employment. You could help me with machinery and if it doesn't work, you won't have lost anything, I shall be the loser, me and only me.'

'And what makes you think you could find them work when we can't?'

'New designs, new ideas.'

'Are you telling me that the designs Dexter's has made its own are worthless? Let me tell you, my girl, that they have been accepted in the finest houses in the country and they'll go on being accepted. Those designs will go on as long as they're wanted and they will be wanted just as they've always been.'

'But don't you think there's room for new ideas, new designs? If we don't produce them, other industries and other countries will.'

'Here we go again, you're talking about the Far East and I've heard it all before from you. How we trained them and how they've beaten us, you know nothing about it, my girl.'

'I know what I've seen in the Far East. I know about the sweat-shops and the slave labour, I know about designs that are so beautiful if you'd give them half a chance you could take something back from what they've taken from you.'

'And I'm not prepared to listen to any more. I won't have my granddaughter telling me how to run my business.'

'Does that mean that you are not accepting my offer to buy the mill?'

'Yes. The engineering business can have it.'

245

'You're afraid to sell it to me? You're afraid of being wrong, you're afraid of competition?'

'I've never been afraid of competition.'

'You're afraid now. You had nothing to fear from competition churning out the predictable time-worn designs, designs that never changed, designs that were unimaginative. Now, because I'm offering something new, something different, you are afraid. Why don't you let me try, if I fail, you'll be able to say I told you so and it will be my money that's been lost, not yours.'

'I'm half-minded to let that happen. It might be the only way to teach you not to meddle in things that don't concern you.'

He stared round the table belligerently and Uncle William said, 'If you take the engineering company's offer, we'll be down thousands, if Amanda wants to take the risk, she's the one who'll suffer from it.'

'You mean you think we should accept her offer?'

Uncle William shrugged his shoulders and Uncle Edwin said, 'What do you intend to call this enterprise of yours?'

'Can't it be part of Dexter's?'

'Dexter's is going into a combine with other manufacturers. You'll be entirely on your own.'

'Then it's something I shall have to think about.'

'Well, I can tell you now, it won't last long enough for you to have much time for thinking,' Grandfather snapped. 'Did you ever hear such a crack-brained thing?'

'I don't think it's a good thing to be condemning it before it's had a chance of getting off the ground. I've seen some of Amanda's designs, they're very beautiful. I think there's room for the time-worn designs and the new adventurous ones,' Phillip said evenly.

'With respect Phillip,' Grandfather said, 'you've never concerned yourself with the cotton industry. Are you the right person to be taking Amanda's part?'

'I'm entitled to express my opinion and I do think that instead of deflating her you could try to encourage her. I would have thought you could find some element of pride in a granddaughter, who's shown some sort of enthusiasm for the industry. I have to confess that my wife has shown none

246

at all.' He looked round and one by one they looked down at the table. 'I can see that you understand what I'm trying to say,' Phillip continued. 'The Dexter women have been more interested in enjoying the money without too much insight into how it is made.'

I was not asked to leave the meeting again, instead I was told tersely by Grandfather that they would accept my offer, but there would be no assistance coming from them with regard to workpeople or machinery.

He regarded my interference in his business as a betrayal of family trust, and that I was a wilful, arrogant woman and if the enterprise failed, as it was sure to, I could expect no help from any of them to recover the loss I would sustain.

He said under no circumstances did he wish to hear anymore about it in his house. It was a business enterprise to be discussed between my solicitor and his or in the mill office and he ended, 'And now young lady I would like to talk to your uncles. Perhaps you will join the other women in the drawing room and leave us in peace.'

Phillip crossed the room to open the door for me. His smile was encouraging but in my heart was a deep and bitter hurt.

Chapter Twenty-Four

I stood in the empty vastness of the ground floor of the mill that was now mine, looking round with a great despair in my heart. The silence was profound and I was remembering the noise, the clanging of machinery, the shouting voices of the women calling to each other across the aisles, the camaraderie.

All I had was a pipe-dream with substance, and my family had shown me clearly in the days since that Sunday meeting that they wanted no part. Even Ralph had told me I had been foolish.

'It won't work, Amanda,' he had said. 'You know nothing about the industry. You're beaten before you've even started.'

I believed him. I had not seen Phillip, although my solicitors had assured me he was very much involved. I did not ask how. I was beginning to lose faith in the enterprise and in myself.

I drifted into the tiny office where there was a telephone switchboard and several desks. I had to find office staff, but before I could do that I had to be sure I had machinery and workpeople who knew what they were about.

I sat at one of the desks looking out of the window. The grey early December day was depressing. The fells were shrouded in mist and it was raining. It always seemed to be raining, I thought miserably. Why did I remember India's sunshine and forget her rain, why did I forget England's sunshine and see only her rain?

A car was driving through the gates and my heart lifted when I recognised Phillip's low-slung tourer. He brought it to rest outside the main doorway and the sound of his footsteps crossing the empty floor echoed noisily in the stillness.

I stared into his eyes across the room and he smiled. 'I thought you might be here, Amanda,' he said. 'Don't let this emptiness depress you, it isn't for ever.'

'I can't help thinking I've been wrong, Phillip. I've been arrogant and foolish, just as Grandfather told me. Look around you, how can it ever come to life?'

'You're not alone, Amanda. I've contacted several manufacturers who are closing mills down. They're prepared to let you have machinery and Stedman's are getting out of block printing – some of their stuff is for sale. I've also found a man who knows something about pattern-making and block-printing. He worked for Arundale's.'

'Doesn't he still work for them?'

'No. Arundale's have been going through a bad patch, they've been worse hit than a great many of the cotton mills. The old man died and the interest went out of the industry. Now they've cut their losses and sold out. Most of their workpeople were made redundant and it's not easy getting back into cotton now that the industry is to be condensed.'

'Would he be prepared to work for me?'

'You need to talk to him, Amanda. He worked for Dexter's a long time ago and he had a difference of opinion with your grandfather who fired him. He went over to Dronsfield to work for Arundale's and he never liked the travelling. Like I said Amanda, he'd like to get back to working in this town but you're a Dexter, a lot of the bitterness still lingers, you'd have to convince him that working for you won't be like working for your grandfather.'

'I'd need others Phillip. If he decides to work for me, would he be able to help?'

'I'm sure he would. There's a lot of unemployment in the town, I don't think you'll have any difficulty in finding winders and weavers, block-printing is a specialised industry, but if you can persuade him to come here he'll be a tower of strength. Your grandfather was foolish to let him go. Apparently the family have put out several feelers to get him back but he wasn't having any.'

He put his hands on my shoulders, looking sternly into my eyes.

'Amanda, you have to make this work, you have to show

249

them that you were right and they were wrong, and I'll help you as much as I can.'

'Will he come here to see me or should I go to see him at his home?'

'He lives in one of the cottages on my land, the last one before you get to the church.'

'Isn't he working at all right now?'

'No. I don't suppose there's much money going into the house.'

'Phillip, you're being so kind. I hesitate to ask more of you. I really don't want to upset Caroline.'

'Amanda, there's something you must understand. Marriage to me is not what Caroline thought it would be. She anticipated a life of long country weekends in stately homes, balls and garden parties, race meetings and foreign travel. That's not for me, Amanda. I have an estate to manage and like most other families the war made a large inroad into my finances. Death duties were crippling and because she made no effort to understand, I stopped trying to explain things to her.'

His expression was bleak. I wanted to ask him about the child Caroline had lost but something stopped me. It was too personal, too sad, and almost as if he read my thoughts he said, 'I thought the child might bring us closer together, but when she lost it everything else seemed to end.'

'That must have made Caroline very unhappy too, Phillip.'

He looked away through the windows at the dripping trees and I knew at that moment that his thoughts were far away from the chill empty room and when eventually he turned towards me I was very aware of the pain in his eyes.

'She didn't want the child, Amanda,' he said flatly. 'She hadn't been well and the doctor had advised her to rest. Instead she danced the night away at the hunt ball and when I remonstrated with her she had the groom saddle her horse and she rode across the fell in a heavy mist. I went out looking for her. She'd been thrown from her horse near a hedge somewhere on the moor and I had to get help from a local farmer to get her home.

'She lost the baby next morning and she was ill for several weeks after that.'

250

'But she was sad?'

'No Amanda, she was relieved. She informed me as soon as she was well enough to get back into the stream of life that she did not intend to have another child. A child would complicate her life and she had never been maternally minded.'

'And you mind Phillip?'

'Well of course I mind. I mind for obvious reasons, but it has also shown me the state of our marriage. We don't have one, except in name.'

'But you will stay together Phillip, for the sake of convention, even though that's all that's left?'

'You're wrong Amanda. Caroline will hang on to me, not because she loves me but because of all the material advantages she derives from being my wife, but I don't have to stay in a loveless marriage for the sake of convention as you put it. I'm prepared to be brave about this, how brave are you prepared to be?'

I stared at him wide-eyed, and with my heart beating wildly. 'Oh Phillip,' I murmured. 'Do you really think this is the time?'

We both knew it was not. He would not have to come to me as a prop for me to lean on. The family would despise me as a helpless foolish woman who had not been ashamed to steal Caroline's husband to help her out of an ambition to prove them wrong. I had to be strong, a successful woman who was able to stand alone so that we could come together out of love instead of gratitude.

He took hold of my hands and gripped them firmly in his. He understood what I was trying to say and when he held me trembling against him we did not need passion to demonstrate the love we had for each other.

That embrace was a promise that one day we would be together,and when that time came nothing and nobody would have the power to keep us apart.

'Don't stay here too long, Amanda. I don't like to think of you in this cold lonely room,' he said gently.

'I'm ready to leave now. Tomorrow I'll go to see the man you told me about, you didn't tell me his name?'

'Tom Kendal.'

'Then I'll call to see him tomorrow.'

'I'll call and tell him you'll be around in the morning. Perhaps he'll come here with you and he'll be able to advise you on a great many things. When shall I see you again Amanda?'

'I'll be spending time here.'

'Either here or at the solicitor's. There's an awful lot of work to be done on this project, Amanda, but I really think you're off the ground.'

He didn't attempt to kiss me and I was glad. I heard his footsteps crossing the room and running down the stone steps to the outside door, then I watched him walking quickly across to his car. He looked up and raised his hand before he got in the car and drove away.

Tom Kendal and his wife received me shyly. I was ushered into the immaculate parlour of their stone cottage and Mrs Kendal immediately produced coffee and warm scones generously buttered.

After we had chatted about the weather, the state of the cotton industry and the changes going on in the town generally Mrs Kendal excused herself and Tom sat back to await whatever I had come to tell him. I was aware that they had been in awe of me. Dexter's granddaughter, Lady Marston's cousin, and I was anxious to reassure him that I had come in neither of those capacities.

'How much has Sir Phillip told you about my plans for the mill Mr Kendal?'

'He told me that ye 'ad some new designs ye were anxious to try out, and that ye'd bought the mill and intended to employ people. Will it be an extension o' Dexter's, Mrs St Clare?'

'I had hoped it might be, but now I know that it will not. My grandfather and my uncles are opposed to my buying the mill so you will understand I'm entirely on my own in this venture. I know very little about the industry, but with the right people around me I hope to learn. Do you think I can succeed without the Dexter family behind me?'

'I wouldn't want to work for Dexter's ma'am. I went to work for your grandfather when I left school years afore, I worked hard and I got promoted, then I did or said somethin' that the old man didn't agree with and 'e sacked mi on the spot. I ate 'umble pie and apologised, not because I thought I'd done anything wrong but I 'ad a wife and children to care for and we needed the money. 'E wouldn't listen to me, 'e said 'e'd got somebody else in the job and I wasn't needed.'

'I'm sorry. I know my grandfather can be high-handed, I've had experience of it from my girlhood in his house. You found something else though?'

'Yes, I went to work for Arundale's and I was 'appy there even when I didn't like travellin'. Now, they've wound up their business and their workforce are lookin' for other work. It's not easy to find these days. The industry's in decline and all the mills are sufferin'. There's nothin' round 'ere for me. I'm fifty years old, there are younger men than me without work.'

'But you have experience in the sort of thing I'm looking for. I intend to start in a small way on two floors. It isn't a large mill but I thought one floor for the looms, the other for the printing. Can you help in finding good weavers? I'm hoping to buy looms from some of the mills closing down, and you will know from experience what sort of help you'll require.'

'Can I take a look at your designs then?'

'Yes. I've brought a book of them here for you to see. I want to get away from the sort of thing Dexter's has been doing for years, I don't want to put it out of business, only to give people a choice of something different.'

I passed the book over and watched while he turned over the pages. His honest stolid face showed no emotion and my heart sank. Perhaps he thought I was asking too much, perhaps he didn't agree that the designs were worthy of a second thought? At last he looked up and handed the book back.

'Don't you like them?'

'They're beautiful, Mrs St Clare, they're certainly different. What sort o' flowers are they then?'

'Lotus flowers, we call them water lilies, and hibiscus, orchids and tropical birds. Believe me, I've seen birds like that in the Far East, and flowers. I thought they would make a change from English roses and ferns.'

'That they will.'

'Can you copy them?'

'Why not? I had no trouble with the roses and the other flowers. I'll enjoy somethin' different.'

'Does that mean you'll come to work for me?'

'It does.'

'And you can find me adequate work people, people you know and are sure of.'

'I can. Some of 'em might 'ave to travel and they might not like that, I know I didn't, but work's work and I doubt if they'll turn up their noses at it.'

'I'll pay good wages, and we'll all be in it together. I know that Dexter's had a good reputation as employers even though my grandfather was a stern and often unfeeling boss, but in this case I don't want you to think of me as a Dexter and it's not going to be known as Number Three mill from now on. I've rechristened it Lotus Mill.'

'That's nice, Mrs St Clare, that's real nice ... When will ye be recruitin' your workforce so that I can tell them to call in to see you?'

'As soon as possible. Shall we say next Monday, morning and afternoon.'

'That'll be fine. I suppose you'll be wantin' office staff?'

'Well yes. I know of a good book-keeper and I'll want a typist, and a girl to handle the telephone and other duties.'

'Mi daughter's bin 'avin' shorthand and typing lessons and she's doin' real well. Our Evie's a nice girl, she's seventeen and she's anxious to get on. Can I bring 'er to see you Mrs St Clare?'

'Yes of course. Will she like working in a mill office?'

'She'll take work wherever it's offered. She'd ideas o' becomin' a secretary to some 'igh flyin' captain of industry, but there's not so many o' them about round 'ere. I reckon she'll settle for working at Lotus Mill.'

I laughed 'In that case, we'll have to encourage her with a new desk and typewriter. We'll make the office look cheerful and we'll put a carpet on the floor to emulate the best Dexter's could do.'

He laughed. 'I'll not 'ave ye spoilin' her, Mrs St Clare, I'll be keepin' my eye on 'er from the mill floor.'

How quickly it all seemed to fall into place after that meeting. The looms and other machinery arrived, and, in days, it was looking less like a mausoleum and more like a working cotton mill. I spent all Monday with Mr Kendal in the refurnished office interviewing my potential workforce, men who had been loom tacklers and women who were weavers, young girls who wanted to learn, seeking employment to sweep the aisles and brew the tea. As well as two young men who Mr Kendal assured me knew a thing or two about block-printing and would be invaluable in helping him.

The small office with its two rooms had an air of efficiency. I had carpeted the rooms and the walls had been colour-washed in cream paint. I had installed a large walnut desk for myself in one room and in the other three smaller desks, one incorporating a telephone switchboard, one adorned with a brand new typewriter, while the other slightly larger, was for my book-keeper.

Eric Vincent was a young man with a large moustache, dark suit and impeccable white shirt. His conversation was studied, his diction precise, but he produced excellent references, and with a twinkle in his eye Tom Kendal assured me that he would prove entirely satisfactory.

I had already interviewed Evie, Tom Kendal's daughter. She was a pretty girl with an open laughing face who, I suspected, would be something of a torment in Eric Vincent's life. The other girl I employed for the office had left school in the summer and failed to find work. She was the daughter of a woman who had been a weaver for Dexter's and whose father had been a tackler, both of them now out of work. Anna was going to nightschool to learn secretarial subjects and told me she didn't want to end up working in a mill like her parents. She was a typical down-to-earth girl from that area of the town that hid behind spotless lace curtains and regularly went to church on Sundays.

I was seldom at home while all this was going on, invariably arriving home long after the family had eaten, which meant that I didn't have to suffer Grandfather's disapproval or Granny's unease. I neither saw nor heard from Phillip, yet strangely I was aware of his presence in the advice I was receiving from his solicitor and in the excellence of the equipment that was coming into the mill.

Strangely enough, it was Ralph who called in to see me in the office late one afternoon, who remarked upon the quality of the machinery.

'How did you manage to get hold of stuff like this?' he enquired. 'I wanted some of it, and was told it had already been disposed of.'

'I heard about it and made an offer,' I replied shortly.

'You mean somebody else heard about it and made an offer on your behalf,' he said with a smile.

When I didn't answer he said, 'Seen anything of Phillip recently, I heard he was away visiting his mother.'

'Really, I didn't know.'

'You couldn't have done all this on your own, Amanda. You've got hold of Tom Kendal and he lives on Marston land. He was the best block-printer Dexter's ever had until he crossed swords with the old man. That was his undoing.'

'Oh I don't know. Tom seems to have been very happy working for Arundale's. I've got his daughter working for me too.'

'He'll have his lad in the business too when he leaves school, you can rely on that.'

'I shan't mind if he's as good as Tom.'

'Seen anything of Caroline?'

'Of course not. I've seen nothing of Alice either, how is she?'

'The housekeeper isn't working out. I'm thinking of sending her away to school. Perhaps the one young Julia's at.'

'Your mother will like that.'

'I know. She never has much time for her grandchildren, it's always Grandmother who gets lumbered.'

'I think Granny might appreciate it if you dropped in to see her one day Ralph.'

'I will, one day when I have the time.'

I watched him walking through the large room filled with

the sound of looms and the voices of the weavers. They treated him with respect, he was a Dexter, a man to be greeted with fingers raised to touch a cap or a bending of the knee from some of the women in the aisles.

It was feudal, a legacy from sterner days when cotton was king in Lancashire, a time-worn ritual of a workforce conditioned to believe that the factory masters were their betters, but to me there was something strangely distasteful in its continuance in my mill.

My great grandfather had worked hard to bequeath the cotton empire to his son and his grandsons, I wondered how many of his great grandchildren appreciated or deserved it.

Chapter Twenty-Five

It was the moodiest, gloomiest Christmas I could remember. There was precious little Christmas spirit at the dinner table and I quickly realised that neither my grandfather nor my uncles had any intention of asking me any questions about my new venture.

Ralph had taken Alice to some country hotel where he hoped to meet up with his golfing friends and his parents seemed to think it was a most unsuitable Christmas holiday for both of them.

Sophie and her husband were still abroad and Julia had decided to spend Christmas in the home of one of her school friends. Caroline and Phillip were visiting his mother.

'Caroline didn't want to go,' Aunt Edith said. 'She says it will be deadly dull and she really wanted to spend Christmas abroad or in London. Phillip said he had no objections if she went away with friends but his mother wasn't well and he had promised to be with her. I advised Caroline to go with him, there's been enough talk already and Christmas is a time when they should be together.'

By the end of the day I was asking myself what I was doing here. I was being made to feel an interloper and the rest of the holiday stretched in front of me in dreary monotony.

The two aunts chatted on how they intended to spend New Year's Eve, both apparently at dinner parties with different friends and I knew what that meant, there would only be me and my grandparents in the house and I knew I couldn't face it.

'What will you be doing, Amanda?' Aunt Myrtle asked.

'I'm not sure. Perhaps I'll visit my grandparents in Devon.'

'Are they expecting you?'

'No, but they'll be glad to see me, I expect.'

'The weather forecast is vile, travelling at this time of the year can be simply awful,' Aunt Edith said.

'Will you be driving there?' she asked shortly.

'I haven't really decided yet.'

But I didn't go in the end. The weather lived up to its dismal forecast with hail and sleet falling from leaden skies and never had the Pennine hills seemed more menacing and hostile.

On New Year's Eve I set out to walk to the mill. A thin drizzle of snow was falling but it was better than staying in the house where Grandfather slept morosely in his chair and Granny's knitting needles clicked endlessly.

As I took out my key to unlock the large iron gates, Ned the watchman came out of the cottage opposite but seeing that it was me he said with a grin, 'Oh it's you, Mrs St Clare. I thown we 'ad intruders, I didn't recognise ye in yer trousers and riding mac.'

He stared at me curiously and I said quickly, 'I need to look at some papers in my office Ned, I shan't be long.'

The empty rooms of the mill without their habitual clatter of machinery seemed forlorn and gloomy. I switched on the light over my desk and sat for a long time staring through the window into the empty weaving shed; a feeling of despair swept over me.

What had I done?

I might be a Dexter but I knew precious little about cotton. Had I really squandered the substantial legacy Anthony had left me in an enterprise doomed to failure? I was imagining the disdain of my grandfather and the rest of them when it failed. I was so sunk in despair I did not hear the sound of footsteps crossing the factory floor until my door opened and Phillip stood staring at me across the room.

'I saw the light from the road, Amanda. What on earth are you doing here on this dismal afternoon with no heat in the place? Are you trying to catch pneumonia?'

I was ashamed of the hot scalding tears that coursed down my cheeks and the sobs in my throat, before he strode across the room and took me into his arms. My voice was babbling on about the mistake I believed I had made, about the intransigence of my family and he listened without speaking, holding me close until the sobs ceased and I moved away from him confused and ashamed.

'What is all this?' he asked gently. 'Where is that girl who had such ambition, such plans that she could do anything she wanted to do, that she would show them all? You're halfway there, Amanda, you have the machinery and the workforce, why are you so sure you've made a mistake?'

I shook my head miserably.

'I suppose you've had a rotten Christmas surrounded by your family, and they won't have made it easy for you?'

'No, they didn't.'

'Well, you've got to prove them wrong Amanda. You can do it.'

'It's everything, Phillip. The atmosphere around the house, even Grandma is disappointed in me.'

'She has to put your grandfather first, Amanda, or at least be seen to be putting him first. I know what they're like. What plans have you made for the New Year?'

'Only to try hard to make this project work.'

'I wasn't meaning that. I suppose it will be the family as usual on New Year's Day, but what of the night before?'

'Nothing.'

'Well, Caroline has decided to invite people to dinner, I don't know many of them, but at least it will be some sort of festivity. I believe she's invited her parents and I'm inviting you and your grandparents. I'll drive you home and ask them when we get there.'

'I can't think they'll come. Grandfather hates having to get dressed up and making conversation with people he doesn't know.'

'Well if they don't want to come themselves they can't stop you coming.'

'They won't approve of my coming.'

'Probably not, but it is my house and I am inviting you. Instead of being difficult, Amanda, perhaps they should try to see beyond what's happening now.'

'I don't know what you mean.'

'I think you do, my dear.'

My grandparents were predictably unenthusiastic about spending New Year's Eve at Caroline's dinner party. I sensed Phillip's exasperation with both of them. At last he said, 'Well, I can understand if you're worried about icy roads, I'll call for you and bring you back and you need not stay longer than you wish.'

Still they prevaricated, and Phillip in some desperation said, 'Very well, if you'd rather not come, I understand, but I think Amanda should come. It will be New Year's Eve after all.'

That was when Granny decided they would go after all. I did not miss the cynicism in Phillip's expression as he made arrangements to call for us.

'We could get a taxi, Phillip,' I said.

'I doubt if it will be possible at this late stage, Amanda. They've probably been booked, now that the weather's turned nasty.'

'Does Caroline know you intended to invite us?' Granny asked pointedly.

'I'm sure she would like you to be there, but in any case, I'm inviting you. Does it make any difference?'

'Well no, Phillip, I just don't want to put her out.'

'Well that's settled then.'

It was not an evening I was looking forward to. Over lunch Granny said, 'What will you be wearing tonight, Amanda?'

'A dress I wore in India, something very plain. The beauty is in the material.'

'I shall wear my brown georgette and everybody will be remembering how long I've had it.'

'I doubt they'll even notice, Granny.'

She smiled ruefully. 'They will if they're Caroline's friends. Her mother says she runs with some very smart people, men who are doing great things in the city and their wives who sit on the committees with her.'

I knew exactly the sort of people who would be there. Women like Caroline who looked at you and knew the price of everything you were wearing, and men, streetwise and successful, but I comforted myself with the thought that they were not Phillip's sort either.

261

On the evening of the dinner party I looked in the long cheval mirror in my bedroom to assess how I looked. The dress was beautiful, and I knew there would be nothing at the party like it. It needed no jewellery to enhance it and the material glowed in shades of jade and turquoise, soft delicate pinks and peacock blue.

It fell in long exquisite folds to my feet and as I walked down the stairs to where my grandparents waited in the hall, I was immediately aware of Granny's long penetrating stare. She would have preferred me in something predictable, something that would not have been a challenge to anything my cousin would be wearing.

'I should wear your long fur coat Amanda. It's very cold outside,' she advised me, and I knew she was hoping the coat would cover the glamour of my gown, hiding it away from any admiration in Phillip's eyes.

Phillip arrived promptly and it was laughable to see how Granny almost pushed me into the back seat of his car to sit with her while Grandfather sat at the front with Phillip.

Lights blazed the length of the hall windows, lighting up the gloom on that cold December night. As we entered the house I was instantly aware of voices and laughter, and soft music, and then a manservant was coming forward to take our outdoor clothing. In the next minute Caroline was there, smiling and embracing and ushering us forward to meet her guests.

Brightly she exclaimed, 'I want you to meet my darling cousin Amanda who has surprised us all by taking on the Dexter empire single-handed. My relatives never fail to surprise me, I have a cousin who is scaring the wits out of us, and a sister who elected to marry a descendant of Genghis Khan and is living somewhere in Outer Mongolia.'

Laughter echoed round the room and she stood beside me with her arm in mine before she turned to appraise my gown with narrowed eyes.

'I'm sure you didn't buy that in England,' she said.

'No I didn't. I believe the material originated in Outer Mongolia which you seem to find so terribly backward.'

'Oh well. I never was any good at geography or history for that matter. Come and meet my guests, most of them are my

262

friends although there are one or two cronies of Phillip's dotted here and there.'

The women smiled and eyed my gown, the men became over gallant and one man took hold of my hand and held it in spite of his wife's annoyed glance.

'So you're the young lady who has taken on the Dexter empire. Don't you think you've bitten off more than you can chew?'

'It's early days yet, so it's impossible to say.'

'I'll bet old man Dexter doesn't approve of what you're doing.'

'Do you know my grandfather?'

'Only by reputation. My father's a member of the same lodge. You haven't got a drink. Come along, I'll help you.'

With his hand under my elbow he ushered me towards the drinks table and while we waited for our drinks he said, 'I'd like your venture to really take off. Caroline's pretty adamant that you'll fail, it would be nice to see her proved wrong.'

'I take it you're not all that fond of my cousin Caroline.'

'Oh she's nice enough, great friend of Alison's, my wife, but I've known her before she was Lady Marston. Caroline doesn't change.'

I decided to remain silent, and after a few moments he said, 'What's all this about Charlotte? Is it true she's married a chap from the Far East?'

'Quite true.'

'Caroline says he's as rich as Croesus. Maybe it's that that is troubling our lady of the manor.'

'I really have no idea. Charlotte and I never discussed money, I do think it's terribly vulgar, don't you?'

I had the satisfaction of seeing him blush, and in the next moment he was saying quickly, 'Tell me a little of your venture in the mill, I'm very interested.'

'It's all really far too soon to speculate, it's something I wanted to do. I can only hope it will be successful.'

'Well if you need a good accountant I hope you'll remember me. We have a very good and lucrative practice in the town.'

'I have an accountant already – Sir Phillip's. He's been very good and helpful since I decided to go into business. I couldn't think of changing him.'

My eyes met Phillip's across the room and he must have read the desperation in them, because in the next minute he had joined us saying evenly, 'I have a friend here I would like you to meet, Amanda, will you excuse us.'

The friend was a white-haired elderly man with keen intelligent eyes and a disarming smile. His name was John Stedman.

'Phillip's told me a lot about you, Mrs St Clare,' he said. 'I'm very interested in what you're proposing to do at the mill.'

I laughed. 'That is what the last gentleman was interested in.'

They both laughed and John Stedman said, 'For very different reasons I feel sure. At least I hope it's for a different reason.'

'John is in interior decorating, Amanda, not accountancy. Tell him about your designs and your plans for them. I'll leave you two together, perhaps I should circulate amongst our guests.'

'Why don't we find somewhere a little less crowded,' he said. 'I've been a guest here a good many times, I always feel most at home in the room I remember best.'

It was the room Phillip had left unchanged from his parents' time, the only room Caroline had left untouched by her taste.

We sat in front of the fire on a comfortable chintz-covered settee and I was aware of gentle colours and an air of good taste.

'I've been admiring your gown, Mrs St Clare, in a room filled with strident colour it stands out like a shaded lagoon.'

I laughed. 'That's a very unusual compliment, Mr Stedman. I can understand why you entered the world of interior decorating.'

'A very successful world, Mrs St Clare.'

I stared at him doubtfully and he smiled.

'I have a great many influential customers, rich people, aristocratic, theatrical, even the patronage of royalty and all of them looking for something different. Your gown is different. If you can produce something as beautiful as this I would be very interested indeed.'

'This material was bought abroad where designs and colours like it have been produced on silk for centuries. I hope to copy my designs on damask and linen, I'm not sure yet how successful I'll be.'

'As I said, Mrs St Clare, if you can produce something as beautiful and elegant as this on furnishing materials, I will be your first customer. Will you keep me informed, allow me to see what you are producing?'

'Yes of course, I'll be happy to.'

'In the meantime I would like to visit you at the mill one day. I know it's early days but Phillip didn't seem to think you would object.'

'No I'd be delighted. Perhaps you'll telephone me when you intend to visit.'

'Certainly. I wouldn't like to pounce on you and find you unprepared.'

'Perhaps we should go back to the others now,' I said hesitantly.

'Of course. We don't wish to appear unsociable.'

The evening passed pleasantly enough, the wine flowed, and Caroline had installed an army of waiters to attend to the needs of her guests. There was laughter and excited chatter, and through it all I saw my grandmother sitting next to Aunt Edith, looking slightly bemused and out of place, while Grandfather had long since departed to sleep the evening away in a quiet room.

Soon after twelve with everybody kissing everybody else I looked up into Phillip's eyes as he embraced me gently and kissed me, the gentle kiss of a brother before saying, 'Happy New Year, darling, the first of a great many more I hope.'

For a long moment he stared down at me, then with a smile he released me and across the room I saw Caroline watching, her eyes hard and angry, and I wanted to go home.

When I reached Granny's side Aunt Edith said sharply, 'We're taking you home. It isn't right for Phillip to have to leave his guests and I think we're just about ready to leave. Stay here with Granny. I'll go and find the others.'

It had started to snow, fine powdery snow that covered the

parkland and shone in sparkling points of light in the car's headlights. Nobody spoke on that journey back to Fairlawn. I couldn't tell if it was because we were tired or for some other reason, but as we took our leave of my aunt and uncle I was dismally aware of Aunt Edith's cold response to my proffered thanks for driving us home.

It should have worried me, but I was too mindful of John Stedman's interest in my new venture to think about anything else. I was glad Christmas and New Year were over. Tomorrow I could return to the mill and hopefully to the realisation of a dream.

At the end of the first month I was still feeling despondent. How long did it take to get established? I was surrounded by empty mills with large *FOR SALE* signs outside and those mills that had gone into large combines were still struggling.

My weavers were producing the linen and the damask but Tom Kendal was unhappy with his printing. He could capture the designs but the colours were not to his liking, and I had to admit that they lacked the subtlety of the oriental ones.

His colours were those he was familiar with. Strong greens and crimson. Bright yellow and an occasional pretty pink, but I knew what he meant when he said, 'They just won't do, Mrs St Clare. They're gaudy. They were all right for roses and peonies, but they're not right for these flowers.'

'What do you suggest Tom?'

'I could ask mi nephew if he knows anybody. 'E's a clever lad, 'e's at Manchester Art College. If 'e can't 'elp he might just know somebody who can.'

'Then I'll leave you to ask him, Tom.'

I studied his efforts carefully and I knew what he meant. They were too bold. They were time-worn colours on new designs and ours had to be something different.

It was several days later when Tom said, 'I went to meet Michael, my nephew last night, Mrs St Clare and I told him the difficulties we were 'avin'. 'E'll be on 'oliday until the end of January so 'e'll come out to see us if that's all right with you.'

'Yes, of course, Tom.'

Michael duly appeared in the company of a fellow student,

266

a small smiling Chinese, whose English was not very good, but he had a ready smile and viewed our designs with shining eyes and some excitement.

Michael showed him what we had already produced and he shook his head adamantly. 'No no,' he said. 'Colours not right, too strong.'

His name was Han Lue and he enthused warmly when Tom showed him the wooden-blocked designs of water lilies and orchids but still he shook his head adamantly over the colours. 'Too strong,' he kept on saying, shaking his head dolefully, but when I asked if he knew how to make them softer he did not seem to understand.

Two days later another and more agonising problem came to upset me.

Julia arrived to spend a week with Granny, and so that she could return after the holidays with Alice who was to go to the same school.

Over dinner on her first evening she said, 'I'm coming down to the mill tomorrow. I want to see what it's like now that you're there.'

'You'd do better to come into the large mills, young lady where you'll see people who know what they're about,' Grandfather said tersely.

'I've been in those a lot of times, I want to see what Amanda's doing,' she retorted.

'Well you'll learn nothing there,' he finished acidly.

When she had not arrived by lunchtime I felt relieved. I really didn't want Julia poking and prying about the place, asking too many questions. It was not to be, however. She arrived at two and I left her to wander around on her own, aware that when our eyes met there seemed to be some hidden amusement which I felt would surface later.

She lingered on until it was time for me to leave, and I was surprised when she suggested that we drive up the country lane and on to the fell.

'But it's cold and blustery,' I protested. 'Surely you don't want to sit up there in a flurry of snow.'

'We can't talk at Granny's.'

'Well there's nothing we have to talk about that Granny couldn't listen to. Will you like having Alice at school with you?'

'She's all right. My friends are looking forward to having her.'

'That's very nice. I hope she'll be happy there.'

'I told them about her mother. We've never had a suicide before. All we've had from the parents are affairs and divorces, suicide's something different.'

'Really Julia! I'm quite sure Alice will not want to talk about her mother's death, I really don't think you should have told your friends anything about her.'

'Well, it's something different.'

'What sort of horrid girls are going to get a thrill out of that? Does your grandmother know what you've been telling them about Alice?'

'I never tell my grandmother anything. I don't like staying there, that's why I come to Great Grandma's.'

I drove in silence, there was something decidedly unwholesome this afternoon in Julia's opinions.

'You can stop here,' she said at last.

'We're not stopping here for long,' I warned her. 'We don't want to get starved to death.'

'Caroline came to see Grandma this morning. They sent me out of the room, but I listened at the door.'

'That wasn't very ladylike, Julia.'

'Don't you want to know what she said?'

'I don't think it's any of my business.'

'That's where you're wrong, it is your business.'

Chapter Twenty-Six

Julia was not pretty. She had pretty colouring and an attraction that might develop later, but in her small shut-in face there was a degree of spite, unusual in one so young.

After a few minutes I couldn't believe that I was listening to this precocious young girl telling me that Caroline had spent all morning at my grandmother's, accusing me of having an affair with her husband.

'She was pacing about the room and shouting at the top of her voice, screaming, that you were only staying on here to steal her husband, that you'd only gone into the mill so that he could help you. Golly, you should have heard her.'

'You shouldn't be telling me this, Julia.'

'Why not? I don't like her, I never have. She's all airs and graces and he's so dishy. He's the sort of man I want to fall in love with, somebody grave and distant, somebody who's real gentry, not an apology.'

'Julia, you don't know what you're talking about.'

'I know what I heard. Caroline was distraught, something had upset her. You and Phillip had upset her. What's he really like, is he an absolutely marvellous lover?'

'Phillip Marston and I are not lovers, we have never been lovers.'

She stared at me in amazement.

'But you must have been, you must be. She wouldn't have said all that if she wasn't sure.'

'I don't care what she said, Julia, I'm telling you the truth.'

'But you do love him, even if you're not having an affair.'

'We're going back Julia. And I don't want to hear another

word about Caroline or Phillip. You should not have listened at the door, it was very wrong of you, and now I suggest you forget it.'

I started the car and drove back down the hillside. She sat beside me in sulky silence. She had wanted me to think that she was on my side, that she approved of everything that might be going on between Phillip and me, but my attitude had knocked all the enthusiasm for scandal out of her.

As soon as I stopped the car outside the front door, she was out of the car and running across the driveway. When I entered the house there was no sign of her, so I could only think she had hotfooted it upstairs to sulk in her room.

As I crossed the hall Grandfather emerged from his study.

'Oh, it's you, Amanda. I thought it was your grandmother, what time is it?'

'Almost six.'

'Where has the woman got to? She said she wouldn't be long.'

'Where has she gone?'

'Over to see Edith and Edwin. I told her it was too cold and wet to go out, but she went off regardless.'

'Is she driving herself?'

'No, not in this weather. She rang for a taxi.'

'I'm sure she won't be long.'

'I hope not, I'm ready for my evening meal.'

Just then we heard a car and as I was halfway up the stairs the door opened and Granny came into the hall.

'Where on earth have you been all this time,' Grandfather snapped. 'It's nigh on six and I'm ready to eat. Amanda's home. I don't know where the child is.'

Grandma looked up to where I was standing on the stairs and there was none of the usual warmth in her glance, only a profound disappointment. That was the moment when I knew I could not go on living in her house: I would have to find somewhere else.

I was even more sure as we sat round the dining table with Grandfather morose because the meal was late, Julia sulking and Granny wrapped up in her own thoughts. After the meal was over Julia went immediately to her room, saying she was playing gramophone records and I excused myself on the grounds of having letters to write.

I had to look around for somewhere to live. I had poured so much money into the mill I knew it would have to be a modest dwelling, some cottage away from the rest of them, but within driving distance of the mill. Consequently on Saturday afternoon I set off to look for something suitable nearby.

I visited estate agents and collected a pile of leaflets and I looked at properties I thought I might find liveable in, but by the evening I knew that I could not live in any one of them. Fairlawn had spoiled me; at the same time I didn't want to clutch at straws.

I was driving back to the house when I spotted Cook walking down the hillside, armed with several shopping bags, so I stopped the car to give her a lift.

She got in gratefully, 'These bags are that 'eavy. I'm shoppin' for mi next-door neighbour as well as miself, she's just out of 'ospital.'

She invited me in for a cup of tea and as in my childhood I found it easy to pour out my troubles.

'Why are ye so anxious to move out of your grandmother's 'ouse. Won't she be very hurt when ye even suggests it.'

'She might conceivably be very relieved.'

'Why's that then?'

'For many reasons, Cook. I've antagonised Grandfather and my uncles by setting up in business at Number Three mill, and I don't think Caroline likes me living there, she's made that very plain.'

'There's bin gossip?'

'Well yes, unfounded gossip.'

'I've 'eard.'

'What have you heard?'

'Well your cousin Caroline's prominent around the town and she never could keep 'er own counsel, even more so when she's angry about somethin'.'

When I didn't speak she went on, 'I've 'eard talk about you and Sir Phillip, that 'e's 'elped ye set up the business, that ye rides with 'im across the fell, that there's somethin' goin' on.'

'And you believed it?'

'Well, I never thought 'e'd chosen the right sort o' wife.

271

Caroline wanted 'im, my 'ow she wanted 'im. The position, the money, the prestige, and what 'as she done to earn it? She enjoys bein' Lady Marston, but that's not to say that she makes 'im 'appy. I allus preferred Miss Charlotte to 'er sister, but Charlotte was made to take a back seat because Caroline was prettier, more assertive, I allus say yer've got to live with a person to really know 'em and Sir Philip never seems a 'appy man to my thinkin'.'

'Caroline thinks we're having an affair. She's wrong.'

'But ye could both be pushed into one, Miss Amanda?'

'I'm looking for somewhere to live, Cook, I have to get away from Fairlawn. The atmosphere is terrible. I've spent all day looking around but I haven't seen anything suitable.'

''Ave ye 'ad a look at that stone cottage on the fell near the old abbey? It might need a bit o' work spending on it but it's been empty since old Mr Lawson went to live with 'is daughter in Lancaster. Ye remember it don't ye?'

'Well yes. I always thought it was a lovely cottage, particularly in the summer when the heather was out and the garden looked so nice.'

'I should take a look at it in the mornin'. It's too dark now to see anything, but I allus thought I'd like to live there if I could 'ave afforded to buy it.'

'Have you any idea what they are asking for it?'

'No I 'aven't. But I know it's out of my limits. Halfords 'ave it in 'and.'

I thanked her warmly for the tea and her advice and left to drive home.

In the days that followed I was increasingly aware that all was not well in my grandparents' house as far as I was concerned. Julia continued to sulk and I saw very little of her. Ralph came with Alice and the two girls spent most of the time in Julia's bedroom playing gramophone records.

The estate agent went with me to look at the cottage and in the first few minutes my heart sank: it needed so much doing to it. Old Mr Lawson appeared to have lived in the utmost squalor for much of his life, but it did have possibilities. The kitchen was well-proportioned and large, in spite of the aged smelly cooker and flagged floor, but the living room boasted a quite beautiful stone fireplace and beautiful views across the fells.

It needed a bathroom, but the two bedrooms were well enough, and I began to imagine what it would be like with my furnishings. At the end of the day I made an offer for it, considerably reduced from the asking price, but when the estate agent didn't seem too dismissive, I began to think the cottage might be mine.

That night after dinner when Granny and I sat alone I told her where I had been and that I was seriously interested in buying the cottage.

At first she looked at me in dismay, then I saw the rich red colour creeping up into her cheeks and I knew she felt discomfited and unsure what to say. Eventually in a small voice she said, 'I hadn't thought you would be wanting to move away, Amanda, but why to that cottage? It needs a lot spending on it. Why not a nice flat in the town or on one of the new estates on the other side of town?'

I was too near the hall, too near to stem any gossip that might arise, and in some exasperation I said, 'I've spent a lot of money on the mill, Granny. My money isn't a bottomless pit, and I do need to be somewhere near the factory. The other side of town isn't a good idea.'

'You have a car.'

'I know. But I don't want a new flat, and the houses are far too expensive for me at the moment.'

'More expensive than what you will need to spend on the cottage and the furnishings?'

'I think so.'

'But you've never had a home of your own, Amanda. You have nothing of your own to put in the cottage.'

'I have enough money to buy good carpets and pick up anything else I might need. I shall go to furniture sales, my grandparents in Devon have furniture tucked away that they never use, I can offer to buy it from them.'

'You needn't do that, Amanda, I'm sure there are things here you can have.'

'I doubt if that's a good idea, Granny. You might be accused of favouritism.'

She had the grace to look suddenly embarrassed.

'Favouritism,' she exclaimed. 'Who would accuse me of that?'

'I wouldn't have to look far for the answer to that, Granny. And it really isn't worth it. It will be nice for you to be able to say I have done it entirely on my own and without any help from you. I'd like you to take a look at the cottage though. You might conceivably see its possibilities.'

She didn't say if she would come but at least I had jumped the first hurdle.

From my parents' letters I knew that Father was thinking in terms of retirement but I knew they would never come to live in Lancashire. Neither of them could understand why I had bought the mill; they wouldn't understand why I wanted to buy the cottage. Indeed Father said he'd never been interested in Dexter's cotton empire and he was surprised that it had skipped a generation and taken hold of me.

I was amazed and touched by the offers of help I received from my workforce at the mill, and from Cook herself, who offered to help me clear the accumulated rubbish out of the cottage.

Tom Kendal introduced me to his nephew who was a painter and decorator and I talked nicely to the gardener at Fairlawn who agreed to look at the garden. I installed a bathroom and kitchen fittings, and then I started to go to furniture salerooms and second-hand antique shops to see what I could pick up.

It was amazing what good carpets did to the place, and I bought rich velvet curtains for the windows, promising myself that one day they would be my designs that would hang there. I managed to find a sofa and easy chair and several small beautiful tables that were expensive, but I had to have them.

It was Sunday afternoon and I was moving furniture around the living room when the door opened and Phillip stood eyeing me with some amusement.

'You never fail to amaze me, Amanda,' he said softly. 'When did you decide to move here?'

'How did you know I was here?'

'The solicitor told me yesterday over lunch. Why did you leave Fairlawn?'

'I thought it was time I had a place of my own. I always liked this cottage.'

He stood looking round the room and after a while he said, 'I must say you've done wonders with it, but why, Amanda?'

'Phillip, I've never had my own home. I never had my own home with Anthony. We lived in married quarters. The furniture had been somebody else's and when we left we took nothing away with us. I know this is a small cottage without any particular style but it is mine, bought by me and furnished by me and I'm going to enjoy it.'

'I sincerely hope you do, my dear. What does your grandmother think about it?'

'I don't want her to see it until I've got it as I like it.'

'How about the others?'

'The others?'

'Hasn't Caroline called to see you? Your aunts?'

'If they called I wasn't here.'

'What's going on, Amanda? This cottage didn't suddenly become imperative. You were pushed into it.'

'You should know by now that nobody pushes me into anything.'

'They've made it very uncomfortable for you to stay on at Fairlawn? I'm not stupid Amanda, if you've been made to feel uncomfortable, don't think I've been spared their condemnation. Caroline's tantrums and sulks, her mother's sly innuendos. If they were meant to make me happy with what I'd got, they failed miserably. I am acutely disenchanted with what I have got.'

I stared at him uncertainly and with a wry smile he went on. 'Caroline and I do not have a happy marriage, Amanda. We have drifted too far apart, perhaps we never had the sort of marriage that was meant to last; on the other hand I don't wish to involve you at this stage. I doubt if you're cut out to be the *femme fatale* your relatives are accusing you of being.'

I stared at him with the tears rolling down my cheeks and suddenly he crossed the room and took me in his arms.

'I'm sorry, darling. Life's a mess but it was a mess before you ever came back here. I have to sort things out with Caroline and I have to make her see that you're not involved.

275

You haven't caused it. It was always there just waiting to erupt.'

'She will never believe you.'

'She will never blame herself. She will blame the world and his wife before she blames herself. You know where I am if you need me, and you know even if we don't meet I am trying to help you.'

'Help me, how?'

'You'll find out in the next few weeks.'

He put me away from him and smiled down into my eyes. How I loved him: his cool grey eyes and the sculptured hair that framed his face, the concern in his remote handsome face and the firmness of his hands clasped around mine. Then he was gone and I sank down onto the nearest chair trembling with emotion.

Phillip had assured me that I would not be involved, but I knew it was a forlorn hope. Sorting things out with Caroline would be traumatic. I found myself remembering the tears and tantrums in her childhood, shouting exhibitions at the loss of a doll or a piece of jigsaw. How much more desperate she would be at the loss of her husband.

Always with Caroline it had been 'me' and 'mine': her toys, her friends, her life; now it would be her husband. She had not been brought up to share things, even with her own sister. If we made friends with her friends we were accused of stealing them: it had been the same with her dolls and her pets. She had been a spoiled child and from a doting parental home she had gone into marriage with one of the county's most eligible and aristocratic bachelors.

Caroline had thought it no more than her due. Sorting things out with Caroline might be more than he could handle, and not just Caroline: behind her was the formidable Dexter family.

I felt suddenly lethargic. I had worked hard for days on the cottage. Now, looking round me, I suddenly lost interest in it. I had to get out into the cold February afternoon with the misted fells before me and the wet country lane and the leafless tossing trees.

I was almost at the bottom of the hill when I saw a small figure plodding up, fighting against the wind so that she had to pause to get her breath, holding on to the stone wall to retain her balance. It was Julia.

I hurried towards her and seeing me staring at her in amazement she grinned as if we had never been estranged.

'I want to see the cottage,' she gasped.

'You could have chose a better day,' I scolded.

'I went home the last time without saying goodbye.'

'I know.'

'I'm only here for a week, it's half term. I told Great Grandma I was coming up here.'

'And what did she say to that?'

'Only to put something warm on.'

'Is Alice with her father?'

'I suppose so. I wouldn't like to live half way up the fell. What are you going to do when it snows and you can't get your car out?'

'Walk it.'

While I made coffee she roamed around the cottage. I could hear her upstairs opening and closing doors and eventually she came into the kitchen to perch on the table.

'It's nice,' she said. 'You've got good taste.'

'Thank you.'

'I was coming earlier but you already had a visitor so I walked on the fell.'

'Not a very good idea on such a cold day. You should have come in, it really didn't matter that I had a visitor.'

'It was Sir Phillip's car.'

'So?'

She grinned, and at that moment I could cheerfully have slapped her.

'You don't come to Fairlawn these days. Granny says she hasn't seen you for weeks.'

'No. I've been very busy at the mill and getting this place decent.'

'I hate it there.'

'Then why don't you stay with your grandmother?'

'I hate it more there. They all came last Sunday as usual and I was packed off to my room as soon as lunch was over. Then yesterday Aunt Edith came and Caroline and they were all in the study talking for hours. Something's going on.'

277

'They always talked together in the study, about business, about all sorts of things I found very uninteresting.'

'They weren't talking about business, I heard your name mentioned and Phillip's. Caroline was upset when she left and so was Aunt Edith. Aunt Edith had been crying.'

'How do you know if you were upstairs in your room?'

'They didn't get rid of me as easily as that. I was at the back of the hall near the kitchen door.'

'What are you telling me all this, Julia?'

'I'm not telling you, I'm warning you. Things can only get worse.'

There was something strangely old and bizarre in this young girl sitting on my kitchen table swinging her long legs, a gleam of expectancy in her eyes, a half smile of derision shaping her mouth.

In some exasperation I said, 'I don't want to quarrel with you again Julia, but you really shouldn't snoop around the house listening at doors and then have the audacity to come here to tell me they've been discussing me.'

'There's going to be trouble and you ought to know. I like you a lot more that I like Caroline. That's why I'm telling you.'

Surely this ridiculous child didn't expect me to be grateful for her concern, which was entirely unwholesome? To change the subject I said 'You can stay for a meal if you like and then I'll run you back to Fairlawn.'

'No thanks, I told Great Grandma I wouldn't be long, that I'd be back before dark.'

'Then I'll run you there now.'

'No, I'll walk. If you take me back you'd have to go into the house and the atmosphere's awful.'

I was glad to see her go, and as I settled down in the evening in front of a bright fire I looked round appreciatively. My little cottage had never seemed so homely and charming. I deliberately didn't want to think about Julia's visit. I'll get a dog, or a cat, I thought. I could picture a contented tabby sitting on the rug before the fire, and a small dog to walk with across the fell, but in spite of my efforts to forget Julia's visit, again and again it came back to haunt me.

Chapter Twenty-Seven

The warmth of the room made me feel suddenly sleepy and it was the insistent sound of the door knocker that made me open my eyes and send me to the door.

I saw that it was eight o'clock by the mantelpiece clock and I could hear the sound of rain pattering on the window and the wind tearing through the trees. In some anxiety I opened the door, amazed to see Granny standing on the doorstep, a small darkly clad figure with a woollen scarf covering her silver hair.

I held the door open wider and drew her inside the house.

We stared at each other without speaking and when she made no attempt to remove her coat I said at last, 'Take off your coat, Granny, and come and sit near the fire. I'll make coffee.'

'No coffee, Amanda, I had some before I left the house.'

'It's a terrible night to drive up here.'

'I know. I couldn't settle to anything, and I thought it was no use sitting at home brooding and making myself miserable, I had to talk to you.'

It was too soon for Phillip to have spoken to Caroline, but not too soon for her to see where her life was leading, and as I took the seat on the other side of the fireplace I waited anxiously for her to begin.

She was sitting nervously on the edge of her chair, twisting the delicate handkerchief she held in her hand this way and that and I knew she was not relishing the part she was having to play.

I waited, thinking miserably, will it ever begin? What will

she expect me to say? And at last in a small voice she said, 'Have you any idea what all this is about, Amanda?'

'I suspect it's about Caroline and the state of her marriage.'

'So you do know?'

'I only know that I had to leave Fairlawn because I was being accused of something I had no part in.'

'How can you say that, Amanda? Caroline is very unhappy, Phillip is distant and she says it's since you came back. He's helping you all he can at the mill and has no time either for her or their life together.'

'We're not having an affair, Granny. I've been very grateful for his help, he's the only member of the family who has even tried to help me.'

'Even if he's neglected his wife to do so?'

'How? How has he neglected his wife?'

'Caroline has tried so hard to be a good wife to him. All his mother's charities, all her interests, she's taken them on as though she'd been born to them. She's played her part, been a fitting Lady Marston. Nobody could accuse her of being anything else.'

When I didn't speak, she said sharply, 'You know I'm telling the truth Amanda. Caroline's worked ceaselessly to keep things going. At the church, on the Bench, charities all over the place, and she's getting precious little thanks from Phillip.'

'I remember Phillip's mother and her charities, Granny. I remember her at the church bazaar busying herself in the kitchen, working tirelessly behind the scenes as well as on the platforms. She hated the adulation that Caroline thrives on, she merely patronised the charities that Caroline loves and where she can travel all over the place spending much of her time away from home.'

'That's very unkind, Amanda.'

'It's also very true. They have no common interests. He has no interest in her activities and she resents everything he enjoys. Ask yourself what they ever do together, where do they ever go together, and, if they have a marriage at all, it goes her way. This is how she wants it and he gave up trying to change it a long time ago, long before I came back here, when I was married to Anthony and without any expectations that I would ever return to Lancashire.'

'But now that you have returned, Amanda, are you here to steal him?'

'If you're asking me if we are having an affair, no, we are not.'

'But you care for him?'

I didn't immediately answer her. I sat staring into the fire, the only sound the crackling of the flames and the rain pattering ceaselessly on the window and she waited, her hands clenched in her lap, waiting for the words that would set her mind at rest, but I could not lie to her. I had never been able to lie to her.

'When I was a little girl, Granny, I thought Phillip was the most beautiful man I had ever met, and I thought Caroline was so lucky to have found him. I was counting the days when I could go with my parents to India because I was never one of you. I was never made to feel one of you, but Phillip was kind to me. He danced with me on the night I was wearing my first party frock, that terrible primrose yellow Aunt Edith insisted you buy for me and when I knew I looked ugly and silly in it, and I never forgot how kind his eyes were and how warm his smile. You are asking me if I care for him and I have to tell you that I do. I've always cared for him.'

'But it isn't the caring of a young girl for a man who is being kind to her, is it Amanda? Now it's something more?'

I nodded. 'Yes Granny, I love him. I suppose I always did, in those days it was a crush, now it's something tremendous, something I can't help.'

'And the fact that he's married to your cousin doesn't matter?'

'Well, of course, it matters. It matters because love isn't enough, there are too many things separating us, too many hurdles to cross.'

'Is Phillip in love with you?'

'He will have to tell you that, Granny. I can only tell you that we have made no commitment and we are not having an affair.'

'And it will not come to that?'

'I can't predict how Philip and Caroline will resolve their problems. If they remain together there will be no affair. If

281

they separate and Phillip loves me, then I will go to him if that is what he wants.'

Her face was white and afraid and at that moment I felt sorry for her. She was too old, too involved with her family to believe that anything would change and she had received no reassurance from me. In her eyes I had caused havoc by antagonising her husband and sons through my involvement with the mill, and now I was a threat to her granddaughter's marriage, a marriage the family had exulted in and which now lay like so much dust around their feet.

Stiffly, she rose to her feet and her small upright figure was so dignified, her expression so disappointed it brought the stinging tears into my eyes. I helped her on with her coat and waited while she adjusted the scarf on her head. Then I went to open the door for her. The sharp wind hit us like a knife as we stood in the doorway, and anxiously I said, 'Let me drive you home, Granny. It's not safe for you to drive on such a night.'

'I'm perfectly capable, Amanda. I suppose you might visit us one day?'

'Yes, of course.'

'Your cottage looks very nice, what bit I've seen of it.'

'I hope you'll come again.'

'We'll see.'

I went with her to the car, with the stinging rain on my face and the wind tearing at my hair. I stood watching the rear lights of her car disappearing along the lane, then I returned to the house. I stood with my back leaning against the door, aware of the warmth, the reflection of the flames leaping on the white walls, the scent of burning logs and I knew in that moment that nothing would ever be the same again.

Caroline would be the injured one, the one demanding all their love and help. I was the one capable of standing on my own, the rebel, the dissenting voice in a close-knit family, I had stood against them once, I wasn't sure if I could do so again.

Neither was I sure how Phillip could stand out against Caroline's intransigence, that what was hers she would keep, come hell or high water, and in my memory I was hearing her small shrill voice proclaiming what was hers. 'My doll, my dog, my friends, my toys. Keep away from them.'

My anxieties were born out forcefully several days later. It had snowed in the night and instead of parking within the mill yard I decided to leave my car on the road outside where gritter lorries had made the road safe. It was late afternoon and it had started to snow again, so I allowed the workforce to leave for home early.

'I'll give you a lift home,' I told Tom and after we had locked the doors, we slipped and slided across the mill yard. Just as we were crossing the road, a powerful car seemed to come from nowhere at great speed and we were suddenly caught in the car's headlights. With a cry of alarm Tom pulled me to the roadside. I heard the sickening crunch as the car took a wing off mine and drove on without stopping.

We stared at each other in disbelief. I was trembling as I surveyed my shattered car.

'Only a maniac would drive at that speed on a slippery road,' I said angrily, and Tom hesitated before he said in a small voice, 'Did ye see whose car it were, Mrs St Clare?'

'No, I couldn't believe what was happening.'

'I'm pretty sure it were 'er Ladyship's car. She drives down the road from the hall as if nobody else should be on the road.'

'Are you sure, Tom?'

'Well I sees 'er in that car every day.'

'Her car will be scratched. I'll telephone this evening.'

I tried telephoning her twice, the first time a servant informed me that she was out, the second time I was told she was unwell and had gone to bed.

Alone in the cottage my anxieties grew. Did Caroline really hate me enough to want to kill or injure me? Or was she so angry or oblivious to us that she had failed to see us? Why hadn't she stopped to see the damage she'd done?

At one time I would have telephoned Phillip, but not now, so instead I got the garage to repair my car and made sure it was always parked in the mill yard.

Apart from the people at the factory I saw few others. My evenings were invariably spent alone, and at the weekends I brooded miserably and wished it was Monday.

I had forgotten John Stedman's promise to call at the mill but at the beginning of March he came to my office. With a warm smile he extended his hand.

'I'm sorry to have taken so long, Mrs St Clare, but I've been in America. I'm staying with the Marstons for a few days so I couldn't miss this opportunity to see you.'

'I think we're getting there, Mr Stedman, far too slowly though. The colours are still not quite right, but I have a young Chinese student coming in to help us, and I really do think he's beginning to solve our problems.'

'Then may I see you designs?'

'Yes, of course.'

I introduced him to Tom and the other men working in the print room and he looked around him with interest. He seemed impressed with the block-print designs and handled the material with a practised eye, then I began to show him the colours we were experimenting with. He said very little, and my heart sank as I thought he was finding them predictable and hardly the sort of thing he was looking for.

We were leafing through several patterns when Han Leu came into the room carrying a piece of material he'd been working on for several days. He was smiling, not his usual cheerful smile at nothing at all, but his small eyes were gleaming with triumph.

He laid the cloth in front of us with great aplomb, saying, 'Thees is good, colours right, you say.'

John Stedman and I stared down at it and Tom came round the table to join us. Suddenly my heart lifted and John Stedman said, 'But this is lovely, I do believe you've done it, Mrs St Clare.'

I knew the design was beautiful, water lilies and trailing ferns, exotic birds and bamboo leaves, and the colours were delicate and ethereal against a pale cream background.

'How soon can you begin to turn out the finished product?' John Stedman asked.

'Very soon now that we've solved the colour problems.'

'I'll give you to the end of the month. In the meantime I'd like to show this to a client of mine, who's refurnishing the drawing room of his stately home. It is open to the public during the summer and he's anxious to have it ready in time for early June. He'll be delighted with this I know. May I take this sample with me?'

'Of course.'

'I'll show it to Phillip this evening.'

When I didn't speak he said softly, 'Phillip and I are dining alone. I believe your work here is a sore point with Lady Marston. I'm mindful that she is after all a Dexter.'

After he had left, we celebrated with cakes from the nearby bakery and I sent out for bottles of sherry which the workpeople were happy to drink from teacups. For the first time in months I felt happy, and that there was a future for us all. It would have been nice to have been able to tell my grandparents that success was on its way, I could cheerfully have worked under the Dexter banner, but they had not wanted it. Now I was their competitor, and, in a battle of designs, mine against theirs, I knew mine would win.

It was my happiest weekend for a long time. I shopped for clothes in the city and treated myself to dinner before driving home, and on Sunday I walked across the fell, revelling in the freshening wind and a blue sky with scudding clouds. I was stoking up the fire when I heard the sound of a car stopping outside the cottage and I went to the window to see who my visitor was.

The car was a very large unfamiliar one, and I stared at the woman stepping out of it. She was swathed from head to foot in expensive furs and I watched her walking to the gate, turning to close it behind her, and before she reached the door I had opened it to meet her.

For several seconds I stared at her in amazement and then she suddenly laughed, 'Don't say you don't recognise me,' she said. 'It hasn't been all that long. Aren't you going to invite me in? It's cold out here and I have become accustomed to more gracious living.'

Charlotte's face beamed out from under her wide sable hat and then larger than life she was in my tiny cottage gazing round her with unfaltering surprise, while I admired her sable coat and air of opulence.

She shrugged her arms out of the coat which she let fall on the floor unheedingly and went to the fire, holding her hands out to the blaze. Her jade green gown was of fine woollen georgette, but it had never been purchased in the west. There was a strangely oriental style about its straight simplicity, then she turned and smiled.

'Aren't you going to offer me a drink?' she asked.

'Yes of course. Do forgive me, Charlotte. You've taken me by surprise. When did you arrive?'

'In London, last week. Here, last night.'

'You're staying with your parents?'

'Yes, for the time being.'

'Is your husband with you?'

'No. He's in Singapore. I knew he'd hate our winters and in any case he'd probably hate my family and they'd hate him.'

'How can you say that?'

'I can say that because I'm not all that fond of them myself.'

I put my arms around her saying, 'Oh Charlotte I am very glad to see you. Have you been happy?'

'Well, it's been different.'

'Your parents will be so glad to see you.'

'It seems they have other things on their mind. Of course they liked to see me wearing silks and sable. I think Mother had the idea that I would be wearing a coolie hat. I haven't seen the grandparents yet. The rest of the family are there today as usual.'

'Didn't they think it strange that you didn't want to go with them?'

'I said I had letters to write, that I'd pick them up this evening to take them home. In the meantime I thought I should see you and hear a little about the mill, and what you've been doing to my sister.'

'What have they told you?'

'That Phillip is more interested in helping you than in spending time with Caroline, that their marriage is on the rocks. That's their side of the story. I expect yours is rather different.'

'Phillip has helped me, none of the others have. They merely resented me. I don't believe their marriage has been happy for some considerable time.'

'But your return here has accelerated their problems?'

'Charlotte, I don't know. I love him, perhaps I always have.'

'From that moment he asked you to dance and you were

wearing that perfectly awful frock, that was chosen purposely so that it wouldn't detract from anything Caroline wore.'

'Even then?'

'Even then, just as my frocks were. I was the one in gingham while Caroline work silk, and when you came along, beautiful and different. The warning bells rang again. You had to be subjugated.'

'But if Phillip had truly loved Caroline, if their marriage had been all it should have been, then nothing and nobody could have come between them.'

'Try telling that to Mother. In her eyes Caroline has been the perfect wife, the perfect Lady Marston, the perfect mistress of Phillip's ancestral home.'

'It doesn't seem to have been enough.'

'No. She hasn't given him an heir and if she's played her part in other respects it's because she enjoys the adulation, the enjoyment of being the centre of attraction. Isn't that what Caroline always enjoyed? They were always her parties, her presents, her guests, and now she has to come to terms with the fact that she's married to a man who no longer loves her and might actually dislike her.'

'I've seen Phillip very seldom, Charlotte. We're not having an affair. There's been no scandal.'

'No? The family are very jealously guarding Caroline's failure as a wife, and if it ever does come to the stage when they can no longer live together, you'll be cast as the scarlet woman, the husband stealer.'

'I know.'

'And Phillip will never let that happen because he's a man of honour. He wouldn't put you through that.'

'It would seem then that there's no future for any of us.'

'There is if you can be like me, Amanda. Follow the man you want to the ends of the earth, regardless of what they might say or do to you. They're glad that I came here alone, they don't particularly wish to meet my husband, because they're afraid that the world and his wife will consider I've married a barbarian from some unmentionable place. You know it isn't true.'

'And I've told them so.'

'And they'll never accept that they're bigoted and ignorant. It will be the same with you, Amanda.'

'I know.'

'They'll all be up there at the grandparents' house, sunk in gloom, rehashing the scandals that have hit the family from Jenny's suicide to you and me. If it wasn't so tragic, it would be amusing.'

'You can find it amusing Charlotte, because you're not staying here. You're going back to the Far East, but I'm here to stay. I'm responsible for a factory employing over a hundred people. I won't fail them, I'll make it work.'

'I want to see what you're doing there, Amanda. I can get precious little information from my father, only some new designs he tells me and designs that will do nothing against Dexter's time-honoured ones.'

'Come down in the morning, Charlotte. Tell me what you think about them.'

'I'll do that. They won't ask any questions but they'll be dying to know all the same.'

'Now can I offer you coffee, a drink? I've been a terrible hostess.'

'I'd better get up there, Amanda. I'll have something with the others at Fairlawn and I'll see you in the morning around ten.'

I watched her wrap her sable coat around her before going out into the night and I stood at the door until the sound of her car's engine faded into the distance.

Chapter Twenty-Eight

In the next few days Charlotte was a constant visitor to the mill. She enthused over the new designs, saying they reminded her of her own furnishings in Samarkand, except that hers were on silk whilst ours were in damask or linen.

'Why don't you come back with me and you can find many more to work with?' she asked excitedly.

'Charlotte, it isn't possible.'

'Why ever not, surely you can leave somebody in charge here?'

'No. This is my baby, I need to be here.'

'Then I'll send new designs out to you. You could make me a business partner.'

I smiled. I never quite knew if Charlotte was genuinely interested in my work or was merely rebellious against her childhood spent in Caroline's shadow. She had said she was staying in England for a few days, but the days extended into weeks and the weeks into months and one day I asked, 'Doesn't your husband mind that you are spending so much time here?'

'I've written to tell him about your work and that I'm here to help in any way I can. Really, Amanda, we're not children, we can spend time apart without endangering our marriage.'

'You have a lot to say about Caroline endangering hers.'

'I know. The circumstances are entirely different. By the way, the brat arrived this morning. I can't think why she doesn't stay with Aunt Myrtle instead of bothering Granny who is getting too old to cope.'

'Don't you like Julia?'

'Not a lot. I can't get through to her.'

There was little liking on either side, I realised, when several days later Julia said bitingly, 'I don't know why she doesn't go home, she's sarcastic, I don't like her.'

The orders were now rolling in, thanks to John Stedman, and through him I was meeting other interior decorators in different parts of the country, all of them enthusiastic, all of them promising work.

None of the family came to see me except Charlotte and Julia. I felt increasingly hurt that Granny stayed away and surprised when Ralph merely afforded me a curt nod when I encountered him in the town.

Charlotte informed me that there was local gossip about Phillip and Caroline, that they were never seen together, that Phillip's mother never visited the hall, and that there was probably some third party, either in his life or hers.

With every new order that came in I sensed Phillip's presence. We did not meet, but somehow he was there behind me, helping me, loving me, and one evening when I dined out with John Stedman he confirmed it.

'You're a very successful woman, Amanda,' he said smiling across the table at me. 'There are times when I ask myself if it's enough.'

'I'm not sure what you mean?'

'To be successful, to see the orders rolling in, to see your workforce busy and happy, and yet you're invariably alone in that cottage on the fell and you are still a young and beautiful woman. You should make room for a great deal more in your life, Amanda.'

'I'm not unhappy, John.'

'Perhaps not, but I am very troubled about two people I like and admire.'

'Two people?'

'Phillip and you.'

When I didn't speak he went on, 'I see Phillip unhappy in his crumbling marriage and I see you singularly alone. He loves you Amanda. One of these days this silent torment is going to erupt and when it does the complacency of a great many people will be shattered.'

'I never see Phillip, John.'

290

'Of course not, he doesn't wish to involve you, but you will be involved, Amanda. Caroline will see to that.'

His words frightened me. All Phillip and I had were our feelings for each other. We were hidebound by conventions we had sworn our lives to, and I had already been made an outcast by a family who considered me a traitor.

I was accustomed to hearing Charlotte's ridiculous high heels clip-clopping across the flagged floor of the mill outside my office, accustomed to see her sauntering along the aisles, occasionally chatting to the weavers, interrogating the men in the print room, gossiping with my secretary, but I was unprepared for the force with which my office door was flung open. But it was not Charlotte.

It was Caroline. Her small pretty face vindictive with temper, her eyes narrow and gleaming, like snake's in her flushed face.

I stared at her with astonishment, and holding the door wide, she said, 'I want to speak to you.'

'Then please come and sit down, and close the door.'

'I prefer the door to remain open. I want everybody in the mill to hear what I have to say. I am here to tell you that I am Phillip's wife and I shall remain his wife. You've known me long enough to know that what I have I keep and you're not going to steal him from me.

'I've told him that I will never divorce him, that he will never be able to marry you, and I'll make this town too hot to hold you. Your days here are numbered. You're not strong enough to take on me and the Dexter family.'

She glared at my astonished face for several minutes before she turned on her heel and slammed out of the door.

I could hear her high heels clattering through the room outside, and I sensed the astonishment of those in that room and beyond.

I sat staring in front of me, trembling with emotion. When, a few minutes later, Evie came in carrying a cup of tea which she placed on the desk in front of me, I could only stare at it stupidly while she left the room without speaking.

I knew that Caroline's words would be repeated around the mill and later in every home the workpeople returned to.

I stayed in my office, afraid to face them, afraid of the

condemnation I might read in their faces, their embarrassed silence as I walked among them, and it was so unfair. All I had been guilty of was loving a man who belonged to somebody else, love that was unfulfilled and destined to remain so.

It was late. I heard them leaving the building to go to their homes and I looked up with surprise when Tom entered the office, looking at me anxiously.

'It's time ye went 'ome, Mrs St Clare,' he said softly. 'Ye shouldn't be stayin' on 'ere on yer own.'

'I have a few things to do, Tom. I shan't be long.'

He looked at my empty desk and the cup of tea I had forgotten to drink and his voice was kind as he said, 'Leave the work 'til the mornin'. Can I ask ye to give me a lift 'ome?'

'Yes, of course, Tom.'

He waited silently while I took my coat out of the cabinet, then he held the door open for me and turned out the light.

Everybody else had left the building and we walked in silence across the stone floor and down the steps to the yard. In silence we walked to where my car was parked and I have no recollection of driving along the road that climbed the hill to the sprawling streets ahead, or turning along the narrow lanes leading to the fell.

''Ere we are, Mrs St Clare,' Tom said. 'Would ye like to come in and 'ave a meal, mi missus will be right glad to 'ave ye?'

I stared at him for several seconds without speaking, but it was the kindness in his voice, the anxiety that had crept into it that brought the rush of tears into my eyes.

'Nay lass,' he said. 'None o' that's worth cryin' about. It'll nobbut be a nine day's wonder, and them as knows ye knows none of it's true.'

'Everything was going so well for us, Tom.'

'That it is, and it'll go on goin' well for us.'

'Scandal never loses anything, Tom.'

He shook his head. 'Eh lass, it's only scandal because it's 'er ladyship accusing ye. In a few days' time they'll be takin' sides and she'll not come out of it smellin' o' roses. She's not well liked in this town wi' her hoity-toity airs. Sir Phillip's

292

liked, 'e's different. 'E's real gentry, and ye're liked too, Mrs St Clare. Yer've given us 'ope instead of despair, and if ye're afraid o' the Dexters yer've done more for a great many of us than they would ever 'ave done.'

'Tom, I'm afraid.'

'Ye needn't be. It'll be interestin' to see if Sir Phillip finds out what 'is lady's bin up to this afternoon.'

What did it matter? Caroline was his wife and would remain his wife whether he loved her or not. Love had not counted in their life for a very long time; what had happened today would make no difference.

In the days that followed I was aware of the whisperings around me, the chatter that ceased whenever I passed by. People stared at me in the shops and in the bank, and it was Charlotte perched on my desk who said brightly, 'So you've had a visit from my sister.'

'Did she tell you she came to see me?'

'Family meeting, we were all informed.'

'And?'

'The parents thought she'd been very brave in confronting you. Granny was tearful, Grandfather said you'd been too sure of yourself for too long, and Ralph and his parents kept their own counsel.'

'And what about you, Charlotte?'

'I think you're the brave one to take on Caroline and the Dexters, I'm just wondering which way Phillip will jump.'

'Are you staying on here to find out?'

'No, I'm going back to the Far East next week. I've decided to start my journey in Moscow along the old Silk Road. I still have the travel bug.'

'You'll come back one day, Charlotte. You'll never really be able to forget your roots.'

'No, I suppose you're right. I wonder how things will have changed.'

'I can't think they ever will.'

'Oh, they will. We're living in a time-warp, Amanda, but things are already changing. Have you never thought that Europe is on the march.'

I stared at her curiously.

'On the march?'

293

'Yes. Awash with dictators all wanting what we've got, all busy empire-making. For years my husband's been predicting another catastrophic war that will engulf the east as well as the west. Time will tell.'

She embraced me, 'I may see you again, Amanda, before I go, but in case I don't I'll say goodbye now. Keep your end up, I'm not sorry to be going back, and I'll send you more designs, I promise.'

Somehow with Charlotte's departure another chapter seemed to have closed. I was glad to be busy. The orders were rolling in and I was taking on more workpeople. The patterns we were producing were not being sold in the shops, because they were immediately wanted in the interior decorating trade, for stately homes, theatrical productions, and even for one of the royal residences, our crowning glory.

It was several weeks after Caroline's visit when I returned home feeling particularly drained after a long day entertaining visiting customers, and when after eating my solitary meal I felt suddenly disenchanted with an evening spent alone. I decided instead to walk into the village to see Cook.

I was about to leave the house when I heard the sound of a car stopping in the lane outside. I looked through the window and my heart sank at the sight of a large dark car which I thought was Caroline's. I made up my mind that I wouldn't go to the door to hear more abuse. Hadn't she done enough by upbraiding me in front of my workpeople in my own factory? She had no right to come to my home. I stood behind the door, trembling, but where she would not be able to see me if she decided to look through the window.

The sound of the knocker reverberated around the room, strident and insistent, then I heard Phillip's voice calling, 'Amanda, please open the door.'

We looked at each other without speaking, but I was dismally aware of the raw pain in his eyes as I stepped aside to allow him to enter the room.

'You were going out,' he said eyeing my sheepskin jacket I had donned for my visit to Cook.

'Nowhere important.'

'We have to talk Amanda.'

294

Indicating a chair near the fire, I shrugged my arms out of the coat and went to sit opposite him.

'I didn't know that Caroline had been to see you until last night,' he said evenly. 'When exactly was it?'

'It's weeks ago now . . . Who told you?'

'Caroline told me.'

My eyes opened in surprise. 'When, when did she tell you?'

'Last night. In one of her tempers and shouting exhibitions I've been subjected to over the last few years. I've asked her for a divorce.'

'Is that when she told you she'd been to see me?'

'Yes. Caroline will blame me and she blames you, that way she exonerates herself. Nor does it matter that I've told her our marriage was over long before you came back. I asked her for a divorce and her reply was entirely predictable.'

'She won't give you one?'

'Her attitude didn't surprise me. She said she would be my wife as long as she lived, that she had given me no grounds for divorce and she would not divorce me. She lives in my house and I have no power to evict her, so where does that leave us, Amanda?'

'Us?'

'Yes. I love you, I want to marry you, I want us to be together but my mind is a blank, I don't know how we are to achieve it. This is a small provincial town and when scandal rears its ugly head everybody is traumatised. Where could we live together in this town without surrounding ourselves with alienation and despair? I'm not concerned about me, but I can't subject you to that.'

'Then, what will you do? Go back to Caroline, live a lie, watch your hatred for her grow day by day and year by year? Is that how it's going to be, Phillip?'

He got to his feet and stood with his elbows leaning on the mantelpiece, staring down into the fire. His attitude was one of despair, dragging me to my feet and into his arms.

I had dreamed of loving Phillip, of having him love me, I had dreamed that our love affair would be a sweet gentle thing, not this deep anguished yearning that left us sated and drained in the hours before dawn.

Our night of love provided no answers for either of us. Brought us no nearer to a solution for the rest of our lives. For the first time since I opened the factory I arrived late, and I felt that everybody I encountered must know how I had spent the night. I could think of nothing except the overpowering passion we had shared, nothing except the feel of him in my arms, nothing except the sound of his voice murmuring endearments against my face, nothing except the desolation of seeing him walk away from me in the early morning rain.

It was Tom saying solicitously, 'Aren't ye feelin' well, Mrs St Clare, get off 'ome, there's nothin' we can't cope with.'

That was when I pulled myself together saying with a smile, 'I'm not ill, Tom. I overslept that's all.'

Mechanically I went about the normal everyday tasks that had made up my life since I took over the mill. I answered letters, walked through the mill and made myself chat normally with weavers and winders, watch the printers at work on the designs I loved, admired the finished results. Quite deliberately, I shut out the ecstasy of the night before and the thoughts I was afraid of regarding.

Did loving Phillip mean other nights of stolen love, secret meetings, a role as his mistress while his wife showed the world a circumspect wronged woman? A wife who was playing her part in the community, faithful and wholesome, involved with good works, remaining loyal to a man who loved another woman, a disloyal member of her own family.

The only answer was to move away, but I had put everything into the mills. I had a loyal workforce and I owed them something. I could not abandon them at a time when there was mass unemployment in an industry that had made Lancashire.

The next few weeks confirmed my bitterest thoughts. Caroline was seen in church every Sunday. She took on more and more charities, even those she had once considered dull and mundane. Now those church-going people were staring at me on the streets and in the shops. I was the wicked woman who was making their wonderful Lady Marston unhappy, I was the rebel Dexter who had taken work away from the Dexter Mills and even in my mill I sensed a feeling of doubt that our good fortune was doomed.

My parents were returning to England now that my father had at last decided to retire from the Indian Army, and, as I had thought, they were not returning to Lancashire. Father came alone to see the family while my mother was busy house-hunting in the south-west, and he went first to Fairlawn to see his parents. When he came to see me that same evening, I knew immediately that he had learned something of my misdemeanours and my involvement with Phillip.

His smile was just as warm as he embraced me, and in the first few minutes he admired the cosiness of the cottage, ending by saying, 'You look tired Amanda, you've taken too much on.'

'We're very successful, Father. We have orders for many many months.'

'I'm not disputing it, what I'm saying is that you look drained. I've strict instructions from your mother to take you back to the West Country with me.'

'It isn't possible, we're too busy, I need to be here at this time, I'll come to see you as soon as I can be spared.'

'You can't tear yourself away from Phillip.'

'They've told you everything, haven't they? Does that mean that you believe all of it, without giving me a chance to give you my version?'

'I'm waiting to hear your version, dear. I know you've set yourself up as a rebel, and that needed some doing against Father. You copied my role, I was the rebel in my generation. I'm not bothered about that. If you've made it work, then I'm glad and I'm proud of you, Amanda. What worries me is your involvement with Phillip.'

'We love each other, Father.'

'And what sort of future can you have together?'

I stared at him miserably and couldn't answer. I didn't have any answers. There were so many things in my life I'd been sure about, but where Phillip was concerned there were only doubt and uncertainty. We loved each other, but was that enough to combat the problems of his wife and the family who had rejected us?'

We talked for hours, and I listened to his reasoning, his logical understanding, and in the end we came no nearer to reconciling the problems.

It was after midnight when he surprised me by saying, 'Well, we're getting nowhere tonight, Amanda, and it's time I was getting back.'

'I thought you would stay here, Father.'

'No love, I'm staying at Fairlawn. I expect they'll all be in bed by this time. I'm only here for a few days on this visit, your mother and I will come when we've got things sorted in Devon.'

'Is that where you intend to live?'

'Devon or Cornwall perhaps. Somewhere near your mother's parents. They've nobody else.'

'I thought you'd never leave India, that you'd stay on in the army for ever.'

'A great many of the senior officers are leaving India at this time, Amanda. There are things going on in Europe that are giving the army great cause for concern. I think the next couple of years will force matters out into the open.'

'Oh Daddy, you like nothing better than to find trouble somewhere or other, that's what your life's been about. Anyway you've retired, whatever trouble there might be can't possibly concern you.'

He smiled, at the use of my childhood name for him, and my assumption that a soldier could so readily forget the things he had sworn his life to.

'Hasn't Phillip talked to you about his fears for what is going on in the world, or are you so immersed in your own problems that you are blind to all the others?'

'We don't talk about politics, or the world's trouble spots.'

'I hope you never have to, Amanda.'

But he was shaking his head as though he did not believe his words.

At the door he embraced me and held me for a long moment in his arms and I said anxiously, 'Shall I see you again before you go?'

'Of course. I'll call in at the mill and take a look at those new designs of yours. I hear you've had Charlotte here for a couple of weeks.'

'Yes, looking expensive and reasonably contented, for Charlotte.'

He smiled. 'I expect before I leave I'll be bombarded with questions about how I could allow Charlotte and you to go off on your own, somewhere unmentionable, where she found some mandarin or other to marry.'

I laughed. 'And what will you say?'

'That I wouldn't like to be responsible for advising Charlotte about anything, neither her, nor her sister. You're up against it, love, I just hope you can handle it.'

'I'm not alone, Father.'

'Perhaps not, but you've both put yourselves in the wrong and society can be ruthless in condemning you, particularly when Lady Marston is enjoying being such a worthy pillar of society.'

Chapter Twenty-Nine

The war caused trauma and tragedy in many homes and many families, but it provided me with a great many answers to too many problems.

The twelve months before we actually declared war on Germany brought an end to exotic designs for the curtains in stately homes, and instead we were weaving cotton for the armed forces. Cotton in Lancashire came into its own again with full employment and every mill working to capacity.

I had made Tom my manager and he proved more than capable, so that I no longer needed to spend all my time at the mill.

Philip was in the Royal Naval Reserve and I sensed his relief that he was ordered to report immediately to Plymouth. He looked sad on that last evening, and seeing him wearing naval uniform the years dropped away, and I was a young girl again gazing longingly at him in that crowded ballroom and wishing then that he was mine.

Now we were lovers, but neither of us knew what the ending would be. He was relieved to be leaving his home and the wife he didn't love or even like, and now I was not losing him to Caroline I was losing him to danger.

'I'm not sure where I'll be, Amanda,' he said gently. 'I don't know if it will be a shore base, a foreign base of a ship, but why don't you come down to Devon? At least until I know something concrete, we can spend some time together.'

'There's the factory, Phillip.'

'The factory will run without you, darling. It's no longer

your baby. It's back to being a Dexter mill again, doing what they're all doing.'

I knew he was right. They did not need me at the mill. I had good people to look after everything there, and faced with a choice of staying in Lancashire and being near Phillip, there was no choice.

I wrote to my parents who had settled in a pretty village not far from Fowey in Cornwall and they telephoned immediately to say I should go there for as long as I wanted.

When I told Tom what I had decided he said, 'I think you're bein' very sensible, Mrs St Clare. Yer not very 'appy where ye are and folk talk without knowin' what they're talkin' about.'

'You've heard some of the talk then?'

'Well o' course. My wife 'ears it every time she goes into town, and when she goes to church. Sir Phillip doesn't attempt to disguise 'is car that's parked outside your 'ouse. If Lady Marston goes to a function 'e doesn't and 'e's not even bothering to keep up appearances.'

'It isn't a happy situation for any of us, Tom.'

'I'm sure it isn't. I should think ye'll be 'appy to get away from it.'

'I'm going to stay with my parents in Cornwall for a while. I'll be in touch constantly to see how things are making out. You won't have anything to worry about at the mills Tom. Full employment will be maintained for as long as the war lasts.'

'They're sayin' it'll be over by Christmas. What does Sir Phillip think about it?'

'He doesn't say.'

Actually when I repeated Tom's sentiments to Phillip he said dryly, 'I know what people are saying Amanda, by the time this war is over the world as we know it will have changed tragically.'

'You think it will last a long time?'

'I don't think we should be complacent.'

He would say no more and when two days later he left for Plymouth I felt singularly alone and lost.

I had packing to do, last minute things to see to at the mill, and the job of closing up the cottage. I intended to drive down to Cornwall and had been saving my petrol coupons for that purpose. I gazed around the room with some misgiving. It looked strangely unlived in with my suitcases standing near the door, devoid of either fruit or flowers, and I had put away in cupboards all my china and ornaments. I started at the sharp knock on the door and nervously I went to open it. Cook was standing shivering in the cold wind and it had started to rain.

'I'm right glad I've caught ye,' she said. 'I 'eard ye were leaving soon so I thought I'd better come tonight.'

'Sit down, Cook. I'll make coffee or would you like sherry or whisky?'

'I'll 'ave a drop o' Scotch, Miss Amanda. I've walked up the hill and it's that cold.'

She took the glass and sipped appreciatively. 'So when are ye leavin' then?'

'Early in the morning.'

'By train?'

'No, I'm driving down, I shall probably need my car in Cornwall, I'm going to stay with my parents.'

Her eyes opened a little wider. 'I made sure ye'd be goin' to stay with Sir Phillip. That's what the talk is.'

'Sir Phillip is back in the navy. I doubt if I would be welcome either at his base or his ship.'

'Well o' course not. It's all talk, and they knows nowt.'

I smiled. Her broad Lancashire dialect somehow brought an air of comedy into a delicate situation.

'Has yer grandmother bin down to see ye, or any of the others?'

'I didn't expect to see them, Cook.'

'Well, as to what they think yer've done, yer still a Dexter. I can't believe yer grandmother's in agreement with all this.'

'It is all very difficult for Granny, Cook. I am her grand-daughter, it's true, but so's Caroline. Phillip and I are the people who have done wrong, everybody feels very sorry for Caroline.'

'That's true, and none of 'em asking themselves if she drove 'im to it.'

I remained silent.

'Where's it all goin' to end, Miss Amanda?'

'I don't know.'

'Well, if 'e doesn't want 'er, can she go on livin' in the 'all? That's bin in the Marston family for generations, she's got no right to it.'

'Cook, I don't know, it's something we shall have to face sooner or later, but for the time being we are having to live every day as it comes.'

I could tell she would have liked to have asked more, but something in my expression forbade it. Instead she said, 'I 'opes Miss Charlotte paid ye a visit?'

'Yes she did. I was glad to see her.'

'Do ye reckon she's 'appy with that Chinaman she married?'

I laughed. 'He isn't a Chinaman, Cook, and even if he were he was a very intelligent and learned man. I should imagine he's widened Charlotte's horizon considerably.'

'She was allus a strange sort o' girl, but then she lived in 'er sister's shadow most o' the time. I'm glad she called to see ye, I expect she's the only one.'

'Well no. Sophie's daughter calls to see me, largely I think to upset them at Fairlawn. Julia's a bit of a rebel like me.'

'And young Alice. I see 'er when she's 'ome from school. She'll not take kindly to any o' the women 'er father's friendly with.'

'I don't know any of them, Cook. I hardly ever see Ralph.'

'Bridie comes to see me occasionally. Little gold mine that shop o' theirs. She allus brings me a little present, cakes and biscuits and the like.'

'That's nice of her.'

'Ay, she were a nice sort o' lass.'

'Well I'd best be goin' afore it gets too late, it's a fair walk down the 'ill.'

'I'll drive you down, Cook.'

'Nay I'll walk, it'll do me good.'

It was only eight o'clock and the long night stretched in front of me. It was too early to go to bed, there was no book I wanted to read and the radio was full of disquieting news. There were comedians trying to bring laughter into our homes and an abundance of patriotic songs, but I was not in the mood to listen to any of it. I got to the stage when I thought I should set out for Cornwall immediately instead of waiting for the morning, but it was not a good idea.

The roads were badly lit and car headlights would have to be dimmed. It was a dark moonlit night and the journey would be a long one, so instead I made coffee and sat in front of the fire drinking it. I decided I would go to bed but would probably lie sleepless for most of the night.

I lay soaking in my bath for a while and was about to get into bed when I heard the sound of a car in the lane outside, and the next moment there was another loud rapping on my door.

I hastily donned a dressing gown and ran downstairs fearfully, hardly daring to open the door in case a glimmer of light fell into the pathway beyond.

I stared in amazement at the figure of my grandmother standing on the path and she stared at me in my dressing gown.

'Where you in bed Amanda?' she asked. 'It's very early.'

'I've just had a bath, there was nothing else to do. Please come in, Granny, and sit in front of the fire. I'll put some more coal on, I was really letting it die down.'

'There's not need, Amanda. I'm not cold, I came in the car and I can keep my coat on.'

'No no, sit there Granny,' and I quickly poked the fire into life and added more coal.

'Here, let me take your coat.'

I hadn't seen her for a long time and she seemed suddenly to have grown old and delicate without her fur coat around her. Her thin white hands held out to the fire seemed almost transparent, and the firelight falling on her pale face and silver hair gave it an almost luminous quality.

'I heard that you were going away, Amanda. When are you going?'

'In the morning. Who told you?'

'Phillip told me before he went away. He came to say goodbye. He said you would be going to your parents.'

'Yes.'

'What about the factory?'

'I have people there I can rely on. We are working on cloth for the government. Everything more adventurous is finished for the duration.'

'I see.'

'Would you like coffee, Granny, or tea? I can soon make it.'

'No really, Amanda. We had dinner late tonight and I'd much rather sit and talk to you.'

We were both finding it difficult, and I was quick to ask, 'Are you keeping well, Granny, and how's Grandfather?'

'We're getting old, Amanda. I'm better than he is. He's always hated the winter.'

'And the others, how are they? It was nice to see Charlotte.'

'They're pleased that the mills are working full time, even if we had to go to war to achieve it. I thought Charlotte might have stayed a little longer. Goodness knows when we'll see her again. Your grandfather seems to think this war will spread. Your father thought so.'

'Yes.'

'Julia is coming to live here until the war is over. Her parents thought it would be safer for her here than in London. She's left school now and she didn't want to go to university. Alice is here also, so they'll be company for each other.'

'Is Julia staying with you?'

'No. She's going to Myrtle. I'm getting too old, Amanda, and Myrtle is her grandmother after all. No doubt she'll be spending plenty of time with me.'

We seemed to have exhausted talk about the family and the silence was a strangely uncomfortable one. I waited, knowing that sooner or later she would speak about the issue closest to our hearts.

'Will you see Phillip in Cornwall?' she asked at last. 'He was reporting for duty in Plymouth.'

'I'm not sure. He didn't know where he was going from there.'

'But that is why you are leaving here, isn't it?'

'It's one of the reasons. I want to see my parents and my grandparents. If it's possible to see Phillip, than I want that too.'

'We've all been very hurt by this, Amanda. Caroline is so unhappy and she's trying terribly hard to cope, to be the sort of wife Phillip needs. Doing all the things his mother did, wearing herself out trying to please him.'

I didn't speak. Caroline had been his wife for many years, trying to please Phillip. Now it was too late.

'Doesn't it bother you that all the town is talking about the situation Amanda? Doesn't it bother you being the other woman in Phillip's life, that you are stealing him from your own cousin?'

'Have you ever asked yourself why Phillip has fallen out of love with Caroline, Granny? I didn't come back to steal him from Caroline, but when I did come back I found a very lonely unhappy man with a wife who did not want his children and who was only interested in the adulation his name was giving her.'

'Caroline realises now that she isn't entirely blameless and she's trying very hard to restore their marriage. Phillip is the unapproachable one, and it is because you're here, Amanda. Without you, he would have gone back to his wife.'

'Has he told you that, Granny?'

'No, but we all think that is what would have happened.'

'Don't you think he thought long and hard about his marriage before he asked Caroline to divorce him? She refused, but that doesn't mean he'll go back to her and forget the empty years that have passed.'

'It has always been my experience, Amanda, that men return to their wives and Phillip has more to lose than many other men. He has an old and honoured name, a beautiful house which has been in his family for centuries and which he will want to return to. My poor child, there are so many dice loaded against you, can't you see it for yourself?'

'You may be right, Granny, but if Phillip leaves me for the reasons you have stated, then perhaps I won't have lost very much after all.'

She stared at me sadly in silence, then with a small defeated shrug of her shoulders she said, 'I have to get back Amanda. Your grandfather doesn't like it when I'm out in the evenings. Give your parents our love and tell them we hope to see them soon.'

'I will.'

'I hope you have a pleasant journey tomorrow, Amanda.'

She did not embrace me and I stood at the door watching her drive away.

When I related our conversation to my parents, Mother shook her head sadly saying 'She could be right, Amanda. Phillip is leaving so much behind him.'

Father was more encouraging. 'He's leaving a selfish inconsiderate wife, and what is there in a name, or bricks and mortar?'

Whenever Phillip could get away he came to stay with us, and on one of his visits he suggested that we find somewhere of our own to live.

'I don't know how long I shall be stationed in Plymouth, Amanda. I could be sent on a foreign base or to a ship, but at least we'll have some time alone together.'

So we went house-hunting and eventually found an enchanting stone house overlooking the sea at Polperro. Virginia creeper crept lovingly along the front of it and the sloping lawns ran down to the cliff edge. It was not large but it was beautifully designed and I enjoyed looking round numerous antique shops for the right sort of furniture. My grandparents supplied a good deal of it and for the first time in my life I felt I had a home of my own.

We were happy in that house overlooking the sea, but it was a tenuous, desperate happiness. Phillip came whenever he could get away and I knew that I was making him happy. The face that I loved smiled more often, gone were the worried frowns and the loneliness behind his smile, but we both knew that our happiness could end at any moment.

Night after night the city of Plymouth was being bombed and on those nights when I was alone I listened fearfully to the drone of German war planes and the sickening crunch of falling bombs. Every time he returned to me I said a prayer of relief that he had been spared, and then on that evening I watched him walking from his car to the house I knew that something was wrong.

I could not have said how I knew, his smile was just as warm, his embrace just as loving, but still I knew, and all through our meal together and later as we sat in front of the fire, wrapped in each other's arms, I waited with dismal certainty for him to tell me.

He went into the kitchen and I listened to him opening

cupboards, followed by the clink of glasses, then he came back carrying a tray with glasses and a bottle of champagne.

As he handed me a glass, he smiled, and I could not keep the tremor from my voice when I said, 'What are we celebrating, Phillip?'

'Four months of happiness Amanda, four months I shall remember when we're apart.'

'Apart?'

He nodded. 'I'm joining my ship in a couple of days' time, I'm not sure when I'll be able to see you again, darling.'

I accepted it quietly because we had always known that one day it would happen. I asked no questions and I did not tell him that I was pregnant. I was determined not to add to his worries. There were sterner things in life at that moment than a baby.

'Will you want to stay on in this house on your own?' he asked me.

'Well of course. Women are on their own all over the country, I shall be happy here, I love this house, and I want you to think of it being here and waiting for you to come back to.'

He telephoned me once from the base but he could tell me nothing about his future movement and I knew better than to ask.

When I told my parents about the baby, Mother immediately suggested that I should go to stay with them but I said I was perfectly happy on my own. I was pregnant but I wasn't ill. I had a good doctor who had promised to find me a suitable midwife who would stay with me for a few weeks and there was nothing for anybody to worry about.

'I suppose you want a boy?' Mother said.

'I really don't mind. Why should I want a boy?'

For a few moments she looked uncomfortable but I knew what she was thinking. Phillip had wanted a son, a son for the title and the hall but my son wouldn't have his name. My son would have no claim to his title.

'Why didn't you tell him?' she asked tearfully.

'I thought he had enough to worry about. Besides he'll know soon enough, he won't be at sea for years.'

But the weeks and months passed and I heard nothing from

him, then two days before my son was born I received a letter from Singapore and although his letter brought me happiness, the oceans that stretched between were overwhelming.

I called my beautiful son John after Phillip's father, I thought he would like that, and he was a robust and well-behaved baby. The young Irish nurse stayed with me a month and I found her warm Irish humour amusing.

'Faith and he's a beautiful baby. Won't his father be over the moon when he sees him,' she said almost every day, and I merely smiled in agreement without telling her my story. I felt strangely sad when she left us, and she wept a little saying, 'Sure and oive loved bein' here. Oi wish I didn't have to leave.'

'You can always visit us, Hilary,' I said. 'John and I will be glad to see you.'

'That'll be noice, and I'd loike a holiday in this lovely house by the sea.'

She left armed with presents from both me and my parents and after she'd gone, Mother said, 'You should get somebody else Amanda, even if it's only a daily.'

So she put a notice in the village post office for a daily woman and I acquired Mrs Pearson who came every morning and kept me entertained by all the village gossip. She knew everybody, having lived in Polperro all her life and nothing and nobody escaped her attention.

Father was busy with his Home Guard duties and Mother with her Red Cross Committee. Consequently I was more than surprised when they both descended on me as I sat in the garden with the baby asleep in is pram. They came with concerned faces to tell me that Grandfather Dexter had died from a heart attack the evening before and they were both going north for his funeral.

They did not ask me to go with them and I was glad. How could I take my baby son to that house of mourning and where his father's wife would be one of the mourners.

Chapter Thirty

I could picture that funeral in distant Lancashire from listening to Granny's memories of my great grandfather's funeral. Those long grey streets and mill chimneys, massive iron gates and silent darkly clad people. The churchyard carpeted with wreaths, the dismal tolling of the bell the shuffling feet of the men and women who had only known him as the master, the being who dictated whether they fed well or starved.

I could picture Grandma, small and slender, her dignity unruffled as she led her family into the family pew. There would be speculation because I had no doubts that Caroline would make the most of her presence there. Beautiful and fashionable as always, arousing admiration and pity as the wronged wife, and there would be more talk when they did not see me among the mourners.

What would be the family's reaction when they learned about my son?

It was several days later when Father came to see me and I received a full account of all that had taken place at the funeral.

'Surely Granny isn't going to stay on in that big house alone?' I said.

'She'll never move, Amanda, but I have asked her to spend some time with us in the not too far future.'

'Will she, do you think?'

'Perhaps. I had thought that one of my brothers might have moved into Fairlawn. After all, the head of the Dexter family has lived there for a great many years and it would have meant that Mother wasn't on her own.'

When I didn't comment he said, 'I didn't suggest it. No doubt I'll get to know more next time I go to see her.'

'Did you tell them about the baby or wasn't it a good time?'

'No love, it wasn't a good time. Caroline was distant, and I rather think she was enjoying her role as the deserted wife, even when everybody knows Phillip is serving in the Navy.'

'Phillip hasn't received any of my letters, and I've only received one from him. I can't think why he's in the Far East. One would have thought a warship was more essential on northern convoys.'

I thought he looked at me oddly and was about to say something, then thinking better of it he smiled and said evenly, 'Come to see us over the weekend love. Stay for a few days.'

'I'll come over on Sunday, but I won't stay. I have this strange feeling that I should be here. It's as if I have to be constantly waiting in case Phillip comes home.'

'Don't get your hopes up, dear. I rather think it will be some considerable time before he comes home.'

His words were brought forcibly to mind when only days later Japanese war planes launched a dastardly attack on Pearl Harbour bringing America into the war, and suddenly the war was worldwide and our territories in the Far East were in jeopardy.

Everyday now we were hearing about Japanese atrocities and it was Father who for the first time raised the issue of Charlotte. Singapore was overrun and Malaysia. India was threatened and Father said, 'She's safe enough for the time being in Samarkand, but Charlotte was a great one for travelling. She could be anywhere in the Far East.'

I was receiving excellent reports of the working of the mill, with the rest of them in full employment and working day and night to fulfil government contracts. I made up my mind that the next time Father went to see Granny I would go with him. I would leave my son with my mother.

We travelled north on the train to Manchester where we

caught our connection for Belthorn and as we drove in the taxi along the streets of the town we could hear the clamour from the factories and see the smoke belching from the chimneys. It seemed suddenly incongruous that it had taken a war to bring newfound prosperity into the area, but with it there was also a staunch determination that we were a people determined to survive and win.

I made up my mind as the taxi climbed the hill towards the fells with the Dexter mills on either side of the road.

'Drop me off here please. I'll walk up to the house later,' I said hurriedly.

'Why not come down in the morning, it's been a long day,' Father said reasonably.

'I know, but I'd really like to look in this afternoon, I won't be too late and you can break the news to Granny that I'm with you.'

It seemed strange to be walking along the aisles of weavers on the old flagged floors. The noise was overpowering, the sound of the looms and their voices above the noise. In those minutes before I reached the office I saw many faces I knew and was rewarded by their bright smiles and mouths shaped in welcome.

I was received by the manager and his staff warmly, and then Tom was there, shaking my hand warmly and asking if I'd decided to return to the north.

'I'm just visiting Tom, but everything seems to be going well even if the work isn't what I envisaged.'

'The war won't last for ever and then we can get back to it,' he said. 'We 'ave to finish Hitler off afore we can think about anythin' else.'

'Well of course Tom. Nothing else really matters.'

'Ye didn't get up for yer grandfather's funeral, Mrs St Clare. All the town turned out for it, the mills closed for 'alf an'our so that the workers could pay their last respects.'

'Yes, my father told me.'

'The old lady bore up very well, one o' the old school she is, they don't show their emotions in public.'

'No. Granny would weep in private.'

'She shouldn't be livin' in that big 'ouse on 'er own. Perhaps one day you'll be comin' back there.'

I smiled but didn't answer and in the next moment he said, 'One of 'er great-granddaughters was stayin' with 'er last week, the one in the Wrens, the one that came many o' time.'

'That would be Julia. So she's in the Wrens.'

'Ay, and mighty pretty in 'er uniform she is.'

I had never thought Julia particularly pretty but time alters many things, and often plain girls blossom into beauty. That she was in the Wrens brought home the fact that I had been long away.

'It seems strange to think that Julia is old enough to join the Wrens, I wonder what happened to the other one.'

'The other one?'

'Yes, Alice, my cousin Ralph's daughter.'

'That's the one the wife told me 'ad gone into nursin'.'

'So much seems to have happened in my absence.'

'Ay, it's funny. When ye stays in a town all yer life like I 'ave nothin' new seems to happen, but as soon as ye goes away it seems all the world changes.'

'No doubt Grandma will tell me all about the changes this evening.'

'There's a big American base on the Bleakstone fell. We sees the boys in the shops and 'ear's their lingo. It's funny that their English and ours can be so different. The lads go to the dance hall and the picture 'ouses and a great many of 'em are out with the local lasses.'

I laughed. 'It isn't taking them long to make themselves at home then.'

'That it isn't. Nice enough lads they are, and their officers are that smart. Lady Marston invites them for dinner up to the hall, I expect they're glad o' that bein' so far away from 'ome so to speak.'

I smiled, and he was saying hurriedly. 'I 'ere all the gossip from the wife, she 'ears it in the shops.'

'Well it's a small town, Tom.'

'Ay, and they 'ave to talk about somethin' I reckon.'

At that moment the manager came to say if I wanted to take a look at some of the books I could make use of his office, but I was quick to say, 'There isn't time this afternoon, I'll see them some other time. I know everything is in order, I have the utmost faith in all of you.'

I knew as soon as I looked into Grandma's face that my father hadn't told her about my son. She embraced me warmly, said I looked well and had been disappointed that I had not been able to attend Grandfather's funeral. Over her head I could see my father's expression of resignation.

'I'm so glad you've come,' she went on. 'There's a memorial service on Sunday for your Grandfather you will both be able to be there.'

I looked at my father with dismay but there was nothing he could say. It would be one more Sunday when they would all be there, including Caroline, and I marvelled that Granny chose to forget all that had gone before.

The church that Sunday morning was crowded with family, people of note in the community and behind us men and women who had worked for the Dexters for a great many years.

I was miserably aware of Aunt Edith's stolid averted profile and Aunt Myrtle's expression of surprise to find us there. Ralph turned his head to smile at us, but there was no sign of Sophie and her husband or the younger members of the family.

Caroline was the last to arrive. Wearing deepest black, but fashionable black from her high heeled shoes to the sweeping brim of her black felt hat. Her pale blond hair and porcelain skin looked well in black and for the benefit of those present she inclined her head graciously in my direction even when her eyes remained cold.

When the service was over the congregation stood while the family made their way along the centre aisle of the church and I was glad of my father's hand holding mine in a firm clasp. I knew what most of them would be thinking, how insensitive of me to be there when there had been so much talk about Sir Phillip Marston and his wife's cousin.

Back at the house a buffet luncheon had been laid out in the dining room and family and guests were already helping themselves to the food.

'It wasn't so bad, Amanda,' Father said evenly.

'It isn't over yet.'

'I know, love, but don't let it get you down.'

People whom Father had known when he was a boy came

to talk to him, and I left him with them to wander around the room. I was not hungry and the sight of them piling food on to their plates nauseated me. I went to stand in the window where I could look at a scene all too familiar from my early days in this house.

It had started to rain, and the leafless beeches were swaying in the wind. Behind me came the hum of voices and I was startled out of my reverie by a familiar voice saying, 'It's nice to see ye 'ere Miss Amanda, I never can think of ye as bein' Mrs St Clare.'

I turned to see Cook smiling at me, her round florid face looking no different from the face I had seen years before across the kitchen table. Then her hair had been hidden under a white cap, now it was hidden under a large black felt hat, and at that moment the years dropped away and I was a girl again listening to Cook and Bridie holding forth about the family and any other gossip they could find to talk about.

'Yer grandmother invited me,' she was saying. 'It was nice of 'er to think of mi.'

'You look well, Cook.'

'Oh I'm not so bad for a seventy-five-year-old. I 'ave arthritis and I 'ave bronchitis this weather, but I can still climb the 'ill there and I go where I want to go.'

'I'm glad. Do you see Bridie at all?'

'I take tea with 'em most Sundays. She were allus a good girl, she's never cut me out.'

I smiled.

'It's taken some courage for ye to 'ave come 'ere today Miss Amanda. Bein' with yer father'll 'ave 'elped.'

'Yes, it has.'

'Yer not eatin' anythin'.'

'I'm not very hungry.'

''Ow long are ye stayin' 'ere then?'

'It rests with my father but I rather think we shall be leaving in the morning.'

'I'll be glad when this war's over. The mills are all workin' to capacity but it's not everything. It'll be nice to see the lads and lassies 'ome and not 'avin' to listen to them German planes comin' over every night. Did ye know young Miss Julia was in the Wrens and young Alice is nursin'?'

'Yes, I still thought of them as children.'

'Well, they're not any more, in no time at all they'll be thinkin' of gettin' married. I do 'ear Miss Julia came on leave with a young officer in tow.'

I laughed. 'Yes I can imagine, it would have to be Julia.'

At that moment Granny joined us and with a smile at cook, she said, 'Mr and Mrs Lewis are leaving now, Cook. They'll drop you off at home on the way.'

I was glad to leave the dining room with its crowd of people and find the solitude of the morning room. Nothing would ever change in this house. Dexter's prints hung at the large windows and covered the chairs and sofa. Delicate patterns of roses and petunias, and the rosewood furniture had been unchanged throughout my grandparents' marriage.

I sat on the window seat looking round the room, surprised when the door opened and Caroline came in. She had taken off her hat and coat and she was dressed in a plain black wool georgette dress, her only jewellery three rows of pearls. I was surprised when she came to sit opposite me, pulling up a chair with every intention of indulging in conversation.

'I thought you were too sensitive to come to Grandfather's funeral, but here you are today. Doesn't local gossip worry you, Amanda?'

'Gossip of any kind doesn't worry me, Caroline.'

'Not even when it's based on the truth?'

'You evidently want to talk to me Caroline. What is it you want to say?'

'I would like to know where my husband is serving, I'm his wife but he hasn't seen fit to inform me. I imagine you will know.'

'The last letter I had was from Singapore.'

She raised her eyebrows. 'So we're both out in the cold.'

I didn't answer, and with a shrug of her slender shoulders she said, 'You must realise, Amanda, that if anything dire happens to Phillip the Admiralty will inform me. I shall have to let you know.'

I stared at her in horrified silence. Her words were callous, but in spite of that I saw the truth in them, and she smiled sarcastically. 'It hurts, doesn't it, but surely you must have known. I do think about him often and how I once loved him,

316

or thought I did. On reflection I don't think he ever loved me. Mother pushed too hard, I was too available. All the same I'm not going to make it too easy for you Amanda.'

'I never thought you would.'

'I said I'd be his wife as long as I lived, but perhaps it was rash of me. I'll be his wife until I've found somebody else. I don't think it will be too difficult. After all, I'm beautiful and rich. I have a great deal to offer the right sort of man.'

I didn't speak and after a few minutes she said, rising to her feet, 'You're not saying anything, Amanda, but surely you must know that I'm not the sort of woman to spend the rest of her life in solitary isolation while you think you can take my place.'

'I'm not taking your place, Caroline. I could never do that because we are two very different people. I love Phillip. You only wanted him. I will be the sort of woman he needs, you were only interested in his title and your needs.'

'Well, it hasn't been all it was cracked up to be I can tell you. All those endless committees and wretched charities, all that adulation for the title and precious little for me, I was often bored out of my skin. If ever you do fill my place, which I very much doubt, you'll find out. I have to make an excuse and leave, I've got a dinner party laid on for several American officers, we have to be generous and welcoming where our Allies from across the Atlantic are concerned.'

I felt increasingly restless after she had gone so that I was more than relieved when Father suggested we take a walk now that it had stopped raining.

'They're talking business as usual,' he explained, 'and since I've never been interested in the mills there is nothing I can contribute.'

'It's as though I've never really been away,' I said. 'The same old arguments, and the aunts trying to outdo one another.'

He laughed. 'I see that Caroline left early.'

'Yes, she had a dinner party for some American officers.'

'She told you, did she?'

'Yes, she also told me that if anything happened to Phillip she would be informed, not I.'

'You know that's true, dear.'

317

'Yes. I simply hadn't thought she would put it into words.'

'Did you tell her about Johnnie?'

'No. I'm sure she'll find out soon enough.'

'Yes, well, we're taking your grandmother back with us. It's unreasonable to expect her to stay on here in the immediate future, the house is too big and she's refusing to leave it.'

'Has she agreed to come?'

'For a short while she says. She'll find out about Johnnie though. That'll be one surprise she won't have bargained for.'

'Would you mind if we took a look at the cottage? I have the keys in my pocket and I'd like to see if everything's in order.'

The cottage had a musty unlived in air about it. It felt cold and a thin film of dust covered the furniture where the dust sheets didn't reach, and without the glow of a fire it was impossible to believe that once I had lived in those shrouded rooms.

'Why don't you sell it?' Father said. 'I can't think that you'll ever live in it again.'

'Perhaps I shall if I have to come back to the mill. Nothing about my future is certain. This is the only place I own and one day when the war is over, the mill will go back to producing furnishing material which is what I had planned for.'

'Why are you leaving Phillip out of your plans for the future, Amanda? He's coming home you know, and you have his son. I can't see Phillip living in the cottage while Caroline holds court in the hall which belongs to him.'

His argument was logical but I couldn't believe in it. There was no way Caroline would move out of the hall to make room for me and she was undoubtedly making the most of her role as the wronged wife. As if sensing my thoughts Father said grimly, 'I expect that young woman's entertaining her American guests with her problems. She'll be the beautiful, deserted wife, and she'll entertain them charmingly, listen to their woes and they'll be left wondering how such a treasure could be deserted by an unfeeling husband.'

I smiled. I could imagine Caroline's version of her marriage to a sympathetic ear. They would delight in the hospitality from the lady of the manor. I had heard that Americans were susceptible to aristocratic titles which they themselves had discarded centuries before.

Afternoon tea was being served when we arrived back at the house and while I helped serve it Ralph said to my surprise, 'I'd like a chat with you, Amanda. There hasn't been much chance to talk before.'

'I doubt if there is much chance of us talking here.'

'We can talk in the kitchen, or better still in the drawing room.'

My eyes met his with cynical amusement. It was a very long time since Ralph and I had indulged in any form of conversation.

While I took my place on the chesterfield, he stood on the hearthrug in front of the fire staring down at me. His eyes were filled with amused speculation, and I thought he had put on weight and seemed a little pompous and more like his father.

'It's a long time since we talked, Amanda,' he began hopefully.

'We talked once, Ralph, in the days before you took sides.'

'I had to take sides, Amanda. I couldn't cross Grandfather or my father.'

'It wasn't easy for me, but it was something I had to do.'

'Perhaps you have more courage than me, anyway you were never really one of us. You were the cousin who opted out just like your father before you.'

'Did you hope that it would fall to pieces round my ears, Ralph? I'm sure the rest of you did.'

'No I never did. I hoped you'd show them, I couldn't afford to let them see that I was really on your side. I think you were right about a great many things. It was time we took a good look at ourselves and realised that we should move on. You proved it.'

'Why is it so important for us to talk about it now, Ralph?'

'Will you be coming back to the business when the war is over?'

'How can I say? How do any of us know what will happen or when it will happen?'

'We'll win the war, Amanda, we have to, and now America

and Russia are in it with us. I don't know how long it's going to take, but in the end we'll win.'

'I hope so.'

'Will you be coming back to take charge then, Amanda?'

Chapter Thirty-One

I remembered that conversation with Ralph long afterwards.

On his part it was a conversation designed to placate me, to soothe and to reconcile and he expected me to be grateful that there was a chance that I would be invited back into the fold.

I was amused by his pains to humour me, but I listened quietly.

'After all, Amanda we're all Dexters, aren't we? When the war's over we can all get together again, doing what we do better than anybody else, Grandfather really wanted it and you know how much it would please Granny.'

'Have you forgotten, Ralph, that I spent a small fortune on something none of you wanted anything to do with? Number Three mill is mine, if I return it to the family then I shall want more than a share in the dividends, I shall want a considerable sum for the fact that I am handing it back to the family.'

'But we *are* family, Amanda, all of us.'

'Then, why is it that I have not been made to feel I'm family for some time?'

'Well, that had nothing to do with the mill. It was all to do with Phillip.'

'He was the only one who had any faith in me. I was glad of his help.'

'And not just his help, Amanda.'

'And now because there's a war on and the future's very uncertain the family can afford to forget all that, and put out feelers regarding the future?'

'Well nothing stands still, does it? When the war's over, we shall all have to pick up the pieces, but things don't change all that much. We'll win the war, of course. You'll come back here because of your stake in the mill and Phillip will come back to the hall. After all, it's been in his family for generations, and no doubt he and Caroline will come to terms.'

'You really think that this is what will happen?'

'I think we have to be realistic.'

'And is that what your father and your uncle think?'

'It's what they hope.'

'What about me? Do I come back to live in the cottage or do I come here? Do Phillip and I talk like polite strangers and does Caroline welcome me with open arms? Really, Ralph, I never heard anything more ludicrous.'

'People tend to know which side their bread's buttered. After all, we're none of us children. Men and women do fall in and out of love, and Caroline is hardly nursing a broken heart these days.'

'What do you mean by that?'

'She's entertaining her American officers, and one American officer in particular. They're seen here, there and everywhere, and rumour has it that he's very rich and very smitten.'

'Ralph, I find this entire conversation silly and premature. Shall we wait and see what happens to all of us when the war is over? In the meantime, Phillip is in the Far East and it is months since I heard from him. I think we have to concentrate on our survival, not in what comes after.'

'You're right, of course. But it is something we all have to think about from time to time. I just wanted to tell you how I felt about it. I want you back in the family firm, Amanda, whatever happens in the next few months, or years if that's what it takes, I'll be behind you.'

I wanted to laugh. He kissed me before leaving the room and then I sat back in amused silence to think about what he had said. Ralph had been somebody I had never relied on, he'd been as transient as thistledown, as mercurial as a cloud. It was only that night when everybody had gone home and I lay sleepless in my bed that I thought again about the future.

I could not come back to Fairlawn if Phillip did not come back to me. I would have to make a whole new life

322

somewhere and then I was remembering the warmth of his smile, the tenderness of his kiss, the passionate fulfilment that had produced our son and I knew that if Phillip was spared he would not come back to Caroline, he would come back to me.

My grandmother came down to the south-west to stay with my parents and a few days later Mother brought her to my house on the cliff so that she could meet my son.

We walked across the short grass to meet them, and when Mother called to him he left my side and ran as fast as his little legs could carry him into her arms.

He looked up at Granny with a shy smile and I knew that she would see immediately a face that was so like his father's, and grey eyes under dark curling hair. He walked between them, holding their hands, and Granny smiled at me gently, saying in the next breath, 'He's a beautiful little boy, Amanda. Your mother's been showing me photographs.'

'I told him his Great Granny was coming to see him,' I said. 'He's been looking out for you all morning.'

We ate lunch and we chatted with every appearance of normality, and there was no reproach in her attitude, only warmth and joy in Johnnie. None of us made any mention of his father and it was only later when she played with Johnnie on the lawn that Mother said softly, 'I had to put her in the picture, Amanda. It would have been too much of a shock otherwise.'

'I'm glad that you did.'

'She took it very well, much better than I thought she would.'

'Has she decided how long she is staying?'

'She hasn't spoken about leaving. She can stay as long as she likes.'

'She'll have to tell the others when she gets home.'

'I suppose so. Perhaps Caroline may be tempted to divorce Phillip after all.'

I had no belief that she would. Indeed news of Johnnie would make her more adamant than ever that she would remain Phillip's wife, but I decided to keep my thoughts to myself.

It was much later when I accompanied them to the car that Granny said, 'I pray that Phillip will be safe, Amanda. The war in the Far East is getting much worse, I worry about Charlotte too, what is happening to her?'

It was only after Grandma had returned home that I learned she had expressed considerable worries about my future and Caroline's.

She had talked long and often to Mother about Caroline's dedication to making her marriage to Phillip work, with all her good deeds, her standing in the community. She could not think that Phillip would lightly forget all this, and that even now Caroline was working hard to make sure the Americans in the vicinity were made welcome at the hall.

Dryly, father had said, 'I very much doubt, Mother, that everybody will see her efforts to be kind to them as entirely circumspect. There are a great many people objecting to our generosity to visiting Americans while their own men are away.'

Granny thought that was outrageous.

'There has never been any scandal about Caroline or Phillip until Amanda came back, and then everybody was on Caroline's side.'

'And you too are on Caroline's side,' Father said pointedly.

Grandma had not replied to that.

After several weeks in Cornwall, she returned home and her parting words to me were, 'I do hope you'll come north to see me, Amanda. You'll want to keep an eye on the mill, I know.'

I wasn't sure if she meant it. She would not want me to take Johnnie I felt sure, there would be too much talk.

I was kept busy helping Mother with her Red Cross work and I seemed to be living in limbo. I had no news from Phillip, it seemed that the Far East was another world away, another lifetime, and the only news we had was from the newspapers, and most of it bad.

The Japanese had overrun Malaysia and Singapore. They had made prisoners of the British people living there and our soldiers were fighting in the jungles. Of the navy there was little news except to tell us of ships that were being sunk almost daily and the air raids on eastern cities.

The war in Europe was over but the Japanese fought on. We did not doubt that they would be defeated but their continuance of the war was a matter of honour. They would drag it on to the bitter end.

It was the atomic bombs on two Japanese cities that brought the war in the Far East to its bitter end, and I was brought face to face with an uncertain future.

I did not know whether Phillip was alive or dead, and if Caroline knew she would not inform me, or anybody else who might inform me. If he was alive, he would come home, but would he come home to me?

I decided to travel north where my business interests lay, and my mother agreed to look after Johnnie. The government contracts for the forces would end, and I had memories of the years after the other war when there was wholesale unemployment and despair in the community.

I did not inform my grandmother that I was returning north, so instead I went immediately to the cottage. The garden was a wilderness of weeds with the curtains hanging limply at windows coated with soot. It would take me days to make it habitable but it had to be done and I set about scrubbing and brushing until my arms ached from my efforts. There was coal in the shed and after the fire took hold I found an old tin kettle which would boil water for a cup of tea. The gas and electricity had been turned off but at least the living room looked more cheerful.

I was making sandwiches, the kettle had boiled and I was brewing tea when I heard a loud knocking on the front door and I hurried to open it, surprised to find Cook and Mrs Kendal standing in the porch looking at me expectantly.

'I saw the smoke from the chimney on my way from the church hall,' Cook said sharply. 'I met Mrs Kendal and we decide to see who was 'ere.'

'Do come in, both of you, I'm sorry the cottage is in such a mess but at least you'll be able to find a chair in the living room.'

They looked around them with some curiosity and Cook said, 'When did ye get back then?'

'This morning around eleven o'clock. I got a taxi in the town and I didn't have much luggage. I've just made a cup of tea if you'd like to join me.'

'Yer surely not thinkin' o' stayin' 'ere,' Cook snapped with her usual forthright manner.

'I'll sleep down here tonight, I'll attack the bedrooms tomorrow.'

'What's wrong with yer grandmother's 'ouse then? It's big enough for a dozen folk. Besides I doubt if there's gas or electricity on 'ere.'

'No, there isn't, I'll have to see about that.'

'The cottage 'asn't bin lived in fer over four years. It'll be damp. Yer'll catch yer death o' cold.'

'I'll soon get it habitable, Cook. I'll keep the fire going all night and I'll light fires in the bedroom. I know it doesn't look much now but in a day or two you'll see, everything will be back to normal.'

'I don't suppose the telephone is workin' Mrs St Clare,' Mrs Kendal said practically.

'No, it won't be.'

'Then I'll go down to the factory and tell Tom you're back. I'll get him to telephone the gas and electricity, and I'll see what he can do about gettin' the phone back on.'

'Oh would you, Mrs Kendal. That would be a great help.'

'I'll do some shopping for you too, if that would help.'

'Oh yes it would. I only bought the basics. I was going to see about something later.'

'I'm sure I can find somebody to help you get this place straight,' she said, and Cook added, 'I'll do what I can, course I'm not gettin' any younger and my arthritis is bad. Still there'll be someat I can do.'

She was sitting in front of the fire, eyeing the limp curtains hanging at the windows.

'Them curtains'll have to come down, I doubt if they'll take kindly to washin'.'

'No, I'll probably have to get new ones.'

'I 'ave some in one o' the drawers at 'ome that might do for ye. I'll find 'em and bring 'em round in the mornin'.'

Mrs Kendal set out on her errands and Cook sat at the table cleaning my brasses. The room was coming alive and I felt a rush of gratitude as I looked at her homely face across the room. It was the face I remembered at Fairlawn, the only kind

326

face I had really known in those early years, discounting Grandma's which had to be shared by so many of us.

'Do you see Grandma at all?' I asked her.

'I sees 'er at the church, but I don't visit now. It's too much of a climb for me to get to Fairlawn.'

'Do you see any of the others?'

'I sees your aunts and uncles drivin' up the 'ill on Sunday mornin' and back again in the afternoon. I often sees yer aunts in the town and I've seen the young girls when they've had a mind to visit.'

'I expect Alice and Julia are very grown up now.'

'That they are, yer'll be 'earin' all the news when ye visits yer grandmother for the usual Sunday lunches.'

'She doesn't know I'm here, Cook.'

'She'll find out.'

When I didn't speak she went about rubbing the brasses and then I was suddenly aware of her eyes gleaming with expectation as she said, 'I notice ye 'aven't asked about 'er ladyship.'

'How is my cousin Caroline?'

'The 'all's been open 'ouse for the Americans at the camp on the fell. O' course they've come and gone over the years, but that 'igh rankin' officer's come back agin and agin to enjoy 'er 'ospitality.'

'People will always talk Cook.'

'And where there's smoke there's fire. 'E's a smart enough fella, and not bad-lookin', but they do say 'e's rich. One o' them rich Americans ye read about and sees on the films.'

I laughed. 'I'm quite sure nobody really knows Cook.'

'Oh some of 'em do. I don't think 'er ladyship'll 'ave kept quiet about his credentials.'

'Well I'm sure the talk will end soon, the Americans will be going home and life here will get back to normal.'

'That's what we 'ope, but for some it'll never get back to normal.'

'No. There will be a great many men who will not be coming back.'

'That's right, and nobody knows if Sir Phillip's safe. Nobody's seen 'im since early on in the war, and when they ask 'er ladyship she just smiles and says that she prays he's safe. I don't suppose you know anythin' do ye, Miss Amanda?'

'I know that he was serving on a battle cruiser in eastern waters, but I haven't heard anything for a long time.'

'It must 'a bin terrible out there. Dolly Jeffries 'ad a brother and 'er 'usband both prisoners o' war, she doesn't know now if they're dead or if they're comin' 'ome.'

The silence that followed her words was a long one. We were both immersed in our own thoughts and dismally I was aware that rain was pelting against the windows and that it was almost dark.

'You'll get wet walking home, Cook, I should have realised it was getting late.'

'It's the storm,' she said, 'It'll brighten up again when the rain stops, then I'll be gettin' off 'ome.'

'I'm so glad that you came, and for bringing Mrs Kendal. You've cheered me up considerably.'

'And tomorrow I'll bring up the curtains and we'll see if they'll do until ye can get others.'

'Oh yes, that would be lovely.'

'And if I sees yer grandmother shall I tell 'er yer 'ere and will be callin' on 'er?'

'I'd rather you didn't tell her until I've had a chance to see her. She may feel rather annoyed that I haven't immediately gone to Fairlawn.'

She favoured me with a long hard look before opening her umbrella and walking down the path. The rain had almost stopped, and I was hoping she would get home before it started again.

I had some good friends. In the days that followed the electricity, gas and telephone were restored to the cottage and Cook arrived with her curtains that were adequate until I was able to find others.

Tom Kendal and his wife arrived bearing offcuts of our early designs and these Mrs Kendal ran up on her sewing-machine to fit most of the windows. When Cook saw them, she said, 'They're beautiful, Miss Amanda, I can understand ye not wantin' mine when ye can 'ave these.'

'But I was grateful for yours, Cook. It's just that they really weren't the right size and you did say you would have them

328

back. Mrs Kendal measured up the windows and ran these up for me.'

Grudgingly she said, 'Ay, she's 'andy with 'er sewing-machine, but they do look right nice. Your grandmother'll be surprised at 'ow quickly yer've got settled in.'

'I'm going to see her this evening.'

'Not with the rest of 'em on Sunday?'

'No. I'm going back to Cornwall for the weekend.'

'Isn't that a long way fer a weekend? Besides, yer've only just got 'ere.'

'I know.'

I didn't explain that I was missing Johnnie and needed desperately to see if he was happy in my absence.

My parents would love having him, but now that the war was over, more and more I was having to think anxiously about my future. Tom informed me that orders were starting to come in from furnishing establishments who had been customers before the war, and slowly but surely normal working was beginning in the factory. In the larger combines orders were spasmodic and already workers were being laid off, and on the evening I went to see Grandma she expressed her fears that the cotton industry was in for another recession and that the uncles were increasingly worried about it.

'But it's so soon,' I said with some dismay.

'It is what happened after the last war.'

'But cotton will be needed for other things besides the armed forces, we're getting back to normal surely?'

'I'm only saying what we talked about last Sunday Amanda. What about your enterprise?'

'Tom Kendal says the orders are surely coming in, and we are a small concern compared to the others.'

'They're all much smaller now, Amanda. Once there were more than sixteen mills around this town, now they're condensed into four. What else can they do?'

I was reluctant to be drawn into talk of changing their designs, altering the methods that had been successful before and which now were dated.

'What is happening to Julia now that the war's over?' I asked by way of changing the subject.

'She's got a string of young men who are interested in her.

Her father's bought her a flat in Kensington. They don't tell me much. I'm not sure if she's going to live in it alone or if she's sharing with another girl.'

Or boy, I felt like saying, but kept my opinions to myself.

'Why are you staying at the cottage instead of staying here?' she demanded. 'I'm sure you would be more comfortable here.'

'I'm happy in the cottage, Granny. I've got it to my liking and it's nearer the mill. Besides I wasn't exactly favourite number one with the rest of them.'

'And you won't be again Amanda when they hear about Johnnie.'

'You mean they don't know?'

'No. It's something for Phillip to sort out when he comes home. Will he go back to his wife, Amanda, or will he come back to you?'

'Have they heard anything from Charlotte?'

'No. Wouldn't you think she would write now that the war is over and at least let them know if she's safe? Charlotte was always one on her own.'

They talked about Charlotte as though Samarkand was just around the corner one day, and in the next as though it was on another planet. But it amazed me that they never seemed to think she was in any danger in spite of the fact that the Japanese had overrun so much of the Far East.

When I said as much to Ralph he only grinned and said, 'I thought Samarkand was part of Russia, or Outer Mongolia. Now that the war's over things'll soon get back to normal.

'One of these days Charlotte's going to come back draped in sable and exotic jewels, simply to show the rest of you that she's survived.'

'You sound very sure.'

'I am, just as sure that very soon Phillip will be back to sort out his marriage and where he goes from here.'

Chapter Thirty-Two

I repeated this conversation to my parents over the weekend. Mother was tearful. Father said staunchly, 'If I know Phillip Marston, love, he'll come back to you. His marriage was over, he has a son and you love him. If he contemplates going back to his wife, he's not the man I thought him to be.'

I wasn't sure. Memories were elusive things and people could change. Phillip had been living for years in the most dangerous part of the world and there was no certainty for me that he would find love important when he thought about the rest of his life.

My parents remonstrated with me over the weeks spent in the north and the snatched weekends in Cornwall. The house in Polperro had been reclaimed by the people we had rented it from, and the only home I could really call my own was the cottage on the northern fells.

Ralph was a frequent visitor in my office. He strolled around the aisles chatting to the workpeople and he perched on the corner of my desk listening to my telephone calls and meetings with my manager until one afternoon I said in some exasperation, 'Why are you here Ralph? There was a time when you never came near the place, now you're under my feet every day.'

'I'm filled with admiration, Amanda, at the way you're coping. I've told my father you're a real Dexter, a chip off the old block, we should cultivate you, not distance ourselves.'

'We're happy on our own. You didn't want us and now I don't want you.'

'A bit unkind to family, isn't it?'

'No. I mean it.'

'I wouldn't like Granny to hear you.'

'She heard you all saying it about me.'

'I know, and she invariably took your part.'

'Did she? I didn't know.'

'She'd like it if we buried the hatchet and got back together again. This is a busy little place, the orders are coming in and your dreams are coming true. I'm here to say we're sorry we ever doubted you. Please come back into the fold.'

He was audacious but seldom malicious. He amused me and exasperated me but I was not to be drawn into anything further.

I had no doubt that he reported everything he saw to my uncles, and eventually invitations came to join them for Sunday lunch, invitations which I was able to decline on the ground of going to Cornwall.

'Why are you always rushing back there?' Ralph said. 'You're a big girl, you don't need to see your parents every weekend, I said as much to Granny, but all she said was that it was none of our business.'

'Nor is it.'

'One would think you'd got a lover down there, somebody you can't afford to miss seeing.'

'I can't.'

'Well, that'll be a relief to Caroline, not that I think she's bothered these days, not with her American colonel dancing attention.'

'How's Alice? You seldom talk about her.'

'Alice is coming home next weekend. If you come to Sunday lunch you'll be able to meet her.'

'I shan't be there.'

'Then come for a meal on Friday evening and you can meet her then?'

'I shall be going to Cornwall on Friday evening.'

'What time's your train?'

'Six o'clock from Manchester. I'm hoping to drive back now that petrol's becoming less restricted.'

'You surely don't intend driving there and back every weekend?'

'No, but I really need my car here.'

'So you're not going to see Alice?'

'It doesn't look like it.'

'If she gets home Friday morning I'll bring her in here to see you.'

'That would be nice.'

Our conversation was always light-hearted and pithy. There was never any resentment and he invariably left with a jaunty smile on his face and good-humoured remarks to the weavers he passed on the way out.

There were times, when out of sheer devilment, I longed to say that I was going to Cornwall to see my son, but since Granny had maintained a discreet silence about his existence I deemed the time was not yet ripe.

Alice was an agreeable surprise. I had wondered if she would resemble Jenny, but only her eyes, large brown eyes in a pretty dimpled face reminded me of her. She was brought into my office in the morning and immediately Ralph asked if he could leave her with me as he had a business appointment in the town.

She looked round her with interest and then with a smile said, 'Dad's tried to get me interested in cotton, a job in the office at Dexter's, but I'm not interested.'

'Haven't you been nursing?'

'I was helping out on the ward, I didn't want to go into the services like Julia.'

'Don't you want to take up nursing then?'

'I'm not sure. I'm a bit squeamish actually. I'm not very good with terminally ill people.'

Her eyes met mine frankly and I knew at that moment she was thinking about her mother. Long before she was ready for it she had been faced with Jenny's histrionics, and her tragic death was something she would never forget; that she appeared as normal as she was said something for her resilience.

'Does this mean that you'll be living with your father for the time being?'

She smiled. 'Not for long I hope, Dad's hardly ever in, he's too busy entertaining his lady friends, I'd be in the way.'

The generation gap between my girlhood and Alice's was becoming more and more apparent. It became even more apparent when she said, 'Julia's got her own flat in London. Her father bought it for her when she said she wanted to move out. I don't want a flat or a house here, and I doubt if Dad'll take to the idea, but I don't want to live with him.'

'Does Julia have a job?'

'Her father's pulled a few strings. She's got a job in one of the ministries, she says he'll do the same for me, but I'm not sure I want to live in London.'

'Couldn't you live with Julia. Isn't there room in her flat?'

She laughed. 'I think she's got somebody living with her, I don't know if it's a girl or some boy or other.'

'Would her father approve of that?'

She laughed. 'He's got no option if it's what Julia wants.'

'I'd like to see Julia. She was constantly up here at one time but now I expect she's more important things to do.'

'I suppose so. She liked you. She said you were the nicest of the older generation.'

When I raised my eyebrows she laughed again, saying, 'Dad's generation I mean. Julia hated Aunt Caroline and she said Charlotte was weird. You were the normal one.'

I could imagine Julia entertaining shy introverted Alice in those early days with her sophisticated views on the family at large. Julia would have derived great pleasure from being in a position to describe us all to the little cousin who had been prevented from knowing us by her insecure mother.

'I remember you coming to the house with Sir Phillip when my mother died,' she surprised me by saying. 'You were kind.'

'Well, of course, Alice. You were too young for all that.'

'Somehow or other things got better. It's an awful thing to say but for the first time I really began to see and do things.'

'I know. I remember your mother when she was young. I tried to be friends with her because I too was very lonely in those days, but it wasn't easy.'

'No. There seemed to be so many of you. I loved Great-Granny Dexter, she was kind, but the others were different, I never felt one of them for an awful long time, now it's different. I go to see my grandmother and I see Aunt Sophie from time to time. Of course they're away a lot.'

'Would you like to look around the mill?' I asked her.

334

'I don't really know anything about what's going on. I've been inside some of the other mills but I hated the noise and the machinery. If you haven't time to talk, I really don't mind.'

'I'll take you along to the print room and you can take a look at the curtain material. When the order is finished it's going to America.'

'Does Dad know?'

'Why should he?'

'Some of Dad's weavers are on half time and here they all are working all out. Did you really set out to steal their work?'

'No Alice. I had hoped to interest them in what I had to offer, they didn't want to know.'

'It's their own fault then?'

'Yes, I really think it is.'

In the print room I watched her enthusing eagerly about the rolls of beautiful damask and linen, her pretty face alive with admiration.

'Oh, I love these,' she exclaimed. 'I love the birds and the flowers, I love the colours, they're so much more subtle than Dad's prints. We have those all over the house.'

'If you find yourself somewhere to live, I'll let you have some of these for your windows. How's that?'

'That's wonderful. I know now why Julia said you were nice.'

When Ralph picked her up later that morning we were drinking coffee and she was chatting animatedly so that his eyes met mine with amused disbelief.

'I must say you're getting on very well. Are you quite sure you don't want to eat dinner with us this evening?'

'Quite sure, I really do have to catch that train.'

'Your parents won't mind if you miss a weekend.'

'I want to go Ralph.'

'Can't you persuade her, Alice?' he asked.

'Not really,' I said laughing. 'Alice and I will meet again I'm sure.'

'You won't forget the curtains, will you?' were her parting words.

It was almost midnight when I stepped down from the train

at Par where Father was waiting for me. I was tired. Exhaustion must have shown on my face and he said gently, 'You can't keep this up Amanda. Sooner or later you'll have to find some other arrangement.'

'I know. I'm staying until Tuesday because it's Johnnie's birthday on Sunday, I need to spend a little more time with him.'

Johnnie was three on Sunday, and when he came into my bed the following morning squealing with delight I realised that I was missing these years. He seemed to have grown into a little boy overnight. He was beautiful with his father's grey eyes and dark sculptured hair. He was tall and robust with health and when he smiled his whole face lit up with enchanting charm.

It was September, a warm golden day with sun-crested waves flecking across the sands and a light breeze rippling the grass. The beaches were empty; only the crying of the gulls disturbed the stillness.

I looked through the window to where my parents were setting out a meal on the terrace and Johnnie sat on the grass with his arm round the neck of Alex, Mother's cocker spaniel.

It was a scene of England at peace, the seashore and a garden, the white scudding clouds and a family at peace with each other, but in my heart was a strange and searching loneliness. Idly, I picked up Phillip's portrait from the top of my dressing table, and I looked long and earnestly at his face.

I was remembering the gravity behind his smile, the low timbre of his voice, the depth and passion of our love-making, but had it been too long?

How long must I wait, and what would Phillip remember after years of danger in a man's world? Surely men wanted to come back to stability, to a remembered peace and tranquillity, not to have to start again to unravel the misery of a broken marriage with all its accompanying trauma?

It was hard for me to maintain a sense of normality when I was torturing myself with uncertainties, but for the sake of my parents and the birthday party for Johnnie, I had to try.

Later in the afternoon Johnnie and I walked along the beach and I watched him eagerly searching shell pools for some treasure he could place in his pail. A small chill breeze had arisen and I called to him gently, saying it was time to walk back, and he turned immediately to run back to me. He was laughing when he reached my side, pointing back towards the house and the cliff path, where I saw a man running quickly on to the sand. At first I thought it was Father coming to look for us, and then suddenly as he walked towards us I realised that this man was wearing a naval officer's uniform and he was smiling, his face alive with warmth and joy.

With a little cry I released Johnnie's hand and ran laughing into Phillip's arms.

It was later that night when we were alone together that we could talk about the future. My parents had left us alone and Johnnie was in bed, there was a full moon and the night wind had suddenly died down. We walked in the garden, savouring the scents of the night and the murmur of the sea and I learned something of the years we had been apart. He talked dispassionately about the cruelties of war, the torment of separation and the terrible fears that it could never end and the disbelief that two devastating bombs on Japanese cities had finally been instrumental in bringing them to their knees.

'In all that time Amanda, I received only four letters from you. There were probably others I never received, but in any one of them did you tell me about Johnnie?'

'No, I never told you. I had to be sure if there was anything left from those years with Caroline. I couldn't use Johnnie to bring you back to me.'

'I love you Amanda. I meant every word I said to you at our last meeting, I'm delighted that we have Johnnie, but it wouldn't have made any difference if we hadn't.'

'I'll telephone you. I want to be with you wherever you are.'

'Then I'll wait until I hear from you.'

For a long moment there was silence. We were all immersed in our own thoughts, then Phillip surprised me by saying, 'Have any of the family heard anything from Charlotte during the last few years?'

None of us had, and Father asked sharply, 'Have you any news of her Phillip? The Japanese were not in Samarkand?'

'I saw her in Singapore. It was the morning before we left and I'd been ashore to see some chap from the embassy. I was on my way back to the ship and I saw a stream of women and children being escorted along the railtracks from one of the sheds. They were a rag-taggle mixture of different nationalities, undernourished, poorly clad, the usual mixture of weary heart-breaking people there'd been all too many of once the war was over, Japanese prisoners-of-war, coming back to civilisation and some sort of hope. I was staring at them without really seeing any one of them, and then suddenly a woman left them and walked slowly across to where I was standing. It was Charlotte.

'I didn't recognise her at first. She was gaunt, sickly, a caricature of the woman I remembered, but she had recognised me and yet she was unable to answer the thousand and one questions I wanted to ask her. She said they were being taken to a derelict hotel in the city for the time being and that she would have to go with the others. I told her I would go to see her there that evening. So many of the buildings in Singapore had been destroyed, the authorities were doing their best.

'She looked a little more like herself when I met her again that evening. They'd managed to feed them and she'd had a bath and was wearing some sort of garment they'd found for her.'

'What about her husband?' Father asked.

'She doesn't know. In between her tears she told me it was her fault that they'd been in Singapore, a longing for the luxury of western hotels, shops and night life. The air-raid on Pearl Harbour had not been envisaged, but after that it seemed the entire Far East erupted overnight. The ferries were crowded, were being sunk at their moorings and everybody thronged to the station with the idea of getting away to some sort of safety. Malaysia, Sumatra, anywhere. She was separated from Sanjay at the station and the last she saw of him he was being herded into a train with a crowd of other men.'

'But didn't he have a Chinese passport?' I cried.

'That wouldn't help him. The Japanese have no love for the Chinese nor would the fact that he had an English wife.

She refused to tell me anything about her life as a prisoner in Japanese hands, and when I asked her what she intended to do, she said she was going home, home to Samarkand.'

'Is she expecting to find him there?' I asked.

'She was expecting nothing. But she was adamant that she was going back to Samarkand. She doesn't know if her husband is still alive, but in Samarkand are things that belong to her. The woman I spoke to in the evening was a far cry from the one I had seen earlier in the day. This was the old Charlotte, a survivor and wanting what was rightfully hers. I'll be able to tell her parents that she's alive and one of these days she's going to surface with or without her husband, and with everything she can conceivably get her hands on.'

I recognised the Charlotte he was describing, but he was describing Caroline too. Another woman who would hang on to what was rightfully hers, come hell or high water.

It was almost a month later when I was told I was wanted on the telephone in my office and my heart leapt when I thought it might be Phillip.

'I'm coming north by train Amanda. I haven't been able to get hold of a suitable car at such short notice. I shall be arriving in Manchester around ten o'clock in the evening. Can you meet my train?'

'Yes of course.'

'We need to talk, Amanda, but not until I've spoken to Caroline. Until tomorrow.'

The conversation had been all too brief and I was glad there was only another day to wait until I saw him. Now that the rest of my life was to be decided soon, I didn't feel ready for it, and yet I couldn't have gone on in limbo. I anticipated tremendous difficulties even when Phillip was optimistic that they could be resolved.

Phillip was wearing civilian clothes when he stepped down from the train and he was smiling his encouragement long before he reached my side. It was a two-hour drive to the cottage and after a while it seemed that normal conversation was banal and we drove in silence. Long before we reached our destination he was asleep, and after I had stopped the car I looked long and earnestly at his face, serene and peaceful and momentarily robbed of the cares and questions which must torment him as much as they tormented me.

Shaking his arm gently I said, 'Phillip we're home. Do you intend to drive up to the hall tonight?'

Sleepily he consulted his watch, then with a wry smile said, 'I think I should. People will talk soon enough. If I could borrow your car?'

'Yes, of course.'

'I'll see that it's returned to you in the morning. Are you able to get a lift to the mill?'

'I can easily walk. I don't always take the car.'

'I'll be in touch sometime tomorrow. If I don't telephone I'll come to see you in the evening. By that time I hope Caroline and I will have been able to talk.'

He gripped my hands and looked long and searchingly into my eyes, then he kissed me briefly before driving off into the night. I made myself a hot drink and sat in the living room. It was eight o'clock the next morning when I awoke, the tea cold on the table near my chair and I was shivering in the chill autumn morning. I had thought to lie awake for most of the night, obsessed with too many problems. Now I faced a new day stiff from sitting too long in a none-too-comfortable chair and overwhelmed by the problems that came rushing back into a new day.

340

Chapter Thirty-Three

I had thought the day would drag interminably but half way through the morning John Stedman arrived, bringing with him two Americans and the rest of the morning flashed past all too quickly. They were enthusiastic, promising trade and inviting me to lunch.

'Are you staying in the town?' I asked John curiously, knowing that he usually stayed with Phillip when he was in the area.

'I'm staying in Manchester with the Americans. I wasn't sure when Phillip would be released from the navy and I didn't want to be a problem. Have you heard from him?'

'Yes. He came home yesterday.'

'So he'll be at the hall?'

'I expect so, but he'll have a hundred and one things to see to. After all, he's been away for five years.'

He nodded. 'I'll speak to him on the telephone when he's had a chance to settle in. Things are really taking off for you, Amanda.'

When I stared at him in surprise, he was quick to say, 'I mean at the mill. Your manager says the orders are coming in steadily and I can promise you business with these two. You'll have to expand soon, take over some of your grandfather's premises.'

I laughed. 'If I attempt to do that he'll haunt me.'

'He might, but I rather think your uncles might be pleased. Cotton's going to be in the doldrums again, they need something new and adventurous.'

Lunch was a light-hearted affair and I was glad of new

341

company which prevented my thinking about other things. It was late afternoon when they finally left, and when I entered my office, my secretary said, 'Sir Phillip telephoned, Mrs St Clare. He says he'll call for you around five.'

'Thank you, Eve. Sir Phillip borrowed my car last night.'

There had been no reason for me to explain to Eve. I was becoming paranoid about what people said or thought. So much so that I waited until everybody else had gone before I left the building.

If there was anxiety in my eyes when they met his, it was quickly dispelled by the warmth of his smile.

'I thought you were home when I saw smoke coming out of the chimney,' he said. 'Who lit the fire for you?'

'I have a daily woman. If the day's cool she lights the fire.'

'Does she make your meal?'

'She would if I asked her, but I had lunch with John Stedman and two Americans. I'm really not very hungry.'

'Then we'll talk over coffee, although there's not a lot I can tell you Amanda. Caroline's not at home.'

'Will she be home soon?'

'The servants didn't know, and of course she hasn't left a note, even when she knew I was expecting to be home any day.'

'She knew you were coming home?'

'I wrote to tell her so. Her absence doesn't surprise me. She was always guaranteed to the do the unpredictable.'

'Have you spoken to her parents?'

'No. It's doubtful if they know where she is. Her frequent absences were a source of annoyance to her mother most of the time.'

The tiny living room looked remarkably cheerful as a result of Mrs Johnson's cleaning and polishing, and a blazing fire added light and warmth to the room.

'This is a nice little house,' Phillip said appreciatively. 'I've spent all my life in large rooms which needed a great deal of heating. There were times when I wished they were smaller and more intimate. I like this little house of yours, Amanda.'

'You wouldn't like to live here, Phillip. This sort of cottage was reserved for your tenants.'

342

'I know, but I could live here with you. I might have to in the immediate future.'

'Are you saying that, if Caroline is still adamant about a divorce, you would leave her and live here with me?'

'I'm saying that I will leave her. Where we live is something we shall have to talk about. We have a son Amanda, we should be together with him. A family.'

I had no faith that Caroline would be accommodating. I made sandwiches and coffee and carried them into the living room on a tray and we ate them sitting in front of the fire.

My immediate future tantalised me. There would be the family to face and the hostility of a small provincial town that had watched the fairy-tale marriage of the lord of the manor and the daughter of a Dexter. That I too was a Dexter would be discounted. I was the scarlet woman who had wrecked her cousin's marriage and in their eyes my son would be a bastard, a child who should never have been born.

I had friends in the town, the men and women I employed and who were grateful to me, people like Tom and Evie, people who had been out of work and I had rescued from poverty, but would it count against the antagonism of so many others?

I had thought there would be so much to talk about but somehow the words wouldn't come. It amazed me that we talked of other things outside our problems, like the years of war, the mill and the everyday normalities, and then at just after ten o'clock the telephone rang and our eyes met in startled surprise.

I answered it, and recoiled at Caroline's crisp voice asking, 'Is my husband with you?'

'Yes. I'll bring him to the phone.'

'There's no need. I'm home, perhaps he'll come here tonight if it's convenient. If not, I shall see him in the morning.'

'I'm sure he will want to see you tonight, Caroline.'

The line went dead and when I replaced the receiver I turned to see Phillip standing in the doorway.

'It was Caroline?' he said.

'Yes.'

'Then I'd better get up there. There's a lot to sort out.'

The night stretched before me endlessly, and all I could think about was the meeting between Phillip and his wife. I made myself a cup of tea and took it into the living room to drink it.

How could I possibly have slept, when within a few miles my entire future was being talked over between the man I loved and the cousin I had never understood or even liked?

It was only just light when I let myself out of the cottage, having bathed and dressed ready for the day ahead, but I felt I could not linger on, waiting for Phillip to telephone or come in person. I walked briskly down the hill to where men and women were already leaving their homes in answer to the shrill hooters from the mills lower down and, if they stared at me curiously, I simply bade them good morning and walked on.

It was at least an hour and a half earlier than I would normally have walked to my office, and inside the mill itself all conversation ceased as I passed along the isle of looms to the office beyond.

I had only just taken off my coat when Tom Kendal came in, acutely surprised at seeing me sitting behind my desk.

'I saw ye comin' into the mill yard, Mrs St Clare. There's nothin' wrong I hope?'

'No, Tom. I didn't sleep very well, I thought the walk would do me good and I decided to come in early.'

'We've got some folk comin' over later to take a look at the green damask.'

'Yes I know, I'll bring them up to the print room as soon as they arrive.'

'It's lookin' very well.'

'That's good then,'

'Mr Ralph was in yesterday afternoon, he just missed ye.' Tom grinned. ''E's gettin' very fond o' looking around 'ere, Mrs St Clare. Would there be a good reason for it?'

I smiled 'I rather think my cousin would like to think that one day we could forget the past and become one concern again.'

'And can we, do ye think?'

'I don't know, Tom. There would have to be a lot of discussion. We would have to forget a great deal of acrimony that has passed between us and I'm not prepared to see them take over everything that we have made so successful without a great deal of reassurance.'

'I should say not, Mrs St Clare. The workpeople have long memories too. We respect Dexter's, but it's you who found us work when they threw a good number of us on the scrap 'eap.'

'Don't worry, Tom. You'll be looked after, all of you.'

With a smile he left and with the arrival of my office staff along came Ralph, smiling amiably, and I was careful not to let him see the amusement in my eyes.

'I called yesterday,' he said, 'but you'd already left.'

'I had to drive into Manchester. Was it something special, Ralph?'

'Not really. I was wondering if you'd heard from Phillip.'

'You've never asked about him before.'

'No. I just thought it was high time he was getting out of the navy.'

'How's Alice?'

'Fine. She's decided she doesn't want to continue with nursing. God knows what she does want.'

'So, where is she?'

'Sitting in the car outside, sulking.'

'She didn't want to see me then?'

'I've given her an ultimatum she doesn't like. Get a job or go back to college to learn something useful. I was never as much trouble to my parents as she is to me.'

I laughed. 'Oh Ralph, how vividly I remember those Sunday mornings when you were in dire trouble with Grandfather and your parents. You invariably relieved the boredom of those Sunday luncheons.'

'There was only Jenny who upset them.'

'And the yearnings to go into the army instead of the mills, and your leanings towards the board room instead of the factory floor.'

He laughed. 'I suppose so.'

Sobering quickly he said. 'You know you'll have to be making decisions quickly Amanda, or is it all going to evaporate into thin air? Will Phillip go back to Caroline, and will you go on being a captain of industry?'

'I'm sure you'll hear in due course.'

'And in the meantime you're saying nothing.'

'There's nothing to say.'

He left with a quizzical smile on his lips and I left my desk to watch him walking airily between the aisle of weavers, treating them to his cheerful smiles and occasional nods of recognition.

It was later in the morning and I was with our visitors in the Print Room when Evie came to tell me that I had a visitor waiting for me in my office.

Her expression was wary and filled with unease so that I asked sharply, 'Who is it Evie?'

'Lady Marston, Mrs St Clare. Shall I bring coffee?'

'I'll let you know,' I answered.

My first thoughts were, oh no! not again, not another scene where we played out our private dramas in front of my workpeople, and as I walked back to the office I was aware of their stares of anticipation. I felt afraid.

Caroline was standing at the window staring down on to the mill yard. She was dressed casually in a long camel coat and she turned quickly at the sound of the door closing behind me. Our eyes met and in that split second she was aware of the anxiety in my expression, the unspoken plea that now was not the time for histrionics.

'I can see you're surprised to see me,' she said. 'You expected Phillip.'

'I didn't expect either of you here at the mill.'

'Phillip knows I've come. There wasn't any other way.'

She opened her large crocodile handbag and reached inside. Then she tossed a bunch of keys on to the desk top.

'You'll be wanting those,' she said brightly. 'They're the keys to the front door, my bedroom safe. There isn't anything in it by the way. All the other locks around the house. I shan't have any more use for them.'

I stared at her in amazement and in the next moment she laughed and picked up a briefcase that had been resting against my desk.

'You'll also be wanting these,' she said lightly. 'They're a list of all those boring charities I've been bolstering up all these years. You'll have to get an accountant on to the accounts. I've never been any good with figures. Oh and there's the vicar of St Mary's, he'll be glad to be rid of me. I was never a very good substitute for the previous Lady Marston.'

'Where are you going?'

'You mean you're interested? Phillip and I talked until the small hours. You've cost him a pretty packet, Amanda. Not me, you, because to have you he's had to give me what I asked for, and believe me it was plenty.

'You'll find out, it's not all it's cracked up to be being Lady Marston. Most of it was a shock to me. I thought it would be balls and parties and all the standard of living in that crumbling pile, but most of it's been hell. If you're into country living you've got it made. It seems I never was.'

'It was what you wanted.'

'Yes, I really thought it was, now I know it wasn't. Drinking tea with the vicar's wife and opening bazaars. Meetings for causes you don't care a fig about and then when the bills roll in and the death duties start mounting up I began to realise I'd sold my soul for a mess of potage.'

'What will you do?'

'My dear girl, I'm shaking the dust of this cool green land off my shoes for ever. I'm going to America where even the poor have a little fun but I'm not going to be poor. I'm marrying my American colonel, who's loaded, a member of an old Bostonian family with a mansion in Boston and a yacht at Cape Cod. We've had our share of sitting on the top, now times are changing. Nobody's going to care a button for the upper classes so I'm going to a country where money talks and aristocratic titles mean nothing.

'I'm getting out, Amanda, and it'll take some time for this close-knit community to forget and forgive your part in the break-up of the lord of the manor's marriage. They will in time, particularly when they see that at least you gave him the son I never wanted to give him.'

I stared at her steadily and after a few minutes her eyes wavered and somewhat nervously she picked up her handbag and turned away. At the door she turned to say, 'We probably won't meet again, Amanda. I don't suppose I'll ever come back to the north.'

'What about your parents?'

'I've said my farewells to them. Mother isn't exactly delighted that she'll no longer be the mother of Lady Marston; being married to an American Millionaire isn't quite the same. They'll come out to see me, and when she gets back to England she'll bore everybody for months about the state of our affluence and no doubt she'll bore me about you and my ex-husband.'

'Are you leaving today?' I asked her.

'I packed days ago. I always knew it would come to this. I'm going to London this afternoon, and I'm sailing to America in three days' time. By the time you get to the hall Phillip will no doubt have removed every last vestige of my presence there.

'We never really got on, did we Amanda? Always at the back of my mind was the feeling that I would have to watch you. Now it really doesn't matter, does it?'

After a long cool stare she turned, closing the door sharply behind her.

I stared down at the keys on my desk and the briefcase filled with papers, then I looked up in time to see her striding through the aisles, looking neither to left nor right.

From the window I saw her hurrying across the yard to her car. She drove away without a backward glance and I sat down at my desk feeling drained of all emotion.

There was no going back for any of us. There would be prejudice and condemnation to be faced, but in my innermost heart I felt no regret. If Phillip's marriage to Caroline had been built on real love and a desire from both of them to make it succeed, I could never have made him love me. Now in the years ahead of us I had to prove to Phillip and to a great many others that what we had together was in the end worth all the heart-searching we were facing now.

Later in the afternoon the telephone rang shrilly in my office just as I was about to leave for home. It was Aunt Edith.

'I hope you're satisfied now that my daughter has left the hall so that you can move in with Phillip,' were her opening words.

'I don't think now is the time to talk about it, Aunt Edith.'

348

'Well I think it is. Have you nothing to say about your part in all this? And I know about your son. Grandma Dexter told me when she knew Caroline was leaving.'

'Aunt Edith, Caroline is happy to be leaving. She's going to America to marry a man she's in love with, and she's not suffering from a broken heart over the ending of her marriage to Phillip.'

'How do we know she isn't? She's being very brave, putting a brave face on everything, showing us that she can survive.'

'Aunt Edith, I expect you to take Caroline's side, she's your daughter. I do think when you've had time to think about things you might realise Caroline's marriage was not the wonderful thing you thought it was. I hope that time will resolve our differences and that one day we can be friends again.'

'I doubt it,' was her reply before she slammed down the receiver.

I decided to wait until everyone had left before leaving myself.

They walked away in small groups, and occasionally one or the other of them looked up at the office windows, and I knew I was the subject of their conversation.

An eerie stillness seemed to have descended now that the clamour of the machinery was stilled,and when at last I went down the steep stone steps leading to the mill yard I began to feel that I had never been so alone in my life.

The night watchman had come on duty and I could see him letting himself into the small office near the mill gates. He raised his cap when he saw me and held the gates open so that I could pass through.

'Are ye goin' for yer car, Mrs St Clare?'

'Not today, Ned. I'm walking back to the cottage.'

'It's a fair walk on a cold day. I reckon I can lock the gates now.'

'Yes. Goodnight, Ned.'

I was almost at the end of the road when I saw Phillip driving my car towards me, and gratefully I sank into the front seat next to him. As we drove back towards the fells, there were groups of workpeople still chatting at street

349

corners and I could sense their eyes staring after us as we drove up the hill.

Nothing would be easy in that north country town where there were conventions people had sworn their lives to, and where people saw their lives in black and white – never in shades of grey.

There would be prejudice to overcome, and I had no doubt that Caroline and her mother had already paved the way for her to be seen as the wronged wife. Caroline on the other side of the Atlantic, would not care.

I sat staring through the car window, lost in feelings of despair, then I felt Phillip's hand covering mine and looking up I saw his smile and the understanding in his eyes.

Chapter Thirty-Four

So, how did they go, those years that came after?

The Marston family had always been highly respected in a community that had grown up in an area where the great house dominated the lonely fells and distant town and villages. Phillip was a respected landowner, a good employer, a decent man and these qualities did not change. I was the one they had to accept and the community was divided in their loyalty.

They remembered that I was the Dexter who had defied the family and found them employment at a time when there was little work. The men and women who had worked for me took my part, the others who condemned me, initially, listened to them and gradually came to accept me.

They saw that Phillip was happy and they liked our son. That I had given Phillip a son weighed very much in my favour and Johnnie was a charming friendly little boy.

In time Caroline's old friends approached me about the committees and charities she had sponsored, but I was wary, unsure about their reasons for approaching me.

Aunt Edith spent a great deal of her time in America and when she returned, the community was left in no doubt that Caroline was living the sort of existence they only saw in lush Hollywood films: their house, their garden, their swimming pool and their yacht, how much her husband adored her, their rich friends and her wardrobe.

Aunt Edith was not to know that her boasts about Caroline alienated them, and more and more they looked upon me as the sort of Lady Marston they wanted. The seal was set on their approval when Phillip's mother came to stay with us.

Her visits had been very few when Caroline was Phillip's wife. Now she mingled with people at the church and at various other functions in the town, telling them she was enjoying her visit and more than happy to be with her grandson.

In the days and weeks of her visit she became my dearest friend and I listened to her advice and learned from it.

She began to insist that I accompany her to flower shows and charity dinners, and when they thanked her for her support she was quick to say, 'Well I really am getting too old for this sort of thing but I'm sure Amanda will be happy to step in for me.'

'Have you decided to leave us again?' one lady asked her, and to my surprise Lady Marston answered, 'I've been very happy here. If my son and his wife can tolerate me, I might be persuaded to come back to the area.'

When I told Phillip he said, 'You know you can come back any time mother. You can have your own set of rooms here and do exactly as you please.'

'Well that would be nice, dear. I'll stay with my sister for several weeks, but we're too much alike and we argue a lot. I'll be happier here.'

'Why did you ever leave?' he asked her.

'I didn't think Caroline would appreciate having me here. She wanted a free hand to be in charge of the house and her destiny.'

Their smiles of understanding said it all.

When Johnnie went away to his father's old school I missed him terribly. Our rides together across the fell, our board games in the morning room when we tried to instruct his grandmother and failed miserably. Now I rode alone and it was on one of those rides that I looked down on another rider approaching the house along the long drive that led from the gates.

I could not tell if it was a man or a woman and urging my horse down the hill I had the strangest feeling that it might be Caroline. There was something about the figure on the horse that made me think of her and as we drew nearer I could see that it was a woman. She pulled in her horse as we cantered along the drive and our eyes met. She smiled and I gasped with surprise, 'Charlotte.'

She grinned. 'Did you think I must be dead?' she asked.

'Charlotte, I didn't know what to think. None of us did.'

'Well, here I am. I'm dying for a cup of tea.'

We left the two horses in the stable yard in the care of a groom and Charlotte said, 'I got him from the riding stables. We no longer have horses at Fairlawn.'

'Are you staying with Grandma then?'

'Heavens yes. I couldn't stand having to listen to Mother going on all the time about Caroline's new lifestyle and my quite obvious poverty.'

'You have an awful lot to tell me, Charlotte.'

'There's a lot to tell you but there are also a great many gaps in my story. Tolstoy could have written it, all that mad flight across Russia, all the waiting and all the trauma.'

She had followed me into the hall and stood at last in the drawing room looking around her.

'We changed a lot of the furnishings, Charlotte. There was so much of Caroline and it wasn't my taste.'

'Well, of course, you changed it. I don't remember it, I came here so seldom. Once or twice I came with the family but never with her friends. As long as I can remember if anybody liked Caroline they didn't like me.'

'She's very happy in America.'

'I know. Mother never lets up. Her house, her yacht, her friends. I don't envy her even when Mother's suggested I get myself off there where no doubt she'll find me a man with plenty of money and in a similar background to her husband.'

I laughed. She was standing near the fireplace staring down into the flames, her expression thoughtful, with a strange elusive sadness about her that would have been alien to the old Charlotte.

'Here, let me take your riding mac, and I'll ask them to bring tea. Sit near the fire, Charlotte I thought it was chilly out there.'

We waited in silence for the tea to arrive but it was not an uncomfortable silence. I knew that she would tell me her story when the time was right.

'How have you weathered the storm?' was her first question.

'I knew it would take time. Phillip's mother has helped

353

she's been such a good friend. And then there's Johnnie. He's a nice boy and people see him as the boy Phillip wanted. I feel more at peace with myself and my surroundings, and your mother keeps everybody informed about Caroline's lifestyle in America. Now that they've come to terms with it, they're largely on my side.'

'And you did find work for a great many people Dexter's had dispensed with?'

'That too.'

For some minutes neither of us spoke and in the face of the woman sitting opposite me I tried to recapture the face of the girl I had left behind me in Hong Kong. There was a stillness about her, a haunting sadness in her eyes that had once appeared so assured, and when she looked up and smiled the sadness behind her smile was troubling.

'There's such a lot to tell you, Amanda. I'm not sure how to begin.'

'Phillip told me he saw you in Singapore, I thought you'd be coming back to England almost immediately.'

'And what did you think when I didn't?'

'I thought you'd decided to stay with you husband in Samarkand.'

'We were all lumped together in Singapore, a group of women who seemed to have been together for always. They were mostly Englishwomen taken prisoner in Singapore, one or two Australians and several Asian women. They were magnificent. We got to know one another well. In fact there never seemed to have been another life, and we had no means of knowing how long we would be prisoners. We heard nothing. All we knew was that the war was being played out and our Japanese guards informed us that they were winning it.'

'Where they cruel to you?'

'Cruel yes, sadistic often, and there was sickness amongst us and never enough to eat.'

'Why were you captured in Singapore?'

Her expression changed and her eyes became suddenly bleak.

'It was all my fault. I wasn't unhappy in Samarkand. For months every year I told myself that I was content, and then

354

for no reason at all I'd start thinking about the luxurious hotels and the shops, the clothes, the music and I'd want us to go to Singapore or Hong Kong. I kept on telling Sanjay how well he always felt in Singapore, that he should spend a few weeks there to equip him for months in Samarkand. He always smiled but he knew that his health was the last thing I was thinking about. I was thinking about me, old memories and the illusion that I still belonged in a world I had thoughtlessly discarded.'

'But you were happy with Sanjay?'

'With my mandarin. Yes, I was happy enough. Every day I spent in that wretched Japanese camp I thought about him sitting in that old house in Samarkand surrounded by his treasures. I remembered how his hands would caress a figure in yellowing old ivory and the smooth coldness of jade. I listened endlessly to him telling me how to assess the carving of old Chinese figurines which the Japanese had never quite been able to capture, and how the colour of jade and rose quartz could assess its worth.'

'Are you telling me that Sanjay remained in Samarkand and you went alone to Singapore?'

'Of course not, we went together. We knew the war was raging in Europe, but in Singapore nothing had changed and I loved it. Right from the first few days Sanjay kept on saying we should think of going back, something was wrong. He was a great one for sensing things. And then came the attack on Pearl Harbour. Overnight everything changed.

'People were clamouring to get out. The harbour and the airport were packed. Suddenly Singapore was like a prison, with the Japanese on the doorstep. We had no chance of getting back to Samarkand. Samarkand is in the Soviet Union and Soviet Russia was an ally of the Americans and British so that we were the enemy. We got separated, and the last time I saw him he was being herded on to a train with other men and taken away.'

'But you know what happened to him, you've seen him since?'

'No. I've tried to find out what happened to him, where they took him, if he's alive or dead, but all I've met is a blank wall. Sanjay would never have stood the rigours of a prison

355

camp. He had a bad heart. I think about him so often, those long slender hands so much like the ivories he loved, almost transparent, and the low timbre of his voice, the changing expressions in those narrow eyes. My mandarin whom I shall never see again.'

'Why have you left it so long before coming home?'

'This wasn't home, Amanda. Samarkand was home, that old beautiful house in an ancient city on the plains of Asia. I knew that if Sanjay was alive he would go back there and for months I waited. Every beggar who walked along the road to the house I thought might be Sanjay, and in Samarkand itself it seemed there were only the old people left, until the young men came home all too slowly, so that life never seemed to pick up its pattern. All my enquiries meet with nothing, and the months passed, and I began to realise that I was living in a museum surrounded by so many riches that might never be mine.

'On those days before I left I packed suitcases with the treasures I wanted. The others I gave to my servants and others I used to procure me a train ticket from Tashkent to Moscow. Then my troubles began. The war was over but the Cold War had begun. I still had my British passport but for days I was subjected to one interrogation after another. Why had I lived in Samarkand? Where was my husband? Why had an Englishwoman married a Russian citizen, and why did I now wish to return to England?

'My treasures went to one official after another, each one promising to get me home to England. The British ambassador tried to help but I was no longer a British citizen, and by this time there was very little left as I bribed my way into a third-rate hotel and pleaded for a flight to England.'

'You have nothing left?'

She grinned. 'I have my ruby, I'd have died before I parted with that. I had one or two other trinkets, the jade and the ivories had long gone.'

'What happened when you arrived in England?'

'I telephoned my father and he told me Ralph was in London, staying at the Dorchester. He said Ralph would give me money and see that I got home.'

She laughed. 'You should have seen their faces at the Dorchester when I asked for Mr Dexter. I looked like a down-

and-out, somebody who'd spent weeks sleeping on the streets, a woman some prostitute would have shrugged away from. I knew they'd warned Ralph what to expect. The manager came with him in case he disowned me, and it was necessary to send me packing. It took several minutes for him to recognise me and assure the manager that it was safe for him to talk to me.

'He treated me to afternoon tea and everybody around us stared until I felt like leaping to my feet to tell them my story.

'He gave me some money and I went into one of the stores and bought a skirt and sweater.'

She laughed again. 'The girl who served me handled my old clothes as if they were contaminated and I told her to dispose of them. I bought a raincoat and a pair of decent shoes and I gave nobody an explanation for the way I had looked. Back at the Dorchester Ralph took me up to his room so that I could have a bath and make myself presentable enough to eat dinner in the restaurant.

'He had a dinner guest. Some woman he knew in London so we couldn't really talk. The next day we came back to the north and I went immediately to Granny's.'

'Why not to your parents' home?'

'I prefer to stay with Granny and wait for Sunday lunch.'

'And that I expect was terrible.'

'My mother will never understand, hence her idea of packing me off to America, the only place where I can live my past down and pick up the pieces.'

'What will you do?'

'Find a job, I can't live on the family, but I'm not sure what I'm equipped for.'

'You could go into cotton. At least you know more about eastern designs than I did when I started. Why don't you talk to Ralph. I'm sure he'd see the logic of it.'

'I don't think I'll do anything in a hurry. I've got the money Grandfather left in trust for me. I expect you got the same, and Dad'll subsidise me for the time being. Maybe I'll go over to America and join my sister in the life of Riley.'

'Why don't you stay and eat with us? Phillip's taken his mother to visit some old friends or hers but they'll be back soon.'

357

'I'm hardly dressed for eating dinner in this impressive pile. Besides I have to get the horse back before the stables close for the night. Are you quite sure her ladyship is ready to meet her late daughter-in-law's sister?'

'Well of course. She met up with your parents at Alice's wedding. It was all very civilised.'

'Tell me about Alice's wedding? Surely there must have been undercurrents between the Dexters and her mother's family.'

'Not noticeably so. Her grandmother and one of her mother's sisters came. Ralph excelled himself in trying to make them feel at home and Phillip and I drove them home after the reception. Granny talked to them most of the afternoon and Alice looked enchanting.'

'I haven't seen her yet but I must call. What's the husband like?'

'He's very nice, a doctor. She met him when she was nursing during the war, they lost touch and met up again.'

'And Julia?'

I laughed. 'Julia's run through the gamut of a host of young men. Rich young men with fast cars, ambitious young men with an eye on big business or politics, but the last one was a poet with long hair, dreamy eyes and an eye for her money.'

'Serious, do you think?'

'I wouldn't think so. One never really knows with Julia.'

I walked with her to the stableyard and watched her mount her horse. She looked down at me with gentle irony. 'I'll let you know what I decide to do or where I decide to go. Get back to the house, Amanda. It's looking like rain. Heavens, how I remembered the rain on those dark dismal hills and how they can suddenly become quite beautiful.'

I walked beside her horse until we reached the long drive to the gates. A chill wind had arisen, sending the autumn leaves scurrying across the grass and I looked up to find her eyes gazing out towards the far horizon, a strangely tormented expression on her face.

She spoke without looking at me, almost as if she was speaking to herself.

'I think that one day perhaps I might go back there. I shall

358

walk along that long straggling street where the shops are open to the sky, I shall hear the cries of the beggars and see the sunlight shining on the most beautiful domes and minarets in the world. I shall see our house on the hillside and find Sanjay sitting on the terrace surrounded by his treasures. His eyes will search for me along the road and I shall take to my heels and run weeping into his arms.'

I did not speak. I could not intrude into a moment that belonged to Charlotte alone. Suddenly, she looked down at me and with a gay wave of her hand and a bright smile she urged her horse onward down the hill.

I told Phillip about her visit later that night, and after I'd repeated her last words, I said sadly, 'Do you really think she'll go back there, Phillip?'

'She's always been unpredictable, but if she does, I doubt if she'll find Sanjay waiting for her surrounded by his treasures. It is debatable if she would find the house still standing.'

'You think there will be nothing left?'

He shook his head. 'I think Charlotte would be wise to forget her mandarin and the Golden Road to Samarkand.'

Phillip's mother was dozing in her chair. She had taken no part in our conversation regarding Charlotte and when Phillip got up from his chair to add logs to the fire she opened her eyes sleepily and smiled.

'How long have I been asleep?' she asked. 'You must be finding me poor company.'

'How were your friends, Lady Rose?'

'Getting old and fragile, rather like me. You were saying Charlotte had called. I never really got to know Charlotte.'

'She'd borrowed a horse from the stables at the bottom of the hill.'

'I heard you say her husband had not returned from the war. I shouldn't think there's much hope that he will do so now.'

'No. She's hoping to plan for the rest of her life.'

'And what will she do?'

'I don't know. I suggested a job at the mill, but Aunt Edith seems to think she should visit America.'

'Well, of course. That I think would be an ideal solution.

359

How long before Johnnie comes on holiday from school?'

'Just a few weeks now. He'll be home for Christmas.'

'That will be lovely. I hope he'll go with me to church. It will be nice to have a male escort again.'

Both Phillip and I smiled. She delighted in Johnnie's companionship for church and any other event connected with it. She would make much of him, show everybody there that this was her grandson, one of the reasons she had come back.

'I think I shall go to bed now,' she said. 'There was a time when your father and I sat up late playing card games. Now I prefer to go to bed early and listen to my radio.'

'There's a fire in your room, Mother,' Phillip said.

'Yes dear. You and Amanda look after me very well. I like the way you've changed things around. This house is really beginning to feel like home.'

'You've been pensive all evening, darling,' Phillip said gently. 'I suppose you're thinking about Charlotte.'

'I've been thinking about the way our lives have been intertwined across the years, how I never really thought of myself as a Dexter and yet I've never really been able to get away from them.'

'Isn't it time you stopped blaming yourself, Amanda, that every disaster in the Dexter family can be laid at your door?'

'I was responsible for a great many of them, Phillip.'

'For standing up to your grandfather – a dictatorial tyrant in anybody's book – who kept his family in a state of constant dread? Even your grandmother. When did she ever have the audacity to express a point of view that differed from his own?

'I saw his ruthlessness in Caroline, and God help me, I gave her the wherewithal to ride roughshod over those she considered inferior. You didn't steal me from Caroline, because for all those years I had never truly loved Caroline – I had never understood the hunger, the pity and the power of love. If you hadn't come back here, I might never have known it. You made me see that my life with Caroline was like living a lie.

'You mustn't tantalise yourself that in some way you're responsible for what has happened to Charlotte. She embarked on her life in Samarkand with her eyes open, and nothing you could have said or done would have made her change her mind.'

I looked across the room into his eyes and I knew that he was right.

When he came to take me into his arms I knew that in spite of his nearness at that moment we were all very much alone. I knew the truth that there was no such thing as happiness without pain, victory without defeat.

In his expression was all the strength and understanding that I loved.